A DARK LIGHT SHINING

Also by Wendy Robertson

Riches of the Earth
Under a Brighter Sky
Land of Your Possession

A DARK LIGHT SHINING

Wendy Robertson

HEADLINE

First published in 1995
by HEADLINE BOOK PUBLISHING

10 9 8 7 6 5 4 3 2 1

British Library Cataloguing in Publication Data

Robertson, Wendy
Dark Light Shining
I. Title
823.914 [F]

ISBN 0-7472-1266-X

Typeset by
Letterpart Limited, Reigate, Surrey

Printed and bound in Great Britain by
Mackays of Chatham PLC, Chatham, Kent

HEADLINE BOOK PUBLISHING
A division of Hodder Headline PLC
338 Euston Road
London NW1 3BH

For Gillian Wales,
librarian, quiet revolutionary
and great facilitator

PART ONE

1

The Arrival

The world was black-grey, endless and all-enveloping. For a second she tried to open her eyes, move her arms, but she couldn't. Later she remembered thinking this is what it must be like just before you die; or just when you are born, before you know your senses are your servants. Her throat came back to her first and she opened her mouth. 'Dad!' she yelled. Instantly she was released. Her eyes snapped open into the welcoming dusk of her bedroom. She knew now she was properly awake.

'What is it?' her father's voice growled from the bedroom below.

'Nothing, nothing.'

She lay listening to the clock on the middle landing strike twelve, then jumped out of bed and stretched as tall as she could under the sloping roof. The attic was hot and airless. She loosened the strings on her nightgown and pulled it away from her sweating neck, then padded across the boards to the low window and pulled at the sash to open it. As she did so she heard a very unusual noise: the coughing chug of a motor-car.

The sound of its chuntering engine winged off the low houses, making the Tait's livery horses whinny nervously into the night air. The screech and thump of the brakes skittered over the large windows of the shops on Mainstreet, most of which were now permanently closed.

Then the motor-car's machine clamour faded, sucked away into the shallow wooded basin, where New Morven lay cupped against the worst ravages of the North-east winters and shaded from the cool sun of its bright summers.

The clump of the car door closing was followed by the rustle of heavy clothes and the scrape and thud of leather luggage, as someone heaved cases and boxes from the boot of the car on to the cobbled road. Then a man's voice started bellowing into the night, screaming and shouting: crying out with animal pain.

That was it. Chamber pots rang as feet crashed against them in

3

the dark. Low muttered curses were swallowed as curtains twitched and blue gaslights blossomed.

'Esther. It's a man, Esther.' Patrick Montague, New Morven's only remaining grocer, was so close to the glass that his breath was steaming it up. 'They've stopped the car at Plush Folly.' This was the big double-fronted house at the end of Mainstreet. 'The man's up on the wall now, Esther, and they're trying to reach him. This woman – she's got this big hat on with a feather – and another man, fat feller. The taxi-driver mebbe. He – the feller on the wall – has an umbrella, holding it like some sword. Shrieking, screaming, can yer hear him, Esther? Here, Esther, look!' He pulled the neat lace curtain up to shoulder height.

Esther, lying rigidly on her back in her own bed, the counterpane draped around her like a sarcophagus, merely murmured in her dry voice, 'Come away from that window, Patrick Montague. Stop your nosing there. You'd think you were Gladys Gregson.'

Patrick put his cheek flat against the glass to improve the trajectory of his view. 'Aye, Gladys's got her nose in. Opened her window, would you believe? And old Hazelwood further down, and the sergeant's lights are on . . .'

'Patrick!' The voice emerging from the sarcophagus had that dangerous tremulous note he'd first heard on honeymoon, and had spent a lifetime dreading. 'I told you about saying *Aye*! Common people say *Aye*. Not respectable grocers. Ooh, my head!'

He sighed, closed the curtains gently, then moved the chamber pot to a place of greater safety far under his own bed. 'Would you like an Aspro, dear? And a nice cup of tea?' He had developed this aggressive mildness through the years, a sure weapon against her invading sharpness. She might just as well try to fight a feather mattress.

Interpreting her stifled grunt an assent, he took his old coat from the brass bedknob and shuffled barefoot across the cold lino out of the room. Downstairs, the kitchen was still permeated with the ghost of the intense heat of the daytime fire. However, the low fire would never have heated the kettle, so he resorted to the gas ring on the scullery window sill.

When he returned to the kitchen, steaming kettle in hand, he found he had company. He smiled.

'Did you see them, Dad?' His daughter, Finn, her fine fair hair fuzzy about her shoulders, looked insubstantial in her long night-shift with its neckstrings untied. She was smiling mischievously back at him.

He poured the water on to the tea leaves, glad that Esther was not there to tell him in her sharp voice about the rule of the teapot-to-the-kettle, not vice versa. She liked to use phrases like that. Vice

4

versa. *Non sequitur. Sine qua non* . . . Half the time he didn't know what she was talking about. And she did like to put her Gs on. Getting. Petting. Loving . . .

'Dad!' Finnuola's voice was sharp.

He shook his head, dislodging the buzzing bee of Esther's voice.

'I said who were they? Those people at Plush Folly crashing around out there waking the dead?' She watched him affectionately as he poured in the last scrap of milk from the jug on the cold window sill.

Finn had worked shoulder to shoulder with her father in the shop since they had arrived in New Morven. She had been seventeen years old then, fresh from a school in Gateshead for the daughters of tradesmen who had aspirations above the shop counter.

In a personal rather than an economic sense, her father was a successful grocer. She loved the way he entered the lives of his customers, exchanging gossip with the women. With the men he swapped racing tips and a bitter, inverted nostalgia for the Great War. She was impressed and at the same time worried at the way he persisted, despite her mother's admonitions, in extending credit to customers with hungry children. She watched tenderly as, in his beautiful copperplate writing, he entered their purchases into the greasy 'tick' ledger, in the full knowledge that he would not be paid. 'Might as well give it all away,' her mother would say morosely. 'He might as well give it away and be done with it.'

'Don't know, pet,' he was saying now. 'Gladys was gabbing on just today about Bella Smith's being in Plush Folly this week, putting fires on and opening windows. But even Bella doesn't know who this pair might be. Spitting feathers with frustration, she was. Lawyer feller from Priorton tells her to get the house opened up, beds aired and made properly. But not a word about who the folks might be. Five shillings she got, for doing it. Big money for her. And Gladys was talking about old Warburton, the old owner. Before our time. He lived at Plush Folly till '28 then snuffed it. Bella says he was so mean he would use tea twice. Had the woman dry the leaves out again on trays. Before our time, anyways,' he repeated.

Patrick Montague had inherited the shop from his Uncle Sep in 1930, grabbing at the chance to come away from the supply business that had folded under him in Gateshead, with the bad times there. His wife had taken one look at this derelict village and acquired the headache which had never left her. The small shop in Gateshead had merely evoked Esther's nervous stomach. At least up in Gateshead, she would say, there was the option of hobnobbing with other grocers' wives; at least there they'd found a decent school for Finnuola, a cut above the thieves' kitchen that passed for a school here in New Morven. Good thing the girl had got her schooling

5

there before coming to this dead end of a place.

A good thing Finnuola was on hand to help. A grand help, Finn. He poured Esther's tea into her china cup. 'I've to get your Ma an Aspro, love.'

Finn followed him through to the shop and leaned on the doorpost, watching as he turned up the gaslight just a bit so he didn't stumble over the potato and flour sacks, the boxes of tins and the stack of brushes, (head up), which he always kept at the end of the counter. Her nose pricked at the smells of slightly rancid butter and old potatoes, and the aroma of coffee and sweet over-ripe apples. This smell was her earliest memory: she had wrinkled her nose at such a smell sitting in her high chair behind the counter in the Gateshead shop, while her dad served at the counter, giving her mother yet another rest upstairs.

She went to stand behind the shop door and peered through an O of the Cocoa sign. She clapped her hands, 'Look, Dad, that man! He's walking right along the top of the wall, now!'

Unlike the other houses in Mainstreet, Plush Folly had a small garden at the front, protected from the street by a long, shoulder-high wall, divided in the centre by a fine wrought-iron gate. This gate had been made, they said, by Stearman Smith, head blacksmith for the old ironmaster who had built Plush Folly. Stacy Smith, Stearman's descendant, had carried on the family's smithing traditions, working as a pit blacksmith right up till the '26 strike. After that he was blacklisted, never to work for legal money again.

Now the stranger, wrapped in a cloak, his face shaded by a very broad hat, was dancing away from his pursuers, parrying their reaching arms with his long umbrella. Suddenly he took a great leap over the stone parapet which divided Plush Folly from the post office next door and came racing down the street, pursued by the woman and the puffing fat man. The woman's heels clicked on the cobbles and her cries were like the mewing of a cat in the quiet watching street.

More lights went on in the houses. More faces followed the progress of the strange trio along the street.

The man's head lifted and his wild eyes lighted on Finnuola, standing in her nightshift inside the door of the little grocer's shop. He skidded to a stop before her.

She stood like a petrified rabbit as he stared at her, gazing back into bright dark eyes, the burning focus of a haggard, furrowed face which had once been handsome. His ragged grey hair, sticking out wildly under his hat, seemed to have a life of its own. He dropped his umbrella and bent to pick it up, never taking his eyes from the girl.

His pursuers caught up with him.

6

Patrick came and put an arm on the doorjamb behind Finn. He did not touch her. Close as they were, he rarely touched his daughter.

'Easy now, sir.' From behind the door they could hear what the fat man was saying. He was pressing a hand to his own heaving chest. 'Easy.'

The woman came to the other side of the tall man and took his arm, trying to drag him away, but he resisted.

He started to shout, 'There, see, Jenny. See the girl? The innocent. The maid.' He swept off his broad hat and held it to his heart. His yelling voice pierced the glass of the door and the large plate-glass window which had been old Sep Montague's pride. ' "There in the moonlight a straight slim figure dressed in a plaitless gown . . ." '

Patrick moved three inches closer to his daughter. Gladys Gregson, at her end of the street, could hear the ringing slap as the woman brought her hand across the tall man's face. He quietened down then, standing up straight but somehow shrinking into himself. The woman stroked his reddening cheek and took his arm. Finn could see her mouth moving as she talked away to the man and led him back down the street through the high gates of Plush Folly. She vanished through the doorway, then came back on her own. She shook her head when the fat man offered to lift the cases into the house, and counted out his due fare from a large purse. Then she went in and the door closed behind her. Now the people of New Morven had, reluctantly, to climb back into their beds.

During the next week in New Morven, gossip bubbled like lava on the subject of the occupiers of Plush Folly. The little community was holding its breath to discover the identity of this strange pair. Fancy! Coming in to live in this village. People did not come willingly to live in New Morven. They usually left here in their droves. People had been leaving it for ten years now. More.

In fact, they did not so much leave, as *flee* – away from the cold decaying houses; away from prosecution for petty crimes committed to relieve the poverty; away from the disused mines and the ghostly rusting hulk of the steel furnace unused for two generations; away from the fighting drunks, rolling off the Priorton train on Saturday – men and some women filled with beer paid for not by work but by errands run and little laws broken; away from the hoarse bellow of Sergeant Corcoran, who had brooked no trouble since his first week in New Morven when he beat Stacy Smith, Bella's powerful husband, to a pulp.

Montague's shop buzzed with speculation about the whys and wherefores of the arrival of this strange pair. Why were they opening the old house? Plush Folly had been left to stew since '28 when the old man died, hadn't it? Oh yes, everybody knew Bella Smith, wife of the mighty Stacy, earned a canny shilling every month to air it. But then she needed every penny, didn't she? To feed her own and Stacy's children, and, it being a second marriage for both, their shared offspring as well. And she needed money to service Stacy's drinking habit, which went barely staunched by the parish money he weedled out of Mr Marchant, the vicar, for his large and needy brood. Things were a bit better for Bella and the children since the Sally Army had set up the soup kitchen. But not much. There were knowing nods and laughs at all these facts in Stacy's absence, but in his presence people were much more circumspect.

But still, no one knew for whom the house had been kept aired, or why. Bella Smith was no help in these speculations. She held daily court in Montague's shop; her every word drunk in by Gladys Gregson, Emily Punchard, an ardent Salvationist, whose penchant for gossip reflected a warm genuine interest in the doings of her neighbours, and Mrs Fosdick, the stout surly housekeeper to the Reverend Hildebrand Marchant.

Bella had to admit to her eager audience that Plush Folly was well furnished in its old-fashioned way, and in good order because of her monthly labours. But when she had called at the house the morning after the dramatic arrival, the new occupant had sent her away with a flea in her ear. Bella savoured her role at the centre of attention, sharing her spluttering indignation with other customers in Montague's shop.

Patrick was filling in a big order for Mrs Fosdick, and Finn was measuring out into screws of newspaper the tiny portions of sugar and tea which were Bella's daily ration.

Bella folded her arms. 'Ah gans there, back door like yer should, and she kept us there, on the doorstep! Dressed like gypsy-lady-muck, she was, but wi' this long black pinny.' The right-hand side of Bella's face twisted with annoyance. The left-hand side of her face was rigid with the paralysis from the blow which had been a honeymoon present from Stacy. Their late marriage had been celebrated by a double family honeymoon spent in a tent on the moor. That would be the year of the Big Strike, when Stacy had been put out of his pit house for good and was in no mood for romance.

The speculation about the newcomers to Plush Folly went on for three days. Then, in the middle of a Thursday afternoon the woman from that house, carrying two large baskets, walked along to Montague's grocery. Patrick smiled as the bell sent its trembling echo through the empty shop. Wouldn't his regulars be disappointed! Not one person here to gawp and whisper: not even his daughter, Finn, who had taken the bicycle with its heavy basket to deliver the regular orders for some farms up the valley.

The woman, quite stout, was wearing a purple skirt, much wider and longer than women wore these days, and a dark red velvet jacket. A closefitting hat moulded her head over a bright scarf. She heaved a great basket on to the counter and placed a list beside it. 'My name is Morgan Loumis. I have . . .'

Patrick came round from the other side of the counter and shook her hand. 'You are over at Plush Folly. Welcome to New Morven, Mrs Morgan Loumis. Mebbe you'd take a chair. It'll take me no time to fill this order.' He lifted the list from the counter and peered at it, then felt the thrill of shock as he looked into her wide face and eyes dark as a woodland pool, and skin whose whiteness was made denser by thistle-fine hair escaping from the bright scarf.

He dropped his glance quite quickly and busied himself with the task of supplying everything from butter to coal-tar soap. He kept his eyes down, even when she paid, in *cash*: pounds shillings and pence! He had assumed she'd *have an account* as did the vicar. Patrick narrowed his eyes as he trickled a little extra sugar from the scoop, closed the blue bag with an expert hand and tucked it into the last corner of the smaller basket. Mr Marchant, the vicar, was one of the few people from New Morven Patrick's wife Esther *didn't* play war about. But the vicar was as hard to dun for payment as any of the unemployed pitmen from the derelict streets of New Morven. Harder.

Patrick lifted the baskets to the floor. 'You can't carry these yourself, Mrs Morgan Loumis,' he asserted. 'I'll bring 'em down for you.'

She laughed: a bright appealing sound. 'I'm no weakling, Mr Montague. I carried them in empty and I'll carry them out full.' She looked around the cluttered shop. 'Do you have wall paint, Mr Montague? I need two gallons of white paint at least.'

'I do that, Mrs Morgan Loumis, but the paint's out the back. I can soon get it.'

She shook her head. 'There's no hurry, Mr Montague. This afternoon will do.' She finally caught his glance and held it. 'Send that girl. Your daughter is it? Send her across with the paint.'

Jenefer Loumis made her way along the street and back across to Plush Folly with her heavy bags. She found the house door, and all the sash windows looking on to Mainstreet, wide open to the weather. As she walked into the hall she could feel the current of air rushing into the house from every window.

She made her way down the passage to the deserted kitchen, heaved the bulky baskets on to the long table, breathed in very deeply, then went back to the hall to take off her coat and hat. She

9

left the bright scarf on her head and leaned nearer the carved mirror, to tuck in the wispy tendrils of hair.

She did not call out for him. She had learned very early that shouting at him or for him intensified his fear. She took her time walking quietly through the house, closing the windows, cutting out the chill spring air. Before closing the back bedroom window she leaned out to steady herself, to stop her mind following his chaotic course.

The day was bright: not bright in the way that France was bright, but not anything like as dark and dismal as it had loomed in her imagination. When the money had just about run out and she knew she and Hubert would have to come here to County Durham, to Plush Folly, her imagination had turned this village into a dark outpost too cold to be called hell.

But New Morven wasn't really like that. Not from this window. No pitheads visible here. In the distance the delicate tones of the bracken on the moor insinuated a line against the blue of the sky, unsullied apart from a wisp of cloud, here and there. The rough grass in front of the orchard, (which had once been the tennis court), was greening up, ready for its spring spurt. Further away the apple and pear trees cut into the sky with spindly untrimmed abandon, their last season's fruit rotted into the ground, or stolen by thieves armed with claw and paw, or the human, two-legged ones, armed with well-aimed sticks.

'Thieves and scoundrels, the lot of 'm.' She shivered slightly as the ghost of her great-uncle's voice crackled and echoed in the empty room. Jonas Warburton had had neither time nor respect for the men who worked in his pits. As a child, her blood chilled by the winter air, Jenefer had flinched at the bleak rasping voice which seemed to contain within it the very essence of this inhospitable land.

Now she smiled slightly as the sound of birdsong cut the air; it issued merrily from the rambling azalea bush which sprawled, unkempt, on to the rough grass. She turned her face to one side in order to hear better: a wren was shouting his territory for all to hear, like some fairground pugilist declaring his intention to take on all-comers. Such a large voice for such a little body. Her gaze moved to the black and white cat crouching expectantly among the winter-wet leaves under the trailing branches.

She pulled down the window and went out to find Hubert.

Her heels sank into the wet ground, and once she slipped on saturated leaves and twisted her ankle. She limped on. She was aiming for the large brick courtyard at the end of the garden. On one side was the old coach house, where her uncle had kept his trap and his small carriage. The horses themselves he had kept at Tait's Livery, just across the back lane. Being appropriately careful with

10

his money, he had expected Alan Newton, his gardener, to drive him around, in addition to his other duties, which varied from cellarman to gardener, messenger to boot-boy.

On the other side of the courtyard to the coach house was the brick cabin – calling it a cottage would be flattery – where Alan had lived with his wife, Susie. Susie scrubbed for old Warburton and anyone else in the village who would pay her for rough work.

The coach house, now housing the wrecks of Warburton's coach and trap, was scattered with discarded tack and storage boxes bound with leather straps, covered with sacking. The air smelled of damp and dust, decomposing vegetable matter and the detritus produced by generations of small mammals.

Going across to one corner, Jenefer pulled aside some heavy sacking hanging across high carriage wheels which leaned drunkenly against a wall: just the kind of close tiny space Hubert liked. This was where Hubert had found refuge yesterday.

It was empty.

She made her way across to Alan Newton's neglected cabin. The door was ajar, but the little room which comprised the ground floor was also empty. She raised her eyes wearily to the ladder, which thrust its way into the sleeping loft. Alan Newton and his Susie had curled up together there like two small animals themselves. One day Susie, trying to cheer Jenefer up, had taken the child up into the loft and shown her the makeshift mattress on which she and Alan slept. Jenefer had fingered the slatted racks with their rows of russet apples which smelled of summer. Bunches of dried herbs hung there too, ready to sell for cures as Susie made her way on her cleaning round, in shops in the village.

That was the day Susie had amazed the young Jenefer with the information of what men and women did together. She had laughed as Jenefer shook her head in mystification and disbelief. 'A lad needs a bit o' comfort, hinney, and a lass too.'

On reflection Susie had been so very right.

Jenefer poked her head through the hole. The roofspace had no window and was only dimly illuminated by light squeezing through the fissures between the tiles. It took a moment for her eyes to adjust to the scented twilight.

Her nostrils flared. 'Hubert?' Tears pricked in her eyes as she heard his sob of fear. 'Hubert. It's Jenefer.' She clambered up right through the hole and crawled towards the corner in the direction of the sound. 'Don't worry, dear little one. Here I am.'

He was curled up closely under the eaves, his forearm pulled up over his eyes. 'No. No. Go away. Away I tell you.' The childlike panic was rising in his voice. 'I opened the windows for you. You're to go away.'

She sat down, put one leg either side of his crouching body and struggled to pull the tense ball of humanity towards her. He was a big man. At first he fought her: he grabbed desperately at her scarf, making her thick hair tumble down, then he slammed at her face with his fist so that her ears rang. She held him to her till the struggles stopped. Then she cleared his hair out of his eyes, stroked his face, and started to rock him backwards and forwards until the trembling stopped, murmuring that he was safe now, nothing would happen. He was safe.

She kissed him very softly at first, then with mounting passion as he began to respond. Then she helped him as he started to pull at her clothes and they made love there in the old dust amid the ghostly smell of apples.

2

Collision

Despite progressively weary legs, Finn enjoyed her Thursday rides to the small farms up the dale. Pedalling hard, she gloried in the rise and fall of the land as it unfolded before her. True, the hills were hard work, but with every toiling ride up a bank she relished the thought of the freewheel down the other side. The nearest thing to flying, she told her father, with the wind in your face and the horizon coming towards you.

The bike Finn rode had belonged to Jacky Burslem, who had worked, man and boy, in Montague's grocery. He first worked for Patrick's Uncle Sep, who had inherited the grocery from his grandfather, Walter Montague. As old Jacky was never tired of telling Patrick, old Walter Montague had opened the shop when New Morven was a thriving village in the 1870s. 'But it was different then, Mr Montague, see? That was before the gaffers at the big ironworks upped lock, stock and barrel, and set up again miles away in Yorkshire. Devil's work.'

When Jacky finally retired, Finn carried on the tradition of doing the Thursday deliveries up to the farms on Jacky's heavy old bike. The farm deliveries were not heavy in themselves. The families up there were self-sufficient in most foodstuffs, growing their own and bartering surplus among neighbours. Sacks of flour for baking would be obtained direct from Priorton Mill on Thursdays, when the farmers went into the Cattlemart. The wives would order other provisions to be delivered on Friday by the Co-operative Society. Some wives would take their goods back with them on Thursday, loaded by the Co-op boys into the trap or on to the farm cart there and then, while the husbands exchanged gossip at the auction, or reflected on a deal well struck over a pint or ten in The Bay Horse.

So Patrick Montague's grocery shop did little enough business with the farmers and their workers in terms of flour, eggs, butter, vegetables or tinned stuffs. But they did call on the grocer for odd things like shoe polishes, pins or needles. Sometimes he would send

13

nice samples of china supplied, 'sale or return', by his traveller, or some nifty little gadget new to the market. And he held an agency for vacuum cleaners where they would order one on credit from a pamphlet he carried, and pay him so much a week till they were paid for. From time to time he would tuck a new book, a romantic story by Ethel M. Dell, for instance, in Finn's basket. Some wife would be happy for a little escape in the long winter hours. Finn knew not to offer it at the farms where people signed their credit agreements with a cross, their schooldays having been spent in the fields, on the moor or in the byre, rather than in village classroom learning their letters.

High Bank Farm, Finn's last and furthest call, was tucked under the last of a series of hilly rises; it was a favourite stopping point. Mrs Fenwick always had a cup of tea and a scone for her, and the children, Anthony and Roddy, were entertaining to watch. And there would be lambs. At this time of year Mrs Fenwick usually had lambs: orphaned or rejected twins in straw around the great iron fireplace.

Finn was hurtling down the final narrow road to High Bank Farm when she crashed into a chugging motor-car and was flung violently to one side. The bicycle went one way and she went the other, rebounding from the bare prickly hedge into a muddy ditch. Wincing, her knitted beret knocked sideways, she crawled out to meet the chilly stare of the Reverend Hildebrand Marchant and the smirk of Clarry Tazewell, his driver.

Clarry's smirk faded as the car engine died. It had taken him nearly five minutes to get the engine to turn over down at High Bank Farm. Now he'd have to get out and jolt his already sore shoulder on that blasted handle again.

The vicar's glasses had slipped to the point of his narrow nose and his black hat was tipped too far forward on his bony forehead. The thin line of his mouth barely opened as he leaned further out of the window to speak to Finn. 'You should watch where you're going, young woman. You are a danger to life and limb, careering around the country lanes in this fashion.'

She started to pile up the spilled goods, ready to put back in her basket.

'What do you say, girl? Have you no apology? You could have caused great injury.'

She looked from him to the sour face of Clarry Tazewell. 'With respect, sir,' she said slowly, 'I left lots of room. Your car . . . your driver . . . came round the corner in the middle of the road. And it's me that's injured.' She winced as she kneeled down to retrieve a patent iron meatmincer from the ditch.

The vicar now had bright red patches on the narrow planes of his

14

white cheeks. 'Will you stand up, girl, and show the respect you're claiming, and get that contraption out of the way of my motor-car?'

She went across the lane, pulled the bike clear and stood watching as Clarry puffed and blowed over the starting handle. Finally the engine turned over, and he climbed back into the car. The vicar adjusted his hat and touched Clarry's shoulder with his stick. The car pulled away, jetting blue coils of smoke into the air. Finn stood still for a second, then she poked out her tongue at the car's retreating rear.

Mr Marchant, glancing backwards out of the window at the chaos behind him, caught sight of the gesture and scowled. Reaching into his inside pocket he took out his notebook and wrote in his neat crabbed hand, 'The old standards of hard work, respect and honour are withering away, to be replaced by idleness, insolence and anarchy. Only by strength and steadiness of purpose will the slide into Bolshevism be arrested. Consider the stirling endeavours of Signor Mussolini . . .'

At High Bank Farm Mrs Fenwick poured Finn a cup of tea. 'Mr Marchant and his horrible contraption, wus it? He wus just here, that vicar feller, going on about tithin'. Allus after money. Ah had ter tell him Tot wus at the lambin'. An' he wus none too pleased, Ah c'n tell yer.' She sniffed. 'Ah's Welseyan meself. It's Tot who's Church of England. An' Ah get left here, tellin' fibs ter his vicar, while he's off skulkin' there in the top barn.' She put her head on one side. 'Here, flower, Ah've got some lineament for them bruises, if yer like. It's not Sloan's stuff, but it works on the hosses.'

Finn shook her head and stretched back in the hard chair, closing her eyes for a second.

A hand nudged hers. 'See Finn, see what Ah got!' Roddy Fenwick was standing before her, struggling to hold on to a lamb, which was bleating pitifully at being removed from the warmth of the fireplace.

She took the animal from Roddy and nuzzled her face against the soft woolly skin, smiling over the knobbly head at Roddy. 'He feels pretty strong, Roddy.' This sturdy little boy had only been a baby himself, crawling around the stone-flagged floor, when she had first delivered to High Bank Farm. She placed the lamb carefully back in the child's arms.

'He's a strong lamb, Finn. Ah called him George, after the King.' He laid the lamb gently back into the straw.

'Nee names, lad! Ah telt yer, yer da sez nee names.' The reprimand was unemphatic. Mrs Fenwick's glance at her youngest was fond. 'Gan an' get yer readin' book an' show Finn how yer knows yer letters.'

Gravely Finn listened to him lisp a complicated story about some

15

children helping an old man to clean his barn. The book was home-made, printed in Mrs Fenwick's painstaking hand.

'He's good, Mrs Fenwick. He's really good. And before he goes to school, too.'

Mrs Fenwick smiled and offered her another biscuit. 'He winnet get the stick for not knowin' his letters, that's one thing. Not like his dad nor his big brother. Ah wus always a good scholar meself. This 'n's for the grammar school. Ah've made me mind up. The eldest'll get the farm but there's nowt for this 'n. He'll need his wits about him ter get work.'

'There's no work down there in New Morven, nor Priorton, Mrs Fenwick. People laid off all over. The towns. Everything. The Means Test is emptying houses of furniture. Hungry people.'

Mrs Fenwick shrugged. 'Ah read it in the paper. But there's jobs for some. There're always jobs for some. I wus asking that vicar feller about it. He gives us one of them sour looks. He canna but agree wi' us, like. Like Ah sez to him, it could stand this bairn in good stead, the grammar school.'

She looked up at Finn. 'Hasn't done that lad of the vicar's any harm. That Daniel Marchant. Do yer know he used ter come down here for the haymaking, the vicar's son? Nah, yer wouldn't. That wus years before yer came, an' he's been out in America this last two years, travellin' they say. Anyway, he's at Cambridge now. Now, that old vicar wus just sayin' he's doin' well, young Daniel. In line for a good job in the gover'mint. Ah asked 'im about Roddy here goin' there, an' gettin' that sort of job. But he said there was no chance. Talked about background. Breedin', he said. Some half-baked parable about sheep and good stock. Looked down that long nose.' She sniffed. 'But you watch.' She filled up Finn's teacup. 'Now tell us some gossip from down there. Ah never see a soul from one day ter the next up here.'

Glad for once to have a real tale to tell, Finn settled down to rehearse the story about the mysterious new people at Plush Folly.

It was an hour and a half later that a drooping Finn wearily pushed her heavy bicycle back up Mainstreet. When she got home Patrick greeted her with the news that she was to deliver two large tins of paint to Plush Folly. The woman (a strange one that!) had not been able to carry it, and had insisted Finn delivered at the first convenient moment.

'Me? Why me?' Finn flopped down on to the customers' chair.

Patrick shrugged 'I don't know. Just be careful, though. They're a queer pair, those two. But she paid cash, so her custom's not to be sneezed at. And this stock's old, had it for years. It's money out of the air. You can take them across on the bicycle. They're heavy.'

She stood up. 'Now?'

'No. Your Mam's wanting her tea. You make that, an' put ours in the oven while I finish putting up these orders for my round tomorrow. Then you can take the paint over before we have our tea.'

Patrick always closed the shop at five so he and Finn could have their tea together. Then he would open it at six and stay open until nearly midnight, the busiest time being just before eleven when the last train came down from Priorton, and late drinkers and picture-goers would drop in to spend last pennies on cigarettes or sweets on their way home.

As she stood up and went through the curtain to the back, his glance followed her, a slight smile on his face. Finn worked as hard as any man alongside him. She worked twice as hard as old Jacky, who was all mouth and not above adjusting quantities in his own favour. Patrick knew that, like himself, Finn enjoyed the work. The bustling shop was their front parlour, the centre of their life. The back room, their kitchen, was dark and stuffy, often as not heaped with stores the shop couldn't take. Upstairs it was different. On the first floor Esther ruled. All that happened up there was painful complaint, the carrying of slop buckets and washing bowls, the providing of food and medicines, and books from the travelling library.

No. The shop was the thing, and his Finn knew it.

Observed very closely by a black and white cat crouching on the gatepost, Finn knocked on the heavy panelled door and stood back as it swung open at her touch. A faint shout from inside seemed to invite her in. She took the tins from the deep basket on the front of her bicycle and walked through the door. The inside of the house was dark despite the late afternoon sun outside. Her feet clattered on gleaming tiles. The cluttered hallway smelled of mint and rosemary, nutmeg and some other arcane spices. And cats. She could feel the cat's tail, a velvet lash, on her calf.

The voice called again. She pushed open the first door and peered into a room. Inside, the curtains were pulled across, so that even at this hour, the room was in deep shadow. From the high mantelshelf a single lamp fought in vain with the smoky darkness in the room. In the wide hearth a fire was struggling to keep alight.

'Jenny, Jenny, why do you do it? Leave me, then come again, changed so?' She flinched as a querulous voice emerged from a curious tall chair, which curled over like a conch shell.

Finn tried not to look at the chair. 'I'm not Jenny.' Her voice came out tinny and nervous. She swallowed and stood her ground. 'I'm Finn Montague from the shop down on Mainstreet. Mrs Loumis asked for the paint to be delivered. I brought it across.'

17

She stepped forward and plonked the tins on the cluttered, heavily carved table which dominated the centre of the room. Then she turned to leave.

'Don't go! Why do you always go and leave me?' The man's voice was even more plaintive and suddenly very young.

She turned back towards the chair and allowed herself to look hard. The first thing she saw were the hands, white knuckled, clutching the arms of the chair as they reached forward. They were large and graceful, long-fingered and marble-white. Then the face emerged from the shadow. It too was large and graceful, with well-cut elongated features topped by the tangle of blackish-grey hair. Pale glittering eyes examined her from head to foot. He shook his head. 'Neither Jenny nor the other . . . thing.' He stiffened. 'Who let you in, child?'

She shook her head. 'The door was open. I heard you call.'

His eyes bored into her. 'It was a long battle,' he said. 'A long battle. There were blood and brains on my sword. And the mud. Clinging mud. But I vanquished him, child. With a single swing of my sword.'

'Vanquished him?'

'Aye, the dragon.' He sat back. 'The greatest of them all.'

She smiled too easily. 'But, sir, there are no dragons. These are modern times. Aren't we just into 1933? There're no dragons.' Her smile faded as he stood up and lunged towards her, then past her.

Now he was bellowing, shrieking. 'There, there, behind you child! Behind you!' He was swinging and sweeping around the empty room, his arm extended as though there were indeed a sword in his outstretched hand. He put out his other hand to grab her. She ducked and tumbled backwards to the door and fled, his screams and shouts ringing in her ears.

She closed the door firmly behind her, and without hurrying, pushed the cumbersome bicycle down the path before mounting it at the gate. As she rode down the street she passed a hurrying figure in a wide green cloak: Mrs Loumis making her way towards those dreadful cries, to be greeted by the sleek black cat with the white face.

Then she could hear Mrs Loumis calling out to her. 'You! Young woman! I wish to speak to you! Come here.'

Finn stopped the bicycle, stood with a foot either side of it and waited for the woman to retrace her steps.

'What is your name?'

'Finnuola Montague. They call me Finn.'

'How old are you?'

'Twenty.'

'Gracious. You don't look a day over sixteen!'

'Now, you are to come to my house to tea tomorrow. Four o'clock sharp.'

'I'm sorry, ma'am, but I cannot. I work in my father's shop at that time.' She hesitated. 'We do close the shop between five and six.'

The dark eyes pierced into hers. 'Five then. Come at five. We will share a glass of wine. Madeira wine. "A beaker full of the warm South."' A hand, none too small, reached out and caught her forearm in a painful grip. 'You have to come, Finnuola Montague. He thinks he recognised you. You will have to come.'

3

Making Calls

Patrick was sitting on his seat behind the counter, reading the paper by the light of the old untrimmed oil lamp which shivered overhead. He kept the lamp for this purpose, thinking gas an unnecessary extravagance for his quiet early evening shift.

He removed his glasses and looked at Finn. 'Well? What are they like, those two?'

'They're a queer pair, Pa. Well, he's mad as a hatter for sure. Thought I was a dragon, or there was a dragon near me.' She took off her beret and smoothed it straight on the counter. 'And I met her, just outside. She asked me to tea tomorrow night.'

He raised a brow. 'She must be a queer'n, wanting you in her house.'

She flicked her beret towards him, catching him on the nose. 'She should be honoured to have me there.'

He laughed. 'So she should. Anyway, you go and have your tea, love. But don't let this highfalutin' company go to your head, will you?' He raised his eyes to the ceiling. His wife was resting in her bed, reading one of the novels from the shop, opening it very carefully so he could sell it on, unused.

Her gaze followed his. 'Don't you worry, Pa. I'm not above standing in here with you, weighing butter and sugar. Better'n working in someone else's shop or cleaning someone else's mess.' She shrugged herself out of her coat. 'I'll just go and see that Mother's all right, then we can have our teas. And then,' she grinned at him, 'I'll spell you in the shop so you can take your walk to The Eagle.'

Finn delayed telling her mother about her invitation to tea at Plush Folly until she was weaving Esther's hair into its night-time plait.

'Plush Folly!' Her mother shot a sharp glance at her through the pretty mirror. 'Those new people! Now that's a fine invitation, Finnuola.' She pulled on her handsome bedjacket. 'So little worthwhile company around here, normally.'

Finn felt an unusual stab of sympathy for her mother. 'It must have been hard, coming here, Ma. Here to New Morven.' She knew her mother liked to air her grievance over her situation regularly. A good moan served to take away her inner pressure, like lancing a boil.

'Hard?' Esther heaved herself into the narrow bed. 'It was hard from the day I married *him*. The very day.'

'Ma!' Finn's voice was sharp.

Esther pulled up the blankets and reached for her book. 'You can't deny the truth, Finnuola. It was a mistake. My mother said it was a mistake. Your Uncle Harold said *he* was a good-looking bundle of nothing . . . well, actually it was "a good-looking nowt", he could be coarse, your Uncle Harold . . . and he was right. And when I saw that dingy little shop in Gateshead I knew they were right. Both of them.' Esther's eyes filled with tears as she thought of her father's house in Newcastle with its long garden, and Megan, the housekeeper, who ran their lives and comforts like clockwork. She started to pleat the eiderdown with her fingers. 'A big mistake.'

Finn plumped up her mother's pillows violently. 'I can't think why you married him, then,' she said grimly.

Esther pulled away from her. 'Don't you shout at me, lady! D'you think if I'd had any choice, if it hadn't been for you, I'd have married him at all?' She lay back against her pillows and closed her eyes. Patrick certainly had charm in those early days, coming with his boxes of shirts for her father's shops. Or yes he could lay it on. The charm.

Finn stood very still. 'Are you saying . . .?'

Esther turned on her side, away from Finn, 'I'm saying nothing, nothing at all. Now haven't you work to do downstairs? There's a draught from that door.'

Downstairs in the little back room, Finn rehearsed the words to ask her father about her mother's remark but she couldn't. She and her father, despite working together so closely, never talked of intimate things. The thought of asking her father whether she had been born out of wedlock defeated her. She could hear the echo of the vicar's voice in one of those Sunday evening services when he fulminated against the sins, seen and unseen, in this community. "Behold, I was shapen in wickedness; and in sin hath my mother conceived me." '

She shivered.

'Are you cold, pet? Shall I put a shovel on the fire?' Patrick was buttoning up his jacket, trying not to be in too big a hurry to escape to The Eagle, and his two hours of freedom. Esther knew all about his visitors to The Eagle but it was never mentioned. In the early years he had drunk deep in a variety of public houses, to numb himself for the return to her cold bed. Then when her illnesses led to the acquisition of separate beds, the need for numb oblivion at night was not so great. But by then Patrick had grown to enjoy the company and the warmth, first of The Midshipman in Gateshead, and now The Eagle in New Morven.

Finn was grinning at him. 'You get away to your friends, Pa. I thought I'd sort and dust that tin shelf. That'll keep me warm.'

Each night Patrick took his walk along to The Eagle, to drink three double whiskies with whoever happened to be in the little snug at the time. Tonight, Tait the livery man was there. And Milton the undertaker. And old Alan Newton, who had once worked at Plush Folly and who now wobbled up on his bike every day to help in the gardens of Banville Hall, home of Sir Oliver Marchant. At ten o'clock Jacky Burslem hobbled into The Eagle, leaning heavily on his stick, and regaled Patrick with rather snide tales of the village shop in its finest hour, under Old Sep Montague. Patrick returned from The Eagle, only slightly the worse for wear, in time to catch the flush of picture-goers coming off the late train from Priorton. Finn had his cocoa ready for him on the counter and grinned her good night before she went, exhausted, off to bed.

The next afternoon Finn took extra care getting ready for her teatime call at Plush Folly. Esther took great interest in the preparations. It was all Finn could do to stop her mother jamming one of her own over-smart church hats on Finn's head.

'No, Ma. I'll wear my green beret, the new one that Mrs Fenwick knit for me at Christmas.' She pulled the beret this way and that over her thick chignon of fair hair. 'Look at this. I should have it all cut off. Nothing looks right on this lump of hair.' She sighed. 'I'm twice behind the times. It's ten years since people had their hair bobbed. Now they're growing it. I should really . . .'

'Rubbish,' said her mother briskly. 'It is your best feature. Unfortunately for you, you favour me, not your father in looks. But your hair is your finest feature. I won't allow you get it cut while you live in this house.'

This business of the hair was an ongoing battle, weakly fought on Finn's side. Deep down she was quite proud of the mane of fair hair, so fine that escaping strands of it would glitter in the light. Finally she just jammed on the beret anyhow, picked up her gloves, and made her way out across the road and along the dirt path towards the wrought-iron gates.

She waited a long time at the door before the woman opened it first a crack and then much wider. 'Ah. The girl. I'd almost forgotten . . .' She was wearing a long, loose smock-like gown of

23

soft material over a narrow skirt. Around her neck was a necklace of beads nearly as large as teacups.

Finn stepped back. 'I shouldn't have—'

'No, no, no. Come in. Don't mind my bad manners. I was preoccupied for a moment. Come in and welcome.' She ushered Finn into the large sitting room.

Finn looked towards the empty shell chair, wrinkling her nose slightly at the smell of something – cigar smoke perhaps – which suggested the strange man had been here recently.

'My . . . Hubert tenders his apologies but has a fearful headache and would be the worst of company tonight. Now sit down, my dear.'

Finn, perched on the edge of a high-backed couch, watched quietly as Jenefer Loumis installed herself next to her by a low round table which was laden with tiny cakes and small sandwiches, and on which glittered a tall decanter and three large glasses designed more for trifle than wine. So she had been expected.

Jenefer lifted the heavy decanter, filled two of the glasses and handed one to Finn. 'Now then, we will drink a toast, Finnuola. May I call you Finnuola?'

'They call me Finn, usually. Only my mother calls me Finnuola.'

'Wonderful! Finn. Fish. A fish swimming, a creature of water. The toast is water creatures!' She held her glass high and drank. Finn did likewise.

Jenefer made her choose a sandwich and she sat back with her plate in her hand, relaxing a little. She looked round. 'You've settled in all right, Mrs Loumis?'

A small plump hand clasped her arm. 'Jenefer, dear girl. Just call me Jenefer.'

Finn blushed. 'I don't think I can . . .' She had called no one by their Christian name since she was at school. Certainly no adult. Busy with her father and the shop, she'd had no chance to make close friends here in New Morven.

The woman looked her in the eye. 'I insist,' she said. 'You simply must. And you must call Hubert by his name. He would want that. Now give me your hand!'

Reluctantly she put her glass down and gave the woman her hand. Jenefer turned it palm upwards and held it towards the light. 'Yes, yes,' she said. 'A long life. Bringing light to others' lives, dark as they are. Three, no four children. And men, three for whom you might provide a conflict, a solution, a resolution. You have conflict inside your life. Darkness. There is envy, malice somewhere near, someone to watch . . .'

Finn pulled her hand away and picked up her glass, smiling to soften the rejection. 'Don't. I don't like it.'

24

The clock on the mantelpiece ticked.

'May I ask you a question . . . Jenefer?'

'Anything. Anything, dear girl.'

'Why did you say he recognised me, Mr . . . Hubert?' She gulped her wine, looking over the brim at the other woman.

Jenefer Loumis nodded, her brow furrowing. 'He dreams of things. He saw you in a dream. Sometimes he dreams of terrible things, sometimes wonderful things. Sometimes things that are true, sometimes things which are the wildest most frightening imaginings. Then he has to do battle. Sometimes things from the future . . . here, let me fill your glass.' She poured carefully to within a fraction of the rim. The wine bellied up slightly into the lamplight. 'I too dream of the future, not the wild or the frightening things, just the truth.'

Finn smiled.

'Ah, the wide smile of disbelief! As when I did your palm. You think I'm a wild mad woman. Many have called me that in my time. But I do see the future and I do cure ailments. And I'm not a witch. The cures I learned from my mother who was born in India and she from her mother who had been stationed in India most of her life. They were simply wives of military men, as was I.'

'Hubert was a soldier?' Finn bit into a sandwich which tasted of egg and some other sweet spicy thing.

'Oh yes, Hubert was a soldier. As was my husband.' She looked Finn calmly in the eye. Finn stopped chewing. 'They were both fine soldiers. Hubert was a brave, fine soldier. Decorated in the Great War for brave deeds. As was my husband. I was there, with Hubert . . . Then he was shelled and the nightmares began.'

'With him? You were with him here?'

'I rented a house in the south and he came whenever he could. Do you know France?'

Finn spluttered with laughter, choking on the last of her sandwich. 'France? Mrs . . . Jenefer. The furthest I've been is Gateshead, where I was born. And Newcastle on the other side of the River Tyne. Durham City. I've never even been to York. My mother has, when she was young. She's always on about it, getting away from here. Having adventures. Always has her head in a book, reading about faraway places. She would have liked to travel herself.'

Jenefer filled her glass. 'You should go. To France. It is a wonderful country. Wide and bright. Pale and dusty. Wonderful people. They are sensual, people of appetite, not to stiff as the English . . . Hubert!'

The door had opened and Hubert was standing framed in the doorway. His feet were bare and he was dressed, Roman fashion, in what looked like a counterpane. He smiled angelically from one to the other. 'The child has come. How lovely. Did you show her?'

'No, dearest boy, but I will.' Jenefer walked over to him, took his arm, and settled him into his chair. She took a notebook from the table beside him and went back to sit beside Finn. She riffled through it, found a page and held it out.

Finn, her head whirling now with the wine and the worry about where the encounter was leading, looked at the page and stared at the drawing. It had been completed in a few absolutely confident lines, and showed herself standing at bay, in her nightshift with the ties undone: a straight image and a ghostly reflection through a glass door.

Finn looked up at Jenefer. 'He drew this from seeing me the other night, when you arrived in New Morven?'

Jenefer shook her head, and leaned closer to read the date at the top of the page. "January 8th." I date them all, to impose some kind of order on this chaos in which we live.'

Finn blinked and stared even harder at it. 'Is he a magician?'

Jenefer laughed merrily. 'No. He just sees through time, as do I.'

'He, you couldn't do that. You . . . Time . . .'

'Time! Just think of time as a swirling pole covered with layers and layers of fine gauze cloth. Sometimes the layers lift as the pole swirls round and we glimpse an event, a person gone before or still to come; sometimes there is a tear in the cloth and we see more clearly. For some people the whole contraption slows down so we get more than a glimpse.'

'And both of you do it?'

Jenefer shrugged. 'He couldn't before he was so injured. He used to laugh at me then and my seeing things, as do others. But now he sees things and doesn't want to see them. He sees too much: great battles . . . the earth rent to pieces. It is all too confused for him. He has no meaning to fix to these things. So it makes him,' fondly she looked over at the beaming Hubert, 'what they call mad.'

Finn stood up, swaying slightly. 'Well, it has been very nice, Mrs Jenefer. I must get back. My dad'll be reopening the shop any minute.'

Jenefer stood up, smiling faintly. 'You will come again? Tomorrow?'

Finn nodded. She knew she wanted to. 'Saturday. It's busy in the shop. But . . . yes. Yes, thank you.' She looked across at Hubert, who was fiddling the fringe on the counterpane where it covered his knees.

'Did you like it?' he said. 'My drawing?'

'It's lovely, Hubert. You're clever to see it so clearly.'

He beamed at this and sat back in his chair. Jenefer went and stood by him, leaving Finn to find her own way out. Then, as she raced down the path, gulping in clear air to clear her head, she tripped over the black and white cat, which went squealing into the house.

The shop was crowded when she got back. Ignoring the stares at her muddy face, she made her way straight into the back kitchen and sat down beside the fire, taking deep breaths to stop her head spinning. The shop bell rang as her father showed the last customer out.

He popped his head round the curtain. 'So what on earth's' happened to you? You're covered with mud.'

She started to giggle. 'I tripped over the cat. And yes, seeing as you ask me, I've had a lovely time. A lovely time. They're both mad as hatters and I think it's catching.' She was roaring with laughter now.

He came closer and put his face beside hers. 'Finn. What have you been doing? Wine!'

She fell against him. 'Too much Madeira wine, my dear dad. Too much Madeira, my dear.'

He held her upright for a moment, his face flushing, then pressed her into the chair and pulled away. She put her arms round his neck. 'Why is it you never touch me, my dear dad. Never touch me.'

He dragged her hands off him and stood back even further, shaking his head. 'That Mrs Loumis wants telling. Giving wine to—'

'Twenty-one, I am. Nearly twenty-one anyway. Never been kissed, kicked, followed home or photographed . . . Isn't that what Gladys Gregson says?' She sat back in the chair and closed her eyes, pleased to shut out the whirling world for a moment.

'Patrick!' The icy tones of her mother brought Finn upright. Esther was standing on the stairs in her nightie. 'What's happening? Look at the state of her! What have you done now?'

Finn smiled at her. 'I did it all myself, Mummy. And aren't I a clever girl getting you out of bed and all the way down here? Like I was clever getting you to marry him in the first place? Wasn't I a clever girl then?'

Patrick gulped back a great rattle of laughter and watched as Esther turned and banged back upstairs, her uncorseted bottom wobbling.

The next morning, as always on a Saturday, the shop was busy with people coming in with their biggest baskets for their carefully considered weekend shopping. Old Hazelwood was waiting patiently at the back for his tobacco and Mrs Punchard, whose quiet personality blazed out every Sunday as she sang at the Sally Army Citadel, was buying black bullets for her youngest, who had a struggle to sit still during the long period of witness, when people came forward to proclaim their salvation by Jesus.

Patrick served Mrs Fosdick, fretting as he added up the generous list, knowing just what it would cost him in the vicar's unpaid account. And Finn served Gladys Gregson, who could not keep her mind on her order for listening to the conversations around her.

Finn was asking for a second time how much bacon Gladys wanted, when out of the corner of her eye she spotted a small dark-haired boy reach out, take a tin of corned beef from a display and stuff it inside his ragged jacket.

'Hey!' she shouted, and the boy shot out through the door, the bell jangling behind him.

'Run after him, Finn,' said Patrick, momentarily distracted from the meticulous demands of Mrs Fosdick. 'Get that back, will you?'

The other customers crowded at the door as Finn gave chase right down Mainstreet, up beyond The Eagle, into the warren of lanes and streets beyond known as the Swamps. This was a damp area of New Morven, in the elbow of the River Gaunt, threaded with the old streets built by the iron company, now offered at peppercorn rents to ensure the properties had legal tenants rather than 'casuals', who assumed ownership of any empty house going.

Here in the lanes, despite the cold, people lived outside in the fresh air, rather than inside the dank cabins: women of all ages were leaning in their doorways calling snippets of gossip to each other. Men, mostly unemployed in this district, squatted on their haunches against the sunny walls, whittling wood, chewing tobacco, reading tattered papers. Or just talking.

Finn caught a flash of the whiter bridge between bared blackened toe and heel as the boy vanished into a long yard which had six houses backing on to it served by three earth closets and a single tap. He swerved into a middle house and the door banged behind him.

Finn paused a little to get back her breath, then quietly walked to the door and knocked on it. She knocked three times, then finally banged it with the flat of her hand.

The door opened four inches and she gave it a push. Two girls aged about eight stood there. Their dark hair straggled down their backs and their bare feet were black. The grubby faces, large-eyed, regular featured with smooth, almost olive skin, were beautiful. They were also identical.

Two pairs of dark eyes stared up at her.

'A boy just came in here,' Finn stated.

The two heads shook as one.

'He did. I saw him. And I saw him steal a tin from my shop. If I don't find him I'll go and get Sergeant Corcoran.'

28

'No boy here,' said one twin. The other shook her head again.

'There is. I saw him!' She reached out to push them aside and was stopped by a deep voice behind her.

'Nancy, Toots, let the lady in.'

Finn stood back and almost fell over a man who had come quietly behind her: a man of about twenty in working clothes with a red neckerchief round his neck and a cap pushed back on to the back of his head. Like the twins he had black hair, olive skin and fine dark eyes, now glittering with aggression. He was fuller faced and heavier built than most of the men in the lanes. He must be in work.

The eyes looked at her with flint in them. 'You demanded to go in, so get yourself inside.'

She flushed and walked into the tiny space ahead of him. Although the day was bright outside, in here it was dark and stuffy, smelling of potato peelings and old dust.

The man stood before the fireplace, a silent twin lodged herself on either side of him. The three dark beautiful faces stared at Finn. 'Now. What was it?' There was no deference in his voice. Usually Finn, the grocer's daughter, was treated with mild politeness and respect.

She stood her ground. 'I'm from Montague's the grocer's shop in Mainstreet and a little boy came in there.' She looked around the bare, deserted room. 'He stole a tin of corned beef. I followed him here.'

'Montague's? They said old Montague had died.'

'Our Michael's bin in Scotland,' said the twin on his right. 'A long time.'

'The one that died was my father's uncle,' said Finn.

'Well, like you see, Miss Montague, there's no boy here.'

The space above their heads was disturbed by a shuffling noise and a swallowed cough. They all looked towards the ladder that led up to the sleeping space.

The man brought her eye back to his. 'Like I say, there's no boy here. So you can get off back to your shop.'

She looked down at the twins again, noticing how the faint shadows under the eyes emphasised their beauty. And she looked round at the cold bare space. 'No. I see there's no boy. But should you see a little boy, bigger than Nancy and Toots here, but with those same lovely eyes . . . if you should see that little boy then you can tell him he can keep the tin of corned beef. It'll make a nice hash.'

There was the faintest glimmer in the man's dark eyes, but no smile on his face.

She held out her hand. 'I'm Finn Montague.'

He looked at it, then wiped his own hand down his thigh before

29

he just touched it with hers. 'I'm Michael O'Toole an' here's me sisters Nancy, real name Alice, and Toots, real name Bernadette. An' the lad who outrun you, he's called Thomas, but we call him Smiler.' He smiled faintly, showing white even teeth. 'Mebbe one day you'll catch up with him.'

She shook her head. 'Next time I won't bother. He's faster than a train.'

'Well?' he said.

'Well,' she said, 'I'll get back to my shop.'

'Yes,' he said and turned his back on her to rattle the coals in the tiny grate.

Her cheeks were burning as she strode back through the churned-up dirt of the yard. Her head was boiling up with anger against the man and his rudeness, and swirling with confusion at the sight of poverty which she knew existed but which she had only ever, so far, viewed from the safe barrier of a shop counter.

That afternoon Patrick took his turn on deliveries, setting out on his longer round up the valley with his cart. After an early healthy trickle of customers Finn was on her own in the shop. She had just cleared round and settled down to read when the bell jangled yet again. She lifted her head from her book and looked straight into the sloe-dark eyes of Michael O'Toole. He banged the tin of corned beef on to the counter.

'I caught up with the boy you were chasin'. That reprobate Smiler. Seems he did pocket this from your shop.'

She stood up and shook her head. 'No. I said he could keep it. Obviously you . . .' She pushed it towards him.

'Obviously we . . . what?' He pushed it back, glaring at her.

'No, nothing. It was just a little child's prank.' She picked up the tin and walked round and put it back on display. 'Thank you for bringing it back, Mr O'Toole.'

He nodded, turned his back and made for the door. His hand on the sneck, he looked back at her. 'I've been in Scotland workin' three years, then was laid off. Me brother Mark was laid off down here with no work an' off now to Canada, no by-your-leave. They were sellin' the furniture to buy food an' coal. Then me mother died, an' I had no idea they were, well, she was, so far down. Things're bad, like.'

'These are hard times, Mr O'Toole.'

'Aye, they are, an' it's time somebody did sommat about it. I tell you that. An' there's them'll do sommat about it in the end. You watch.'

The door clashed behind him and the bell trembled for a full minute before it stilled. Finn's hands were shaking as she found her place in the book again, and the print danced before her eyes as she tried to read words about the brave British soldiers in battle against the insurgent natives in North-west India.

4

Pastoral Duties

Widowhood had come upon the Reverend Hildebrand Marchant as a surprising delight. He had found the whole business of taking a wife irksome. Being the youngest son of an eminent, though more recently impecunious, Durham family, holy orders had been his only option if he wanted to continue a life of some gentility. Hildebrand's faith in God was a matter of custom and convenience, a vehicle for power unobtainable otherwise.

When it came to the point, it had been no easy task to select a suitable wife, who was superior enough to sit at the dinner table at Banville Hall, home of Sir Oliver Marchant, Hildebrand's bachelor brother; genteel but strong enough to withstand the rigours of a near derelict, impoverished Northern parish; and sufficiently pleasing to engage his own legitimate carnal interest. Above all, he searched out a woman who would be pious and retiring, grateful for the attention of himself, a scion of the eminent Marchant family, a descendant of the legendary Tolly Marchant about whom songs had been written.

Yet he had found the paragon in Harriet Bartram, fifth daughter of the widow of a dean, brought up in the shadow of a cathedral but at the time of his courtship enduring genteel poverty. His courtship had been authoritative. He was clever enough to woo the mother rather than the daughter. The good lady had found his pedantic charms hard to resist and she eventually ensured her daughter's compliance.

However, once installed in the vicarage, with her staff and her status, Harriet, this paragon, gentle lamb, had turned to a raging lioness, her excesses only to be curbed by her husband's nightly, sometimes twice-nightly, insistence on his God-given nuptial rights. Apart from that, he had left Harriet to rule her kingdom and gone about his own business in the parish and the wider county. As a Marchant he dined at the better tables, even hunted on horses kindly lent to him by his brother, Sir Oliver.

31

From the start, being so persistently confined by pregnancy, his dear Harriet had not been able to join him in the pleasures of his brother's table and extended social circle. Unfortunately, contrary to appearances, her family stock cannot have been strong, as she kept losing the children: two stillborn and two further lost at half-term. It was Hildebrand's custom that they pray before their nuptials, and he began to add special prayers that she might be strong and bear him the son that was his right and would be his brother, Oliver's heir. She must make her body welcome the child into the world rather than snuff out the life before it was lived. Then he insisted she say her amen in a louder, clearer voice before they embarked again on their nightly joining.

Then his son, Daniel, was born. From his study at the far end of the house, Hildebrand could hear the shrieking, lusty voice proclaim his entry into the world. Following previously agreed instructions the nurse brought the baby, pink and clean and wrapped in a snowy shawl, through the long corridors of the house to the study for the paternal inspection.

He pulled the shawl aside with a long finger. All the parts were there. 'Does it thrive, nurse?' he said.

She pinched Daniel's cheek and he began to brawl. 'He thrives, Vicar,' she said. 'A fine boy. He thrives.'

Hildebrand contrived, with the help of the local nurse, and then a grander creature whom he had hired from Newcastle, to keep the baby away from Harriet. The money for this superior nurse came from Oliver who, maintaining sturdy bachelor status, had no heir and fully intended to take a special interest in this new Marchant pup, Daniel James Oliver Marchant.

When Harriet cried for her baby Hildebrand would take her hand and say gently, 'The babe needs care and you are weak, my dear. You must get strong and he is in good hands.'

She had looked at him then through red-rimmed eyes. 'You think I'll hurt him.'

He patted the hand. 'No, no, dear. You are quite mistaken. Just get well and we'll see.'

He did his part. He left her alone at night, denying himself his nuptual rights. Strangely, at the safe arrival of his son, his own pressing carnal desires died. It was a relief to put from him that act which, though distasteful, he had always considered a legitimate response to his baser nature, properly ordained by God.

For three long weeks Harriet had ranted and raved, and that dreadful wailing permeated the vicarage. Then she became strong enough to move out of her distant room into the main house. By that time she showed no interest whatsoever in the child, even going down the narrow backstairs to avoid the nursery door.

She would burst into the kitchen at the most inconvenient moments. The cook had objected to this invasion of her territory, but the vicar told cook to wait, to give Mrs Marchant time. This strange behaviour would soon pass. But it didn't. Poor Harriet began to indulge in embarrassing rages and, when she climbed on to a window sill to babble some rubbish about Mary Magdalene, she had had to be forbidden to enter the church. He did ensure, though, that she had the benefit of her own private communion and the preparatory ruminations for the sermons which were the highlights of his services.

And there was the terrible episode when she had been found on Priorton Railway Station dressed only in her nightdress and top coat. Then, on the very day Dr Lewis was to come to take her to Sedgefield for some treatment, she did that final terrible thing. Hildebrand shuddered even now. It was so much worse, because the men who found her, taking the short cut over the fields were lewd pitmen: Nonconformists of the worst type, who had little respect for the Church. Hildebrand's heart stilled a moment as he thought of their coming upon her, lying exactly in the centre of a newly ploughed field, blood trailing from her cut wrists which were crossed demurely over her ample breasts.

He shook his head to shake the distant past out of it. Then he rang the small silver bell which always lay by his plate. 'Mrs Fosdick! More marmalade, more marmalade! This house is getting slacker by the day. Just look at the daily papers. Don't you know there's a queue of women from here to Doncaster just waiting to supplant you and your idle minions?' He glared at her, unsmiling, and she bustled off, her sour heart warming towards him in the peculiar way it always did when he bullied her.

She brought the marmalade back in its silver dish, curtsied as neatly as her bulk would allow, and said meekly, 'Sorry, Vicar. That May Lynn has gone off again on her wanderings.'

His fist came down on the table. 'I have told you before the folly of employing vagrants and gypsies. They may be cheap workers but have you seen them in the lanes? They're barely human.'

'Begging your pardon, Vicar, but she *is* very cheap and works like a donkey when she's here. This is a big house . . .'

'Go! Go!' He fluttered a narrow hand at her to dismiss her, but she stayed. 'What is it, woman?'

'Mr Daniel said he would be back by ten. He's hared off on that bike of his, visiting his Uncle Oliver for the horseriding. He'll be back by ten.'

The vicar nodded, watched her go from the room, then spread the marmalade thickly, a meagre smile flickering across his face. Daniel was sensible about his uncle. Knew which side of his bread his own marmalade was spread. Every vacation apart from this recent long spell in America, he had spent time at Oliver's: riding, visiting the farm and the mines, making the right noises; hiding the relish with which he anticipated his inheritance. The school and university had done their jobs there: Daniel had an easy manner, a blend of deference and high intelligence which would get him a long way in the world. Talked some nonsense now and then, of course, but that was youth. Hildebrand bit into the toast and the thick marmalade oozed at the side and stuck to his chin. He finished the whole slice before bothering to wipe off the marmalade with his snowy napkin.

Within a few weeks Finn was going across to Plush Folly after tea each day to deliver one large white and one small brown loaf of bread. On the Thursday of the second week she was pounced on by Jenefer, pressed into a chair and, refusing more Madeira wine, handed tea and biscuits.

Jenefer questioned her closely about the shop and its customers. 'I've had both Mrs Gregson and Mrs Punchard here this week on some pretext about simples.'

'Simples?'

Jenefer laughed. 'Medicines, pills, potions. Mrs Bella Smith had apparently been talking about the pots and jars in my kitchen, and the herbs hanging in my back bedroom. I'd told her I made medicines. Do you know these women, Finn? Mrs Punchard was asking for jam jars for her Salvation Army mission, and Mrs Gregson asked if I was cheaper than the doctor.'

'Nothing happens in this village that Gladys Gregson doesn't see. Eyes like a hawk. And Mrs Punchard's nice enough. Collects jam jars for the Salvation Army, who sell them to factories in the South. Or sometimes my dad'll buy them off her if a supplier's asking for them. They buy hymn books with the money.' Finn shrugged. 'Yes, I know the women. I know all the village, from the other side of the counter, that is. Gladys jaws on about everyone and everything. I wouldn't tell her my secrets. Mrs Punchard is nice except when she goes on about Jesus.' She paused to drink her tea. 'I can't say I know people properly. I didn't grow up amongst them.'

'Mrs Smith keeps coming. She's never off the doorstep, telling me how she always cleaned for old Uncle Warburton.'

'She has a hard time, Bella. Works her socks off for her family.'

'Well, she was helpful on the first big clear-up but I can't have her here to clean. Either she'd scare Hubert to death or vice versa.' She paused. 'It must be nice, helping your father in the shop?'

'It's interesting enough. Good when we're busy. You get some funny people in, though. Had this woman in causing a stir the other day, hanging round for two hours till I got back from my rounds,

34

because she wouldn't ask my dad for what she wanted.'

'What did she want?'

Finn coloured. 'Open drawers for her Granny. We always have some put by, but the women like me to get them for them.'

Jenefer laughed loudly. 'Those old-fashioned knickers? Nanny used to have them. My Richard used to laugh when he saw them on the line.'

'Richard? Is that your brother?'

Jenefer glanced at the floor, then her eyes met Finn blandly. 'No. Richard was . . . is my son. I dreamed about him last night, funnily enough. Old Nanny was his nanny.'

'You've a son?'

'I bore my husband a son. I nurtured and brought him to the age of four. Then I left him. So I suppose I have no son.'

'You haven't seen him?' said Finn, frowning slightly. She felt certain that even her own mother, cross-crabbed and self-absorbed as she was, would not have abandoned her daughter so easily.

Jenefer was smiling faintly at her. 'You think I'm a bad mother?'

Finn shook her head uncertainly.

Jenefer sighed. 'Perhaps I am. Perhaps I was. It seems such a long time ago now.'

Finn took a breath. 'How did it happen? How could you leave him?'

'He seemed to belong to everyone else. To his father, who adores him, and his grandmothers, who'd both lost sons early in the Great War, to Old Nanny and young Nanny. I was supernumerary, unrequired. He didn't seem to need me at all. Nor did his father need me. My husband, Arthur, was wedded, dedicated to the army and the war, as you might expect. Then I met Hubert.' She leaned forward and filled up Finn's fine china cup. 'He was actually on Arthur's staff: devoted to the war in his turn. But he needed me from the first time he saw me.' She picked an invisible thread from her brightly coloured skirt. 'And I needed him. Oh so much.' She looked up and laughed. 'Now I'm embarrassing you.'

Finn shook her head, struggling to retain her composure. 'And have you not seen your son . . . Richard . . . since?'

'Seen him? Oh, many times in the early years. I would go to stand near his school at the end of term and watch him load his luggage into his father's car. I would stand at the gates of the house that Arthur had in Hampstead and see him walk out with the man Arthur employed as a holiday tutor. I went to Oxford when he graduated and saw him among his friends.'

'What did he say when he saw you?'

A laugh barked forth from Jenefer's fine-lipped mouth. Say? My dear son never even saw me. And I know boys don't like to be embarrassed. So I just stood and watched. I wrote, of course, but I didn't receive a single reply.'

Finn thought for a second that the woman must be a witch, if she could make one feel sorry for her when she was in the wrong, leaving her young son like that. She stood up. 'I must go. My dad'll be busy.'

Having shown Finn out, Jenefer turned away from the front door and the silence of the house invaded her. She began to make her way along the landings and passages, searching, listening for Hubert. There was no sign of him there, no signs in the garden nor in the outhouses. Sighing, she put on her fringed cloak and tasselled cap and went to look for him in the streets of New Morven.

She was brought up short on the pavement outside the Memorial Hall, which was crowded with men. Two of them were holding a limp banner declaring their allegiance to the Unemployed Workers' Union. Sergeant Corcoran and a gangly constable stood head and shoulders above the crowd, their uniforms standing out blackly against the bright pea-green paint of the double doors.

Jenefer went up to Corcoran. 'What is it, Sergeant?'

Corcoran shrugged himself to one side so she could see the poster announcing that Mr K. Hilson, MP would be 'at the Memorial Hall talking about War in Europe.' Inside her head she glimpsed the notice through Hubert's eyes, and knew he would be somewhere in there listening to some speaker holding forth about the last war, Hubert's war, which they now believed had really been The War to End All Wars. She knew the rage which would be coursing through Hubert.

'I have to go in, I think my husband's in there,' she said.

The sergeant scowled. 'I don't know about that, missis . . .' he began.

Then a car chugged up and the crowd parted with instinctive respect. The policemen stood to attention outside the great double doors. A resentful mutter spread through the crowd like a contagion as they recognised the Reverend Hildebrand Marchant and his brother, Sir Oliver.

Corcoran saluted, then leaned forward to open the car door. He stood back deferentially and Jenefer could smell the damp wool and stale sweat from his uniform as he squashed her against the wall to make room for the visitors. She ducked under his arm and squeezed out to follow the men through the green doors. Corcoran did not stop her.

Jenefer stood by the wall watching. The speaker paused while the two men were ushered to two seats at the front. She could see Hubert sitting halfway down one aisle: behind the darker mass of dignitaries and in the front of the ranks of men sitting, caps in their laps, hair slicked back.

The speaker returned to his subject. '. . . The situation is now critical, gentlemen. Other countries appeal to us, to England, to keep the balance. And we are vulnerable as never before. With the engineers taking war into the air no power on earth can protect you, even in these far northern parts of Britain from the bombing which will ensue . . .'

Hubert let out a great groan and the speaker paused. Necks twisted to catch sight of the groaner.

The speaker glared at him over his glasses. '. . . You may groan, sir, you may groan. We need vigilance, we need to prepare.'

Hubert leaped to his feet. 'No more, no more!' He was holding his head and shrieking. 'No more!'

A burly man stepped down purposefully from the platform and the vicar, looking on with narrow distaste, sent a boy back outside in search of Sergeant Corcoran. Jenefer watched as a young dark-haired man sitting beside Hubert jumped up, putting an arm out to protect him. A blond man stood up beside him. The dark man spoke. 'Your man here is right to groan. Sirs, you want nothing, talkin' about war an' puttin' money into weapons when there's people starvin' in the very street outside. You come here from London with your tales about war, an' you can go back there with *our* tales if you like, about starvation an' suicide, about children without shoes an' men who fought in your last war beggin' on the street, cheated by the Means Test . . .'

The platform man dodged him and started to grapple with Hubert, who fought back with surprising strength. The man finally wrestled him to the floor and was sitting over him with his fist raised when the dark young man pulled him off, only to get socked hard in the face for his troubles. He was then set upon by Sergeant Corcoran and caught in a muscular arm-lock.

The blond man stood watching anxiously, his fists curling at every new attack on his friend.

Jenefer finally reached Hubert and pushed the platform man away from him. 'Let me. He's my husband.' She pulled Hubert to his feet and brought her face close to his. 'Now, dear, darling boy, you have no need to fight. There are no dragons. The man's merely using words here, neither fire nor claws. Now come on, my darling, come on!'

The crowd melted before them as she led him away, followed by the burly sergeant, who still had Hubert's dark-haired defender, twisting and wriggling, under one arm and the blond man at one elbow.

The speaker on the platform gathered his notes again and the wooden benches creaked as people settled back to listen. Mr Marchant stared at the hairs on the white backs of his hands and concentrated on the speech.

Outside the hall Jenefer turned to the sergeant. 'Let the young man go, Sergeant. He'll do no harm now. He was helping my husband.'

The blond friend nodded vigorously. 'Only defendin' the bloke, he was.'

The sergeant twisted his arm further on the boy's neck, so that he had to fall to his knees on the dusty pavement.

The friend jumped towards him but the gangling constable held him off. The crowd standing in the street started to mutter.

The sergeant met Jenefer's gaze. 'It's the cells for him, the boyo needs to cool his heels.'

'All he did was stop that man beating my husband to a pulp.'

'He attacked an officer of the law. He spoke sedition,' Corcoran growled.

'I didn't see that. Or hear it.'

Corcoran unclasped his arm from the young man's neck allowing him finally to stand up. 'I'll have yer name and' address, lad,' he said, taking out his notebook.

'Me name's Michael O'Toole an' I live down in the Swamps in a house that feller in there wouldn't put pigs in.'

The blond-haired man spoke. 'You shouldn'ta' telt him, Michael. You shouldn't a' telt him.'

'They need tellin', Tom, I keep tellin' you.' Michael O'Toole, glared at the sergeant, wriggling his shoulders, and rubbing his quickly bruising face. 'I only helped your man here as was set on by that hooligan in a suit. An' what he was sayin' was right. These bloody princes and bigwigs've no right comin' up here tellin' us what noble folks we are, what—'

Corcoran made a lunging punch towards him, holding his forearm in a painful grip. 'Addin' treason to yer list, are you?'

The young man called Michael O'Toole ducked the blow, then smiled sweetly down at the hand grasping his arm. 'Only in a manner o' speakin' Sergeant.'

Now the men in the crowd pushed towards the sergeant, a low grumble of the threat in their joined voices. Blond Tom strained against the clasp of the gangly constable.

Keeping one hand on Hubert, now standing rigid beside her, Jenefer reached out the other to grasp that of the young man. 'I'm very pleased to meet you, Michael O'Toole. I wonder could you help me to get my husband home? That beating quite took the stuffing out of him.'

Michael O'Toole shook off the sergeant's hand and put an arm round Hubert's shoulder. 'I'll do that, missis. Pity to miss the meetin', though. It was just warmin' up.' He looked across at his friend. 'What about you, Tom?'

His friend nodded his head back at the double door. 'Ah'll get back in there, marrah. Need an eye keepin' on them, these bliddy capitalists, ah can tell you. Thi'll have us back at war in a blink.'

After a few paces Hubert threw off Jenefer and Michael's support and walked with them quietly enough. Then he strode straight into Plush Folly without glancing at either of them. Jenefer stood at the gate and looked up at Michael.

'I cannot thank you enough, Michael O'Toole. My husband sometime gets so agitated . . .' She turned her hands out. 'I haven't my purse here, if you'll wait . . .'

'We might be out o' work, missis, through no fault of our own, but we don't need payin' for bein' human,' he said curtly.

Jenefer went red. 'I'm sorry I . . .'

They were standing there awkwardly when Hubert came striding back out of the house and grasped Michael's arm and started dragging him along with him through the sidegate and down the side of the house. Michael followed without protest, smiling slightly at the sheer strangeness of the man. They walked through the garden, past Alan Newton's cabin, to the coach house and into its wide high space.

At one end of a heavy plank was set up on two trestles. Beside it, two large buckets of white paint.

Hubert turned and put a hand on Michael's shoulder. 'I have a lot of work to do in here, I have to show the dream,' he said. 'But first I must paint all these walls. Will you help me, Michael O'Toole?'

Michael glanced at Jenefer, his face unsmiling. 'What price the job?'

'Half a crown a day till the job's done,' she said quickly.

'Done,' he said, shaking her, then Hubert, by the hand.

Hubert beamed, the dragons in the Memorial Hall now forgotten. 'Can you start now?'

'I can, but,' he cocked an eye upwards, 'I have this feller to see, from the meetin'. What if I turn up first thing tomorrow?'

Patrick Montague, whose cart had been held up by the crowd of men in the street outside the Memorial Hall, clicked his tongue at his horse to set away again and followed the little procession right to Plush Folly. He was thoughtful as he stopped in front of his shop to reload. That Mrs Loumis, a strange woman, though lady-like enough – what did she want with that rapscallion from the Swamps? Thieves and vagabonds, the lot of them. Best keep your distance, he always said. He did have a bit of time for the women down there, who cut and contrived to manage their big families and hulking

39

menfolk on virtually no money. But he had little patience with the men themselves: hanging round street corners, not shifting for themselves. Or even worse, listening to rabble-rousers and causing trouble. All right, all right, it was terrible to be unemployed. But that marching. That gathering together. The paper had called it 'undisguised exploitation of the unemployed', and they'd just about got it right.

Patrick, running his little shop and extending his credit to the point where he was in debt to his suppliers, lived a life only a little ahead of the people around him. True, unlike them his family did not have to worry where the next meal was coming from. And they had decent enough clothes, bought wholesale, with one set for Sunday. He could just about afford the elaborate range of medicines that Esther seemed to need to keep going. But even to live in this modest fashion he had to work fourteen hours a day, six days a week. His only respite was a couple of hours off each night for his socialising in the snug at The Eagle. Things had been so much better since Finn had finished school. She was a gem, that girl.

Weighed down by a sack of potatoes, he pushed the door open with his shoulder and the bell tinkled. Finn was behind the counter dealing with a queue of people. She was taking very little cash, entering most items in the greasy tick book. Not one of her customers bought more than two small items.

Florrie Sallis, Emily Punchard's next-door neighbour, having waited ten patient minutes, finally reached the front of the queue. She pushed an Oxo cube across the counter. Finn looked at her blankly.

'Can Ah hev me penny back on that, hinney?'

'Don't you want it, Mrs Sallis?' said Finn, her head on one side.

'Ah dinnet need it now, hinny. Ah got it last night off yer da 'cos the old bugger was hevin' a bad time an' ah thowt a bit Oxo in some boilin' watter'd feed him, like.'

'Didn't he want it, then?'

'Nah. T'owld bugger died in the night, didn't he?'

'I'm sorry, Mrs Sallis.'

'Dinnet worry, hinney. My Bert was a bad owld bugger. He was no angel when he was here, so now he has his chance to try being an angel in good company. Ahv'e bin his slave all me life. Worked twice as hard when he came off work. All day long, "Give us this, hold that, do this, do that." Not a minute's peace. But the Good Lord saw fit ter give us just a bit of time on me own, a bit of peace, afore Ah snuff it mesel.' She grinned her toothless grin and leaned forward. 'So can ah hev me penny back, hinny?'

Patrick twitched an eyebrow at Finn as he raised the flap to walk through.

Finn slid a penny across the counter into Mrs Sallis' worn

black-nailed hand, and retrieved the slightly battered Oxo cube.

Patrick was on to his second cup of tea when Finn finally came through the curtain. He poured her a cup. 'Plenty business?' he said.

She threw up her hands. 'Plenty of customers. But goods? A bit of this, a bit of that . . .' She picked up her cup. 'And it's, "Put this in the Ticky Book, Miss Montague. Yer da says I can go this week too . . ." Two and threepence cash sales all afternoon.'

Patrick smiled faintly at her. 'Don't tell that to your ma. She'll have us back on Tyneside in no time, sweeping up for your Uncle Harold.'

'Don't you ever wish you were back up there yourself, Dad?'

He shook his head. 'Back to your grim aunties and your sainted uncle? No, thank you. Anyway, I wouldn't go if I couldn't afford me own place. This was the cheapest place I could get after losing the money on that place in Gateshead and I couldn't even give it away now.'

She frowned, cast down suddenly by her normally cheerful father's mood. 'Oh, Dad.'

He smiled. 'Don't worry about me.' He thought of something to sheer her up. 'I tell you what. I just followed your friend Mrs Loumis down from Chapel Street. That husband of hers was in a kerfuffle outside the Memorial Hall with Sergeant Corcoran. I think they'd thrown him out of that meeting where the MP's talking. He looked drunk, Loumis.'

'Drunk?' she said, colouring, remembering herself falling about after the excess of Madeira.

'Anyway, Mrs Loumis had help. It was a big feller, handsome brute, from the Swamps. He's been in here for porridge oats a couple of times. Must eat plenty porridge in that house. Troublemaker back down from Scotland.' He poured more tea. 'I tell you who it was. Brother to that scallywag you said pinched the corned beef.'

'He came for porridge?' she said.

'Yes. You'd be on deliveries.'

'Anyway, what'd happened there at the Hall?'

The shop bell tinkled and Finn stood up.

'The lad'd be there heckling, shouting the odds, shouldn't wonder. A bit of it about these days. And the Loumis feller was fighting drunk as far as I could tell, screaming like fury. Corcoran was stotting mad. Doesn't do anyone any good, getting on the wrong side of Corcoran.'

Finn thought about Michael O'Toole. Probably sitting on Jenefer's sofa at this very minute, being plied with Madeira.

'Did he go into the house? Into Plush Folly?' She felt uncomfortable at her own interest.

'They took him round the back. Mebbe giving him a bit of gardening. Must'a been reading the paper. Says there we should be "giving the unemployed what work we can." '

'What about us? Couldn't we do with someone to help?' She pushed a precarious mountain of boxes with a tightly laced shoe. 'We could do with a hand here. Sweeping up, tidying round and things.'

He laughed at that. 'Next thing you'll be wanting that thieving young tike of a brother of his in here, wielding a brush.'

'We could do worse. The boy would do it for pennies. It's heavy here. You seem out such a lot. Your deliveries are taking longer and longer.

The bell rang again and she stood up.

Patrick stroked his chin. The deliveries *were* taking longer and longer. It was pleasant to linger a bit with the farmers' wives, drinking tea and eating fat bacon. They welcomed the company, with their men up on the hills and not seeing a fresh face from one week to the next.

'What do you say, Dad?' Her voice was quite sharp.

The shop bell rang again.

'Can't afford it,' he said.

'I know as well as you, Dad, what we can afford. Even these widow's mites we take across the counter add up. It's no fortune, I know, but it would only be pennies to pay for the boy.'

'Hey, Mr Montague!' Gladys Gregson's voice came through the curtain. 'Mrs Fosdick's stanin' here waitin' for eggs for the vicar's supper!'

He stood up. 'I have to finish unloading.'

'When you've finished I could go and see if the lad would do it. Sweeping, not thieving, I mean. It'd have to be after school,' Finn persisted.

'Patrick!' Esther's voice floated down the stairs.

He grinned at his daughter. 'Seems we're wanted from all quarters. All right. You get the lad. I'll find the pennies.'

Esther was lying back on the bed, bathed in sweat, in a state of agitation. She pushed a large envelope across at him. 'I've been waiting and waiting for you to come. Didn't you hear me call?'

'I've just been having a cup of tea, dear. Been to the warehouse in Priorton and those sacks take some lifting.' He opened the letter. 'What's this?'

'The postman came. This is a money draft from my brother. He is off to America on some errand which will take him six months. He wishes us to put this away for Finnuola and give it to her on her twenty-first birthday.'

'Fifty pounds.' Patrick whistled.

'Yes,' she said, settling back on to her pillows complacently.

'Harold has always taken his godfather role seriously.'

'Seriously.' He allowed himself a disbelieving tone. 'He has never been near here, and never near this family in two year.'

'He is a busy man! He has a business to run, workers to support, Patrick.' She leaned over and lifted the curtain to peer into the street. 'Anyway, who would come here to this den of iniquity if they didn't have to?'

Even after these tricky years, Patrick felt some love for his wife, but there were times when, quite literally, he could have killed her. Just leaned over and squeezed that white neck and killed her.

'It could come in handy, this money,' he said. 'I've wholesalers' bills to pay.'

She snatched the envelope from him. 'No! This is a sacred trust. It is for Finnuola on her birthday. From her Uncle Harold. And it is not going into this grubby little shop to pay the debts of those grubby folks who get your eternal elastic credit.' Turning her face away from his she tucked the money into the handbag that she kept beside her pillow.

He turned to go.

'And, Patrick. Please don't, under any circumstances, tell Finnuola. It is to be a surprise. Her uncle insists.'

It was an hour before Finnuola had served her last customer. But then she set out for the Swamps, making her way up behind Chapel Street and down Viaduct Row. To her right was the broad stretch of allotments, neat parcels of land already green with successive sowings that would keep some more prudent families fed right till the winter. One man stood up from his labours and shaded his eyes from the flat evening sun and watched her coolly as she passed.

She made her way towards the courts named Primrose, Violet and Mallow by the keen builder who, fifty years before, had thrown them up at minimum cost on the instruction of the Iron Company. As she walked, the conditions underfoot and the quality of the air became worse, and she thought again that the nickname Swamps was well derived. Here the men were not working, even on their own allotments. On some corners they were leaning on walls and squatting in gutters. The faces were older than their years and the conversations were spasmodic as every topic had been worn to a shred through months, years of inactivity.

A young man with a dark unwashed face called across to her. 'Now, pet. Lost yer way?'

There was a ripple of interest and crusty amusement around him.

She went bright scarlet and stumbled. 'I know my way,' she squeaked. There was a ripple of hoarse laughter behind her before they settled back into the half-dream in which they spent their days.

A small beetle-browed, crop-haired girl stepped in her path, opening her arms wide to stop her passing. 'You wanna pot o' broth, missis? Me ma meks good broth. Only a penny.'

Finn's anger at being obstructed died as she saw the anxious light in the child's eye.

'Yes. Yes. I'll have some broth.' She felt in her pocket while the child vanished, then returned holding up a two-pound jam jar with soup slopping around inside it. 'Here, missis.'

Finn proffered the penny. 'Thank you.'

The child clung to the jar. 'Another penny on the jar, missis. But you can bring it an' get it filled next time an' not pay.'

Finn felt in her pocket again and found a threepenny bit. 'Here,' she said, gently disentangling the girl's clutching hand from the jar.

She left the girl staring in disbelief at the shining coin, pleased to do something positive in this dreadful place.

The twins answered the door, at first denying any knowledge of their brother.

'Can I come in, then?' The girls stepped back and Finn bustled past. She stood in front of the fireplace looking from one dark sharp face to the other. 'Toots and Nancy, isn't it? How does anyone ever tell you apart?'

They regarded her gravely. 'I'm Toots,' said one. 'An' our Micky and our Smiler, they know. Our Mick, he put this fingermark on me when I was born so he would know the difference.' She pulled the rough tangle of hair away from her neck to show a red mark the shape and size of a fingerprint.'

Finn laughed. 'But you'd have to tie your hair back with ribbon so anyone would know.'

They nodded gravely. Then Toots said sorrowfully, 'No ribbon.'

But Finn had come prepared. She put the jam jar of broth on the rickety table and from one deep pocket she produced a brush, and from the other a bundle of ribbons. They both clapped their hands, then Nancy reached tentatively towards the bundle.

Finn laughed. 'Choose!' she ordered.

Nancy chose a bright yellow check and Toots picked a red stripe.

Finn sat on the only chair and held Toots between her knees as she worked the brush through the tangles. She talked in a loud voice as she worked away. 'It was your Smiler who I really came to see. I have a little job for him in the shop, not much but . . .'

There was no mirror in the house but Nancy and Toots did not need one. They stood face to face, viewing their own mirror-image improvement with delight. They were squealing with glee when there was a thump and a shuffle in the loft and Thomas, called Smiler, dropped lightly on to the floor beside Finn. She jumped, pretending to be surprised.

'I'll have that job you were talkin' about,' he said.

A rattle at the sneck, and Michael O'Toole came in with a blond man. Their sheer mass darkened the little room and made it seem even smaller. Finn stood up.

'What's this then?' Michael took in the ribbons and the jar of broth at a glance. 'Lady Bountiful, is it?'

'No,' Finn said defensively, 'I was passing and this little girl was selling her mother's broth—'

'An' I bet you paid over the odds. Ha'penny's the going rate. What d'you pay, twopence? Threepence? Healin' the poor natives?'

'Steady on,' said the blond man. 'Steady on, the woman—'

She was bright red now. 'I don't need you to defend me, Mr . . . Mr . . .'

'There now, I'm forgettin' me manners.' Michael O'Toole swept off his cap. 'Miss Montague from the shop, this is Tom Farrell, no great shakes with his fists, ex-horsekeeper at the pit, writer of pamphlets, organiser of marches, who's just told the big feller at the meetin' where he can get off.'

Tom Farrell's cap was off too. 'Michael, Ah'd better—'

'Nay, stay. Miss Montague is just goin'.' He leaned over and handed her the jar of broth. 'An' she's takin' the slops with her, an' her ribbons. You two! Give back the ribbons!'

'No, no!' They squealed, and ducking under Michael's arm, they raced from the house.

Finn took a breath. 'I have to go now anyway.' She turned to the boy. 'Straight after school tomorrow, Smiler. Don't forget.'

She was rewarded, as she swept past him, by the look of puzzlement on Michael's face. But as she walked quickly, then ran through the Courts to get back to Mainstreet she vowed never to go back to that house and that bitter hard man. He might have the face of a dark angel but inside he was as black as the coal he was so keen on digging.

5

Riding Out

Finn's steps slowed when she reached Mainstreet, unwilling to
re-enter the closed world of Montague's shop. Michael O'Toole was
right, of course. She had been enjoying the Lady Bountiful feeling.
It's an easy thing to do, she thought, to hand out thruppences to that
street urchin and ribbons to turn the twins into Cinderellas. And it's
easy to turn up your nose at the men on the corner, forced to pass
the time away till bedtime. Their world's so dark. Dark alleys, dark
houses, dark lives.

Michael and that friend of his Tom Farrell weren't like that. They
were doing something, at least, with their marches and protests.
Getting up off their bottoms and doing something. Not that it'd
come to anything. Dad was right when he said that.

She jumped as her ears were assaulted by an almighty gurgle and
rattle, forcing her to leap aside as a motorbike drew alongside her.
Her eyes widened as the rider stood up and removed her helmet,
goggles and red silk scarf to reveal the broad face and the gleaming
eyes of Jenefer Loumis.

'What on earth . . .?'

'Do you like it?' Jenefer grinned broadly.

'Where did it come from?'

'Tucked away in a barn in France. One of my few remaining
capital assets, apart from Plush Folly. Got a good friend to set it up
again for me, and ship it over. A boy rode it from Darlington
Station, to deliver it. He was in seventh heaven.'

'Can you ride it?'

Jenefer hooted with laughter. 'Ride it? Ridden it since Hubert
used to come winging home to me on it during the war. First thing I
did was make him teach me how.'

Finn touched the saddle.

'Want a spin?' said Jenefer. 'The light's going but there's time for
a quick ride in the lanes.'

Finn looked down at her skirt, 'I don't know that . . .'

Jenefer followed her gaze. 'That is a bit on the narrow side. Go and borrow a pair of your pa's plus fours and I'll wait for you,' she ordered. She lifted a leg, sticking her foot out at a right angle. 'These are Hubert's plus fours. Used to wear them for golf, when he played.'

'Right,' said Finn. She raced into the shop, nodded at her father who was serving, then raced upstairs.

'Mmm . . . What is it, mmm what is it?' mumbled her mother, roused from her early evening nap.

Finn poked around in the cupboard which did service as her father's wardrobe. 'I want to borrow Dad's army trousers.' She said avoiding her mother's gaze.

Esther sat bolt upright. 'What?'

'Mrs Loumis is going to give me a ride on her motorbike.'

'Her *what*?'

'Her motorbike. She's had it since the war in France and has just been up to Priorton Station to collect it. She says I can have a ride.' Finn held her father's old khaki trousers against herself and peered into the scratchy mirror in the door to her mother's wardrobe.

'Patrick! Patrick!' shrieked Esther.

By the time her father had bounded upstairs, thinking his wife was dying, Finn had the trousers on, and was bunching the bulky waistband into his Sam Browne belt. 'What's this?'

'This, Patrick, is your daughter. She's wearing your trousers. In order,' Esther gulped, 'to go riding on Mrs Loumis's . . . motorbike.'

He stroked his chin. 'I thought I heard a racket out there.'

'Tell her she can't. Tell her she can't, Patrick!' moaned Esther.

Normally he would have supported his wife, but since he had had the murderous feeling towards her, the tide was turning in him. 'It can't do much harm,' he murmured.

'Patrick! Look at her.' Esther banged the woven counterpane with a nervous hand. 'Standing there in your trousers like some gypsy boy.'

He put his head on one side and smiled faintly at Finn. 'You remind me of a young private in my regiment in the war. Nice lad. Lied about his age to get in. Dead at seventeen.'

Finn pulled on her woolly hat. She looked hard at her mother. 'I want to do this, Ma. Sorry.'

Esther threw up her hands and glared at her in something akin to hatred.

Finn made for the door. 'I'll be back in time to make your supper. Promise.'

Esther looked grimly up at Patrick. 'What's happening to her? What's happening to us?'

48

He put a hand out to pat hers but stopped himself. 'She's just young, dear, trying out her wings.'

She looked at him coldly. 'Wings! My whole life with you, Patrick Montague, has been a trial. You're stupid, thoughtless, lazy and sentimental and always were. Now your daughter is going mad and you're encouraging her.' She turned her shoulder away from him. 'I wash my hands of you, the pair of you.'

He looked at the hefty shoulder, the quivering back. In the whole of his married life he had only made love to his wife twice. No, once, if you called it *love*. You wanted to call it love. Once when they had made Finnuola. He smiled slightly. His daughter had been made in the pale brightness of a Northumberland afternoon in the winter. Esther had tried everything to get rid of the baby but the little creature inside her had clung on for dear life and Esther resigned herself to having her. After that, he had not been allowed near Esther until the hurried wedding three months later.

In that time he had written her love letters, but they were returned, with the spelling corrected, in Esther's brother Harold's handwriting. Even when Patrick and Esther were properly married there was no question of *bed*. They were living in her parents' house, she in the bedroom of her girlhood, he in a small second-floor room next to the housekeeper. The hatred towards him in that sober Church of England household was so strong that he felt that if one night he slipped into the Tyne and drowned, there would be celebrations.

He was kept away from the baby when she was born, finally making her acquaintance when she was six weeks old. That day the house was empty. Esther wanted to wallow in one of her interminable baths and he was deputed to watch the sleeping baby. He sat staring at the round closed face fearing that if he took his eyes from her she would vanish. She must have felt the power of his gaze, because her eyes, pale and bright, fanned by thick sandy lashes, opened. They widened and the lips trembled and then broke into a smile which was all chuckling delight. He touched her porcelain cheek in wonder, and made up his mind there and then to be the perfect husband, the perfect father, rather than lose this beauty, this child of his own.

He had blotted his copybook just once. He'd had what was called a good war, escaping death by bomb and mortar, bullet and trench fever, ending up commissioned in the field when four more of his officers were killed. On his final leave from France, coarsened by his war experience, encouraged by his success with the French girls in the *estaminets* behind the lines, he had tried his chance again with Esther. She repulsed him and he persisted, tearing into her with the pent-up fury of his lost youth and the dereliction of war. Rape not love.

'Patrick! Patrick! Stop standing there in a daze!' His wife was talking to him, her back still towards him. 'That shop bell's ringing. You have customers in that grubby little shop of yours.'

He leaned over and pulled her roughly round to face him. The smell of too much sleep and sweat wafted upwards towards him. 'I was wondering, dear, why you took me back after that thing . . . in the war. Why you bothered.'

Her smile creased back into her round cheeks. 'Well, for one thing I didn't fancy being the deserted wife. And for another, Patrick, that would have been just too easy for you. You had to pay.'

'Don't you see, stupid woman, that you've paid too?' He growled and turned on his heel and left the room, slamming the door behind him.

Outside, a crowd, mostly children and young men with a great deal of time on their hands, had clustered around the motorbike, asking Jenefer questions. One of the boys caught sight of the demure daughter of the shopkeeper done up in men's trousers and gave a long piercing whistle.

Above the shop front the curtains at Esther's window fluttered.

Jenefer put on the helmet and stood up straight to make more room. 'Hop on behind me,' she said.

Awkwardly Finn climbed on to the pillion seat behind her.

'Hold tight!'

Trembling, she clasped the woman tight round the waist, even tighter as the motorbike set off at a roaring pace along the street. The houses whirled past like flattened paper, and the noise of the engine filled her ears. The all-consuming rattle of the machine seemed to reverberate through her body. Faces, turned in their direction as they passed, melted to pink orbs punctuated by startled eyeholes.

Finn's hat whipped off and her hair flew away behind her. She blinked as the cold air streamed into her eyes. In minutes they were in the lanes. The trees reared over them and the hedges seemed to lean out to touch them, tapping at their faces with green fingers. Farm dogs raced yapping to the wide gates and cows mooed, troubled by the racketing sound.

Jenefer swerved to a stop on a stretch of grass on a bumpy clearing by the River Gaunt. She stood up, one leg either side of the saddle, then hopped off. She removed her helmet. 'Come on, young lady, stretch your legs,' she ordered.

Stiffly, Finn alighted. Her knees felt weak. Her head and her body were ringing with the sound and the vibration of the machine.

Outside her body, at what seemed like an interminable distance, she could hear the water rushing over the weir, the rustle of the wind in the high trees and the evening twitter of birds.

'Like it?' Jenefer was lighting a cigarette.

'Like it? It was wonderful,' shouted Finn, through numbed lips. Her voice came out louder than she'd intended, competing with the sound of the engine in her head. 'Wonderful! Like it must be to fly!'

Jenefer nodded, satisfied. 'You should get away more from that shop. It brings out the best in you.'

They stood side by side looking out over the river, their backs against a broad tree. 'My dad says he saw you coming away from the memorial Hall.'

Jenefer sighed. 'Yes. Some fool was beating a drum for war and my poor Hubert got himself into one of his states. Frogmarched out. Rescued by this young surly sort of fellow who helped me home with him. A very grumpy young man, but very beautiful. Must be good in his heart but it didn't show.'

'I know him. Michael O'Toole. He's from the Swamps. His little brother stole a tin of meat from the shop a few weeks ago.'

'The Swamps?'

'A bad area behind Chapel Street. They're all out of work, the people there. The houses are dirty . . . dreadful.' She paused. 'I'd never been there before I went chasing after this little lad, Michael O'Toole's brother. It's really awful.'

Jenefer bent, picked up a stone, and sent it skimming across the water. 'Hubert's asked him to come to Plush Folly to help him, you know. Is it a big family?'

'There's this little brother, Thomas, who they call Smiler. He's going to come to the shop to do some jobs for my dad. And there are twins, Nancy and Toots. I can't remember what their real names are. No ma and pa.'

Jenefer clapped her hands. 'Twins! Fascinating. My father was a twin, he and my uncle would go into a shop in towns a hundred miles apart and buy the same jacket, or the same pipe. They look absolutely alike even now, two grizzled old men.'

'These two are like as peas in a pod. But there being no mother, they're quite wild.' She hitched the army trousers higher. 'So he's coming to your house, Michael O'Toole?'

'Yes. Hubert took a fancy to him. He wants him to help to paint the coach house. I think Hubert wants to paint pictures in there. So the boy, somewhat unwillingly, will give him a hand. We'll pay him, of course.'

'The money,' said Finn. 'You can buy a man's soul these days, with money. It's getting dark. Can we go?'

51

Jenefer buckled her helmet. 'Dark? There's something dark about you, Finnuola Montague.'

Back in New Morven, Jenefer ran the motorbike up behind Plush Folly and into the broad yard beside the coach house. The last of the daylight had faded and the sharp light of a lantern cut its way through the gap in the great doors. Jenefer took Finn by the arm. 'Come and say Hello to Hubert.'

Finn allowed herself to be bustled into the high space.

Hubert was standing on a tall trestle, slapping on paint with gusto, his shape a hard-edged shadow against the newly white wall.

His hand paused mid-swipe as he turned to see his visitors. 'Ha!' He pointed the dripping brush towards them, then took up a precarious fencing stance. 'Marauders! Army infiltrators.'

Jenefer's laughter pealed out. 'Hubert, you know very well who we are.'

He peered closer and his dripping, paint-sodden guard dropped. 'Ah! The Queen and the maid. A fine disguise.' He clambered down the pockmarked ladder and shook Finn by the hand. 'Good morrow, maid.' He turned to Jenefer and bowed low, so that his smock swept the floor. 'And greetings, great Queen.'

Then he touched Finn's hand. A heavy, evocative scent filled her nostrils and her body prickled with feeling. She swayed and Jenefer caught her.

'There, Hubert, you've quite knocked the child out with your foolery. I'll take her for some tea and you can get up there again and finish that wall. It'll give you a start tomorrow when the boy comes.' Her tone, though threaded through with laughter, did indeed have a regal edge to it.

Two women were standing at the back door. They nodded to Jenefer and Finn as they approached and followed them into the scullery. Jenefer sat one woman down on a chair there and smiled at the other and asked her to follow her into the kitchen.

Finn sat down on a chair at the back of the kitchen, in the shadow of the great dresser.

Jenefer invited her visitor, a heavily built woman who could have been anything from thirty to fifty, but was probably nearer thirty, to sit down at the scrubbed kitchen table. 'What can I do for you?' she said.

'Why, missis, Ah hev this problem with me . . . er . . . *doings*. You know, *down there*. Like . . . er . . . scabs. Mona Golightly sez you give her sommat and it got rid of them in a trice. But she wouldn't lerrus 'av a go. So Ah hev ter come here mesel'. Ah wouldn't bother, like, but me man, he's, like, allus at us an' . . . it, well, it hurts.'

'I'm sure we can find something for you. Where is it? Will you let me see?'

The woman glanced at Finn, who turned her face to one side. When she turned back a few seconds later the woman was seated again and Jenefer was busy filling a small dish with part-spoonfuls of powders from a range of jars on a shelf. Each jar was painted with a different undecipherable symbol in scratchy gold paint. She tipped the mixture into a screw of white paper and handed it to the woman. 'What you've got's not the same thing as Mrs Golightly. This is different. Make it up like tea and drink at least a pint of it morning and night. And wash that area down there, clean as you can, every morning and every night. A week or so and it should be all right.'

The woman stood up. 'Thank yer, missis.' She pulled a purse out of the pocket of her pinny. 'Now what do Ah owe yer?'

Jenefer shook her head. 'Nothing. Nothing at all.'

The woman took two pennies and tried to thrust them in her hand. Jenefer pressed them back. 'No. You keep it.'

The woman thanked her effusively and almost backed out of the room. The second woman came in and, with a glance at Finn, whispered something into Jenefer's ears. Again Jenefer went through the ritual, plundering different jars this time. Again the woman's pennies were refused.

Jenefer closed the door behind her and looked at Finn. 'Now! Tea!' She paused. 'What are you shaking your head for?'

'That was wrong.'

'What, what was wrong?' A crease marred Jenefer's full brow.

'You should have taken their money.'

'Why? They're poor women. And in New Morven terms I'm not. They can't afford the doctor. Why should I take their pennies?'

'First, because they offered it, and that was their right, their dignity. You offered pay to Michael O'Toole for doing that job. What would you say if he refused the money? Second, if they don't pay for it they'll think it's worth nothing. They won't value it. And when they get better they'll think they would have got better anyway and it's none of your doing. So you're worth nothing either.'

'That's shopkeeper talk. I'm not a shopkeeper.'

Finn stood up, muttering almost under her breath, 'Beneath you, you mean? Well, I wonder you can be bothered with us shopkeepers at all, Mrs Loumis.' She stormed out, brushing past Jenefer.

Jenefer followed her to the back door and called after her as she raced across the yard, 'Finn, Finn, come back, you silly goose!'

Hubert, in his workman's cap and smock watched the drama. 'Is the maid in a hurry?'

She stood to one side and let him in. 'I think I've offended her. My tongue too quick for my brain.'

He pulled her to him and she could smell the pungent scent of fresh paint. 'Your tongue is neither quicker nor slower than is

53

perfect. Perfect for everything.' He kissed her and his tongue found hers. He pulled away. 'Perfect.'

She picked a flake of paint out of his hair. 'You need this washing out of your hair, and you need a bath,' she said tenderly. Then in a more commanding tone. 'And you're not sitting down at my dinner table in that state.'

He tugged at her braces, his knuckle brushing her erect nipple. 'And will you sit there in trousers, watching me eat?'

She chuckled up at him. 'If you are very good, and make yourself very clean, dear boy, I will sit there watching you eat in nothing at all.'

'Mr Montague! Mr Montague!'

Obedient to the raised umbrella, Patrick pulled his horse, Bessie, to a stop. He removed his cap. 'Morning, Vicar.'

The vicar and his son were standing on the country road, sticks in hands, stout shoes on feet, midway through the morning walk which was their custom when Daniel was at home, and not called to attendance by his uncle.

'I would appreciate a word with you, Mr Montague.'

Patrick clambered down and turned to face Mr Marchant and the tall lanky figure beside him. 'You know my son, Daniel, Mr Montague?'

Patrick shook his head then grasped the slightly damp hand of Daniel Marchant. 'Pleased to meet you.'

The young man nodded, his full lips moving into a bare smile. He had the slightly yellowed skin sometimes induced when fair people spend too long in the sun.

'My son has been travelling in America and Africa,' said the vicar, 'but is now back at Cambridge to continue his studies.'

Daniel was looking two inches to the left of Patrick's right ear, his boredom painfully obvious.

'What can I do for you, Vicar?'

'Well, I was wondering how your wife was, Mr Montague. I have missed her at church these few weeks.'

'She's as well as ever,' said Patrick. 'Very tired. I get her tonics from the traveller but they seem to make no difference.'

'Poor woman.' He turned to his son. 'A much more refined person than one meets here. A cross indeed, that she lives in such a dreadful place.'

Patrick's jaw went rigid. 'Well, if that's all, Vicar, you'll have to excuse me. I've deliveries to make up the valley . . .' He turned to climb up on to his wagon.

The vicar put a hand on his sleeve to restrain him. 'There is another matter, Mr Montague.'

Patrick turned round and stared at the hand till it dropped from the sleeve of his work coat. 'What's that, Vicar?'

'There is the matter of your daughter.'

'What about her?'

The vicar put a narrow hand to his mouth and coughed. 'She, like her mother, has not been to church.'

'She goes to the Methodists with me,' lied Patrick.

'Be that as it may.' The Vicar paused. 'There was an incident a while ago when she, er, crashed into my vehicle. And was subsequently less than polite to me. I have been waiting to catch you.'

Patrick thought that it was more likely the other way round. 'My daughter is always very polite,' he said.

The vicar ignored him. 'And now, it has come to my ears . . .'

An image of sharp, fat Mrs Fosdick, the vicar's housekeeper, rose in Patrick's mind.

'. . . that your daughter has taken up with . . . er . . . the new incumbent of Plush Folly, Mrs Loumis?' He turned to his son. 'The lady has a motor bicycle. This lady, as far as one can tell, is neither Chapel nor Church in persuasion. Worse, she is said to be the purveyor of noxions and potions associated with the darker arts.'

'A witch, you mean?' said Daniel, now fractionally more interested.'

'Well,' Mr Marchant coughed again and peered threateningly at Patrick, 'no fit companion for any girl with aspirations to refinements, the daughter of her mother.'

Bessie whinnied, the sound echoing into the still morning air.

'Well, Vicar,' said Patrick slowly, his glance moving from the weak supercilious face of the son to the narrow hawk-like face of the father, 'in my dealings with Mrs Loumis, she's ladylike enough. And I hear the women in my shop talking about her tinctures and her potions. Seems to help them where the doctor is too dear or won't find the time.' He put one foot on the metal step, ready to heave himself up on to the wagon, and spoke over his shoulder. 'But what I really like about her is that she pays cash for all her purchases and doesn't run up bills which make a poor grocer poorer.'

He jumped up lightly and took his seat, so that he was looking down on both of them. 'I can understand tick when a man's out of work and wants to feed his family. But it's the gentry that puzzle me, Vicar. You wouldn't believe it! Can't get a penny out of some of 'm.' He clicked his teeth and the horse moved on quietly, the clack of her hooves muffled on the pressed-dirt roadway.

Daniel turned to his father. 'Typical petit bourgeois. Obsessed with money, scraping pennies off the poor . . .' In any conversation Daniel only ever heard what he wanted to hear.

'I don't know where you get these strange ideas,' Mr Marchant

55

snapped. He was generally tolerant of Daniel's wild opinions, seeing them as part of the general excrescences of youth, but the grocer had touched a raw nerve. 'The man's insolent, like his daughter. I shall tell Mrs Fosdick that we will not patronise that shop. It were better closed than housing the ungodly.'

Patrick settled by Mary Fenwick's table, tucking into fruitcake and apple wine. 'By, this is good, Mary. Nobody makes it like you.' He looked around the neat farm kitchen. 'No children today?'

She shook her head, dimpling. 'Colin, lad that helps Tot, took 'm down his cottage ter show him the new chicks.'

He bit into the fruit cake. 'And Tot?'

'He's up by the high pasture doin' a bit of hedgin'.' She leaned towards him. 'There's a bit of raisin on yer tooth,' she said.

'Is there now?' He caught her by the waist and pulled her on to his lap. 'What are you going to do about it?'

She settled comfortably. 'Here.' She took out a clean handkerchief from her apron pocket, and held his chin in her hand. 'Open wide.'

She wiped off the raisin skin, closed his mouth and, pursing her lips, kissed him.

His clasp tightened and he kissed her back, relishing the soft warmth of her breasts and thighs. They kissed till they were both breathless and pulled away, laughing.

'I've got something for you.' He reached into the pocket of his work coat and pulled out a small package wrapped in tissue paper. Eagerly she unwrapped it.

'Aw, Pat, it's lovely.' It was a small silver brooch in the shape of a swallow.

'Thought you'd like it,' he said complacently. 'I got it at Walbrook's in Priorton. New stock.'

'Can Ah put it on?' She started to pin it to the neck of her blouse.

He shook his head. 'No. It's not for there.'

She dimpled. 'So where is it for?'

'Sit still while I show you.' He slipped off the straps of her apron and with a slow awkwardness he unbuttoned her blouse and pushed that off to her waist. Then he pushed off her vest straps and she pulled her arms through the armholes.

'There.' Very carefully he pinned the brooch to the point where her brassiere met, below the deep cleft where her breasts fought with its substantial confines. 'I wouldn't like to prick you,' he said solemnly. He kept his fingers behind the pin, and dug them deeper into the voluptuous flesh. His nail encountered her hard nipple and he turned his finger so its soft pad started to rub against it.

'Aw, Pat!' She caught his head and pulled him to her. Her hand

56

went behind her and the brassiere fell and his face was kneading both breasts, his mouth and cheeks and eyes engulfed in their curious firm softness. His fingers came up again to tease her nipples. Then he held one tight and his mouth was on the other, and he licked and sucked it till his lips and other parts of him itched and tingled. One hand went to her waist, then between her legs over her ample skirts.

Her hand came over it in a slight slapping motion. 'No!'

'Oh, Mary,' he groaned.

'Never mind, "Oh, Mary". Ah've telt yer afore: so far an' no further.' She disentangled herself from him, and stood up, bringing her brassiere up and fastening it, carefully removing the swallow brooch. Then she pulled up her vest and blouse and fixed the brooch at her neck. He watched all this, savouring every action.

'Now,' she said, 'do yer want more apple wine, or a bit o' tea with that cake?'

6

Bright Images

Mrs Loumis came into the crowded shop, basket swinging, and the buzz of conversation faded. She lingered at the back of the queue quietly enough, fingering a crossover apron which Patrick Montague had hung in the corner of the display cabinet.

Then Bella Smith turned again to Gladys Gregson. 'So like our Stacy says, if a feller can't do a bit extra work ter help feed his family, the world's gone mad. Now they're gettin' him in court for false claimin'. Then prison, likely, 'cause we can't pay the fine. So where does that leave us? Without him even ter chop a few sticks or go an' pick a few coal off the heap ter keep us warm.'

Patrick looked past Emily Punchard to Jenefer Loumis. 'Can I help you, Mrs Loumis!'

She shook her head. 'I'll wait. I'm in no hurry. I have the time.'

'Time!' spluttered Gladys. 'We've all got plenty o'time. Costs nothing, time.'

There was a murmur of agreement around her as Emily Punchard opened her clinking bag and carefully unloaded the jam jars on to Patrick's counter. He counted out the pennies which she put into the back of the battered purse that she kept specially for her charity collections.

'Thank you, Mr Montague. God bless you.' Emily turned to Bella. 'You know there's an extra session for soup at the Hut on Saturday?'

'Aye. Our Bobby telt us when he came back this mornin'. They'll all be down there, Ah can tell yer, Emily. Trust me ter be cussed with kids that're all appetite.'

By the time Jenefer got to the front of the queue, it had multiplied with new people behind her.

'What can I do for you, Mrs Loumis?'

'I really wondered if I could speak with Finnuola, Mr Montague.'

'She's just in the back there having a cup of tea. I've been out all morning and she's been run off her feet. I'll get her for you.'

59

Jenefer cast an eye back towards the crowded shop. 'If I could go through? It's a private word I need.'

'Certainly, Mrs Loumis.' He lifted the flap, and, to the astonishment of the onlookers, she walked through. No one, apart from Mr Montague and his daughter, went through that flap. If you wanted to see Mr Montague as a *person*, you went round and knocked on the side door.

Patrick lifted the curtain and ushered Jenefer through. 'Finnuola, you've a visitor.'

Finn's feet came down from the fender with a crash and her cup of tea wobbled in her hand, 'Jenefer, what on earth . . .?' She stood up, looking around in despair at the back room, cluttered with heaps and piles of stock, and barely furnished with the battered chairs where she and her father took their infrequent rests.

'Sit down, Finn. May I?' Jenefer sat down rather heavily on Patrick's chair.

'Can I get you some tea?' said Finn, still standing.

'No, no. Sit down and rest.' She paused. 'I just came to apologise for being such a tease the other day.'

Finn coloured. 'Oh . . . well . . . that's good of you.' She would not say it didn't matter because it did. It was odd, being looked down on, not looked up to, because you were a shopkeeper.

'And I've brought you these, as a little peace offering.' She handed over a pile of books and brochures, and one rolled piece of paper. 'Unfurl it,' she urged.

Finn unfurled the small poster and held it towards the light from the window. It showed a great boulevard with trees and elegant buildings. Above them the sky was a shining blue, and across to their left the sea gleamed and glittered to the horizon, the whole scene intertwined with letters.

'See! N-I-C-E. Nice. The loveliest place in the whole of France!' said Jenefer, with the satisfaction of a magician who has just produced peacocks rather than pigeons from her tall black hat. 'Hubert and I had such wonderful times there. There're the guidebooks and some hotel bills and some prints by famous artists, people who've worked there.'

Finn lifted each one and looked at it closely. 'It looks wonderful. So bright. Such colour. Wonderful.' She sighed.

Jenefer leaned forward. 'You must go.'

Finn roared with laughter. 'You are funny, Jenefer. You are not in this world.'

'You could,' said Jenefer. 'Have you no savings?'

'Even if I did, how would my father manage? I . . .'

Jenefer threw up her hands. 'This shop, this village, is full of women who would love to help him.'

60

Finn looked at her sharply, sensing a double meaning but Jenefer looked back innocently enough.

Sadly she put the papers and books into a pile and pushed them back at Jenefer. 'It's a kind thought, Jenefer, and very cheering. But impossible . . . Unthinkable.'

'Nothing is impossible. Nothing. Keep them by you Finn.' She looked round. 'Would there be hammer and tacks in this establishment?'

Finn stood up. 'Yes, in the drawer in the dresser here.'

Jenefer peered in, selected the hammer and tacks, and without more ado stood up on her chair and pinned the poster, and a print of yachts bobbing on an emerald sea, on the wall above the dark mantelpiece. 'There!' she said. 'Every time you come in here you'll see it. Then you'll be more determined.'

Finn sat back in her chair and surveyed them. She flicked through the books. 'It must be a wonderful place. So bright and clean.'

'You can save up,' said Jenefer eagerly.

'Save up?' Finn laughed. 'To save up you'd have to have a wage, wouldn't you?'

'You get no wage? For all you do here?'

Finn shrugged. 'It's family. My father takes no wage either.'

'But I'll bet . . .' Jenefer stopped her tongue just in time. She had observed Patrick Montague's nightly visits to The Eagle, and had seen him just last week buying brooches in Walbrook's, the jewellers in Priorton. Mr Walbrook senior had been mending a watchchain of Hubert's while she waited in his little back cubby-hole. She recognised Patrick Montague's faintly nasal voice, bargaining for a good deal on three silver swallow brooches of no small value.

'Well,' she said rather lamely, 'just remember the labourer is worthy of her hire. You have value. Remember that.' She tucked her hair back into her hat. 'I have to go.'

Finn stood up. 'Thank you for the pictures, and the books. I can't think of any way I could get there, out of here to that place. But just seeing the pictures makes me feel cheerful.'

'And do you forgive me for my crass tongue?'

Finn blushed. 'No, Jenefer, you shouldn't apologise to *me* . . .'

Jenefer put a hand on her shoulder and kissed the burning cheek. 'What did I tell you, dear girl? Value yourself. You have value. And someone – anyone – who's offended you should apologise.'

And she was gone, leaving the scent of geraniums behind her and Finn's head swirling with new thoughts, and images of a shining place as unlike this dark back room as heaven to hell.

Patrick popped his head round the curtain. 'What was that about?' he said.

'She brought me these pictures and books,' Finn said.

He put his head on one side to see them at a better angle. 'Brighten the place up,' he said.

'No, they're . . .' She stopped herself. It would be too much to explain and she was very tired.

The shop bell rang and his head vanished again, calling behind him, 'Get us a cup of tea, love, will you?'

She opened the book and read, ' "NICE is noted for its fine situation, its lovely bay of clear blue sea, its abundance of sunshine and its variety of attractions. The Promenade des Anglais is one of the most magnificent seafronts in the world." '

She glanced up again at the bright picture on the wall. Then, sighing, she stood up to pour her father's dark tea into his familiar cup, a favourite memento of the King's coronation.

After the present of the pictures and the guidebooks, encouraged by the welcome she received, Finn started to call into Plush Folly in spare moments on most days. The painting of the outbuilding was coming on quickly, with Michael O'Toole's assistance. According to Jenefer, the young Irishman said very little, working at a furious pace.

'Never spills a drop,' said Hubert, in the kitchen one day for a cup of tea with Jenefer and Finn. He opened his arms. 'Look at me.' He was spattered with paint from top to toe. 'Half the white on me, half on the wall.'

'What is it you want to paint on the walls?' asked Finn.

Hubert's smile faded and he turned abruptly to Jenefer. 'The boy. He needs sustenance too. Why didn't you send him sustenance?' He marched out, clashing the back door behind him.

Jenefer met Finn's startled gaze. 'Don't worry. He's . . . not thinking of you. He's back inside himself.'

'Why is he like that? How . . . what happened to him?'

'It happened to so many of them in the war. Wounded twice. Back to the fighting. Blown up again. Then back home. He was very ill at first, but seemed better. We had some good years in France. He painted and I had some money from my mother and then Uncle Warburton, who had this house.

'Then we were in Marseilles once. There was a shooting, nothing to do with him or me. This sent him back into his old states, haunted as ever, doing stranger and stranger things, things which worried people. He went berserk in the apartment of a friend, broke everything breakable, and set it on fire. Our dearest friends began to look warily upon us and I thought it was time to move on. My money had just about run out by then. This place was all that was left so I decided to come back here.'

'It must be hard for you. Both of you.'

Jenefer smiled. 'Not all the time. There is enough of the old sweet Hubert there to keep us going.' She paused. 'But you should have seen him before, Finn. Handsome, glamorous in the true sense. Funny, clever. And then he was the most wonderful dancer. And sing – he could sing the latest songs! Before these last attacks, his painting was receiving a lot of attention. Then he started painting strange medieval images and they started to laugh at him. That hurt badly . . .' Now tears were dribbling down her cheeks, clinging to her chin. She stumbled to the teapot and poured a large mug of tea. 'Here, take that for the boy.'

'Jenefer, I'm sorry. Can I . . .?'

'Take it! Take it!' the other woman shrieked and Finn bolted through the door, frightened of Jenefer in grief for her lost Hubert.

In the coach house the two men were into the last corner, painting shoulder to shoulder in companionable silence. The high space was filled with reflected light. Michael was stippling paint into the awkward spaces. Hubert had a finer brush and was making black strokes on the plane of white before him.

They both turned as Finn entered. Looking into the dark unsmiling face of Michael O'Toole she reflected on Jenefer's comment about 'the boy's beauty'.

'Ah! The maid!' said Hubert, his recent rancour entirely forgotten. 'With a libation for the craftsman.'

Michael made no effort to take the cup from Finn. 'I don't need no tea,' said Michael. 'The job's nearly done.'

'You cannot refuse, once offered,' said Hubert with a certainty which made Michael put down his brush and take the cup.

'Thanks,' he said, hardly looking at Finn.

She looked round at the building, now almost blinding in its whiteness. She put her head on one side to study Hubert's black squiggles, but they made no sense to her. 'It all looks very clean.' The minute the lame words were out she could have bit her tongue.

Hubert beamed at her. 'It will be a great canvas, little maid. A great canvas. A canvas for bright images.'

Michael O'Toole took his nose out of the cup. 'What will you paint on it, Mr Loumis?'

Finn held her breath.

Hubert shrugged his big shoulders. 'Something will come, dear boy, something will come.'

Finn wondered at the mildness. 'Well, I'll just go now. I need to get back to the shop—'

Michael interrupted her. 'I forgot to say to you. Thanks for the ribbons for the girls. They was cock-a-hoop over them. Little enough colour in their lives. An' Smiler seems to like doin' jobs for your pa. I was sour the other day . . .'

'That's all right, I've—'

But he was turning back towards Hubert. 'Is that about it, Mr Loumis? There's a meetin' of the Unemployment Union I want to get to.'

A rational light sparkled dimly in Hubert's eyes. 'And do you think all that will do any good, Michael? All these meetings and marches in which you indulge?'

Michael looked at him carefully. 'No indulgence, Mr Loumis. Only thing keeps us human. At first, when I came back down from Scotland, I thought it was a waste of time. Then I met up with an old marrah I'd been to school with. Tom Farrell. He's keen on all this, says we've nothin' to lose. So he kind of pulled me in.' He was washing the brush in a bucket of water and drying it with an old bit of sacking. 'Jonty Clelland, our old teacher, is in on it too. He was a conchy in the war, an' says those old war-mongers'll make another one – a war that is – before this unemployment thing is sorted out.'

Hubert shook his head violently. 'No, no good. No good!' He started to shriek, kicking the ladders till they fell so close to Finn she had to jump out of the way. He grabbed the old chair he had just been sitting on and started battering it against a newly clean wall.

Finn went up to him and caught his arm, wrestling with him till he stopped. 'It's all right, Hubert, it's all right! Jenefer . . . your queen . . . she wouldn't want you to spoil all this bright space, would she?' he stopped flailing around and stood still. 'Now, look at that wall, poor Michael'll have to paint it again, won't you, Michael?'

Michael unclasped Hubert's hands from the chair, stood it straight, then quietly sat him in it. 'So I will, Mr Loumis.'

Hubert protested.

'It'll be no trouble, no trouble at all. You just sit there an' I'll cover them in just a moment, sure I will.'

'No, no, dear boy,' said Hubert, absolutely calm now. 'We can't have you missing your meeting, can we? Too important. Take him across to the kitchen, little maid, and Mrs Loumis will give him his money. I can touch those scuffs up in a moment, as you say. Go and get your money. The labourer is worthy of his hire, don't you know?'

As Finn opened the kitchen door Jenefer looked up from the table, where she was head to head with Bella Smith. 'In a minute, Finn,' said Jenefer, her voice distracted.

Finn backed off, straight back on to the toes of Michael O'Toole's boots. He caught her by the upper arms to balance her, She could feel the imprint of his fingers even after he let her go.

64

They stood in the scullery, unable to avoid hearing Bella's strident voice as she pleaded with Jenefer.

'Ah know yer'll have sommat, Mrs Loumis. Ah know yer will. Just give us a try.'

The murmur of Jenefer's quieter voice.

'Ah know it's against God, Mrs Loumis. God forgive me for that. An' the devil. But what he did ter her is against God. Ah know two wrongs don't make a right but . . .'

More murmurs.

'Can Ah bring her ter see yer, just?'

Michael's hand was on Finn's arm again and he was pulling her into the yard.

She looked up at him. 'What was that about, d'you think?'

He scowled. 'Don't you know?'

She shook her head.

'You don't see much behind that counter of yours, do you? There's people half dead with hunger an' mad for want of work. There's mothers dyin' from overwork and' fathers dyin' from the sheer black thoughts of havin' to live another year in this pit of a place. There's people gettin' comfort where they shouldn't, an' bairns being born out of place . . .'

The light dawned. 'Bella? Is that what Bella was talking about? She . . .'

'Not her from the sound of it. But somebody . . . Anyway, here she is.'

Bella bustled past them, not glancing in their direction at all.

Inside, Jenefer had Michael's money neatly stacked up waiting for him. 'Thank you, Michael. Hubert could not have done without you. I think he feels comfortable with you.'

Michael shrugged. 'He's a queer old coot, but he's no harm.'

Jenefer smiled at him. 'Finn was telling me you have twin sisters. I'd love to see them. My father was a twin. A strange phenomenon, twins.'

He looked round the warm cluttered kitchen which smelled of herbs and smoky geraniums. 'They want nothin' here, Mrs Loumis. You'll forgive me.'

She smiled straight into his eyes. 'Well, Michael, if those twins fall sick, or if they need anything, you bring them to me.'

He put his cap back on his head. 'Thank you for the pay.' He paused. 'If you want anythin' else done you know where to find us.' He turned on his heel and left.

Jenefer turned her smile on Finn. 'I think I've made progress with that young man, Finn.'

Finn leaned back against the dresser. 'You turn your charm on the lot of us, Jenefer. We're all sows' ears into silk purses.'

65

Jenefer looked at her. 'I can't think what you mean, dear,' she said mildly.

'Can I ask you a question? What was Bella here for? Medicine?'

Jenefer's face closed up slightly. 'I can't say. It would be wrong to say.'

'Did you give her something?'

Jenefer looked at her for a full minute. 'There are some things you should leave alone, Finn. Turn away from. Secrets work to help things stay together, move along. And this is one of them. Tell them and things blow apart. Now,' she looked round, 'another cup of something, or is too early for a glass of Madeira?'

Patrick popped his head round Esther's door. 'There's a visitor downstairs for you.'

Esther shot up in bed, pushing at her hair. 'Me? Is it our Harold?'

'No. Mr Marchant.' Patrick's own heart had failed when the tall gaunt figure thrust itself through the shop door; for him the shop bell seemed to toll, rather than give its usual merry ring. 'He says he wants to see you.'

Esther had her feet on the floor. 'Put him in the parlour, put him in the parlour. He wants nothing standing in that pokey shop.'

Patrick opened the door of the little front bedroom which had to make do as a parlour. It smelled of dust and old smelling salts. He drew back the half-drawn curtains and opened the window a crack, to let some light into the shadowy room.

He looked around. He never liked this room. Each item in the room, though it showed the shallow patina of newness, was years old. It had never been sat on or at except on high days and holidays and there were few enough of those. It was dusty too. Finn got little enough time to come up here with her dustpan and brush.

He shepherded Mr Marchant up the narrow stairs. 'Sit down, Vicar. My wife'll be in in a minute.' Then he vanished.

The vicar lowered himself carefully into the heavy moquette.

After ten minutes Esther entered the room. Her hair was only slightly awry, but her cardigan was buttoned up wrongly and the belt of her dress was undone. The vicar rose to his feet and loomed over her, poking out a narrow hand for her to shake.

Solicitously he asked after her health and commiserated with her on the punishing nature on the fates which would lay one so low. Then he embarked on a meticulous rundown of her family's failings: a daughter who has been so infected by this derelict place that she has entirely lost her manners and who is, moreover, running wild in the company of a woman, who, to put no finer point on it, has very suspect theological views and who was eccentric to the point of perversity and who, from her class, should know better. And now

66

her own husband, Mr Montague, has taken it into his head to make insolent allusions. 'To the point, dear lady, where I feel impelled to take my account away, loath though I am to fail to support a local business in this fashion.'

Esther put her head in her hands. 'No.'

'My sympathy, dear lady, is with you, a person of genteel disposition, fragile in health and brought down to living,' he cast an eye round the dusty room, 'in such a place.'

Esther sat up straight and pinned up a floating hair. 'I think perhaps you are mistaken. I can't imagine Finnuola being rude to anyone. She's not been brought up to it. I think I told you once she was at private school in Gateshead. A refined school.'

'As I suggested. Infected by this place. Perhaps she has learned rough and ready ways since she has lived in New Morven?' he suggested with snakelike softness.

'This is a terrible place. A dark place.'

'It is indeed.'

'And my husband is a busy man. Perhaps you mistook—'

'Incivility is unmistakable, Mrs Montague.'

'But to take your account away . . .'

'I hesitate to make the final decision.'

'Just give him another chance, Vicar. I know he wouldn't mean anything by . . .'

He put his fingers together into a little steeple and pressed the point to his pursed lips. 'Well, perhaps one more chance. That would be just.' It would also please the abominable Mrs Fosdick who liked to lord it in the little shop. She had reminded him humbly several times that they had a six-month bill standing with Mr Montague, and the shops in Priorton were nothing like so tolerant. Her oily stubbornness had won him over.

Now, he changed the subject. 'And I see none of you at church these days, Mrs Montague.' He held a hand up. 'Now I know you've been unwell. I do think, however, it would be beneficial to you to come to church, and good for that daughter of yours. Perhaps, bring her to a greater moral sense of the world around her.'

Esther nodded, eagerly welcoming the price of reprieve. 'Perhaps it would do me a bit of good, Vicar.'

He stood up. 'I must go. I have a diocesan meeting.' He put up one hand. 'Do not struggle to get up, my dear lady. I will see myself out.'

She sat tight in the chair until she heard the distant tinkle which signalled his exit, and then went to the top of the stairs. 'Patrick!' she yelled.

He came to the bottom of the stairs. 'What is it?'

'Come here!'

'I'm too busy.' Unusually there was no apology in his voice. 'What is it?'

He clattered upstairs and put his head round the door. 'You and our Finnuola've offended Mr Marchant by your goings-on. He was going to take his business away.'

'Some business,' said Patrick gloomily.

'Anyway I've persuaded him not to,' said Esther triumphantly.

Patrick groaned and his head vanished. She followed him on to the landing but was left there, shouting for him in vain.

When Finn got back to the shop from Plush Folly Patrick was busy with a single customer.

'Mr Marchant's been,' he said. 'Putting his oar in.'

She made her way straight through to the back of the shop, only to hear her mother calling to her. She plodded upstairs.

'Where were you, Finnuola? I've been shouting and shouting. Your father just ignores me. I don't know what's got into him nowadays. At least he used to do as he was told. Where were you?'

'I was at Mrs Loumis's,' said Finn, plumping up her mother's tasselled cushions and lifting the counterpane in a billowing movement before setting it down again, to lie much more smoothly.

'Huh! I thought so. You're there too much nowadays. Can't think what you get up to. Silly, a woman like that and a girl like you.'

'She's my friend.' As soon as Finn said it she knew it to be true. 'I haven't had a friend since I was at school.'

'Friend? Stupid. She's a grown woman. And you're a—'

'Grown woman. I'm nearly twenty-one, Mother . . .'

'Anyway you're to stop seeing her. I can't approve of it.'

'What do you mean? You were happy enough in the first place.'

'But I didn't know then that she was this wild harum-scarum . . . that motorbike . . . now all these things about magic brews.'

'It's not like that . . .'

'It is like that. I was told.'

'Who told you?'

'I was talking to the vicar . . .'

Finn was at the door. 'Dad said he was here. He's a very mean man, Ma.'

'But he knows what's right, and . . .'

'He's just out for himself, Ma. Anyway, I've work to do.'

'You can't say that, you can't . . . Finnuola, Finnuola!'

But her daughter had gone, slamming the door behind her. Esther leaned back against the pillows, wondering just what she had to do to get proper attention from those two downstairs. They were too bad, just too bad altogether.

7

Family Affairs

During the vacation, unless Daniel Marchant was dancing attendance on his uncle, Sir Oliver, he and his father ate breakfast and supper together at the vicarage served by the watchful Mrs Fosdick. Their conversation covered everything except religion, which interested neither of them.

They did talk about politics in that energetic fashion peculiar to the half-informed. During the years Daniel was growing up, these discussions had been homilies from Hildebrand which his son echoed and approved with thoughtful nods. More recently he had taken an increasingly opposite view to that of his father.

Hildebrand regularly voiced his irritation at the prevarication that was fashionable now in government. 'The English need strong, distinctive leadership, Daniel. All this namby-pamby stuff about the League of Nations sets my teeth on edge. The English people need to know who they are, where they are going and what they are expected to do. All this shillyshallying means that they don't. So we must suffer these strikes and the harassment of these marches. It defeats me that we can lead in an exemplary way in the colonies with our people there . . .' Hildebrand had had a satisfying three years in his youth in Africa, converting the poor Africans, who knew no better, '. . . so why not here at home?'

Daniel smirked. 'You'll be saying next you think this beggar Hitler's on the right tracks, Pa.'

'Ah! In Germany, Daniel, there you have the wrong man on the right tracks. The wrong sort. Plebeian. No patrician sense of service. He'll go off the rails, I assure you.'

'Or off the tracks,' chuckled Daniel.

Hildebrand swept on. 'There are signs of his misjudgement. I think the burning of the books was regrettable. And I can't agree with his actions towards those of the Jewish persuasion. Although I fear to some degree that the Jews tend to bring opprobrium on themselves, marking themselves out with such eccentric manners

69

and habits, wheedling their way to powerful positions, flaunting wealth which is bound to attract envy and a reflection of their own inordinate greed.'

'Pa!' Daniel put down his fork and sat back.

Hildebrand's narrow pointing finger came up. 'It has to be said.' The tone suggested one who knew he had the God-given truth. 'No doubt you disagree. And what views are those reprobates in Cambridge pouring into your young ears?'

Daniel chanted, 'I learn about the sovereignty of the people, the rights of the proletariat, the just division of labour, the inevitable historically determined downfall of capitalism.'

'The babblings of a Jewish émigré who had a vested interest in the death of decent Christian society,' snorted Hildebrand.

'More to it than that, Pa.'

But Daniel left it there. He had more in common with his father's views than he would disclose. In fact, Daniel's own views might be said to go much further than those of his father. The solution to the Jewish question was a nettle that had to be grasped. In Britain, of course, one wouldn't deal with it in as crude a fashion as had the Germans, but that was the German character. The British were more civilised than that. Best, though, that his father thought Daniel was genuinely playing with the ideas of Bolshevism. It was one of the tests, not letting your family know, and Daniel enjoyed the game.

He put his knife and fork together and sat back in his chair. It was a fact that his father had never known what was really in his mind. Even as a child, coping with the shadow of a mother who had, disgracefully, committed suicide, Daniel had always been very good at playing up to whatever company he found himself in, gaining people's liking and trust. He had nurtured that quality.

'So what are your plans today, Daniel?' Hildebrand rang the bell for Mrs Fosdick to clear.

'I'm to travel to York with Uncle Oliver. He needs to see a new gunsmith. He says we may stay over with a friend of his, Denis Consadine. Do you know him?'

'Consadine? Sound man.' And rich and powerful, thought Hildebrand with satisfaction.

'And you, Pa? Do you have a busy day ahead?' Daniel did not listen to his father's reply, something about dealing with a recalcitrant shopkeeper. His mind was already on the meeting in the house of Denis Consadine, where men of power considered their role in the fate of England.

Finn slowed down and stopped her bike, her legs aching. The final rise before the drop into New Morven was just too much. She

70

leaned the bike against the fence and put her elbows alongside it. Two butterflies, the colour of cinder toffee, danced around a cluster of yellow toadflax just below the fence. The heavy scent of meadowsweet drifted towards her, its floating heads shimmering above the grass. The woodland beyond the field was lush now in its high-summer green, and the continual grinding noises from the Old Morven pit nearby were interspersed with the rushing spurt of birdsong. She wished for the hundredth time that she could recognise one bird from another.

These sounds were all familiar, but her head turned when she heard an unfamiliar rasping noise in the distance. She climbed over the fence and made her way through waist-high grass towards the source of the sound. She crept a little way into the wood and stopped stock still. Just ten feet away there was a small deer, not much bigger than a dog, darting round the base of a large tree pursued by a buck, who was the source of the urgent rasping call.

Finn smiled and moved towards them softly. The deer darted away, flickering across the grass and vanishing in seconds. Beneath the tree, their footsteps had left clear marks. Fairy rings. Her father had told her they were fairy rings when, soon after they arrived in New Morven, they had walked in these woods. She smiled. A better name would be lovers' rings, considering the urgency of the stag's pursuit.

She was still smiling when she got back to the fence, to find a tall young man was leaning over it beside her bicycle.

He lifted his cap. 'Good afternoon. I have to tell you that, striding through that meadow, you are a true vision. Persephone personified.'

'Persephone?' Finn pulled her bicycle away from the hedge and wheeled it on to the road. 'She's the goddess of spring. It's hardly spring.'

'Well, the goddess . . . what is your name?'

'Finnuola.'

'Finnuola the goddess of high summer. A goddess on wheels.'

She laughed. 'And who might you be? Do I know you?'

'I'm Daniel Marchant.'

'Oh, the son of—'

'Yes.' He held up his hands. 'But don't blame me. And you work for Mr Montague, do you?' He indicated the painted sign on the bike.

'He's my dad.' She held up one hand, steadying the bicycle with the other. 'And you can blame me all you like.'

He laughed, put a hand on her handlebar, and said, 'May I? It's a long push up that hill.'

She handed over the bicycle and he pushed it, while she walked alongside him.

'I've glimpsed you before in New Morven but you seem always to be bustling about,' he said.

'It's a busy life, running a shop.'

He proceeded to ask her assiduous questions about the deliveries, and how far up the valley she had to ride. She asked him about his work and he told her about Cambridge and how he had just returned from a long stay in America.

'Were you there to work?'

He shrugged. 'Not what you would call work. My uncle paid for me to find out . . . what life was like there. What the people's attitudes were.'

'What for?'

He glanced down at her. 'Just because he likes to know what goes on. What people are thinking.'

'Why?'

He laughed. 'How many questions for a little shopgirl!'

She grabbed her bicycle from him. 'And you've a lot of cheek considering you're only a little vicar's son.'

'Hey! Hey! I meant nothing!' he laughed, trying to wrest the bicycle back from her. She clung on to it, not letting it go.

Suddenly the bicycle was wrenched from Daniel's hands and planted in front of her. 'Here. It's yours,' said Michael O'Toole.

'I say!' said Daniel. 'Go easy, old boy.'

From the far pavement the twins were watching with identical wide-eyed interest.

'It is your bicycle, isn't it?' said Michael O'Toole to the silent, startled Finn. He turned to Daniel. 'Shouldn't fight in the street with a lady, mister.'

'Michael, I . . . He didn't . . .' spluttered Finn.

He looked from one to the other. 'Oh. My mistake. Sorry to push me nose in.' And he marched towards Plush Folly, the twins trailing behind him.

Daniel looked after them. 'Lout,' he said.

'No,' protested Finn. 'It's not that at all. He thought you were . . .'

'And was I?' He put his head on one side and gleamed his smile at her.

She shrugged. 'I suppose not.'

He left her at the shop gate, raising his cap and saying he was sure they would meet again.

Esther heard Finn tiptoeing along the corridor when she went upstairs to change her clothes. 'Who was that boy? That son of the vicar's, wasn't it?' she asked.

'Yes, he walked me up the hill,' she said.

'Mmm.' Esther flopped back on to the pillows. 'Seems like a very nice boy.' How much better this was. More suitable.

'He just walked me up the hill, Ma.' She rushed downstairs to where her father was waiting anxiously for his tea before his nightly sojourn at The Eagle.

As Finn put the pies in the oven and the peas and potatoes on to boil she wondered what Michael O'Toole and the twins were doing up this end of New Morven at this time of day. Perhaps they were going on the train to the pictures in Priorton. She shook her head. No, there would be no money for that. Or would there? Perhaps he had saved some of the paint money.

Her thoughts moved from Michael to Daniel Marchant. He had been polite enough but there was a watchfulness about him that made her uneasy. She suddenly thought of a mistress at school who had collected butterflies: the loving tenderness with which she pored over the cases; the precise care with which she lay them out, spread their wings and pinned them into place.

She shivered a little and looked up to the pictures of Nice above the mantelshelf. They would have butterflies down there in the south, she thought: large ones which flapped their wings in the sunshine.

Jenefer Loumis shook hands gravely with Toots and Nancy. 'Charming names,' she said.

'We're really Alice and Bernadette,' said Toots, 'but our mammy gave us other names to frighten off the little people.'

'They come to take you if you're as like as two peas, like we are,' volunteered Nancy. 'But they canna do that if they don't know your name.'

'Do you know any little people?' said Toots, peering round the crowded kitchen with interest. 'Our Smiler says they say you're a w—'

'Toots!' said Michael. 'Mrs Loumis, that mouthy one has a rash an' its gettin' bigger. Now the other one's started. One gets sommat, they both get sommat . . . Here, Nancy, show the lady.'

Nancy started to pull up her skirts to show Jenefer but Jenefer put her hand on her. 'No. I won't be able to see anything with all that grime.' She looked up at Michael. 'They need a wash before I can see to do anything for them. Would you mind if I took them up and washed them first?'

Michael looked at her plump white hands. 'I try my best. There's one tap to six houses across in the Swamps.'

'I know about that. Well, young Finn Montague told me about it. But, believe me, whatever it is, a wash would help.'

He stood uncertainly fingering his cap.

Jenefer poured two mugs of tea from the great teapot and put them in his hands. 'Here, take this to Hubert in the stable. He's

73

made a good start and he'll like to show you what he's done.'

Hubert was working, by the light of three bright lamps, on a vivid section of the back of a dragon which stretched from one wall to the other. He was painting just below the raking cockscomb which traversed its arching back.

Hubert smiled his delight when he saw his visitor. 'Hah! The painter. What do you think of my fine dragon?'

Michael handed him his tea and stood back to look at it. 'It's a rare fine monster, Mr Loumis.'

Hubert gulped his tea. 'Yes it is, my boy, a rare fine monster. Here sit down.' He removed a palette knife to make a space for Michael on the battered bench that had been there since Alan Newton looked after the horses for old Warburton. 'Now, tell me how you are. Have you found a job yet?'

Michael laughed mirthlessly. 'That's the funniest thing I've heard for a week.'

'Is there nothing you can do? Nothing?'

Michael shrugged. 'They've set up some workshops in the school-rooms in Priorton. Teachin' them cobblin' and' tailorin'. An' they teach them to paint there.' He looked up at the wondrous dragon. 'The feller's nothin' like as good as you, mind.'

'Didn't you want to try something there?'

He shrugged again. 'They mean well there but me, I'm a pitman. Been that since I was twelve. I want to work, to win sommat with me hands, me strength, like. Not fiddle on, doin' women's work. I want to do the work that's been taken away from me. From all of us. Me and Tom Farrell an' them like us want to win it back, to force them to give it back to us.'

Hubert shook his head, he had tears in his eyes. 'We must do something. We must do something.' He started to tremble all over.

Michael took the mug from his shaking hand. 'Aw, it's none of your affair, Mr Loumis. Look there, there's the old dragon waitin', that bit just under that third gill is still to do. You've missed it.'

'Have I, have I?' Hubert mopped his brow then picked up a lamp and peered closer. 'So I have.' He leaned over to pick up his paintbrush and started to peck away at it, Michael's troubles forgotten.

When Michael arrived back in the Loumises' kitchen the twins were there, pale clean ghosts of themselves, their wet hair in fat pigtails. They were sitting at the table, great mugs of milk before them, devouring chunks of bread.

Jenefer handed Michael a cake of carbolic soap and a screwtop jar with what looked like sticky ointment in it. 'They've got the ointment on now and I've showed them how to anoint each other. Can you make sure they wash that area every day – I know it's hard

– before they put the ointment on?'

Nancy piped up, 'Jenefer . . .'

Michael shot a look at Jenefer, who laughed and nodded at this use of her name.

'. . . Jenefer says it's the baths that'll do the trick an' we're to come here once a week to have a bath.'

'You should see it, Mickey. There's this big geyser an' a big bath an' two of us can get in at once. An' there's a fireplace in there. An' this towel, you've never seen such a big 'n . . .'

'I don't know about—' he said.

'The baths will do the trick,' interrupted Jenefer. 'And they'll keep other things at bay too.'

'I can't p—'

She put her hand up. 'If, like your young brother, you listened to the gossip in the village you would know I always refuse payment for my cures. I can't make an exception for you.'

Michael was curious, despite his determination to resist this disarming woman. 'Why don't you take pay, then?'

'Well, I've little enough myself, but it is riches to the people here. And if I took money for what I do, then the scandalmongers would have more to chew on. Call me a profiteer, I wouldn't doubt. It always happens. One has to be very careful. I've been asked to do these cures wherever I've been, as did my mother and her mother. Money, or even any concrete return, pollutes it.'

As they returned down Mainstreet, the lights of Montague's shop were still on and Michael could see the shadow of Finn Montague moving about behind the counter as she tended to the customers.

Nancy put a hand in his. 'Can we have a ha'p'orth of liquorice, Mick?'

He shook off her hand. 'No, no. No ha'pennies for liquorice. We have to get home. Didn't we leave Smiler stirring the stew? It'll be just about ready now. Come on. Let's run!'

Patrick watched Finn as she brushed her hair and perched a battered linen hat on top. 'What is it over there that you do?'

At first he had watched the increasing frequency of Finn's darting along the road to the big house with complacent affection. Then he started to miss her help in the shop. The boy Smiler did a few jobs but he was no substitute for Finn. Her absences affected his visits up the dale to the extent that they were now merely for the purpose of business, with no opportunity for special tea and cake with Mary Fenwick and the two other farmers' wives with whom he had a more than friendly relationship. Two remaining swallow brooches still nestled in his wallet, aching to be presented to the buxom women. Even so, with Esther objecting so much to Finn's friendship with the

Loumis woman, Patrick had taken sly pleasure in encouraging his daughter to go across there.

Finn smiled at him through the mirror. 'We drink tea. We talk. She shows me pictures of when they lived in France. Sometimes they dance to the gramophone.'

'Dance?' His brows shot up into his thick hair. 'You too?'

'Well, Hubert's showing me the foxtrot but I'm a bit slow on the uptake. He's a lovely dancer, when he's in the mood.'

'You want nothing dancing,' he said stroking his chin. 'Your ma'd have a fit.'

'What the eye doesn't see . . .'

'The women're swearing by these skin cures Mrs Loumis gives out. Of course, your ma says they should go to the proper doctor.'

'They can't afford it. You know that. And . . .' she blushed, 'sometimes it's woman's things. Things they wouldn't go to the doctor's for.'

He smiled. 'Aye. I've heard that whispered too. Sometimes they think I'm deaf and blind behind that counter.'

'Well,' Finn said, pulling on her crocheted gloves, 'The shop's not busy at all now. I won't be long.'

'Try to get back by one,' he said, trying not to sound too anxious. 'I've deliveries to do up the dale.'

There was no answer at the front door of Plush Folly so Finn made her way round the back to find the house empty, the back door open and the yard deserted. Following the sound of children's voices, she was drawn to an area beyond the coach house where the garden had high walls on two sides and Jenefer was struggling to establish a vegetable and herb garden. She came upon Jenefer in her broad straw hat attempting to cut down tall grass with a great scythe. Alongside her the O'Toole twins were gathering the weeds in their arms and heaping them in the corner where two walls met. Occasionally one twin would fall with the weight of her load and all three would shout with laughter. The twins had caught the sun and, with their glossy black hair tied back with the remnants of the ribbons Finn had given them, they looked foreign, like pictures of Italian and Spanish people she had seen in Jenefer's books.

'Ha! Finn!' Jenefer stood up and wiped her brow with her scarf. 'What good helpers I have.' Noting Finn's enquiring glance, she added, 'They came on their own, although I think their brother knows they're here.'

Finn started to peel off her gloves. 'Let me help.'

Jenefer laughed. 'No! No! You're far too tidy. The girls and I can manage quite well. You go and talk to Hubert. He's making great strides with his wall.'

Finn turned back towards the coach house, her uncomfortable

left-out feeling enhanced by the shouts of laughter behind her.

Hubert kept the big doors closed, so that even on a bright day like this he could use lamps to work by. He was crouched in a corner, totally absorbed and did not notice her when she came in.

The last time she had seen his wall it had been totally white. Now it was inhabited by a great writing creature which curled and coiled across its surface from a great dragon head to three thrashing forked tails. It was painted in patches, in a fashion which made it look red from one angle and green from another. She drew nearer and with her nose to the wall finally saw each scale was an elaborately worked image of some scene of war. One scene represented knights in armour in the lists; another a gun emplacement surrounded by heaps of bodies; another a dugout writhing with soldiers scrambling to the top; another a shell hole with arms, legs and heads exploding in random array around it; another showed rank upon rank of miniature soldiers marching with rifles at the ready.

She shuddered and looked across at Hubert, who was still absorbed in his task in the corner. Then she climbed the ladder to get a closer look at the dragon's head. She nearly fell to the floor when she saw the way in which Hubert had done the eyes. The pupils consisted of bullets stacked point out from a tin can. The iris was a wondrous weaving of what looked like naked bleeding bodies of men and women writhing in their final agony in a circular dance round the pupil.

'Oh!' Her strangled gasp finally caught Hubert's attention. He stood up, then looked up and smiled at her. 'Ah, the maid. How lovely to see you.'

She climbed down the steps.

'What do you think of it, Finn? My dragon?' he said, his eyes wide open and piercing.

'It's very dramatic,' she said, then paused. 'Do you really see him like that?'

He nodded slowly and placed his palm across his own forehead. 'He is to be vanquished, don't you see?'

She put her hand on his arm. 'Hubert, I . . .' She stopped as her glance dropped to the figure in the corner which Hubert had just painted. Now she was looking at a perfect image of herself, standing at bay in that same nightshift which she had been wearing when Hubert first saw her. Her hair was wild but the face was unmistakable as was the body, slightly heavy-breasted, under the shift. She might as well have been naked. 'Oh no, how could you, Hubert?'

'What is it?' he asked. 'You see the maid? She has to be protected against him.'

'But, Hubert, you can't . . .' She looked into his inward-focused face and knew it was not worth making the protest.

77

He put his hand towards her and she pulled away and turned to run. She ran through the garden, ignoring the calls of Jenefer and Nancy and Toots as she passed them. Jenefer caught her and held her arm. 'What is it, Finn? Has he done something?'

'Have you seen the thing he did, Jenefer? Me with nothing on? How could he? How could you let him? You're using me, both of you.'

Jenefer's anxious face smoothed, her hand dropped from the arm and Finn ran on. At the gate she fell pull pelt into Michael O'Toole. She could feel the length of him against her. He held her for a second as she struggled. 'Get off me,' she hissed.

He let her go.

The shop was still quiet when Finn returned. Patrick, pleased at her early reappearance, went to load up the cart for his delivery. Among the parcels was a special delivery of china for Mrs Harrot up on High Stone Edge Farm. She would be very pleased with that. He sneaked a look in his wallet to check the silver swallow brooch was there. She would be pleased with that too.

Finn hooked her bottom on the high stool behind the counter and rested there, her blood still boiling. They had used her, there was no doubt about that. All she was was an image to be transferred. A creature to entertain. She felt as if Hubert had stolen her very self when she wasn't looking.

After that she stayed away from Plush Folly for several days, and the time in the shop was reduced to routine more mundane than before. One day, after she had served fifteen people in a row, nine of whom had no money to pay, the door rang and in walked Daniel Marchant. He asked for some cigarettes. He looked round, his nose wrinkling ever so slightly. 'You seem to sell everything here?'

'We like to stock what people want,' she said. 'We are a shop. Are you enjoying your holiday?'

He shrugged. 'Not much of a holiday. Have to dance attendance on Pa and Uncle Oliver.'

'You're lucky to get a holiday at all.'

'Can't you get away from here?'

'There's nothing to do if I get away.'

'Would you come to the pictures with me in Priorton? There's one cinema there that isn't a fleapit.'

She blushed. 'Yes. Yes. That might get me out of the doldrums.'

'In the doldrums, are we?' He smiled his narrow smile.

The shop bell rang and Bella Smith walked in.

'Saturday night at six o'clock then?' said Daniel.

She nodded, avoiding Bella Smith's broad knowing wink. She waited till he had gone out before turning to serve Bella.

Bella winked again. 'Ye're deein' awright there, pet. But Ah'd watch him. Yer can tell he's a sly one. Keep yer hand on yer—'

'What did you want, Bella?' said Finn fiercely, remembering that Daniel hadn't paid for his cigarettes. She would have to put them in the book, on Mr Marchant's perpetually unpaid account. What games they all played, she thought.

'Ah said have yer any Quaker Oats?' said Bella patiently. 'That lass of mine is eatin' us out o' house an' home. I dinnet knaa where she gets her appetite from.'

As Finn scooped the dusty oats into a packet she pondered on the fact that they both knew where Bella's daughter got her appetite from. Wasn't it called 'eating for two'?

8

Swelling Sound

Stanley Punchard, whose wife had deserted the True Church for the Salvation Army in the early years of their marriage, was savouring the grand joy of the opening chords of 'Jesu, Joy of Man's Desiring'. The glorious sound released by his fingers winged its way from the great pipes across to the walls of the ancient church and re-entered his ears like the sweet concord of heaven. As he played this music before the service, his weekly offering, Stanley's heels tingled with the satisfaction that he was serving God in the best way he knew how.

The Sunday services at St Benedict's were the centre of Stanley's life. He thought, planned and practised all week to make sure that God got his dues on Sunday. The vicar showed little interest, and within the structural constraints of the Christian year, allowed Stanley to have his head entirely in the choice of hymns and music for the services.

Stanley had been unemployed for four years but the great organ at St Benedict's had kept his body and soul intact. As well as the music, there was the timely remittance from the Church. And Emily was a frugal manager, the very personal epitome of the miracle of the loaves and the fishes – a quality which was very much valued in the ranks of the Salvation Army, as well as by Stanley and their three surviving children.

Now in his personal capsule of delight, Stanley added an extra flourish to the chord at the end of verse two in tribute to Emily.

Down below, in his elaborate medieval pew, Hildebrand Marchant wriggled with distaste at the emotional excess assaulting his ears. Punchard would have to be told. It was getting too much again. The man'd had one reprimand after the tasteless display he had put on on Easter Sunday. On that day, Hildebrand's brother, Oliver, had voiced his dismay at the pagan excess of the music during that service. And Punchard had had the insolence to lecture him on the delight of the Risen Lord.

Hildebrand gripped his hymn book more tightly. Punchard would have to be told. Better still, he could be replaced. Oliver had mentioned a man, a protégé of his, who had served him in the war: a man with passing knowledge of the organ, who knew how to obey orders.

Smiling slightly in satisfaction at a decision made, Hildebrand sang on with greater vigour.

Finn watched the vicar's Adam's apple move up and down as he sang. He had a mean and scrawny neck, she thought, then glanced across at the crucifix asking silent forgiveness for such an unkind thought in this beautiful place. She had forgotten how darkly elegant St Benedict's was, how powerfully imbued with the sense of age. She remembered how enchanted she had been when they first arrived at New Morven to see this beautiful building in the derelict village. On those early Sundays she had been happy to come along and lose herself in the sheer beauty of the building: the bright glass, the polished pews and the twinkling brass of the lightholders, all kept bright by Win Gregson, sister-in-law to gossiping Gladys. Even then, the services were poorly attended; according to her father the chapel on Gunn Street was bursting at the seams. Emily Punchard was not the only refugee from the mean harangues of the Reverend Hildebrand Marchant. Disgruntled and patronised believers had trickled off to the chapel as well as the Salvation Army.

Even today Finn was an unwilling participant. The shock had started when she had got up from her Sunday 'lie-in' to find her mother fully dressed, corsets creaking under her best dress, which was covered by an apron till the second before she covered it with her best coat.

'You've got your clothes on, Mother,' Finn had said, stating the obvious with a sinking heart.

Esther beamed at her. 'Yes, dear. I feel so much better today. I thought church would be the thing for us.'

'Us?' said Finn, glancing at her father who was crouched beside the fire reading Saturday's paper.

He shook his head. 'If I go anywhere I go to the chapel.' He stood up, shook out the paper and folded it neatly. 'Yes. I'll go to the chapel.'

Esther glared at him. 'I can't fathom you out at all, Patrick Montague. A Catholic mother, your father nothing at all. Can't think why you don't go to St Benedict's. It'd suit you much better than that place full of bawling miners.'

'You know perfectly well, dear woman, that I chose the chapel, because it lacked priests. My poor mother died thinking she'd go to hell because of a vicious priest. And I'll have none of them.' He stretched up to get a clean celluloid collar from the top of a cupboard and peered into the mirror to fix his stud. 'And the bawling miners sing a very good song. From the heart.'

Now in the church Finn thought about the grandmother after whom she was named. There was a photo of her in her father's drawers: an upright woman with the barely contained mass of fair frizzy hair which was the bane of Finn's own life. Bridget-Finnuola was an Irishwoman who, in service to a grocer's family in Berwick, had married Bert Montague, a commercial traveller who called at the house where she worked. She was widowed early and had died shortly before Finn's birth. Just because she was an unknown quantity, Finn liked to think she was like her: her mystery allowed Finn to feel that anything was possible.

She blinked, coming back to the present as her mother tugged at her coat and she realised that she was still standing after the other people were sitting down. She sat down and exchanged an embarrassed smile with Daniel Marchant, who was openly smiling at her gaffe.

Almost despite herself she had enjoyed the evening at the pictures with Daniel. He had been a perfect gentleman, paying her rail fare into Priorton, and for the best seats in the Picture Palace, and escorting her to her door without putting a foot wrong.

Esther, noting the exchange of smiles, sat back in her hard pew with smooth satisfaction. That was worth getting up early for. That Marchant boy was much more the ticket than any of the trash round here.

The vicar rose to the high pulpit to make his sermon. He spread out his papers before him. Then he looked down at his scattered congregation. Then, sighing, he put on his glasses to read the notes on the lectern before him. After a second he took them off again to peer once more at his congregation.

He cleared his throat. 'In a recent sermon, our Bishop referred to three events fresh in the memories of most of us. The status and outlook of women . . .' he looked directly at Finn, who looked at her brightly polished laced shoes,' . . .which has had its own vexatious consequences. The Great War, which robbed Britain of the very flower of her manhood and laid waste to the civilised world. And the revolution in Russia . . .' His eye flicked towards his son, in the front pew. '. . . This third, as the Bishop says, has laid an axe at the root of civilisation itself, setting in motion an aggressive atheism which threatens the total ruin of Christian morality.'

There was a rattle as Stanley Punchard's foot fell off the organ pedal during his customary mid-sermon doze. Hildebrand snorted. Even from where she was, Finn could hear the breath whistling down his nose.

Hildebrand turned over a paper. 'And we see at our very doors the consequences of this, the disruption of our lives: self-indulgent secularism, pleasure-seeking.'

Finn, the image of the Swamps and the hollow-eyed children rising to her mind, glared at the vicar.

'Consider the rising tide of whining, of complaint we hear against poverty, and yet are not the public houses full to overflowing? Do not the three cinemas in Priorton have queues every night? And I am told on good authority that the last train from Priorton into this village is a disgrace – carousing and drunken fights – a shame on our community.'

Finn flicked a glance at Daniel. Pompous tittle-tattle over supper at the vicarage, she thought angrily.

Hildebrand leaned forward. 'As the Bishop has so wisely said,' he banged his fist on the lectern and then dropped his voice so that they all had to strain to hear it, 'and I repeat what the Bishop has told us all: "Sin thrusts a veil between man and his maker and blocks the door through which Christ may enter." '

He let the words hang in the ensuing silence for a moment. People started to cough and shuffle their feet.

Hildebrand took care to omit any reference to the next part of the Bishop's sermon which referred, with rather inconvenient sympathy, to the dreadful plight of the unemployed.

He went on to preach of his favourite St Francis. '. . . Did he not give away his wealth, even his clothes? He did not go on to the streets to demand his rights to wealth and fine clothes. Did he not desert his fine house? He did not go whining and protesting, blaming others, demanding food and presenting himself to the political agitators like a lamb to the slaughter . . .'

He had to pause as the Montague girl was overcome with a fit of coughing which got worse as he watched her. He flicked a glance at his son who, with affecting solicitude, made his way back to escort the girl outside.

'I can't believe it!' Finn gasped, patting her cheeks with her handkerchief. 'Hasn't he been out in his own parish? Can't he see the sheer despair of the men, the children who are hungry?'

Daniel still had his arm around her. Now his hand travelled down and settled on her waist.

She pulled away. 'I know he's your father, but he does talk some,' she thought carefully, then said deliberately, '. . . unfeeling rubbish.'

He shrugged his shoulders and his short lower lip pouted. 'Am I my father's keeper? Are you?'

'I know my father wouldn't come out with stuff like that,' she said fiercely. 'My father knows *his* customers' lives. Some of them survive by his charity.'

Daniel shrugged again. 'Society's changing. Someone has to suffer. It's in the order of things.'

She looked at him. 'It's so easy for you, living in your house, with your dinners cooked by Mrs Fosdick, to say that.'

He put his hand towards her face and she pulled away. 'I'm all right now,' she said. 'My mother'll worry about how I am. We'd better go in.'

Inside, Stanley Punchard's soaring chords were pulling people to their feet in readiness to sing about worshipping the Lord in the beauty of holiness. Esther was busy riffling through her hymn book to find the number when Finn took her seat again. 'What was that about?' she hissed. 'It was very embarrassing, Finnuola.'

'Just a frog in my throat, Ma.'

As they came out of church, Esther shook the vicar's hand heartily. 'Wonderful sermon, Vicar. Inspiring.'

He reached out and gripped Finn's hand in his narrow vicelike grip. 'And you, Miss Montague? What did you think?'

'I have to admit, Vicar, there was a lot there that I couldn't agree with. In fact, I agreed with not one thing you said.'

Esther let out a strangled moan and a muscle in the vicar's cheek twisted. 'It is not for you to disagree with me, miss. You listen and you learn, that is why you are here.'

He turned on his heel and stalked back into the church, cornering Stanley Punchard beside his organ, to give him a glacial reprimand at the music-hall excesses of his playing. And to give him his notice.

Daniel caught up with Esther and Finn at the church gate. 'I wondered if we might take a walk, this evening, Miss Montague? After Evensong?'

'I won't be coming to Evensong,' said Finn.

'Finnuola!' said Esther.

'I will meet you at the shop after Evensong,' he persisted. 'I have to go to tea with my Uncle Oliver, or we could have walked this afternoon.'

'She'll be there,' said Esther firmly, before grasping Finn by the arm and turning purposefully for home.

At the tall lych gate they, and Gladys Gregson who was close behind them, were nearly knocked over by Stanley Punchard, who rushed past them, his highly polished Sunday boots striking sparks off the pavement.

'Now what's knocked his pint over?' said Gladys.

'Isn't that the organist?' said Esther speculatively. 'He *is* in a hurry.'

'Aye, that's him. Our Win – she cleans the church, yer know – our Win says Stanley's dead keen on his music, like a mad man over it. Him and the vicar argue over it, but Stanley stands his ground. The vicar doesn't like the way he plays, yer know. Never has.'

Finn thought of the swelling sound. 'Stanley's music was the only thing I liked about the service,' she said.

'Mebbe the vicar's telt him off. Aye, that's it. The vicar has a sharp tongue in his head. Made me feel like goin' down the Baptists more 'n once, I can tell yer.'

Finn lay sweating on the bed, trying to take her throbbing mind away from the raging ache in the small of her back. She had borrowed one of her mother's books, *Huntress of Death*, to take her mind from the pain, but she had flung that to the floor in petulant despair.

Normally her periods were no trouble. If anything, she felt better while menstruating, unlike her mother who buried herself into deeper invalidity during what she called her time-of-the-month.

Her mother's voice assailed her ears now. 'Finnuola, he's here! Daniel Marchant's here for you.' Esther was calling from the bottom of the attic stairs.

'Go and tell him I can't come,' Finn's voice was muffled by the pillow into which she had thrust her aching head.

'What?' Esther laboured up the steps and peered through the narrow door at Finn. 'What is it?'

'You know. Time-of-the-month.'

'But you don't have trouble with that, Finnuola. Not like me, I'm a martyr to it, as you know . . .'

'Well, I'm having trouble now, either that or acute appendicitis. So please go and tell Daniel Marchant I can't go for a walk with him tonight.'

'Oh, get up and move around! You'll soon feel better.' Esther was thoroughly cross at this lost chance with Daniel Marchant.

Through the aching maze Finn had the thought that she was a fine one to give that advice.

'Try, Finnuola! Daniel is such a fine young man, so suitable. Reminds me of your Uncle Harold when he was young.'

'He could be the Prince of Wales and I couldn't see him. Please, Mother, go and tell him.'

Esther was fulsome with excuses to Daniel. 'She is so unwell. Prostrate. Some infection, I think.'

'Well . . .' Daniel turned on his heel.

She caught his arm. 'She would have loved to have come, believe me.'

He looked at the hand on his sleeve then smiled blandly down at her. 'Well, I'm certain we can do it some other time, Mrs Montague. Don't worry about it.'

Esther watched him as, with almost military style, he made his way towards the station. Then she went upstairs to the cold cluttered parlour where Patrick was smoking his Sunday pipe and looking through the previous week's *Northern Echo*.

'What was that all about?' he said from behind the paper.

'That Marchant boy wanted to take our Finnuola for a walk,' she said, plumping herself down on the moquette seat. 'And she says she is too . . . unwell . . . to go. It's too vexing.'

He put down his paper and took his pipe from his mouth. 'That's not like her. What's the matter with her? She looked all right at teatime.'

Esther coloured. 'Woman's things,' she said.

He lifted his paper to his face again. 'Don't know why you're so excited about that Marchant boy. Just dallying while he's on holiday. She wants nothing with him.'

'It's not like that, Patrick. You should see how he looks at her.'

'It's not one of your novels, Esther. This is real life. Stay out of it.' His tone was curt and she looked at the back of his paper with resentment. Patrick had been so sharp lately, so unwilling to please. She was not used to that.

'She needs to meet young men, Patrick. Suitable young men who'll give her a better chance in life.'

'Ah,' said the voice from behind the newspaper. 'Just like you did, you mean?'

'Give that to me.' Jenefer Loumis leaned over Hubert's shoulder and took his drawing book away from him. He clung on to it for a second, then let it go. As she closed the book and put it on the table she caught sight of the last of a series of quick, neat drawings of terrible events, real and mythic, which he had been scratching away at with frenetic vigour all evening.

She leaned towards him and started to strike her hands down his face, smoothing out the dark furrows of over-focused concentration, occasionally bringing her hands down to the shallow hollow at the base of his throat, underneath his Adam's apple.

Then she pulled his head against her bosom and started to kneed and stroke first the back of his neck under his loose shirt, then his shoulders, still as muscular and strong as they had been the first time her fingertips had touched them. She smiled, thinking of that first time, when he had come to her with a message from her husband and had stayed to spend the night and the following day with her in her husband's bed.

The knotted muscles started to relax and the savage tension went out of him. His arms went round her waist and he moved his head against her breasts, working his way like a nuzzling lamb through the flowing wrap to the generous naked flesh underneath. 'You smell of violets,' he said.

87

She drew him to his feet. 'You've been working so hard, dear boy. You need some rest, you know you do. Sleep.'

He turned to her. 'But first, some adventures. Adventures, then sleep?'

She laughed and led him out into the wide hall and up the stairs.

Two hours later, she was watching his peaceful sleeping face when the doorbell rang. He stirred fretfully, then settled down again. She peered through the window to see who it was, then went down to open the door to a rather wan-faced Finn Montague.

'I'm sorry if I'm disturbing you, Jenefer . . .'

She held the door open wide. 'No. Come on in.'

Finn looked around the hall.

Jenefer shook her head, smiling. 'Hubert's upstairs sleeping like a baby. He's had a hard day but he's had the best sleeping draught there is.'

'One of your medicines?'

'You could say that.' Jenefer's eyes twinkled. 'We call it adventures.'

Finn went bright red.

She took Finn's arm. 'No need to worry about those things, Finn. If you know how to go about them they are a delight. Here, sit down, you look all in. What's wrong?'

Finn's face retained its high colour. 'It's . . . well, I can't sit, stand or lie for this ache . . . It's my time-of-the-month, see? Normally I hardly notice, but . . . I feel terrible.'

'I'm certain we can do something for that.' Jenefer stood up and came behind Finn's chair. 'Just relax and sit back, Finn. Close your eyes.'

Finn obeyed. She could feel Jenefer's thumbs touching her scalp and then her fingers came down and pressed lightly on her temples. Finn's head felt very hot, as though all her body's blood had rushed to it. A great heat travelled through her body in waves, untangling the muscles in her shoulders and her diaphragm.

Then she felt the extra weight as Jenefer placed her chin on her locked thumbs, which were pressed firmly on Finn's cranium. She could smell Jenefer's musky perfume and a ripple went through her own body. It was as though the bones in her pelvic girdle unlocked. The pain was gone. She relaxed and for a second was suffused by such relief that she was tingling all over.

Jenefer took her hands away and came round to face her. 'Floodgates opened?' she asked.

Finn nodded. 'How does that work?'

Jenefer shook her head. 'I have no idea. I just know it does. My mother did it for me. Now, dear girl, to celebrate the opening of the floodgates, a glass of Madeira!' She waved away Finn's protests.

'Just one! I'm in need of sustenance myself. The adventures take more out of me than they used to.'

Later, walking back to the shop, lighter in heart and body, Finn wondered if the muttering that went on in the shop was right, and that Jenefer really was a witch.

'Witch!'

It seemed that her very thought was plucked from her head and was being roared behind her, accompanied by great crashes and splintering of glass. She turned to see Stacy Smith picking stones and cobbles off the street and heaving them with deadly accuracy into the windows of Plush Folly, using all the strength of his blacksmith forebears.

He was bellowing like a bull. 'Witch! Bloody crazy witch! Bitch! Murderer!'

Finn started to run.

9

Under Siege

Finn raced to Bella Smith's house in Queen Street and battered at the door, to be let in by Bella herself, who had a black eye and a bruise down one side of her face.

'Your Stacy's smashing every window in Plush Folly, Bella. You've got to come and stop him.' She stopped, looking closer at Bella's grim countenance, ashen where it wasn't livid with bruise. 'What is it, Bella?'

'It's our Alice. She . . . there was a bairn, an' it came early an' . . .'

Finn peered past her in the gloom. 'Alice? She's had a baby?' Finn knew Alice was one somewhere in the middle of the large family. She was still at school; couldn't be more than thirteen.

'She's dead. Alice. An' there's no bairn, just blood . . . An' Stacy's gone crazy. Funny that, seein' he's the cause. It was him that did it to her . . .' She put one hand on her mouth as though to stop the words coming out.

Finn digested what Bella had just said. 'But what's he doing down at Plush Folly?' she said, grabbing the other woman's arm and making her look directly into her eyes. 'What's he doing down there?'

'I got stuff from her, that Mrs Loumis, to stop the bairn,' said Bella dully. 'An' somehow it's all gone wrong.'

Finn dropped her hand. 'We've got to stop him, Bella. He'll do murder there.'

Bella looked at her. 'Mebbe that's what she's done here. Murder.'

'Don't say that, Bella. It's not true. We've got to stop him.'

'Get the poliss,' said Bella wearily. 'That Sergeant Corcoran's the only one who can do anything with our Stacy when he's in one of his fits.' Bella turned away wearily. 'Anyway, I've got the bairns to see to. And the Co-op man to send for. Alice was the only one of them we had a penny a week on. Funny that.' She gave a small sound, more like a bark than a laugh, and was gone.

Sergeant Corcoran, a crowd of eager onlookers behind him, was already there when Finn got back to Plush Folly. He had Stacy by the arm and was leading him, yelling, away. The crowd stayed in the street, muttering and looking up at the silent shattered windows.

Finn went up to the door, then turned round to face them. 'You can go now,' she said. 'It's all over.'

They muttered and two men at the front moved towards her. Suddenly her father was beside her. 'You heard what my daughter said. It's all over. You get back to your homes.'

She stood watching them trickling away, then turned to ring the bell. There was no reply. She rang again, desperately, thinking that Jenefer, or Hubert, or both, must have been hurt in that welter of flying glass.

She leaned down and shouted through the letter box. 'Jenefer! It's me. Finn. They've gone now. Let me in.'

The door opened and Jenefer was standing there, the light from the hall lamp glinting off the shards of glass on her dark wrap. Blood was trickling from a tiny cut on her right cheek. She was shaking.

Behind her on the hall bench was Hubert, blood flowing from a cut in his temple. He had a heavy service revolver in his hand. When he saw Patrick he leaped up and started to wave the revolver in the air.

Jenefer put a hand up to bar Patrick. 'You'll have to go, Mr Montague. He sees you as an enemy. One of many enemies,' she said wearily.

Patrick looked from her to Finn. 'Are you sure?'

'You go, Dad. I'll help Mrs Loumis.' She went out into the vestibule with him. 'I'll see what I can do.'

'It's dangerous in there, him with that gun. All that glass,' he said anxiously. 'What happened?'

She looked up and down Mainstreet, which was now nearly deserted. 'Stacy's daughter, Alice, you know that middle, gangly one? She's died of a haemorrhage after . . . losing a baby.'

'Alice? But she's only a little girl herself.'

'Well, that's what happened.'

He looked up at the house. 'So what has it to do with them?'

'According to Bella she got stuff from Jenefer which started the . . . miscarriage and caused the problem.'

Patrick shook his head. 'What a business.'

She looked at him carefully. 'It's worse. According to Bella, it was Stacy that was the cause . . . Stacy and Alice . . .'

'No.' He put a hand over his eyes for a second. 'This place,' he said. 'This place.'

'I'd better get back into the house,' she said, 'See what I can do for them.'

Patrick walked back down the street, his head whirling, his face hot at the thought of Stacy and his daughter; he thought of himself and Finn, and how, for some years now, being too near her young form had caused him problems. He lengthened his step, went to the shop and filled a flour sack with bread and cheese and ham, and made up bags of different sweets. Then he set out for Bella's house. There was one thing a grocer could do.

Esther opened the window and shouted down to him in the street. 'What's happening, Patrick?'

'I'll tell you when I get back,' he said briefly, and set off.

Inside Plush Folly Jenefer was sitting on the bench, slack with exhaustion. Beside her Hubert was sobbing uncontrollably now, the gun on the floor by his feet. Jenefer bent and picked it up. She hauled herself straight and went to put it in the back of the hall cupboard.

When she returned she said, 'There's nothing wicked in what I do for them, you know, Finn. All my cures are things of nature. I want you to realise that. This thing that has happened to the girl would have happened whatever I did.'

Finn nodded slowly. She looked round. 'Now, let me make a start clearing this.'

Hubert suddenly dried his eyes with a silk handkerchief and looked at her. 'Get the painter,' he said. 'He will make all secure.'

'Hubert, it's late,' protested Jenefer. 'She can't go across to that terrible place at this time of night.'

'Oh yes I can,' said Finn, relieved to do something.

The streets were dark and unlit as she made her way across the Swamps and she stumbled into the wrong stinking place before she finally found Primrose Court.

Michael's face beneath the tousled hair broke into an unforced grin when he saw her. 'Well, this is a pleasure, Miss Montague.' He ushered her across the threshold.

'They want you up at Plush Folly.'

'What, now?'

'Stacy Smith smashed all the windows in and it all needs clearing up and making safe. Hubert'll only have you to help.'

Michael reached for his cap. Then he looked up at the faces of his sisters and brother, who were peering down from the lofthole. 'You come too. A few more pairs of hands'll help.'

They did not need telling twice.

Walking back through the dark streets, Finn found herself between the twins, a small hand in each of hers. Michael and Smiler, walking ahead, whistled 'Lillibullero' together, absolutely on pitch. Finn wondered what it was about this family which made her feel so very alive.

Back at Plush Folly they all set to with a will. Hubert reverted to the role of efficient army officer managing the efforts of his troops. The twins and Smiler were deputed to sweep up the shards of glass very carefully into piles so that he and Michael could shovel them into sacks. He ordered Jenefer and Finn to don gloves and go over the chairs and beds with hard handbrushes to ensure no pieces of glass lurked there.

While the twins were helping Jenefer to heave the sacks outside, Hubert called on Finn to hold sheets of canvas across the windows while he and Michael hammered tacks into them to secure them.

Tapping away with his hammer, he glanced at her. 'Are you my friend now? I was afraid I'd lost you when—'

'Don't worry, Hubert. That doesn't matter.'

Suddenly he was telling Finn about himself as a child. How tight his life was, how confined. Then came the time he first met Jenefer and fell under her spell. 'The French say *coup de foundre*, don't you know? Struck by a thunderbolt. That was just it. She was a queen, above all those around her, such eyes, such glittering deep eyes. People were healed just by coming near her. When I was with her, all those terrible years in school and with my grandfather were transformed into their positive elements. And then, in the trenches and those final days in the shell hole, the image of her rose before me, talked to me, sustained me.'

Finn shivered and thought again of the terrible pictures in the body of the dragon. She sagged, despondent herself in the light of his terror. Compared with all this, her own little world with her father and the shop was a cul-de-sac, a small place where nothing of significance happened, except perhaps that Patrick, in his own way, kept some families alive, afloat in their own despair.

Hubert stood back and surveyed the canvases, tight as sails, stretched across the sitting-room windows. 'There, Michael, that should do it.' His tone was neutral.

Finn exchanged glances with Michael. It was as though Hubert's recent confidences had not happened.

Finally, by two o'clock, the house was clear and safe. They were all exhausted. Hubert started to tremble uncontrollably again. He looked across at Jenefer. 'I will go to bed now,' he said flatly, and walked wearily out of the room and up the stairs.

Jenefer looked at Michael. 'There'll be more to do tomorrow. Can you stay and help?'

Michael shrugged. 'Happy to,' he said.

'Can we have a bath?' piped up Nancy.

'. . . a bath,' echoed Toots. 'We're dirty.'

Jenefer glanced at the clock on the wall, then laughed. 'Why not? You're covered with my dust. You too, Smiler?'

'Nah. Ah don't need no bath.' He yawned widely. 'Can Ah not just lie on the floor here?' He eyed the deep hearth rug. 'Ah'm asleep as Ah'm standing.'

Jenefer nodded. 'And would you walk Finn down the street back to the shop, Michael? I'm certain she'll be safe but it's so dark down there. And after what happened . . .'

Michael nodded and reached for his cap.

Their feet echoed as they walked down Mainstreet shoulder to shoulder. 'All that that Hubert said makes me see what a dead end life is here. We potter on day by day . . .'

'It's not a dead end,' said Michael. 'Me friend Tom Farrell and our old teacher Jonty Clelland, and their pamphlets, would say it's part of everything else that's happenin', connected like a long chain. It's connected to the so-called War to End All Wars and heroes from that war beggin' on the streets here and in Germany. It's connected too to the pitmen's strike in '21 and the big strike in '26. It's connected to the right of some people to wear diamonds while others have to look for bread . . . Sorry, Ah'm goin' on.'

'No, no, Michael. It makes me . . .' She paused. His way with words, the pamphlet litany, flowed over her. She fumbled for something to say. 'But where do people themselves come in all this? People like me and my dad, the twins and Smiler, poor Hubert and Jenefer?'

Michael smiled faintly down at her. 'You're a good friend to that queer old pair,' he said, edging away from his own rhetoric.

'I like them,' she said. 'They're kind of true. True to themselves. I like that.'

He reached out and pulled her arm through his. 'So do I.'

Inside the doorway of the shop he held on to her hand, then leaned and kissed her on the cheek. His lips were soft and she could feel the sharp push of bristle on unshaved early-morning chin. 'I think I like you, Finn Montague. You're "kind of true" too, I like that.'

And he was gone.

She leaned back against the glass and listened to the steady crunch of his boots as he walked away. She put her fingers to her cheek. The softness of his lips had surprised her. It must mean he liked her, that kiss. It must mean that. She put her key in the lock. She certainly liked him. That leap of life deep inside her every time she saw him, or even when she saw the twins or Smiler because they were close to him and had his likeness in their faces: that must be liking. Perhaps much more than that.

First thing the next morning Finn made her way across to Bella Smith's house with a quarter of tea, a loaf of bread and a bottle of

95

lemon cordial, in a basket. Three old women were sitting with Bella in the bare kitchen, the advance party of mourners.

Bella took the provisions from her. 'Good of yer to come, Miss Montague,' she whispered, one eye cocked towards the ceiling. 'Kind of yer. Yer da brought stuff too. Stacy's out for the count. Corcoran gave him whisky. Can yer imagine?'

The women by the hearth murmured.

'Would yer like to see our Alice? Mrs Donkin's laid her out nice.' The trembling thread in Bella's voice was the only thing which betrayed her equable, accepting demeanour.

Finn nodded and was led through to the capsule of a front room where the childlike figure of Alice Smith lay under a sheet. Her hair had been combed in long locks over her narrow chest, her eyelashes down over a face like white china. She looked much younger than her thirteen years.

'She was a good bairn,' said Bella. Then her voice hardened. 'Too obligin' half the time.'

Finn coughed. 'Will you do anything about . . . that?' she said.

'About what?' said Bella, the thread in her voice hardening.

'About . . . y'know, what you said about Stacy.'

She shrugged. 'Nah. It's the way. I got our Joe like that. Me da got carried away one night. Me ma brought Joe up. Like a brother to me.' She opened the middle door and ushered Finn back through to the tiny kitchen. 'We lost him in that first bout of flu after the war.'

Finn refused to sit down. She would not complete the circle round the fire. At the door she faced the other woman. 'Every window's out at Plush Folly, Bella. The house is a real mess.'

Bella shrugged. 'Stacy got mad. It's the drink, you know. Anyway, that stuff she got for our Alice . . .'

'It was harmless. But you got it from Mrs Loumis, Bella. You gave it to Alice. So isn't it your fault too?'

Bella set her lip. 'I didn't want her to go through the same as me. Too young.'

'I know you didn't mean badly. But what about Stacy? He—'

Bella took hold of Finn's arm in a grip that hurt, and brought her face so close Finn could smell her rancid breath. 'You shut up about Stacy, ahm tellin' yer, Miss Stuck-up Shopgirl. Stacy's all the man Ah've got an' Ah'm not upscuttlin' any applecart.'

Finn shook off her hand. 'Well, you just stop talking about Mrs Loumis like that,' she said sharply, 'or I'll be going to Sergeant Corcoran with another story. Mrs Loumis has enough on her plate with Mr Loumis. And like I said, it's you who bothered her to get that stuff.'

Bella heaved a great sigh and her body sagged. 'Aye yer right,

96

lass. Neebody can throw the first stone here.' She put a gentler hand on Finn's arm. 'And thanks for the tea and things, pet. It's appreciated.'

When Finn got across to Plush Folly a glazier's cart was at the gate and three men were up ladders, tapping broken glass out of the frames and chipping away at the old putty. Jenefer was in the kitchen, carefully slicing up tomatoes for some kind of casserole which was just about ready for the oven. Finn could smell some nutty herb and some aniseed. A pan of onions was sizzling on the stove. 'That smells nice,' she said.

'Ah, food is good for the troubled soul,' said Jenefer. 'When you get to France you make your way out of the town and eat at some countrywoman's table. Then you'll know good food.'

Finn sat down at the table unasked. 'How's Hubert?'

'He's complaining about the draughts, but apart from that he has wiped the whole thing out. He's across in the coach house, working.'

'And how about you?'

Jenefer's nose wrinkled as she gave the onions a stir. 'As long as he's all right, so am I. It's not the first time we've been under siege, encountered shattered glass. When I first went to Hubert, my husband sent some hefty minion to do the same to the house where we were living.' She laughed. 'He didn't lower himself to come and do it. No passion, you see!'

She put in some scraps of ham and pork to join the onions, followed by a handful of herbs. 'And before that, fire. The house where I lived with my mother in India, that was burned once by someone who had tried her powers and found them wanting.' She smiled mischievously at Finn. 'The women in our family, for good or ill, raise fire in other people's lives.'

Finn said nothing then, but on the way home thought that true even in her own life. Once a person met Jenefer Loumis, they were never the same again.

When she got back, the shop was busy with early morning customers, but her father signalled her to go up to the parlour.

'You've got a visitor,' he said.

Daniel Marchant stood up as she entered the room. 'I hear there were great dramas in New Morven last night,' he drawled.

'I don't know that I'd call it that,' she said slowly. 'Just a bit of drunken loutish carrying on.' She put her head on one side. 'Did you want something?'

'Well, I've got a project for you.'

'For me?'

'My Pa's received a whole van load of things from some charity drive in the parish where he was curate in the South of England.

97

People with a social conscience, you know? Clothes, shoes, blankets, that kind of thing, to share out in the parish. He's recruiting volunteers to help with the distribution. Started with me and I thought you might help. I told him I knew just the person.'

She blushed, feeling angry and flattered at the same time. She didn't particularly like Daniel Marchant but there was something, just something, about him that appealed, that got under your skin.

'I am too busy here,' she said.

'Ah! I thought you were concerned about the folk in this place. Their hardship, their poverty.'

He shook his head in mock despair and Finn knew, however unwilling, that she would have to do his bidding.

She was certain, though, that this was about something more than sharing a few cast-offs from some affluent people in London. She didn't know much about Daniel Marchant, but she knew he was out for himself.

Then she thought of Michael O'Toole's brief kiss in the shop doorway. She touched her cheek.

10

Old Clothes

Finn had to do battle with her father about taking the time to help with the clothes in the church hall. 'I'm single-handed here, don't forget, Finn,' he grumbled. 'Seems you're going off all the time these days. There're the deliveries to do, you know.'

'I'm still working fifty or sixty hours in the shop, Dad. And I race through my deliveries on Fridays.' She looked at him speculatively. 'You seemed to be taking longer and longer these days on your rounds . . .'

'It's that business that keeps us afloat, don't forget. Farmers pay, in kind if not in cash,' he said shortly. The third silver swallow was almost pecking a hole in his inside pocket. He'd seen Mrs McGillivray, his final favourite call on his rounds, twice since he had bought the swallows, but her husband, Stuart, had been around the house. So Patrick wasn't in his usual position to take his modest and somewhat partial advantage of the situation.

'What about Mother? Why can't she help? She could do an hour now and then.'

'You know your mother's not . . . strong. Not well enough to stand here behind the counter all day.'

She looked him in the eye, wondering whether he really believed it. 'She's stronger than she looks, Dad. You must know that. She's been to church three times in the last few weeks.'

He stroked his chin. 'Do you think you could get her to give a bit of a hand in the shop?'

She grinned. 'I can give it a try. Do her some good to get on to her feet now and then.'

In the event Esther agreed with surprising alacrity. She listened to the tale of the vicar's charitable enterprise with interest. 'And young Daniel asked you, did he?' She heaved her legs out of bed. 'I suppose we all have to do our bit, Finnuola,' she said solemnly. 'These are difficult times.'

Finnuola was still smiling at this when she fought through a

99

disorderly queue of people to get into the parish hall. She was let in by Mrs Loxley, the cobbler's wife, who immediately bolted the door behind her.

Mrs Fosdick, in a close-fitting hat, her large figure wrapped in an unseasonably warm coat, was very much in charge. She ordered the ladies about with an authority which belied her subservient attitude in the vicar's presence.

'Young Mr Marchant said you might come to join our happy band.' She smiled thinly at Finnuola and nodded across towards the far corner of the hall.

Daniel beckoned to her. He was unloading the clothes from great boxes, and carrying them across to the trestle tables which were lined up around the walls. The items were all clean and only marginally crumpled. Some of them were fine clothes with famous labels, very little worn.

Stationed at each table were ladies of the Reverend Hildebrand Marchant's wider parish, some down from Priorton on the train, especially to help. Two of them were holding the clothes up speculatively against themselves. Mrs Loxley tucked away a Fortuny gown she had found crumpled at the bottom of a box. 'A waste to pass it on to these people; they'd be scrubbing their floors in it,' she said to Mrs Colney, whose husband had the flourmill in Priorton.

'From what I see,' said Mrs Colney, 'the floors that get scrubbed down here are few and far between.'

The clothes and shoes all unpacked and organised by size and type around the tables, Mrs Fosdick stationed a lady behind each table. She held up a hand to quieten their chatter. 'Ladies! For those not familiar with our custom,' she glanced at Finn, 'only one item of clothing, and one item of footwear per family member. And keep a sharp eye out for the thieves. Half a chance and they'll steal anything to sell to the second-hand man in Priorton market.'

Then she opened the doors and a great draught of fetid air preceded the crowd, mostly mothers trailing children, who rushed in, knowing that first there would get the best choice and the best fit from this second-hand bounty.

Half an hour later the crowd had thinned out a little. Finnuola was just fitting a pair of unlikely brogues on to the bare feet of a bow-legged eleven-year-old when she became aware of a presence at either shoulder.

'We came for shoes,' said Toots.

'An' a frock. The teacher said you had frocks here today,' said Nancy.

Finn looked past her into the grinning face of Smiler and the rather wooden face of Michael O'Toole. 'They need shoes,' he said simply. They all looked down at three pairs of bare young feet rimmed with dirt between the toes. 'I tried to do the soles wi' cardboard but they broke down in the wet.' Michael paused, and Finn looked at the mouth that had kissed her cheek, the mouth that had been on her mind for days. 'If I'd 'a thought you'd be here I'd 'a thought twice afore coming.'

Finn's cheeks became pink as she felt his acute embarrassment, the prickly edge of his pride. 'They'd still have needed shoes, Michael. These are bad times. That's neither their nor your fault. Isn't that what you told me you're fighting against?'

He scowled and she turned from him, taking some trouble finding decent dresses for the twins. Toots and Nancy fought over a pair of red shoes, then neither would have them because the other couldn't. Smiler tried on four pairs of boots before he found a pair that fit reasonably well.

Finn looked up at Michael. 'What about you?' She willed him to smile, to be the Michael who had walked her home from Plush Folly.

He pushed his cap further back on his head. 'Nah. No rich fellers' handouts for me,' he said. Then his face softened a little and he did smile faintly. 'Here I've brought something for yer.'

He thrust a pamphlet into her hand. It was folded in two, printed on cheap fragile paper. She turned it over to read it. 'Take action for yourselves!' it said, in bold lettering. 'Take control over your own lives!' It went on to announce a meeting to discuss social issues in the Memorial Hall later that week. The speaker would be Tom Farrell, the political activist.

'Tom Farrell?' asked Finn.

'You saw him. That first day at my house. Blond feller. Tom and me were at school together. He was a pitman before they blacklisted him after the '26 strike. Tom says the only road forward is through political action, not charity.'

'How does he live, if not through charity?' she said sharply. 'People would starve if it weren't for Emily Punchard and her Sally Army soup. Charity. People go to Jenefer Loumis for her pills and potions. Charity. Everybody without work manages on some charity, whatever fancy name they give it.'

'Tom Farrell takes no charity. He makes a bare living on the books and booklets he writes. They've raised a bit of interest in them about the county. One of his called *The History and Trials of the Working Classes* sells even further afield.' He was watching her carefully.

'That sounds very dull. How d'you say you knew him?'

'He and me were at school down in Priorton together. He came and sought me when I got back from Scotland. He's mates now with our teacher Jonty Clelland, famous round here for being a conchy in the Great War. Got many a beatin'-up for it. Jonty edits Tom's pamphlets these days, turns 'm into King's English and helps to distribute them.' He dipped into his pocket. 'Here, I'll sell yer one for sixpence.'

'Hey, missis, are you givin' out shoes or what?' A burly woman towing two equally burly children was glaring at her. Finn took the pamphlet and gave Michael sixpence, which he deposited carefully in a cotton bag he had in an inside pocket.

The O'Tooles left her then and worked their way through the crowd, handing out notices of the meeting and, here and there, selling a copy of the precious pamphlet.

Near the door Michael came upon Daniel greeting his father and uncle, who, having had a late if somewhat substantial breakfast at the Gaunt Hotel, were taking their customary royal progress around their charitable enterprise.

Michael put a notice and a pamphlet into the vicar's hand. Hildebrand looked casually at the leaflet, then ducked his head closer to read it. 'What's this? What's this? Who gave you permission to . . .' He threw the papers to the floor. His brother spoke softly into his ear and Hildebrand's white face gained two red spots at the sharp points of his cheeks. 'How dare you come here and pollute the work of good people with politics?' His voice was icy with contempt.

Michael stood up straighter. 'The work of these good people, handing down from the greedy to the needy, ~is politics, Mr Marchant. The need for people to come on their bellies begging for crumbs from the rich man's table is politics. The need for them to take . . .'

There were some murmurs of approval from the crowd which was gathering round them, watching with interest.

'Need? Take? The good people of this community do not need your weasel words to tell them they do not need to be properly grateful—'

'Their work's been taken from them, their dignity . . .' Michael interrupted.

The vicar's stick came up, and flicked Michael's cap to the floor. 'You will show me and my brother, Sir Oliver, some respect, young man, and you will take your poisonous papers and,' his eye dropped to the twins, 'your brattish helpers out of my parish hall.'

Michael retrieved his cap from the dusty floor and replaced it carefully on the back of his head. 'It's a free country, unlike some. I'll take my pamphlets where I fancy.' He put a hand on the shoulder of each of his sisters. Smiler stood beside him, grinning.

Hildebrand turned. 'Daniel, you will eject this malefactor and his lieutenants immediately.'

The murmur in the crowd took on a threatening tone.

Daniel shot a veiled glance at his uncle, who was standing leaning on his cane silently watching the drama. 'No, Father. I don't think that is wise.' He picked up a notice from the floor, and dusted it down. 'I may attend the meeting myself. It looks very interesting.'

Finn finally fought her way through the crowd and took Michael's arm. 'There's no need for this, Michael.'

He allowed her to pull him away out of the hall, the twins and Smiler trailing behind. When they were into the road she turned on him. 'What was that all about? What was your complaint? That was a good thing happening in there. People who had nothing were being given something. Barefoot children were being shod. What's wrong with that?'

'It all makes me so mad,' he said. 'Is it a real gift when you get shoes from somebody who buys twenty pairs a year? Clothes from somebody who has hundreds of pounds worth every spring and every autumn?'

'Yes, when people need them,' she said stubbornly.

His face grew very grim. 'Those people crawling on their bellies there have just as much of a need, maybe a greater need, to come to Tom and Jonty's meeting, to think about what's happening in the world. To know what action they can take. They shouldn't leech on the patronage of people like you, your "charity". Here!' He kneeled down at Nancy's feet and unbuckled the shoes. 'Get these off. You too, Toots, Smiler. We dinnet need their charity.'

His brother and sisters, stunned to silence by his uncharacteristic rage, obeyed and stood there in the dirt, barefoot.

Her fury heightened at his lumping her together with Mrs Fosdick and the others. 'People with empty bellies and bare backs . . .' She was shouting now.

He interrupted her. 'You should go to Tom's meeting yourself, Miss Montague, learn something about the world outside. You've the vote now, after all! You'd think the women's vote never happened, the way you go on.'

'I wouldn't go to your stupid meeting if it was the last place on earth!' she shouted.

He shrugged. 'Suit yourself.' He turned his back and she watched as he set off down the road followed closely by Toots, Nancy and Smiler, their blackened soles flicking into the air as they walked.

Patrick fluttered his whip over Bessie's ears in some contentment. He had made ten calls up the valley and been paid in cash or kind at every one. And he had had a kiss and cuddle at Mary Fenwick's. Even better, up at McGillivray's smallholding he had tasted the full fruits of Mrs Mac's gratitude; that is barring the early finish to prevent accidents. Mrs Mac had welcomed him with open arms, saying Mac was off with his axe, working in Canter Forest for Sir Oliver and would not be back until well after dusk.

Patrick licked his lips and made a little kissing sound into the air to encourage Bessie to further efforts. He was just approaching a narrow corner when he heard the eerie sound of mournful singing, a resonant baritone voice skimming the surface of the steady clop of Bessie's feet. ' "O worship the Lord in the beauty of holiness . . ." '

Patrick turned the corner and was forced to pull up, to avoid hitting a man who was occupying the middle of the road. Stanley Punchard was standing there, his arms open wide, singing up towards the sky with tears streaming down his face. "Bow down before Him His glories proclaim. With truth in its beauty . . ." ' He dropped on his knees in the dirt.

'Now, Stanley!' Patrick called. 'Nice morning for a bit of a sing.'

The other man turned a haggard face towards him.

'What is it, Stanley? You look bad.'

Stanley shook his head. 'I am clad in the raiment of shame. Everything's wrong, Mr Montague.' He held out his hands. 'See these hands? Even they are useless now. No soaring chords, no juicy sound. Might as well have them cut off.'

'Don't talk silly, Stanley. Hop on and I'll give you a ride down home.'

Stanley shook his head. 'Can't go there. Can't give Emily her wage, see? Can't eat her dinners.'

'Why not?'

'I reckon it like this, see? No work, no eat. It was bad enough when me pit wage stopped. But now not even any money from the music. And no music to feed the soul. She's busy doing her soup for the poor souls down there. But I can't take none, see? So I goes up to the viaduct to throw meself off, but I haven't even the guts for that,' he said sadly.

'Get up here, man,' said Patrick impatiently. 'You're talking claptrap. You're dead on your feet.' He waited quietly as Stanley scrambled up beside him. 'Now get yourself a pie from that box on the back, friend, and don't be so bloody soft.'

Tom Farrell leaned across Jonty Clelland to speak to Michael. 'You've done some good work letting folks know, marrah.'

Jonty nodded his agreement. There was a fair number for a village meeting. A scattering of people sprinkled themselves across the series of concentric circles of chairs that Jonty and Tom Farrell had set up in the Memorial Hall. Jonty and his wife, Susanah, and son, David, sat with Tom and Michael and a few other regular supporters in the inner circle. Behind and in front of them people

104

sat in clusters. They were mostly men, but here and there sat man and wife, and there were several pairs of women.

A solitary girl, her fair hair held in some control by a beret, sat in the very back circle on her own. Michael tried to catch Finn's gaze but she determinedly looked elsewhere.

There was a stirring and a turning of heads as Daniel Marchant walked in. Even those who didn't know who he was, knew from his well-cut jacket and the snowy shirt that this was no working man.

He sat quietly at the back and listened as Tom presented his ideas on a society where the owners of labour and the owners of capital met as equals, where rank and respect were awarded according to the contribution an individual made in society . . .'

'Hear! hear!'

Necks craned to locate the source of the clipped, slightly nasal comment.

Tom looked up from his paper. 'What was that, sir?'

'I say I agree with you. And as Mr Marx says, this will not be achieved until the workers take over the means of production.' The speaker was Daniel Marchant. 'Don't you agree with me, Mr Farrell, strong, even violent action is no high price for building a more just society?'

One or two people applauded. Michael glanced at Tom and stood up. 'Well, lads, here's a feller born with a silver spoon in his mouth setting us up so we can be done for sedition,' he shouted.

'You're wrong, sir,' Daniel called back. 'I'm no *agent provacateur*. I'm a student, I come to learn.'

'I say throw him out,' growled Michael. 'Feller brings trouble.'

Tom frowned from one to the other. 'A feller has to have his say,' he said. 'That's what we're on about here. But, sir, your lot's had all the say so far, so I think yer should hold yer tongue in this assembly, unless asked. And if . . .' he pulled himself to his full height, his fair hair gleaming in the light, 'provocative agent or not, you're asking if I'm for the revolution, the answer's yes. You can put that in your little black book.'

Daniel looked round mildly. 'I tell you I'm with you, Mr Farrell. I'd go to the very end, upturn the order of things . . .'

There were shouts, both of shame and approval from the audience.

'He's an informer, I can smell it on him.' Michael was lunging towards him. 'With his grand clothes and his grand airs – you should have seen him this afternoon with his cronies, lording it over the poor and the destitute of this village. Standing there in a fifty-pound jacket, giving away old clothes.'

Daniel waited till he reached him and looked him in the eye. 'If you mean was I there when you were scrounging clothes among the more deserving, I was.'

Michael's large fist connected with Daniel's cheekbone and he fell to the floor. In seconds they were pulling and thumping each other and wriggling all over the floor in the dust.

They rolled towards Finn Montague, where she sat in the very back row. She stood up and hauled at Michael so that he fell back and landed almost on top of her on the floor. He turned on her, struggling to disentangle himself from her. 'Get out of my way, woman, will you?'

She went fiery red and pushed him away from her.

Daniel scrambled to his feet and dusted himself down, adjusting the immaculate crease of his trousers. He smiled his thin smile at Finn. 'A heroine to the rescue.'

'Are you all right?' She stood up.

Michael leaped at Daniel again, only to be held back by Tom Farrell. 'Leave 'm, Mickey. Thi're all alike. Only look after their own,' he said.

Finn, brushing dust from her skirt, glared at him. 'Who? Who is this *they* may I ask?'

He looked at her coolly. 'Capitalists. And their lackeys.'

She brought a hand back and cracked him hard on the cheek. 'I work as hard as any person here. I'm no . . . lackey, did you call it? I work fifty, sixty hours a week. How many here can say that?' She looked round at the interested audience.

Tom Farrell rubbed his reddening cheek. 'Chance'd be a fine thing, missis. Haven't you noticed from behind that counter that nine out o' ten men here in New Morven have no work at all? Fifty or sixty hours might sound like sweet music to some of 'm but it seems ter me yer exploited, Miss. Yer should join a union.'

Daniel had a hand on her arm now, his thumb moving over the flesh. 'Come on, Finnuola. You want nothing here.' He drew her arm through his and they left, ignoring the glowering face of Michael O'Toole, the supercilious face of his friend Tom, and the jeers of the crowd behind them.

In the street Daniel fell into step beside her as she made her way back to the shop. 'What idiots, what fools . . .' he began to laugh.

'They're not that,' she said. 'They do want to do something to stop all this rot; they have some ideas.'

'Ideas! Too stupid to know what's needed,' he said. 'Animals.'

'Daniel!' she protested.

'Anyway,' he put her arm through his again. 'Why trouble about them? Let's go for a walk. There is a good deal of daylight left.'

She removed his hand. 'No. I've got to get back. My mother's holding the fort and she'll be frightening off more custom than she wins.'

'Tomorrow then? Tomorrow afternoon! A bicycle ride up the valley?'

'I've no bicycle. Just the shop bike.'

'That will do. Come on!' He pulled her round to face him, his face innocent and pleading. 'Do come. It's so boring round here.'

In spite of herself she laughed. 'All right. My father's delivering. If I can get my mother to stand in for me I'll come.' She knew that because Daniel Marchant was involved, her mother would leap at the chance. Anyway, it was good to get her up off that bed and into the real world.

'Good, good! I've to be at my uncle's for lunch, but two o'clock? By the bridge over the Gaunt?' He flicked a glance up and down the deserted street and leaned over and kissed her. 'Do you know you're awfully pretty?' he said. And then he strode away, whistling.

'Impudent . . .' She put her hand on her cheek. His lips had been dry, almost rough. Not pleasant at all. As she opened the shop door and the bell rang, she wondered just what she had let herself in for with Daniel Marchant.

11

Wreckage

Hubert sat bolt upright in bed, dragging with him the heavy woven-silk cover.

The chill evening air poked its fingers into Jenefer's considerable expanses of flesh. 'What is it, sweetheart?' she murmured, her mind still half in the world of sunlight and unforced laughter which filled her dreams these days.

'Do you hear it, Jenefer? They're at the door: the butts of rifles, hilts of swords, banging, banging. They're upon us.'

She hauled herself up beside him, and turned him round, forcing him to face her. 'We're here, Hubert, in our bedroom in New Morven. That's someone banging at our door. Someone for me. Now turn over and lie down again. Go to sleep.'

Obediently he lay back and she stroked his broad brow. 'Now dream, Hubert! Dream of those days by the sea with Pierre and Marianne. That sea! Do you remember? Royal blue into pure silver just towards the end of the day.'

His hand relaxed in hers and she knew she had transferred her dream to him. She yawned. Every time she did that dream transfer now, it drained her to the very heels.

Walking down the stairs she felt very heavy, her back and her legs were threaded through with weariness. How long had it been since she had done a single thing purely for herself, when she had connived to meet her own needs, her own desires? Perhaps as far back as that first time she had given herself over to the pleasure of Hubert's pleading hand, before the great interval of passion which had made her forever his protectress, his queen.

The banging was coming from the back door. She fumbled her way through a house only illuminated by the grey light leaking through the half-open doors of the rooms leading off the hall.

She opened the door and took a step back. Bella Smith was standing there, her sheer bulk filling the doorframe, the smell of sweat, new and old, wafting from her into the house.

'What is it?' Jenefer kept her voice neutral.

'Ah need help, Mrs Loumis. Our—'

'I can't help you, Bella. Helping you leaves me windowless.'

'Eeh, Mrs Loumis, yer canna blame me for our Stacy when he gets a skinful. Like a man off, he was. Sorry enough now. Ah ken tell yer . . .'

Jenefer hesitated, then stood to one side, letting Bella in before her. 'Come in, Bella,' she said wearily.

She pulled out a chair for the woman to sit at the kitchen table. 'Now what?' she said.

'It's our Nicholas, the bairn, has something on his chest. Summer flu, the doctor says. No question that he's dyin', like.'

'Go for the doctor. Here, I'll give you the money.'

'Doctor's been. Says he can do nothing. In the hands of the gods, he says. He can do nowt about it.'

'Then neither can I.'

'Yer can do . . . something. Say a few words? Some special words?'

'Get a priest.'

'The vicar came an' talked sommat about going into the arms of Jesus. But . . .' her voice took on a wheedling cunning note '. . . don't yer know some special words?'

Jenefer suddenly roared with laughter. 'A spell! You want a spell! Last week you were smashing my windows and nearly killing my poor husband, and here you are asking for a spell.'

Bella sank her head on her chest. 'Missis, me bairn's dyin'. Last week me other bairn died. Ah'll do anything.'

Jenefer put a hand on Bella's burly forearm. 'I'm sorry, Bella. This is no time for laughter. But you see I'm no witch, black, white or sky-blue pink. I just know some simples, some cures that my mother taught me, that her mother taught her, right back in our family. Sometimes things work because people think they will work. Sometimes things work because I make people wash as well. And I know that's nearly impossible round here. Sometimes the things have the true effect. I'm not always sure which is which myself.'

Bella heaved a great sigh which seemed to come all the way from her solar plexus. 'You and me know it's more 'n that, missis.'

Jenefer shrugged. 'Sometimes I see through the veils and curtains that envelope us all. But that doesn't save a dying baby.' She stood up and moved heavily across to her cabinet. She spooned some powder into a screw of paper and pushed it at Bella. 'Here, make this up like tea and let it cool. Give it to him on a spoon. It may help. And I'll say a prayer myself. That may help.'

Bella shivered it into her apron pocket and stood up, satisfied. 'Ah thank yer, missis.'

110

'It won't stop him from dying, Bella, if it's meant. But if he does die it will be easy. There'll be no pain.'

'An' don't you worry about Stacy, missis. Ah'm keepin' him on a tight rein.'

'I should hope so too.'

Hubert stirred again as she got back into the bed. 'What was that?'

'Another citizen wanting me to be witch, wizard and soothsayer all in one.'

He turned her towards him and put his face against hers. 'What's this,' he said. 'Tears?'

She sniffed and pushed her hand up her face and into her hair to sweep them all away.

He held her to him. 'Honey, sweetheart, you cannot cry. You must not cry.' But the tears still flowed for Bella, for Bella's lost daughter and soon-to-be-lost son, for her own young friend Finn Montague, condemned to live in this grim half-world there death stalked the innocent and half-formed, where women grew old before their time and work was a dignity and privilege for only a few. And the tears came too for that all-too-brief time of delight known to herself and Hubert, before the dark closed in on them as well.

Daniel was waiting by the bridge, leaning by his bicycle, which glowed with the sable-gleam of newness. Immediately Finn perceived the scruffiness of her own machine and the incongruity of the basket on the front and the advertisement on its crosspanel. 'This is silly,' she said gloomily, 'me riding this and you on that monster.'

'This?' he said airily. 'A present from the doting Uncle Oliver. The trick is, though, never to be satisfied. Never let them rest. I'm angling for a motorbike now. They're all the go, I can tell you.'

'My friend Jenefer Loumis has a motorbike. Riding on that is like riding with the wind. Anyway,' she hauled her machine round to return the way she had come. 'Like I say, this is silly.'

He wrenched it back in the other direction. 'It's you who're silly. A silly goose. This is a chariot.' He reached up and took a great branch of wild rose from the towering hedge and placed it carefully in the basket. 'There! A flowery chariot for Persephone.' He pushed the handles back at her. 'Now shall we go?' He mounted his bicycle and started to pedal, twisting the machine back on itself in a zigzag to stay in front of her. 'Come on!'

Smiling faintly, she removed the branch, then remounted her bicycle and set off to follow him.

They rode through the lanes, at times racing each other, then riding along sedately, side by side. Finn told him about her days at school in Gateshead, and about her grandfather who had had three shops in Newcastle. He told her about America and the infinite sense of space there, the infinite wealth and power of many of the people he met. He was obviously greatly moved by this. 'The problem is all this power's sometimes in the hands of the wrong people. All that power for good, for efficiency, in the wrong hands.'

'You talked about revolution in Tom Farrell's meeting.'

He executed a wide turn in the lane and came alongside her again. 'There are all kinds of revolution, of course,' he said. 'Now what about that great handsome brute of an Irish fellow? Seems to have taken quite a shine to you.'

Her face went hot. 'No. No. What a stupid thing to say.'

'Stupid? Stupid? Me? Top of every class in which I ever studied.'

'Anyway. He's nothing to me. Nothing at all.'

'Good thing too. He's a great Irish brute. Troublesome lot, the Irish. They should all be put down, every last one of them. Put in a boat in the middle of the Irish Sea and the plug pulled out.'

Finn fought back the desire to defend Michael and the whole of the Irish race, including her own grandmother. She came to a stop by a broad farm gate. 'Look! Down there. That's Tot Fenwick's farm. Mrs Fenwick was telling me you used to go down there to play when you were a lad.'

Daniel stood with a foot on either side of the bicycle. 'Well, I never! So I did. One of my uncle's tenants, if I remember rightly.'

'I know. Let's call to see her. She'll give us a cup of tea and we can play with her little boys. They're very bright. Do you know she teaches them? Wants a schooling for them?'

Daniel shook his head. 'Clodhoppers.' He was disappointed by the turn of events. He had remembered the place. And he remembered there was a patch of woodland beyond High Bank Farm. Yes, a sheltered patch of woodland.

'She'll be so pleased to see you,' Finn persisted.

Reluctantly he acquiesced and they dismounted and walked their bikes down the bank to the farm. When they turned the corner into the farmyard they were confronted by the Montague delivery wagon with Bessie patiently standing chewing at wisps of hay that someone had stuck in a hedge.

'My dad must be here,' said Finn. 'That's funny. This is my call, not his.'

'Ah. Do we have to go in?' said Daniel.

Finn nodded and made her way towards the farmhouse. Stopping at the small side-window, she peered in, then froze and put out her hand to stop Daniel going any further. 'No. You're right. We won't go in.'

'What is it? Let me see.' He pulled her roughly to one side and

112

peered in himself. The sight that met his eyes brought a smile to his lips. There was the good grocer with the buxom farmer's wife on his knee. Her blouse had been pulled down to her elbows and his face was very close to her half-naked breast.

Daniel composed his face to meet the startled eyes of the grocer's daughter with some sobriety. 'Poor girl!' he said, touching her shoulder with what he judged to be just the right level of consolation. 'Come away now. You should not be here.'

They pushed their bicycles back up the pathway. Then he turned his towards the patch of woodland. Unthinking, she followed him. In minutes they were into dense, overhung, tangled pathways. He leaned his vehicle up against a tree and did the same with hers, taking it from her unresisting hands. Then he took her arm. 'Finnuola, you look entirely wacked. We'll find somewhere to sit while you get your breath back.'

She pulled away for a second, then allowed herself to be drawn along narrower pathways, ending up under a tree, whose widespread canopy nearly touched the ground.

He heaped some leaves together. 'Here. Sit here. You look all in.'

She took off her coat, spread it over the leaves, and sat down with her legs straight out in front of her. Her face was white and her eyes were blind and inward, imprinted as they were with the image of her father and Mary Fenwick.

Carefully easing his trouser creases away from his legs, Daniel sat down beside her. 'You must be upset by all that,' he said gently.

'Wouldn't you be?'

He let out a short bark of a laugh. 'The very idea of my father with the likes of Mary Fenwick has a bizarre charm, but is not of the real world, I fear. Pa's had no blood sport since, to his relief, my dear mama took her own leave of this vale of tears.'

'Sport? You call that blood sport?'

He laughed a faintly nasal laugh. Light piercing the tree's canopy highlighted the sweat on his cheek. 'Looked sporty to me. Nuzzling away at Mary's generous proportions.'

Finn blinked, startled out of her torpor.

'Of course,' Daniel was continuing in an almost dreamy tone, 'Mary is very well-endowed there. Do you know I once saw her naked when I was a boy? Up there after the harvest, exploring he bedrooms, and there she was, preening herself in front of the mirror. Of course we both pretended it hadn't happened. Yes, she's very well-endowed in all departments.'

His hands came from behind Finn and cupped her breasts over her blouse. 'Not like you. Like sweet grapes these, to her pomegranates.'

113

She was rigid now, with fear. His hands suddenly nipped and squeezed her painfully.

'Beautiful, though,' he went on dreamily. 'Ripe and untouched.'

Finally she unfroze, wrenched herself away and leaped to her feet. Laughing, he jumped in front of her and put his arms out wide to stop any escape. 'Come on, little shopgirl,' he said.

She moved to one side and he blocked her, then to the other and he did the same. Then she dived under his arm and started to run. He raced after her and caught her in a very well-practised rugby tackle. She crashed to the ground, the wind pressed out of her, her hat flying off.

In a second he was on her, turning her and straddling her across the waist. She could feel his thick hard thrust through the layers of clothing. One by one he pulled her arms to her sides and brought them under his knees. She started to shout and he slapped her face, then took off his tie and tied it tightly over her mouth. His eyes were gleaming down at her. She turned her head away so that she couldn't see them.

He unbuttoned her blouse with some care and pulled it down to her waist. 'Lovely, lovely!' he murmured. 'I knew the shoulders would be perfect.'

He pulled at her petticoat, unclipped her brassiere straps and, none too gently, lifted her breast free. 'Ah. Perfect. Perfect,' he said softly.

He was in a world of his own. And she was nothing beneath him, bred for his use. He searched for some phrase his uncle had used to Mr Consadine, about brood and show mares, but the precise details failed him.

He put a hand out and forced her face round so that she looked into his eyes. 'What would you like, little shopgirl? Shall I kiss them? Shall I bite them? Or . . .' That's what they had said. Something about marking your stock. With difficulty he fished out a scout knife he kept in his top pocket. 'Shall I carve my initials on them.'

She yelped into the tie around her mouth and closed her eyes tight to deny him them at least.

'No? Oh well, I'll think about that.'

He eased up a little so that he could pull up her skirt and petticoats. 'Oh,' he said in disappointment, 'no corset.' He lifted a hand to tap her quite hard on the cheek. 'Next time you must wear a corset and stockings. They are interesting. We'll make a lady of you yet.'

He pulled at her knickers. She could feel the hardness of his hand, and wriggled to no avail. 'Oh, lovely, new as a pin,' he said thoughtfully. 'For a second I thought, perhaps the big Irishman . . .

114

now then, should I make a way, perhaps? What do you think?'

She felt his weight shift as he leaned away, picked up a stick and turned it over in his hand. 'This should do. From the toothmarks someone's been throwing it for a dog. Just the thing for a little overclosed shopgirl.'

That was when she started to pray with all her heart. She closed her ears to his sticky insinuating voice, his probing invading hands and prayed to the bearded God of her Sunday school pictures, the Jesus who hung at the front of Daniel's father's church. She promised to be good, to work harder, to help the people. Even to forgive her father.

From their left, from beyond the ring of woodland came the dull crack of gunfire. Daniel jumped. Then there came the laughter of children and the deeper booming voice of Tot Fenwick. Daniel leaned down and whipped his tie from her mouth.

Then all was black and she was floating high above the wood, peering down to try to make out the struggling girl in the darkness.

Stacy Smith frowned, concentrating on his task in utter silence. The light from the bucket of hot cinders glowed up at him, bright and potent, pulling from him the memory of his father at the black-smith's bellows, and his grandfather who in turn could remember his own grandfather . . . Stacy shook his head. He was breaking that circle. No work for blacksmiths now.

There was no one about.

He had lain low until Bella was fast asleep on her back, her mouth and eyes wide open in that strange way of hers. She was sound, full to the belly's brim of pre-funeral gifts of food and the half-pint of beer sent down from The Eagle.

On his way out of the house, Stacy had peeped at the baby, Nicholas, in his rough orange box on a chair in the scullery, waiting for the morning and his final journey. Bella'd wanted the bairn in the front room with them, where he had slept in life, but Stacy had had the shivers and had forbidden it.

Now, for this job he'd had to wrench an iron railing from its place outside the chapel. It'd needed chipping away at first but in the end it came out with a scraping plop and a puff of dust in the air. Then, in his bare feet, he had crept like a cat down his street and round the corner on to Mainstreet.

He ran an appreciative hand over the fine work on the gates of Plush Folly, fashioned by his grandfather. Keeping his fingers over the pineapple finial, he looked up at the house. The gleam of the moon picked out the glitter of new glass in all but one of the windows; the narrow one to the side of the porch was covered with rough wood.

115

Stacy picked up the railing by its ends and grunted with effort as he bent it to form an elbow which he could dunk into the cinder bucket to help him bend it even further.

'Yes!' he whispered as he felt it give. Not many feats of strength were beyond Stacy Smith. Who was it won the annual Strong Man Competition at Priorton Gala? Compared with that, this was easy.

When he task was finished, he grinned bleakly down at it in the darkness. 'That'll show ye, bairn-killer.'

Patrick served the customer, the last traveller off the last train from Priorton, with unusual sharpness, hustling him out and locking the door behind him. Then he raced up the stairs two at a time.

Esther was by the window. She whipped round and looked at him, her eyes wide and worried. He went and stood by her shoulder and peered down into the dark street. 'Still not back,' he grunted. He moved across to the cupboard to get his best jacket. 'I'll get down that vicarage.'

'Patrick. You can't do that! There'd be a scene. What will the vicar think?'

He caught hold of her shoulder. 'What will Mr God Almighty Marchant think?' His voice squealed in cruel imitation of hers. 'What will the vicar think? What do you think, Mrs Montague, about your daughter, out till this time with that . . .' he licked his lips '. . . supercilious clot?'

'Patrick!'

But he was gone.

Mrs Fosdick answered the vicarage door in her dressing gown, her head garnished in curlers looking curiously skittish above her massive face. Her scowl deepened at his enquiry. 'I'm not waking Mr Daniel. He's been in hours.'

He grasped her flannel-wrapped arm. 'You'll get that young feller and bring him here, or I'll—'

She wrenched her arm away and stared at him. Beads of sweat were forming in the hairs on his heavy upper lip. Then she half-closed the door against him and turned away. He breathed hard, listening to her weighty tread on the thin-carpeted stairs. Then he leaned against the doorjamb and lit a cigarette. He was halfway down the cigarette when Daniel Marchant, in a navy dressing gown, his hair tousled, pulled open the door and stepped back so that Patrick could move into the hall.

Daniel listened politely to Patrick's questions, and slowly shook his head. 'I cannot understand it, sir. We had a fine ride. Came by High Bank Farm. Finnuola seemed to think that you might be there.' His thick lashes dropped over his eyes. 'But she didn't seem to fancy calling on Mrs Fenwick herself. So we came home and she

116

raced away from me at the end of the village. She seemed quite preoccupied.'

Patrick took a step back, crashing into the glass door, a bolt of shock rippling through to his fingertips. Finn had seen him and Mary Fenwick. She had *seen*.

'Now, you will excuse me, sir? I need to complete my sleep. I'm off shooting rabbits with my uncle in the morning.' Daniel turned on his heel and walked steadily up the stairs.

Mrs Fosdick grasped the handle of the vestibule door. 'Now, Mr Montague,' she said sourly, 'if you please. An' if you come another time could you come to the back? There's a plate there saying tradesman's entrance.'

Patrick looked at her strong, thick-fingered hand, and wished he could chop it off, starting with the little finger. Then he turned and walked out of the house, and the stained glass shook as he banged the door loudly behind him. He made his way slowly back along the street towards the shop, passing the bulky figure of Stacy Smith without a glance.

Esther was waiting for him downstairs. She was fully clothed and was wearing her outdoor shoes. Her normally slack face sharpened with concern. 'Well?'

He shook his head.

'Oh.' Her face crumpled and her shoulders sagged. He put a tentative arm around her. She looked up at him. 'We'll have to get the sergeant, Patrick. Something's very badly wrong.'

Sergeant Corcoran was with them a minute after they knocked on his door, pulling up his braces and buckling his big belt. 'Ah ken see why yer concerned Mrs . . . Mr Montague.' However rough and peremptory he was with the grocer's customers, he was never less than deferential with the grocer himself. He pulled on his jacket and ducked into the back room to get a lantern. 'Now let's go and see,' he said.

They found Finnuola wondering without much direction on the Priorton Road. She was coatless and hatless and her face glowed white in the moonlight. She was shivering in the cold night air. She leaped towards her mother and clung to her. 'Mummy,' she whispered, tears coursing down her cheeks.

Esther took her in her arms and Patrick removed his coat and put it round them both. He touched Finn's shoulder. 'What is it, pet?' he said.

She flinched away from him, closer to her mother. 'I want to go home,' she said dully.

Esther turned and guided her footsteps, calling behind her, 'We'll take her home, sergeant. Thank you.'

The sergeant turned to Patrick. 'I should talk to her, Mr Montague,' he said.

Patrick shook his head. 'We'll get her home, Sergeant. If there's anything . . . I'll come to see you in the morning. The girl's upset.' He scurried after his wife and daughter, and Corcoran plodded after him, thinking again about his bed and the languorous warmth of Bridget, his compliant and comfortable wife.

Inside the kitchen with its overlay of daytime warmth, Esther turned anxiously to Finn. 'What happened? What did he do?'

Finn looked across at her father who was just coming in. 'He tried to do what men do,' she said sombrely. 'Then there was a disturbance – boys, and the gamekeeper, I think – maybe Tot Fenwick. And he left me. And I think I fainted then. I came round in the dark. It was so cold.' Tears welled up in her eyes again.

Esther brought her close. 'Come on upstairs. We'll get you out of those wet clothes. They're . . .' she picked a dead leaf off Finn's blouse '. . . filthy.' She drew her up the stairs, saying down to Patrick, 'Boil some water, Patrick. Bring it up. She needs a wash.'

The fire was too far down to use so Patrick lit the gas ring. He watched the water run into the heavy kettle. Usually it was he and Finn together, sidestepping and sideswiping at Esther. Now it was he who was well and truly out in the cold. He lifted the enamel bowl and placed it on the table beside the cooker.

Above him Finn flopped down heavily on to her mother's bed. Esther started to pull at her blouse. 'Here, let's get this all off,' she said, with uncharacteristic energy.

Finn placed a hand over her mother's. 'No,' she said. 'I'll do it myself.'

Esther put her hand by her side and Finn turned her back before she started to peel off her sodden clothes. Esther watched her for a moment, then said abruptly. 'I'll go down and get you some water. He'll have it heated by now.'

'Thank you. Ma . . .'

'What is it?'

'He didn't manage to actually . . . you know. I fought him off.'

Esther, walking steadily down the stairs, suppressed the panic which had been welling up in her since they had come upon Finnuola and it had become clear what Daniel Marchant had done.

She stopped halfway down the stairs and took some deep breaths. Unwillingly she was living again the long minutes when Patrick, not drunk but loosened out and emboldened by drink, had lost his temper when she turned her back on him in bed. He had forced himself on to her and into her with an alien violence, leaving her so bruised and battered she had to stay in the house for a week, rejecting invitations from her family on the pretext of illness.

She had prayed that night to die. Her prayer was not answered. Neither was she reassured by Patrick's abject apologies the next day, and the day after that. But gradually she realised she could survive and he would get his punishment, day by day, year by year as he lived out the penance for his evil act.

Patrick looked up from his place beside the gas ring. 'How is she?'

'She's been through the mill, I think. That dreadful boy.' She looked him directly in the eye. 'She fought him off. She is luckier than some. And no doubt he'll be full of compunction tomorrow too. And the next day.'

He put his hands to his head. 'Esther, it's not like . . . We were married.'

'Oh yes it is, Patrick Montague. Here. Pour that into the dish. I'll take it up.'

'Can you manage?' Normally it took all her time to lift a hairbrush.

'Oh, yes,' she said grimly, 'I can manage.'

In half an hour she returned with the empty bowl. 'She's tucked up in her bed now. I did try to get her to sleep in my bed, then I could have slept in yours and kept an eye on her.' She handed him the bowl which he emptied in the scullery sink. He watched her anxiously and she relented. 'She does seem all right, Patrick. She is just very shaken.'

He turned down the gas mantle, and, taking up the lamp, followed her upstairs, then past her up the rickety attic staircase. He had to knock twice on Finn's door before he got a response.

The light from his lamp, as he entered, filled the tiny space, illuminating the hump in the narrow bed where Finn had burrowed under the bedclothes.

'Are you all right, Finnuola? Finn?'

'What? Oh! Yes. I'm all right.' Her voice was muzzled.

'Can I do anything for you?' He put his face close to hers. 'I'm worried about you, Finn.'

She turned over and stared up at him, unblinking. 'I saw you with Mary Fenwick, Dad. How could you do that? I go there to play with the boys. I thought she was my friend.'

'She's a nice woman, Mary Fenwick. Warm.'

'Dad!' She sat up now, her face shining clean, her hair in fuzzy fair plaits down her back. She looked about twelve years old. 'How could you? My mother would—'

He put a hand on her shoulder. 'How would she know unless you told her?'

'Oh, I won't tell her,' she said scornfully. 'But what is the matter with you? You let yourself down. And me. I think it was seeing you there that made Daniel think he could—'

'Finn! No!' He was horrified.

119

She shrugged. 'Maybe not. He's a bad lot, I think.' She remembered her promise to God to forgive her father.

'I'm going to see him tomorrow. Take Corcoran.'

'Don't do that,' she said sharply. 'No one must know . . .'

'Corcoran knows already. That there was some kind of attack.'

'Appeal to him for me.'

He nodded slowly. 'I'm still going to see that . . . brat. To tell him what for.'

She slid down in the bed and said wearily, 'Do that if you want. Now I'm tired. Good night, Dad.'

He pulled the counterpane straight then, hesitating. 'I'm sorry, Finn. I'm very, very sorry that you saw. I'll never go there, never do it again. Please, Finn . . .'

She remembered again her wild promise to God. 'I have to forgive you, Dad. I have to. But I can't forget what I saw.' He tried to kiss her on the brow and she turned her face into the pillow away from him.

His wife was apparently asleep when he got into the bedroom, and with well-practised silence removed his clothes, got into bed and crept beneath the bedclothes.

12

Revelations

'Hey, missis! Do you know some joker's tied a knot in your gate?'
Jenefer looked up from her baking bowl into the handsome,
normally serious face of Michael O'Toole, now lit with the faintest
gleam of humour.

She followed him out of the kitchen door and down the side to the
small front garden. 'What the . . .!' She put her hand out and
rattled the gate, pulling and pushing at the alien iron bar which was
ingeniously woven around it.

'It'd take a blacksmith to do that,' said Michael.

'Stacy Smith,' she said. 'The baby must have died.' She looked
angrily up and down the deserted street, then stormed off towards
the coach house where Hubert was painting.

She burst through the door and exploded at him. 'These people!
These bloody people!' She stamped her foot. 'I hate them, small-
minded, superstitious, ignorant . . .'

Michael, shuffling his feet, said quietly, 'We're not all like that,
missis.'

Hubert put down his brush and led her to the small basket-weave
chair. 'What now? What is it?'

The fear and anxiety in his voice calmed her down. She could not
risk disturbing him. She took two deep breaths, then stood up
laughing shrilly. 'No, no, don't worry, Hubert. Don't worry at all.
Nothing the matter at all. I'll deal with it.' She pulled her heavy skirt
round her knees. 'Men!' she said.

Hubert and Michael held their breath as she swept away, both
feeling guilty for being men.

Then Michael looked at the wall. 'That's comin' on, Mr Loumis!'
The scales of the dragon were now fully painted, each one a tiny
image of some aspect of war. In the space around the dragon were
clusters of people in different aspects of domestic activity: a nanny
sewing, with a boy in a sailor suit at her knee; boys playing football;
four men, one in uniform, playing cards round a table; a man and a

woman dancing, a man and a woman swimming. 'It's coming on,' he repeated. 'There's a life there.'

'Good of you to say so.' Hubert picked up his brush, smiling. 'Now what can I do for you, young feller-me-lad?'

'I was wondering if there was any more jobs you wanted doin'. Me sisters need shoes an' our Smiler is eatin' us outta house an' home.' Michael had thought for some days before coming back. He had had a lecture from Tom Farrell about going cap in hand to anyone. But he had patched the twins' shoes again this week with cardboard and decided that in this case pride must be swallowed.

Hubert paused mid-stroke. 'Could you get up on the roof here and see where the tiles need replacing or renewing? I had buckets in here last week catching the rain. Jenefer'll tell you where the hammers and things are. There are ladders in the corner. But first you can follow Mrs Loumis for me, to see she comes to no harm?' He smiled slightly. 'She's so full of fire, Jenefer.'

Then he turned to his painting, Michael and his problems, Jenefer and her problems, quite forgotten.

Jenefer had ignored the twins, hanging around the gate, and strode off through the streets, stoking her anger with thoughts of other times, when her acts and intentions had been misinterpreted. Her mind was driving on. 'That's it. That's it. We'll have to go. This can't go on. Can't go on.'

'Steady on, Mrs Loumis. You take some keepin' up with,' puffed Michael, finally reaching her side, the twins in tow.

Outside Bella Smith's house was a small knot of people, drably dressed, faces keen with a combination of sympathy and curiosity. As Jenefer and Michael watched, the vicar emerged, followed by Stacy carrying the coffin under his arm. The coffin looked not unlike one of the orange boxes which were normally stacked outside the back of Montague's shop.

Bella was clinging to Stacy's arm, her face pudgy and blotchy with crying. At her shoulder and clinging to her skirts were the other children, frightened by the rage and the dejection around them without quite knowing the reason why.

The men at the door removed their caps as the vicar set off along the pavement at a stately pace which was swifter than it looked. Stacy and Bella, with their orange-box burden and their knot of ragged children, ended up scurrying to keep up with him.

'Bad business,' said Jenefer, glancing sideways at Michael.

He scowled. 'Bad business? Accordin' to Tom Farrell an' old Jonty more babies die here than in any other part of England. Poverty sits on us like a big fat hen, pickin' us off one by one, like peckin' grains of corn. Doctor'll only come when he chooses, then he'll leave a bill you canna pay.'

The vicar did a very short off-hand service by the hole under the graveyard wall where the baby's sister Alice already lay. Needing a cheap burial, Stacy had been at his weedling best. He had persuaded the vicar to reopen Alice's grave to put her little brother beside her. He had caught Hildebrand Marchant in a benevolent moment when his son, before going off to shoot with his uncle, had been excessively charming with him.

Stacy had redug the hole himself, stopping when his spade had clanged against Alice's coffin.

Jenefer wondered out loud where even the simple costs of this burial had come from.

'Where d'you think? People have a whip-round with their pennies and farthings.' Michael watched as the vicar, head and shoulders above the crowd, intoned the final rites.

Bella started to shout and moan and Stacy had to pull her back, to stop her jumping into the hole. Jenefer was visited by the ridiculous thought that, had she succeeded, Bella would have been stuck in the hole and it would have taken more than Stacy to pull her out.

The vicar stalked away, glaring malevolently at Jenefer as he passed.

Jenefer and Michael were the last to file past the bereaved family. She shook Bella's grimy hand and looked Stacy in the eye. She did not offer to shake his hand. 'My condolences for your great loss,' she said.

He returned her look for look. 'We all know how he died,' he said. 'There're those—'

'Mr Smith,' she interrupted him, 'this might be an inappropriate time but I am sorely in need of someone with the skills of a smith to disentangle some iron from my front gate.'

'Is that so?' he said, sticking his large chin out.

'I'd be willing to pay good money for someone to put it right,' she said. 'It's so inconvenient.'

Bella nudged Stacy. 'Good money!' she hissed.

Stack shrugged. 'It's true I'm a smith.'

'Will you do it?'

Bella punched Stacy in the ribs.

'Aye, missis, I'll dee the job. Mind it maks nee shap what Ah think about other things . . .'

Another sharp stab in the ribs.

'Aye. Ah'll dee it. Be there this noon.'

'Thank you, Mr Smith,' said Jenefer. 'Thank you, Bella. And again, I am very sorry about your little boy. Very sorry indeed.'

That irritating little grocer Patrick Montague was sitting in the hallway when Hildebrand Marchant returned from the 'dreary little funeral'. He didn't really mind these affairs, tedious as they were; they did serve to remind him of the grace he brought to the dark and colourless lives of the indigent. He relished the way he had waved away their stumbling offerings of payment, their piles of pennies and farthings, saying that his brother, Sir Oliver, had instituted a fund for just such contingency. Then how he had nodded graciously as that great reprobate Stacy Smith had fingered his cap and stumbled through such thanks as he could articulate.

Standing at the vicarage door he had rubbed his hands at the thought of hot chocolate on a silver tray brought in by Mrs Fosdick. This and the *Church Times*, followed by a chapter from Isaiah at his desk, which had been carved by the craftsman who fashioned the altar at St Benedict's . . .

In the hall his pleasure faded as he saw the little grocer Montague sitting on the high-backed hall chair clutching his trilby on his tightly closed knees.

Mrs Fosdick was standing beside him, her arms folded. 'Vicar, Mr Montague . . .'

Patrick stood up. 'Vicar, I've come to complain . . . that son of yours.'

Hildebrand glanced at his housekeeper. 'That will be all, Mrs Fosdick. Mr Montague, if you please . . .'

He swept past and led the way into his study and Patrick was forced to follow him and stand while the vicar sat down behind his vast old desk, on a chair which seemed to lift him above common mortals.

Slowly Hildebrand took his glasses from their case, polished them, put them on his nose, then finally looked over them at the grocer. The little grocer and his family were getting more troublesome these days. 'What is it, Mr Montague?'

Patrick had not been asked to sit down. 'Your son, Daniel, Mr Montague.' Patrick put his shoulders back. 'I want to see him and give him a good thrashing.'

Hildebrand sat up straighter. 'What do you say, man?' he barked.

'My daughter came home last night from an . . . outing . . . with your son in a very distressed state. He had attacked her in a . . . indecent fashion. She was distraught. He should be punished.' Patrick looked towards the door. 'Is he here? I've no need to say this behind his back.'

Hildebrand put his fingers together. 'No, Mr Montague, he is not here. At this moment he is with his uncle, Sir Oliver. You may say all to me.'

Patrick moved from foot to foot just as he had years ago on the carpet before his headmaster. 'I had considered going to the constable, but've been prevented because of the delicate feelings of

124

my wife and daughter.' He paused. 'Your son needs a good thrashing and I am here to give him one.'

The vicar stood up then, his figure loomed over Patrick, blocking out most of the light from the thickly curtained window. 'What are you saying, man?'

'He attacked my daughter. They went out for a bicycle ride and, him being your son, I saw no objection. And he attacked her violently with lascivious intent.' Patrick's head went down. 'She had bruises on her arms where he . . . kneeled on her.'

'She claims he hit her?'

'He leaped on her like a beast. It is only because she fought him off, and others came along, that she's still . . .'

Hildebrand's narrow head poked forward towards Patrick. 'My son is not here, Mr Montague, but I can tell you unequivocally that it is a lie. My son is a gentleman. He would force himself on no one. Not even,' he sniffed, 'a village girl.'

Patrick threw his hat to the floor. 'My daughter's not some village girl, sir. She's refined, educated . . .' His voice faded as the vicar raised his hand, palm out to stop the torrent. 'You have my deep sympathy, Mr Montague. I have noted for some months you have trouble with your daughter.'

'She is not a trouble—'

The dry voice drove through Patrick's protest. 'I have observed myself that she is rude, pert and disrespectful.' He flipped open a black notebook on his desk. 'I made a note of it.'

'You make a note of these things?' said Patrick incredulously.

Hildebrand fanned the pages of the book, closed it, then tapped its leather back. 'This is a useful volume. Knowledge of the minutiae of individual deviance is a great aid in the writing of both my articles and my sermons.' He glanced at the pages again. 'Now I have it on good authority . . .'

Patrick's eye flicked to the door, where he knew the said 'authority', Mrs Fosdick, was lurking.

'. . . on good authority that your daughter associates with individuals of lewd disposition and irreligious demeanour. She is seduced by the false glamour of those she may see as her betters. Mrs Loumis is not a suitable companion for any young woman . . .'

'I cannot agree, I—' Patrick was nonplussed at finding himself defending Finn rather than attacking Daniel Marchant.

'And now, it seems, this daughter of yours who has been running wild for months, has pursued my poor son, so he informed me this very morning, to the point of embarrassment.' He sniffed. 'No doubt he is what is called, in the lower echelons, "a good catch".'

'That's not true, Vicar. Not true!'

'So I will thank you, Mr Montague, to keep your predatory daughter away from my son.'

Patrick smashed a fist on the desk. 'It is not like that, Vicar, I tell you. He attacked her and left her. She could have been dead.'

Hildebrand looked at the hand as though it were something he'd rather not have on his shoe. 'Then it is some other village Lothario who has pressed his suit, and your reprobate daughter is trying to blacken my son's name. I tell you he would not stoop to such an association. Now . . .' He rang a silver bell which stood on the table. The door opened instantly and Mrs Fosdick bustled into the room. 'Will you show Mr Montague out, Mrs Fosdick? No, Mr Montague? Then, Mrs Fosdick, you may go and get the sergeant. I am sure he will be pleased to investigate this thoroughly. The girl's reputation will be exposed and my son vindicated. Good day, Mr Montague.'

Patrick picked up his hat from the floor. Mrs Fosdick opened the door wide. Patrick backed out. 'It's not the last you'll hear—'

Hildebrand smiled thinly. 'Then you must go to the sergeant yourself, Mr Montague, and put your mind at ease.'

Patrick hunched his shoulders as he walked back to the shop. His despair deepened when he saw Finn in her usual place on her high stool behind the till. She looked enquiringly and he stumbled angrily through a version of the conversation he had just had with the vicar.

She laughed bitterly. 'Go to Corcoran? We'd not win against that man and his son. I want you to leave it. If we pursue it I'll not be able to go out of the door. Here or up in Priorton.'

'If that's what you want.'

'It is.'

He stumbled on, trying again to apologise to her for what she had seen at Mary Fenwick's.

She looked at him coldly. 'I've no wish to talk about that either. But you must see you've got to stop all that or it's not me, it's you, who'll be the talk of the district. Mother'll look a fool.' She paused. 'And so will you.'

'I won't. I won't go on, I promise, Finn.' He took her hand across the counter. 'It was just . . . your mother . . .'

Finn pulled her hand away. 'I don't want to know anything about that, Dad.'

They both looked round as Jenefer Loumis bustled into the shop. 'Finn, dear, I've been so delayed today. Would you believe that reprobate Stacy Smith has tied an iron knot in my gate? And then I went to the funeral of that baby of theirs. Poor mite, in an orange box, would you believe? And the scrappiest words said over him by that dried stick of a vicar . . . Finn, what on earth is it?' She lifted

126

the flap, moved round behind the counter and put her arms round the girl.

'Oh, Jenefer.' Finn started to cry, then sob violently. The shop bell pinged and Emily Punchard bustled in.

'Take her in the back, Mrs Loumis,' said Patrick, moving swiftly behind the counter, relieved to return to a role which he could handle. He smiled cheerily at Emily Punchard, his head racing with regret at his own impotence. He could not even defend his own daughter, a daughter whom he loved more than anyone in the world: a daughter who now looked on him with contempt. Wrapping up a quarter of butter and two ounces of sugar for Emily, he thought what he wanted most in the world was a very large whisky from under the bar of The Eagle. But he wouldn't get away that night, with Finn so put about. Yes. He would send out for some. That was it. Catch one of the lads and pay him a penny to fetch a gill of whisky. He would leave it beneath the counter. No one would know.

Emily Punchard handed over the pennies and carefully put her meagre groceries in her string bag. 'Our Stanley's not himself these days, Mr Montague, not himself at all, since the vicar stopped him playin' that blessed organ.'

'It's a bad business, Mrs Punchard,' said Patrick absently. His mind, still on a possible glass of whisky, did not even rise to the reference to the vicar.

'The allotment needs diggin' over but Ah cannot get him to do it. Ah try to get him down the Army Citadel but he won't come.'

Patrick shook his head and watched her go. The echo from the shop bell had hardly faded from the air before he was through the door himself to look for a lad to run along to The Eagle and get him a gill of whisky.

Hearing the low rush of Finn and Jenefer's voices in the back room, Esther made her way downstairs. She bridled when she saw the distinguished face and the flowing skirts of the woman from Plush Folly. 'Finnuola . . . are you all right?' She almost pulled her daughter away from the other woman.

Jenefer's hands came down to her sides. 'She seems very upset.'

'So she should be, she—'

Finn's tears dried. 'Will you stop talking about me as though I were a lump of lard?'

Jenefer eyed the cluttered back room. 'Why not come across to Plush Folly, Finn? You can rest there, and tell—'

'She's not going anywhere,' said Esther grimly. 'This is her home. It's all the gallivanting that's caused—'

'What?' Finn wrenched her arm away from her mother. 'Are you saying it was my fault? That it was me who turned Daniel Marchant

127

into an animal?' She grabbed her old coat from the peg and jammed a beret on to her head.

'Where are you going?' said Esther.

'Come with me,' said Jenefer. 'It's quiet there . . .'

'I'm going up to High Bank Farm. I promised those boys some old school books of mine. They'll be waiting.' She paused. 'And my best coat's up there somewhere in the woodland. And my hat. I can't afford to lose them.' The door scraped as she shut it and the two older woman were left alone.

Jenefer looked enquiringly and with some authority at Esther.

Esther shrugged. 'That Marchant boy attacked her. Very nearly had . . . his way. But he was disturbed.'

Jenefer went bright red. 'You should go to the police. She should . . .'

Esther shook her head. 'No. She wouldn't let us. Probably she's right. We'd get nowhere – his father a vicar, his uncle a magistrate.' She sat down heavily and started to rock backwards and forwards. 'I don't know what to do.'

When Patrick came into the back room ten minutes later the two women were drinking tea, made by Jenefer, and she was holding Esther's hand, the very image of mutually sympathetic motherhood.

It was a subdued Mary Fenwick who greeted Finn at High Bank Farm. 'The lads're off with their da,' she said soberly. She shook her head as Finn offered her the books. 'No. I'm sorry, Finn. Tot wouldn't have them in the house. Says we have to change grocers. Use Simmons in Priorton.'

Finn watched Mary closely. 'Why's that, Mrs Fenwick? Why's he taken against us?'

The other woman shrugged. 'He's a funny feller, Tot. Gets these things into his head.'

'Did he see my father here yesterday?'

'Saw the van . . .' Mary's head came up sharply. 'How d'you know?'

'I saw you too, Mary. But not just the van.'

Mary's broad face, marred today by a livid weal on the left-hand side, went brick-red. 'Eeh, hinny. What must yer think?'

'I think my dad's a stupid man, and you . . .'

'Eeh, Ah'm that sorry, hinney. No harm meant, yer know. A bit o' comfort all round.'

'Comfort!'

'Well, hinney, yer da's a canny man. A lonely man. A kind man.' She thought of the silver swallow brooch nestling among her pillowcases. 'An' up here it's, like, ahm just another bit of stock, like some prize sheep o' Tot's, fattening up for the Stanhope show.

Your da made me laugh . . .' Her voice tailed off for a moment. 'Yer right, hinny. There's no excuse,' she said humbly.

Finn thought of the animal brutality of Daniel in the woods, and the puppy-like nuzzling she had witnessed in Mary's kitchen. She put her hand on Mary's well-upholstered shoulder. 'Water under the bridge, Mary. There's worse things.'

Mary frowned slightly at her. 'Yer mean yer not tellin' yer ma?'

Finn shook her head.

Mary breathed out. 'Tot'll say nowt just to keep face.' She fingered the weal down her cheek. 'He give us a good hidin', like, for his own satisfaction. Dinnet blame yer da, hinny. He's a good man. A kind man. A nice talker to a woman. Yer dinnet meet many like that.'

'He's stupid.'

'Well, yer take that fer granted, hinney. They all are, one way or another. Every last one of them,' said Mary glumly, bringing a faint smile even to Finn's face.

'But you can have the books, Mary. You read them to the boys.'

Mary shook her head slowly. 'Nae use, hinny. Tot says Ah ken feget all that stuff. The boys'll work the land like he has, an' no fancy learnin' needed.'

'You can't just take that, Mary,' said Finn hotly.

Mary fingered her cheek again. 'Oh yes Ah can, hinney. Ah've got to.'

Finn hugged her, recognising now Mary's need and even that of her father to be human and turn for comfort where they could.

She refused Mary's offer of a last cup of tea and made her way off out of the farm up towards the woodland to retrieve her coat and hat from under the wide spread of the old oak tree. The coat was flat on the ground, spread out like some tipsy body and her hat was tangled in brambles close by. She picked up the clothes and shook them, watching the dried leaves float away into the clumps of grass. She closed her eyes and felt again the punishingly tight tie round her mouth and the prying, sly insistence of Daniel Marchant's hands and his whole body in his savage attack. She heard again the soft insinuations in his voice, and she leaned against the tree, her body shaking.

Her back lay along the tree and she could feel the flow and ripple of the bark beneath her skin. She stayed there very still for fifteen minutes. Then slowly her body started to relax. The tree seemed to be blotting up her anger. She took some deep breaths and the shaking stopped. She knew then that she could stay angry at Daniel, but not with herself and her hapless father. And she knew, as though the tree were speaking to her, that she should not worry. Daniel would rue what he had done. She was certain of it.

She folded her coat carefully and put it in the bicycle basket on top of the books. The books – she would take them to the Swamps for the twins. That was where she would go. To Michael O'Toole's house. She started to think again about the night Michael had walked her home and kissed her in the shop doorway. She put her own hand to her cheek and felt the kiss again.

When Jenefer got back to Plush Folly she prowled restlessly around the kitchen, then took a jug of hot lemonade across to the coach house. Hubert and the boy Michael were there, standing shoulder to shoulder looking up at the nearly completed wall. Hubert's face was beaming as he turned to her. 'You must have read our thoughts, my dearest. Michael and I are just resting . . .' His voice sharpened. 'What is it? What has happened?'

Carefully she put down the lemonade, then she heard her voice stumbling through some kind of explanation about Finn, the brisk, practical façade she had shown across in the shop crumbling. 'Oh, Hubert, how could he? That little girl. That dreadful man, he . . .'

Hubert groaned and moved across to squat in front of the section of the wall where he had painted the maiden, the girl in the plaitless gown. He started to rock backwards and forwards. 'It can't happen,' he said, 'It can't happen – it can't happen – it can't happen – it can't happen.' His voice was rattling out, taking on the force of an engine.

'Oh, Hubert,' said Jenefer. 'Not now. Not at this moment.'

He whirled round at her. 'He needs horsewhipping. He will not get away with it. It can't happen, I tell you.' He turned to Michael and said almost rationally. 'I saw it, you know. In France. My soldiers moved into a village just after them. A girl there, lying, the blood coming out of her. Blood – blood – blood.' He was rocking again.

Jenefer said dully to Michael, 'Will you go now? I'll see to him.'

When Finn arrived at the house in Primrose Court the twins and Smiler were playing a game with stones in a patch of sunlight which fell on the black dirt outside their door. Toots' smile lit up her grimy face. 'Miss Montague!' she said. 'Our brother isn't here.'

'Isn't he off gettin' money for us to have some new shoes?' said Nancy, flexing her bare toes in the dirt.

'D'yer want a game of chucks?' asked Smiler. 'Ah'll len' yer my boss ter start. Ah've got a spare.' He held out his hand to her, palm up. Resting in the middle was a large pebble, pyramid-shaped with rounded edges.

Finn jumped off her bike and leaned it up against the narrow window. 'I haven't come to see your brother. I've come to see you.'

She fished the books out of the basket. 'I brought you these. Would you like a look at them?'

Toots eyed the bright pile indifferently. 'We never had no books.'

'We can't read,' chimed her twin.

'Not read? Big girls like you? What do you do at school?'

'They learned, but they forgot. Not that often at school since Ma died,' volunteered Smiler.

'Why not?'

He shrugged. They all looked at her with round eyes, then Nancy said impatiently, 'Do yer want a game of chucks or not?'

'When I was little it was called fivestones.' She looked at the scuffed soil where she would have to squat.

'I'll get yer a cracket,' said Nancy. She raced into the house, returning with a small stool not much bigger than a book itself.

Finn squatted down. 'Right. I'll play with you. If I win, you have to show me how you can read.'

'You'll not win,' said Toots. 'Our Smiler beats everyone in the Swamps.'

That was how Michael found Finn, crouching in the dirt, in a bright patch of sunlight playing chucks with his sisters and brother. He had already been across to the shop, to be told by Mr Montague that his daughter wasn't there and anyway it wasn't any of his business where she was. Patrick softened a bit when Michael produced money to spend. He counted out the cost of the items and the change very carefully.

Michael had then scoured the streets of New Morven and even gone down the Priorton Road in search of Finn.

He had hung around the gates of the vicarage, frustrated when that bumptious fool Daniel Marchant had failed to appear. He passed poor Stanley Punchard, wandering down the street muttering away in a world of his own.

Outside the Memorial Hall he bumped into Tom Farrell and old Jonty and poured out his anger at the tale he had heard from Jenefer Loumis. He would wring the man's neck. Just let him find him, the supercilious brat.

Tom took him by the shoulders and shook him. 'Stop it, Michael, man. Ah keep tellin' yer it's nee good sayin' you'll beat this or that man. It's all of them. The whole class. Arm yersel', keep yer energy for to rout all of them. Lift yersel' from the serfdom of individual reprisal, to class action.'

Michael had twisted away from him. 'Oh, you, Farrell, talkin' like a text book, as cold as ice. Isn't it ink that flows in your veins not blood?' Blood – blood. Hubert Loumis's voice echoed on and on in his head.

Tom's hands dropped helplessly to his sides. 'Better ice than fire, that burns itself out at a single puff.'

'Don't let's quarrel among ourselves, lads,' old Jonty had said then, a hand on each shoulder. 'If we do, they've won over us without a word or a blow. Where'd the world be without ice and fire both?' He turned to Michael. 'Go and find the girl and comfort her, Michael. Be her friend. It seems just yesterday I was all fire for my Susanah.' He laughed. 'And I'm still warming myself at that hearth, even through the coldest of days.'

Smiler saw Michael first. 'Here's our Mick.' He jumped up, knocking Finn's hand so that her throw was aborted. Finn scrambled to her feet, brushing the dirt from the hem of her pleated skirt. 'Hey, Mick, Miss Montague's a canny hand at chucks. Nearly beat me, she did.'

'So I would have, if you hadn't knocked me!' said Finn, giving him a friendly cuff. She brushed her hands together and looked up uncertainly at Michael, her colour rising, her heart lifting. 'I . . . brought some books for them. Maybe they'd like to read at home, seeing as they don't get to school much . . .' her voice tailed off.

Michael smiled down at her, relieved. She was pale, but she didn't seem all that different from usual. She was not the shivering wreck he had imagined. 'That was really kind,' he said gently, 'but they'll be able to go to school now.' He lifted up the sack he was carrying and tipped out two pairs of tough stout shoes and a pair of heavy boots. Finn recognised her father's stock. 'No excuse now. You'll all have to go to school. Mr Loumis gave me money on account for some roof work I'm doin' for him.

The twins and Smiler groaned in unison. 'School! Can't we just read Miss Montague's books?' said Toots, her sister nodding in agreement.

Michael hugged her to him. 'You can do that as well.' He lifted his eyes to meet Finn's and looked deep into hers. He wanted to ask her about it all, how she felt, and tell her he would kill that twerp if she wanted. But he knew he couldn't speak, and she wouldn't say a word about it. 'That is, if Miss Montague's happy about that.'

Finn smiled, the strain and the stress of the day and the night slipping entirely from her face. 'Oh yes, Michael. I'm happy about that. Shall we start now?'

At Plush Folly Jenefer Loumis moved desperately from room to room, looking for Hubert. She had finally given him one of his draughts and, so she thought, had settled him down on the bed. But he was gone. The coach house was dark and padlocked and Hubert was nowhere to be found. She shivered.

13

Victims

Getting the rope out of the house had been a problem. She was so watchful. Of course, that was loving care, you knew she did it because she cared. Her intentions were so good. She was a good woman.

He had wondered about the rope. He had never seen a man hanged. Did it take a long time? He had seen them shot, of course, in the war. Played his part in a firing squad once, for some poor soul who had run rather than stayed. That had been quick, but the man had been terrified: sobbing his heart out and saying Hail Marys all at the same time, then dropping like a stone in mid-hail.

It was important to find the right place. He'd thought hard about the problem of where to do it. It would have to be the right place. They should not find out till long after the deed was done. It might take some time after all, the process of dying.

Finn came back from her walk to find her father in the shop in a rather overrelaxed state. He declared himself pleased to see her looking so much better, the walk must have done her some good, really she should put it all behind her, the feller wasn't worth a spit . . .

She put her face close to his. 'Dad, you've been drinking whisky.' She looked around. 'Did you close the shop?'

He heaved a theatrical sigh. 'No, Caught a lad in the road and he got me a gill from The Eagle.'

'In the shop? Dad!' But her tone was not too sharp: she was still suffused with the good feeling induced by spending time with the family at Primrose Court. Michael had offered to walk her home, but she refused, saying she was a big girl now. One part of her had longed to say yes, to feel his hand in hers, his lips on her cheek again. He had looked at her hard, willing her to tell him about her bad experience. She resisted his unspoken plea, but she knew that he knew all about it. That hurt her; she resented the sulky evil of

Daniel Marchant seeping into this precious and delicate new friendship which was beginning to mean the world to her.

Now she sighed and turned to her father. 'You go upstairs and get your feet up. Dad. Sleep it off a bit. I'll take over here. Can't face Mother just at the moment.'

An hour later, having 'slept it off a bit', he came bounding down the stairs. 'I've been up at the window, Finn. There's some kerfuffle on down the other end of the street. Can you hear?'

They went out and along the street and when they got nearer The Eagle they could hear cheers and laughter, catcalls and whistles. Patrick grasped Finn's arm. Her eyes widened.

There, reeling around drunkenly in the street was Daniel Marchant. His face was bruised and he was wearing just a shirt. His long white legs were bare and his buttocks and his private parts were smeared with evil-smelling cow dung. He reeled in front of Finn and she met his eyes, which were full of tears. She forced her own eyes to sweep him from head to foot. 'You should get yourself home, Daniel. You're making an exhibition of yourself,' she said.

'Poor lad.' It was Emily Punchard, hurrying across with her own threadbare coat. She wrapped it round his waist and grasped his arm, 'Come on, love, let's get you home.'

The landlord of The Eagle told them the tale was that the vicar's son had been riding his horse up near his Uncle Oliver's place and someone had jumped on him. According to the horsekeeper, the animal had returned to the livery stables under its own steam hours ago.

'Well, fancy that!' said Patrick, as they walked back to the shop. 'He got his comeuppance all right. Wish I'd had the wit . . . or the courage.'

Finn linked her arm through his. 'Dad, all you can do is be you, not some false hero.'

'Who did it, do you think?' said Patrick eagerly.

'I have a very good idea.'

'Who?'

'Michael O'Toole.'

'The Irishman?' Patrick's tone was less jaunty. 'I know he carries a torch for you, but—'

'There's no one else, Dad. Unless that man's been hurting someone else. I suppose that's quite possible.'

Esther was in the back room waiting for their story when they returned and was so pleased at the cause of the mêlée she actually made them a cup of cocoa with her own hands.

It took Emily Punchard a while to get some response at the vicarage, but when Mrs Fosdick saw Daniel she opened the door wide and ushered him in, her shriek of horror so loud that it brought the vicar along the landing in his battered velvet smoking jacket.

'Come up here, Daniel.' He stood impatiently as his son made his way up the stairs, clutching Emily Punchard's coat to his waist. He peered over the banister at Emily. 'What happened here, Mrs Punchard?'

'Seems someone pulled him off his horse, Vicar. And . . . attacked him.'

Hildebrand did not put a hand out to Daniel, who was now swaying beside him. He wrinkled his thin nose at the stench. 'Thank you, Mrs Punchard, for bringing him home,' he said dismissively. 'We shall take care of him now.'

Emily took a breath. 'Vicar?'

'Yes?' he said sharply.

'Would you reconsider about my Stanley? He's in a terrible state without his organ. Bad enough, out of work. But no music! He's like a man off.'

'In the first place I will not reconsider. I never go back on my word. In the second place I must reprimand you for your crudeness, your insensitivity in bringing that up when my son is in such distress. Mrs Fosdick, will you show Mrs Punchard out? Then draw a bath for Mr Daniel?' He turned to his son. 'I will wait for you in my study.'

The door closed with a click behind Emily and she stood there in front of the closed door, put her hands together and closed her eyes. 'Lord forgive him for he knows not what he does.'

Later at the vicarage, Hildebrand looked at his son, standing before him in his dressing gown, white and subdued.

'Now then, what is all this?'

'I was pulled from my horse and attacked.'

'Why should they attack you?'

Daniel shrugged. 'Hooligans, misfits. They need no reason.' He wouldn't meet his father's eye. 'There's chaos here in the North, Father. Like Uncle says, it needs bringing to some kind of order before the whole country falls apart.'

Hildebrand stroked his chin, considering the bad association with his son in the last few days. 'I think it's time you went back up to Cambridge, Daniel. This is no place for you. You must have reading to do.'

Daniel nodded. 'You're right. There's no life here for me among these . . . halfwits. To be honest, Father, I can't see how you stand it.'

Hildebrand put his fingers together. 'Ah. It's God's work, son. Not done without suffering.'

The next day Finn did a full day's work, then asked her father if she could go off for an hour.

135

'Off to see Mrs Loumis?'

'I'll call on her on my way back. I . . . want to go across to see Michael.'

'Him?' he sniffed.

'Yes, him.'

Michael was standing in the doorway at Primrose Court. When he saw her he stood up straight, knocked out his pipe and put it in his pocket. 'Finn Montague!' he said, pleasure opening up his face.

She stood before him. 'I've come to say thank you . . .' she started.

He laughed. 'For what?' He opened his arms. 'Come here, lovely. Come on in here.'

She ran to him and his whole body seemed to enfold her. She grasped him round the waist, then hesitated as she smelled his pipe tobacco and the colder acrid smell of poverty and hardship. But the hesitation was wiped out as she felt the softness of his lips on hers and his arms like whipcord around her. Then his lips became hard and insistent and she could feel again the tie with which Daniel had stopped her mouth. She started to struggle.

'Hey, come here, Nancy, here's our Mick kissin' Miss Montague!'

Finn broke away with some relief to stare down into the bright dark face. 'Toots!' She started to laugh. The identical face loomed beside it. 'Nancy.'

'Is he a good kisser, Miss Montague?' asked Toots.

Nancy nodded. 'I bet he is. He's handsome, our Mick. Everybody says that.'

Michael touched her elbow. 'Are you all right?' he said. 'That wasn't . . .'

She shook her head looking at him soberly. 'I'm fine. It was fine. It was just that I remembered . . . Jenefer told you, didn't she?'

He was pulling her into the house and his voice was in her ear unheard by the twins. 'Sure, all that'll go away, Finn. That'll fade away. Just wait and it'll go. It's no more meaning than if he'd cut you with a knife. It'll heal.'

They were in the dark room and Smiler was stirring the low fire. Michael sprawled in front of it and grinned up at her. 'I hear that rapscallion vicar's son got a good drubbing.'

'That's what I'm here for. I thought you . . .'

He shook his head, got out his pipe and started to light it. 'I wish it'd been me. I went down the vicarage looking for him, but there was no sign.' He shrugged. 'Maybe that mouth of his's made him more than one enemy.'

Toots was tugging at Finn's coat. 'I was lookin' at this book you brought, with the pictures of the black-faced boy and the babies in the water an' our Smiler said you'd read it for us when you came.'

136

Finn took the copy of *The Water Babies*, already grubby from dirty clutching hands. She stopped herself from telling them they should wash their hands before they handled the books. That would involve a trek across the muddy yard to fill the water bowl, by which time the desire to read would have gone. Better to have soiled books.

She patted the bench beside her. 'Come and sit by me so you can see the pictures. I'll read the first page and you have to try the second and Nancy has to try the third.' They snuggled in, one at either side. With Michael watching, they all settled to the task. They had struggled through to page four when Michael leaped up.

'Mr Loumis!' he said.

'What? What about him?'

'He did it. It's gotta be him. He was so wild when Mrs Loumis told him about it. I wouldn't put it past him. He had one of his wild things on. Me grandda in Ireland used to get them on him, when he was in the drink.'

Finn closed the book and stood up, her pleasure at the story and the twins' fascination with it fading. 'I have to go to him. To her. She'll be worried . . .'

He stood up. 'I'll come with you.'

'Is it Mrs Loumis you're going to?' said Toots. She stood up and linked Finn's arm. 'Didn't she say we could have a bath again soon, Nancy?'

Nancy nodded vigorously and put a thumb in her mouth. She leaned on Finn on the opposite side and they set off, leaving Smiler to tend the fire and give a message to Tom Farrell, whom Michael was half expecting.

The old walls of Plush Folly were vibrating with loud music, which was thumping its way through the open door as they arrived. Jenefer, when she came to greet them, was dressed in a long purple skirt, had flowers in her hair and a fine crystal Madeira glass in her hand. 'Come in! Come in! We are dancing in celebration.'

She took Finn's hand. 'How are you, my dear? You look wonderful. Come in! Come in!' She pulled her towards the drawing room door without waiting for an answer. 'Come in, children, join the party.'

Hubert, standing by the fireplace, leaned over to lift the needle from the gramophone. The clamour of music was stilled. He smiled anxiously at Finn. 'Are you all right little maid?'

She nodded. 'Yes. Yes, Hubert. More so now that—' She turned to Jenefer. 'Someone did terrible things to Daniel Marchant. I thought . . .'

They all looked at Hubert.

Jenefer went and stood beside him. 'Hubert went running off, as

Michael knows. I went in search of him. He was nowhere to be found, not anywhere in the village. So I set out on the Priorton Road and there he was.'

'They said Daniel had been pulled off his horse,' said Finn.

'I didn't pull him,' said Hubert. 'I stood before him, challenged him with being a miscreant. And he started to laugh. Such a strange loud, neighing laugh he has. The poor horse no sooner heard that than it reared high twice, and crashed the feller to the ground.'

Jenefer took up the story. 'I passed the cantering horse on the road before I saw them. And there they were, the boy lying cursing on the road and Hubert looming over him. The boy took one look at me and called me horrible names.'

'So I punched him,' said Hubert with relish.

'And I told him what a beast he was for . . . attacking you, Finn.'

There was a pause.

'Then what?' said Michael.

Jenefer shot him a sparkling glance. 'Then I sat on him while Hubert stripped him of everything but his shirt . . .'

'He was crying by then,' supplied Hubert, his eyes on Finn.

'. . . then Hubert went into a field and heaped up cow's business into the boy's coat. And he brought it back and I . . .' there was relish in her pause '. . . I applied it.'

Michael glanced at Finn, who started to laugh. She laughed so much that she began to hiccough, and had to sit down to retrieve her breath. They all joined in, including the twins, who were not quite sure what all the hilarity was about, but a laugh was a laugh anyway, wasn't it? And they didn't want to be left out of the fun.

In ten minutes they were all sitting down drinking Madeira and eating Jenefer's cake, the visit turning into a celebration of the bizarre rout visited on the son of the vicar. The twins asked for, and were granted, their bath and Michael and Finn progressed to tea and fine biscuits.

Hubert wound the gramophone again, put on a record, came across and, with a graceful bow, ask Finn for the pleasure of her company in a dance. Jenefer pulled Michael to the floor and they waltzed round the room, Finn laughing over Hubert's shoulder at a bemused Michael, who was clumping about avoiding Jenefer's feet as best he could. The twins came down, damp and shining, and joined in the fun.

It was an hour before they got away, and the high spirits of Plush Folly stayed with them as they made their way back to the shop.

Finn laughed up at Michael. 'My father'll feel deserted. I must have been out of the shop three hours.'

'Do you want me to come in and tell him about it?'

She shook her head. 'I can look after myself, thank you. Look at

138

those girls. They're all in. They need their bed. Too much wine and dancing for their own good.'

'No. No. We're not tired,' said Toots.

'Not tired,' echoed Nancy.

Michael laughed. 'Just look at the pair of you, aren't you dead on your feet?' He glanced up and down the street, leaned over and planted a kiss on Finn's cheek. 'We'll be away, then.' The girls continued to murmur their protestations but, in the end, quite meekly, allowed themselves to be led away.

Patrick, marching backwards and forwards in the shop, swung round as the tinkling bell heralded her entry. 'Where in heaven have you been?' His face was black and full of thunder. 'After last time—'

'I was at Michael's and then at Jenefer Loumis's.' She took his arm. 'What is it? Dad, what is it?'

He leaned against the counter, his face ashen. 'Corcoran was in here. Finn, poor Stanley Punchard's dead! He hanged himself, up there in the woods. Seems like the place where you . . . where that feller took you. They say the log was there four feet away that He'd stood on and kicked over.' He put his hands over his face. 'Poor feller. Poor Emily. No work. That's what it does to 'em. No work, no meaning.' When his hands came away from his face he was crying like a baby.

Across at the Swamps, Tom Farrell was breaking the same news to Michael. Stanley was his father's cousin, an 'uncle' in his family. Tom was rigid with anger. 'It's time something was done, Mike. It's overdue. Time people like you stop mooning up there on the fence, and come down and fight by our side. None of them'll help us. We have to help ourselves. We've got to let them know we'll not stand half the world starving while the other half lives off the fat that even this land still has.'

Michael held up a hand. 'Stop! No more speech-making, Tom. What shall we do? I'm with you on this. Always was. I'm with you all the way.'

14

The Apple Loft

After the routing of Daniel Marchant and the death of Stanley Punchard, the Reverend Hildebrand Marchant's congregation was reduced, not just by the Montague family but by others who had witnessed his son's humiliation and had heard the reason for it on the village grapevine. Finn was popular in the village and they counted her now as one of their own, more so than that snooty vicar's son who turned up now and then. And there were even more who had been disturbed by Stanley's dismissal, and guilty that they had taken no action.

So the Salvation Army Citadel gained more souls, as did the Primitive Methodists and the Wesleyans: after all, both these latter were safely led by their own people, sons of miners.

Hildebrand, relishing as ever the sound of his own voice echoing through the graceful arches of St Benedict's, was confident that his flock was being depleted by the increasing godlessness in this benighted community. He had foretold it, after all.

Stacy Smith and Bella did, however, continue to attend, as Stacy's weedling could still tap the vicar's charitable pocket. For Hildebrand, Stacy represented all the poor, indigent and mean. This meant that irregular donations in Stacy's direction, accompanied by a small sermon, allowed Hildebrand to hold forth at dinner parties about judicious giving being the key to charity these days. He would give Stacy Smith as a 'for instance', concealing the fact that he was the only recipient of his charity.

Michael continued to do odd jobs for the Loumises. There was a good deal to do; Plush Folly had been neglected for many years. He now called openly on Finn, much to the discomfort of both her parents. Finn and Michael could now be seen walking out together quite regularly. Sometimes they even walked arm in arm. As well as visiting Plush Folly, Finn now spent some time across at Primrose Court, continuing to read with the twins, although Smiler resisted the lure of the books.

She and Michael had little time alone: a thing which was in turn a source of relief and frustration. Every time they kissed and became physically close Finn was still made rigid by the shadow of Daniel Marchant. Michael saw this and understood, contenting himself with a closely held hand, a kiss on the cheek.

Sometimes now Michael vanished for days at a time, off with Tom Farrell to meetings and marches in Newcastle and Manchester. Tom had taken a fancy to a new woman politician caller Leonora Scorton, whose views chimed with his, and he would travel many miles to hear her speak.

The two men were also involved in other more shadowy, less public activities. Finn asked Michael about this, but he would just shrug and say, 'Things to help. More than one way of charitable giving.'

There were reports in the papers of thefts from great houses, of motor cars with cut tyres. Emily Punchard and her fellow workers would turn up at the Salvation Army Hut and find sacks of potatoes and other vegetables, and battered cardboard boxes containing clothes and boots. One cold morning there was a once-white flour sack spattered with blood, containing a neatly butchered sheep.

The Salvationists mentioned this to Sergeant Corcoran, who came and confiscated the precious meat to moulder away as evidence. After that, they cooked and distributed such bounty without telling the sergeant. Or, as Emily would say with a perfectly straight face, wouldn't it be a mistake to let all this bounty of the Lord, who worked in His mysterious ways, go to waste?

Since the death of her husband, Emily had lost weight and her demeanour was less chirpy. But she worked on in her cause with even greater zeal, dedicating every working hour she could spare from her family to cooking and providing for the queues which were increasing each day at the door of the Hut. Stanley's nephew Tom Farrell would turn up at the house at odd times, to take the lads off for a game of football, or to talk to her about Stanley and the music he had loved.

Michael fought with Tom Farrell about his work for the Loumises. Tom called it 'lackey's work'. Michael protested that it wasn't like that, the Loumises were funny folk, strange, but not like that. And the money was little enough, but it put a bit more food on the table. Tom said gloomily that *they* were all *like that*, just some disguised it better than others. Then he left the matter, ignoring Michael's work as though it were some dark guilty secret.

Michael was enjoying the sheer activity of working on the building of shelves, or the repairing of attics. He particularly liked standing alongside Hubert as he worked in the coach house, listening to his tales of battles, real and imaginary, in which he had taken part. Or thought he had.

Finn listened to Jenefer's tales about her own and Hubert's life among the artists in France. Sometimes Finn asked about Jenefer's earlier life, before she had met Hubert. But then Jenefer would become vague, talking about the army and protocol, and cages and prisons.

People continued to come to Jenefer's kitchen door for small cures and advice. Finn watched her one day attend to a woman who came in with a painful limp. Jenefer made the woman take off her dress and lie on her belly before the kitchen fire. Then she started to pull at the woman's arms and legs, ignoring the screams and groans this caused. Then she got some oil from the big dresser and, pulling up the woman's shift, rubbed her bare back and buttocks with long billowing strokes which pulled and moved the flesh in every direction.

The woman finally stood up and stretched, and took a cautious walk round the room. 'Aye,' she said, 'that's better. Ah'll be able ter get back ter work, only one day missed.' She told them she worked in the laundry room and the house of Sir Oliver Marchant, hard physical work when she was there and a four-mile walk in both directions.

'You should rest,' said Jenefer. 'Only gentle exercise.'

The woman made a rasping noise which might have been a laugh, then walked out, painless and without a limp after failing to make Jenefer accept sixpence.

Finn listened when other women brought more obscure needs to Jenefer's kitchen. She heard Jenefer making lyrical allusions to another life, another Side, to times past, and to scenes in their own lives which Jenefer herself had not witnessed. The women would nod then, exchange glances.

One night, walking home with Michael, Finn started to talk about these powers which Jenefer seemed to have.

Michael shook his head. 'Mumbo jumbo,' he said. 'Sure, she's a great woman, but she's got you all mesmerised. She's had old Hubert mesmerised since the first day he saw her.' He chuckled. 'Me too, I think.'

Reluctantly Finn nodded her head. 'I sometimes think she's playing the part of the wise woman, the fortune-teller. She believes it and they believe it. But what she says is so loose that it can mean what they both want it to.' She looked up at him earnestly in the light of the street lamp.

He smiled back at her, then, glancing up and down the deserted street, pulled her round into the shadow of a narrow ginnel. He held her close and she could feel his hand on the side of her face. 'Talkin' about being mesmerised, it's you who mesmerised me that first time you came to read the Riot Act to our Smiler. Standin' there with that cloud of hair . . .' he stroked it back from her face '. . . an' those grey eyes . . .' She could feel his fingers on her eyelids. 'An' a mouth like velvet raspberries just off the cane.' Her lips itched as his fingers traced their shape.

Tentatively she put her hands to the back of his head and pulled him towards her. He kept very still. Then with her lips she grazed his cheek, then his left eye and then his lips.

'Oh, Finn,' he groaned, 'don't do it if you don't want.'

She pressed harder with her lips and brought her body in line with his, so that her puckering breasts just touched him. In their kiss and those which followed, all shadows of black feeling associated with Daniel Marchant began to dissolve, leaving a clean space inside her.

Suddenly there were men's loud voices in the street beyond the ginnel and, guiltily, Finn and Michael leaped apart. 'I have to get home,' she whispered.

He nodded slowly and they waited for the men to pass before slipping out to walk decorously along towards Montague's shop, the picture of mutual innocence.

He kissed her on the cheek before letting her go, and she raced through the crowded shop, avoiding her father's quizzical glance. She raced up the stairs two at a time to hang up her best jacket in her room, before returning downstairs to help her father.

'Finnuola!' Esther's plaintive voice followed her on to the landing.

She opened her mother's door. Esther was standing beside the window. 'You let that Irish boy kiss you!' she said accusingly.

'If you mean did I kiss him, I did,' said Finn.

'You'll be getting a name.'

'I only see Michael, Mother. We only walk from Plush Folly to here, or from Primrose Court to here.'

'But he's not our—'

'Sort? Ma! We live in a village of poor people. We're barely more than poor ourselves. Folks up in Priorton'll see us as poor. And Michael and all them, the only thing wrong with them is they have no work. The bad is done to them, they are not bad themselves. They do not have the mark of Cain. They are not a different species.'

The outburst subdued Esther. The girl was right. Being shop-keeper here was not like being a shopkeeper at Gateshead. Here, they were 'the poor' themselves. Hadn't she gone on and on at Patrick about the life they were forced to lead here, little better than beggars themselves?

She tried another tack. 'He's a Catholic. All those Irish are . . .'

144

'My father's not a Catholic, and wasn't his family Irish, and Catholic – his mother at least? Wasn't she one of those Irish? Anyway, Michael never goes to church. And even if he did, I '. . . her voice tailed off.

'Are you that keen, Finnuola, that affected by him, this boy?' asked Esther soberly, bewildered at witnessing a depth of feeling that had never been her own experience.

Finn nodded slowly. 'I think so, Ma. I think so.' She took her mother's arm. 'Now, Ma, why not get back into bed? You must be cold there by the window. Let me brush your hair and put it in its plait and you'll be more comfortable.'

Daniel Marchant moved about quietly, preparing for bed. His rooms at his Cambridge college were more comfortable than the average. The fires didn't smoke, for one thing, and his scout was very biddable. The civilisations of cushions and curtains supplied by Harrods, courtesy of his Uncle Oliver, and the port which came from his uncle's own wine merchant, all contributed very satisfyingly to his level of comfort.

He had shut himself here in his room for a week after his return from the North, while he licked the wounds of his humiliation at the hands of that mad pair from Plush Folly.

But in time, his tutor, and the men who thought they were Daniel's friends, drew him again into the gatherings which had been so much of his life before: gatherings where the wine flowed and the talk was wild and idealistic. Here he picked up titbits which were crucial, according to his uncle, to the ongoing intelligence process. This would be their armoury in the future in the new order of things.

In these meetings of the group he could talk now with some authority about the sufferings of the proletariat and his own role in the North in raising people's consciousness, making the poor aware of their exploitation, giving them some understanding of their international responsibilities.

In addition, he was getting quite good at feigning acquiescence in the subtle homosexual undercurrents that sometimes characterised these gatherings, even though they did make him sometimes sick to the stomach. When this got very bad, after he had made his customary note to send to his uncle, he would put on his coat and hat and visit a compliant woman who, for a ridiculously small amount of money, would allow him to express just how much of a man he really was. He was no pansy.

This was all so much better than being in that filthy little village with those dirty people. He could not think how his father had stood it all these years. The old boy was tainted with it himself, this darkness, this dereliction. If his Uncle Oliver weren't close by he

145

would never go within ten miles of the place again.

He got into his pyjamas and froze for a moment, reliving again the humiliation of that witchwoman's hand smearing cow dirt all over him, chuckling quietly as she did so. Even while he thought of it he had a throbbing erection, just as he had when she was about her evil work. They were all the same, women. Witches and whores. Look at his own mother, stripping naked to lie in the corn to die. And that was after abandoning him to housekeepers and maids years before! Abandoning him to people who pinched and slapped you in private, and fawned over you in public; who taunted you as they bathed you, playing with you and making you hard. Making you scream.

Witches and whores, that's all they were.

He worked away, getting rid, in his usual fashion, of the painful erection. No, he would go directly to his Uncle Oliver's in future. Never back to that place. Never again.

Finn popped her head up into the loft space and watched Michael for a moment before he saw her. He was sitting, hammer in hand, astride a beam in the apple loft above Alan Newton's old cottage. He was wearing an old checked shirt of Hubert's and his muscles moved under the soft well-washed fabric as he reached up to secure the wooden strapping under the slates.

'Michael.'

He swung round, a delighted smile lighting up his face. He had a gloss about him these days: his hair shone and his skin glowed. The extra money from Hubert, Jenefer's perpetual French stews and the weekly Plush Folly baths which he and the twins, and even the unwilling Smiler experienced now, had transformed him from the gaunt, pinched man who, although handsome, had looked older than his years, into the shining boy before her.

She put the ladling can of soup on the plank floor and pushed it towards him. 'Jenefer asked me to leave you some of her spicy stuff on my way home and said to tell you you should finish soon and get home to those twins and Smiler.'

'I've other things to do before I go home. I need to see Tom Farrell.' Michael rolled off the beam and crawled towards her. He could not stand up to his considerable height in this space. 'Come on up off the ladder. Isn't this a snug space? Can you smell the apples?'

'Apples?' She pushed herself further up the ladder and he took her hand to help her up. 'Yes.' She looked round. 'Where are they?'

Holding on to her hand, he shook his head. 'What you're smellin' is just ghosts of apples laid down here years ago, long since eaten. It's in the rafters. Come an' see this.' He pulled her along the length of the roof space, half bending, to the end wall where into the stone

146

apex which supported the steep roof was cut a small crudely glazed window in the shape of a fleur-de-lis. 'See this? A shamrock. Sure, didn't some Irishman draw it up an' cut it in stone all those years ago? An' look!'

They peered through the window at a perfect view down the Gaunt Valley, over the heads of the mean houses, past the silent gantries of the pits, towards the gentle rise of the green hills within which were folded trees, like bundles of protected wool, in dips and gullies. 'See that? It might be bits of Ireland I remember from when I was a small boy . . .'

Her heart caught at the thought of the little Irish boy looking solemnly at his own green hills for the last time. She was bristlingly aware now of her hand in his, the heat of his cheek close to hers.

Then his lips were pressing her cheek. 'An' look at this.' Right under the eaves were three rugs pulled on top of each other to make a neat couch. 'It's Hubert's, I think. You know when he goes missin' an' Mrs Loumis has to go in search? Doesn't the poor man hide here like some harvest mouse in the last ears of corn?' His lips moved to her ear, feeling their way through the cloud of loosely tied hair. 'Come lie with me, Finnuola Montague. Lie with me.'

She allowed herself to be pulled into the narrow space and relaxed on to the blanket couch. He lay there beside her and cradled her head in his arm. Against her cheek he whispered to her how she was beautiful, like the purple pansy or the late spring bluebell. How her hair was like spun silk and her skin like velvet. How her lips were like new raspberries . . .

'Oh Michael, talk about kissing the Blarney Stone!' And it was she who kissed him to stop the talk; it was she who stroked his face from temple to neck, reaching inside his collar so her fingers could touch the soft skin of the nape of his neck. It was she who undid the buttons of the soft check shirt.

Then he was kissing her hard, almost burning his way into her, his lips forcing her mouth open to allow his tongue to flicker on the inside like a mother bird feeding its young.

She pulled her mouth away. 'I want . . . I want . . .' she murmured.

When they made love he lifted her over him, so that this first time held no shade of memory of the pressing, choking embrace of Daniel Marchant. They laughed when their coming together couldn't happen, because she was so tight. 'There's no space, no place,' she giggled, half gasping, intoxicated with their play. Then gradually, gradually it did happen and then she was gasping with searing, half-welcomed pain and breathless with dawning and explosive delight, as, for an enormous stretch of seconds, she was at one with him and at one with the dancing dust in this apple-haven in

147

Plush Folly, at one with Morven Hills and the streams running through them, at one with the lowering sky and the birds that were hammering their way through their evening chorus in the woods.

Then it was over and they were lying side by side staring at the rafters and the evening light gleaming through the tiles above them.

Finn closed her eyes and waited for her body to stop ringing like a struck bell. After a few minutes Michael's breathing slowed. He turned towards her and, supporting his head on his elbow, he stared down at her.

He pushed back the hair, now sticky, from her brow. 'You are a true beauty, Finnuola Montague, a true delight.' He paused. 'An' I'll always love you. Always remember this. Whatever happens in this world, I'll always love you an' I'll always want to be with you.'

She smiled up at him. 'I know,' she said. 'You make it all so good, Michael. We make it all so good. Something's begun here.'

'So it has, darlin' girl. So it has.' He took her hand. 'I'm off again with Tom for a couple of days, but I'll find you the minute I get back. The very minute, I promise you.'

On the way home Finn was pleased of the darkness in the streets. There was only one patch of blood on her petticoat and she felt sure it wouldn't show through. But she felt equally sure that anyone looking into her face would know what had happened, would know that tonight she had travelled through that one-way arch.

In the shop Patrick had two customers, but called across as she dashed through, 'Can you come down, Finn, when you're ready? There's things I want to see to.'

She took a bowl of water upstairs and washed and changed, brushing and pinning her hair very carefully. She looked at the brown-edged mirror and thought that her very face had changed. It seemed full and very white and the lips seemed permanently wide and smiling. She felt that she could never scowl or cry again.

Her mother called out for her and she went into the bedroom, still not able to suppress her smile. She looked her mother in the eye and she knew her mother knew. She also knew that neither of them would speak of it. They would never speak of it.

'You had a nice time, dear?' said Esther.

'Mmm,' she nodded, pulling the counterpane straight on her mother's bed. 'Dad wants me downstairs, Ma. I've left him too long.'

Her mother looked at her keenly and turned back to her book. The door shook in its frame as Finn clashed it behind her. Esther turned a page in her novel, finding to her astonishment that the strongest feeling in her heart was not anger about what her daughter was up to, but envy at her obvious and radiant pleasure.

Downstairs, once Finnuola was ensconced behind the counter,

Patrick went for his coat. She smiled at him.

'You're looking very pretty tonight, Finnuola,' he said absently.

She sketched a quick curtsy. 'Are you off to The Eagle?'

'Time for just one whisky, I think. I'll be back before the last train so you won't have to handle that rush yourself. There'll be things to talk about down there. They say Sir Oliver's closing the last pit. Putting his money abroad, so they say. And there's talk of trouble. Corcoran was in here. Said they've had word there'll be big trouble right here on our doorstep.'

The expansive sense of pleasure which had filled Finn for the last two hours drained away. She knew as surely as the sun would rise tomorrow that the trouble would be something to do with Tom Farrell. And inevitably with his friend Michael O'Toole. She tried to turn her mind back to the apple loft and what had happened there. It was not easy.

15

Prison Bars

The entry drive into Banville Hall was circular. From their vantage point inside the gates, Jonty Clelland, Michael O'Toole and Tom Farrell could see the motor-cars as they swung through the high gates. They proceeded at a dignified speed, then stopped to discharge their passengers at the shallow steps and the big double doors. Then their drivers took the cars on another circuit of the drive, to take their place behind the line of parked cars. That done, the drivers locked their cars carefully, then made their way round to the back of the house. There in the kitchens they knew they would find a nice cup of tea, and hefty sandwiches made from last night's beef.

The passengers in the cars were dressed for dinner. The men wore black, some with old-fashioned high collars, others with more modern softer linen. The women also spanned the fashions of the last twenty years: some, under their furs, were sporting the new sinuous swirling cross-cut gowns; others were corsetted and round-bosomed like the Queen, necks laced in with high collars, hair uncut and still piled high.

Almost at the last came the Reverend Hildebrand Marchant, in splendid isolation, in the car driven by Clarry Tazewell, who did his garden and drove his car, as he had the day of his collision with Finnuola Montague.

Just before seven the trickle of cars stopped and a heavy-set man in a black suit closed the tall doors against the damp night.

Michael relaxed. He leaned against a trunk and lit his pipe. 'So that's it, is it? People who're what's what at this end of County Durham, all under one roof?'

'So they would have you think,' said Jonty Clelland, coming out of the shadow behind the tree.

'Did you see that jewellery, those furs?' said Tom bitterly.

'The cars?' said Michael, with feeling.

'Three mine owners there, who've just shut their mines altogether.

151

Did you see that Lord Somervell, with the silver hair?' said Jonty. 'The one with the high hat? He was the mine owners' hero in the '26 strike. Held out heroically against the "recalcitrant miners" till the last, according to their papers. He writes a canny letter to the papers, does old Somervell.'

'And that younger feller with the black moustache?'

Tom nodded. 'With the lass with short hair?' The girl was very beautiful but with her small stature and very short hair might almost have been taken for a boy. 'Yes. That's Sir Denis Consadine. Associated among others with Sir Oswald Mosley in an attempt to arouse all of us workers to save ourselves from all those terrible foreigners and follow them into the promised land, like their mate in Germany. Bloody Fascists. Should hear that MP Leonora Scorton on about'm.'

They crept around the side of the house to the wide, finely arched window of the dining room. The curtains were still open and they could see lit candles flickering on the long empty table, which was dressed with heavy, glittering cutlery and two great silver trenchers of fruit.

The three drew back as the big man in black came into the room and moved across to close the heavy curtains.

'Good!' said Tom.

He and Michael, earlier in the afternoon, had unscrewed the catch on the sash so that the windows, although they looked closed, could easily be lifted with the hooks they had screwed to the outside.

They slid down and sat with their backs to the wall, their heads beneath the window sill. They could hear music inside swell and cease as the guests made their way from the drawing room to the dining room. They could hear high-pitched nasal chatter, then a pause.

'Old Hildebrand says grace,' whispered Jonty.

Then the chatter again.

'Now?' said Michael.

'No,' whispered Jonty. 'Wait till they're in the middle of the meat course. More of a lesson there.'

Then more chatter and the scrape of spoon on bowl, the chink of bottle on glass.

They waited for what was the longest half an hour in Michael's life. Then, 'Now!' said Tom. Very gently, with almost maternal care he lifted the sash till it was fully open, wedging it with a stick which he had earlier measured and cut to the required length.

There was a whispered altercation as Tom Farrell tried yet again and in vain to persuade old Jonty to leave it to him and Michael, not to join in this part. The older man chuckled quietly and shook his head. 'I'm coming,' he said.

So all three of them stepped over the shallow window sill and stood behind the curtain listening to the muffled chatter on the other side.

'Now!' said Tom, pulling the curtain to one side and stepping into the dining room.

The boyish girl with Sir Denis Consadine uttered a shriek. The chatter stopped, and the clatter of knives and forks was stilled. Michael had thought there would be outright panic, but their entry was greeted with muttered imprecations, worried murmurings and one loud voice.

'What in heaven . . .?' bellowed Sir Oliver.

Michael held up a hand. 'We've brought no danger, sir. We wish to talk.' His arm went out towards the table, still sumptuous in mid-course. 'Have you no shame? Don't you see what's around you? I come from New Morven where what you have eaten tonight'd feed a family for a quarter. Sure, in just one street this last month four people died for want of real food. Last month a man, uncle to me marrah here, killed himself,' he glared at Mr Marchant, 'because the dignity of work was denied. That dignity'll be further denied seein' as you're closin' this last pit, Sir Oliver.'

'Money safer elsewhere, I hear,' said Jonty absently. He started to move round the table, pushing sheets of paper in front of each plate. 'Tom Farrell, the lad by the door, wrote this . . .'

'It says in that paper that yer should give over the pits an' the workshops to the people,' said Tom. 'That wealth for the country and dignity for the people'll only come if you an' your sort come in with the people an' share their plight.'

'Paper warriors.' Sir Denis Consadine spoke for the first time. His voice, light and affected, had the steel edge of contempt underneath. 'I might have known. Irishmen and Bolsheviks. The Bastille being stormed in North-east style. With paper swords.' He neighed with laughter, then cast a glance round the table, raising responsive sniggers. The men stood up and closed in on the intruders. Jonty, true to his pacifist principles, gave in to his captor straight away. However, Tom and Michael fought hard, Michael only finally being crushed by the lash of Sir Oliver's riding crop, brought with unrestricted power down his right cheek.

'Now, Oliver,' said Sir Denis Consadine gently, 'is there such a thing as a police force in this benighted part of the country?'

'They did *what*?' Jenefer's voice peaked with incredulity, a grin breaking out on her face.

'It's no laughing matter, Jenefer.' Finn was still gasping from her run. 'It happened last night. They're in Priorton cells right now. Sergeant Corcoran told my father they'll definitely go to jail for it.

153

They've been hard put to find a magistrate that wasn't actually at that party.' She paused. 'Corcoran was on his way across to the Swamps to get the twins and Smiler. They're to go to Priorton Orphanage, or Carhoe. He doesn't know which.'

'What?' Jenefer was reaching for her hat. 'Come on! How fast can you run?'

Corcoran had taken a leisurely ride across the village on his bicycle, acquainting several cronies with the drama at Banville Hall on the way. When he got to Primrose Court he met the velvet-clad woman from Plush Folly and the Montague girl coming out of that kennel of a house, hand in hand with the twins, followed by the glowering boy who had a sack under his arm.

'I'm here to tek them across to Carhoe,' said Corcoran, standing astride his bike.

'No, Sergeant,' said Jenefer gently. 'These children are not homeless. They're to stay with me.'

'I don't know that I can allow—'

The twins clustered to Jenefer's skirts. 'They've a right to be with me. Aren't they my own second cousin's children?' Her voice suddenly had the very faintest allusion to an Irish accent.

The sergeant took off his helmet, looked inside it as though he were conferring with some authority and said, 'Well, ma'am, I think that will be in order.'

And he rode off, whistling.

Finn helped Jenefer to sort out bedrooms and bedding for the children, who, very subdued, did exactly as they were told. Only Toots alluded to the reason for their presence at Plush Folly, asking Finn if the police would shoot Michael, like they did to her mammy's Uncle Stephen in Ireland.

When Finn finally got back to the shop she had a visitor, sitting silently in the upstairs sitting room. The woman was stately in build, silver threading through her dark hair which was swept up from a beautiful unlined face.

She smiled faintly as she stood up to shake Finn's hand. 'I'm Susanah Clelland. Seems my husband's down in the cells with your friend Michael. I had a note from him asking me to take you down there. Emily Punchard's already been down to see young Tom Farrell, her nephew, you know. Wedded to the cause, is Tom Farrell. Jonty always says that. The sergeant might just let us have a word with them if we go over there.'

'I'm breakin' rules, mind!' the sergeant grumbled in a routine fashion, and let them into the cluttered front room which did as an office. 'But Mrs Punchard's been in to see that nephew of hers. So fair's fair. No trouble, mind!'

Michael and Finn sat on opposite sides of the table. Underneath the table Michael brought out his feet and enclosed hers in his.

She was shocked by the ugly weal on his face, purpling now to a bruise. 'What on earth is it, Michael?'

'War wound,' he said briefly.

'Did you go there to fight?'

'Nah . . . Didn't we go to talk to them, to tell them to be ashamed of themselves? To show them what they'd caused?'

'Oh, Michael, it's all foolish. What good will that do?'

'It gets us off our knees. Tom's wrote this paper about how things should be, *A Message from Durham Miners*. We handed it out to 'm. The newspapers have it. It'll be in the newspapers.'

'Will it make much difference? Any difference?'

He shrugged. 'Like I said, we had to do sommat to get up off our knees. I had to help Tom. It's being talked about at least.'

'You'll go to prison.'

He shrugged again.

'Oh, Michael, just when we . . . when I . . .'

He put a hand out and took hers. 'We'll still be here in ten, twenty years. Look at Jonty and Susanah.'

The older pair were sitting side by side by the door. They were simply holding hands, the love between them warming the chill air in the room.

In the month following Michael's arrest, Finn went round in a daze. Their time in the apple loft had roused a new side to her, a new awareness of the barbed relationship between her parents, of the strange erotic bond between Jenefer and Hubert. And a new view of Bella and Stacy Smith, and just what must have gone on between Stacy and his daughter to make that baby. That made her shudder afresh.

Jenefer had given her another pile of books about France, in the middle of which was one about married love by a woman called Marie Stopes.

Esther had come upon it on the table at the top of the stairs. She had got very upset, saying only a loose woman could use such a book. 'There's only one way not to have a baby,' she had said quietly to Finn.

Finn cocked her head. 'So what's that?'

Esther's cheeks were bright red, 'Restraint,' she said, 'Abstention.'

'From my observation, Ma, that's not a recipe for lifelong happiness,' said Finn, blushing, amazed that she had got the words out.

All the same, Finn had taken the book back. 'This got in among the other books, Jenefer,' she said.

Jenefer pushed it back to her. 'It was no mistake, Finn. It's a book any woman should read these days.' She paused, 'Always remember knowledge and freedom go hand in hand.'

Finn looked down at the book. 'I'll have to hide it from my ma,' she said.

'So be it,' said Jenefer. 'It's a price worth paying. Put it in a brown paper cover.'

In the end, Jonty, Tom and Michael were sentenced to six months imprisonment by one of Sir Oliver's fellow magistrates.

It was a long dreary month before Finn and Susanah Clelland were allowed to visit. In that month Finn plodded disinterestedly through her work at the shop, spending all her spare time at Plush Folly. At least there Jenefer would talk about Michael, about how he was a man of principle which was to be valued above rubies, or about his physical beauty. 'Doesn't that beauty make your toes tingle Finn?' she said one day.

'Toes? What do toes have to do with it?' Finn said stiffly.

At that Jenefer hugged her. 'How can anyone reach twenty years old in this day and age, in this Godforsaken community, and be so innocent? Just one thing that makes you so special, Finn. And I'm sure Michael O'Toole thinks so too.'

After the initial shock of so much soap and water and the reintroduction of school, the twins and Smiler settled down to a fair life with Hubert and Jenefer, who seemed to relish the unfamiliar role of mother. 'I never had this much to do with my own boy, Finn. Never. Nannies and nursemaids make an impenetrable barrier, you know. Especially seeing that my son's nanny had been my husband's nanny and he worshipped the ground she walked on. Her word was law.'

When the time for the prison visit finally arrived, Jenefer offered to take Finn there on the motorbike, but Finn chose to travel on the bus with Susanah and Emily Punchard. Susanah was as tranquil as ever, but Emily was nervous, chattering for the whole journey, talking about Tom and how he was more than a son to her, and how she admired him as a man of principle, even if he were no Christian. 'Ah couldn'a kept going these months after what Stanley did if it's not bin fer our Tom. Not that Stanley hadn't gone to a better place. I know that. But that Tom Farrell! Tower of strength he's been. A tower of strength.'

When they finally met them, Michael looked grey-faced and Jonty looked gaunt and ill. But Tom Farrell was bouncy, looking quite his old self, talking away to Emily from the minute he saw her.

Michael was awkward with Finn, making it very difficult for her to say all the things she wanted to say, things she had saved up, about the twins and Jenefer, and how she herself felt about the way things were between them, and how there was a future for them, and . . .

But nothing of all this came out under Michael's stiff and stony gaze. The few minutes seemed to stretch to an hour. When Finn was finally through the heavy clanging door again her heart was heavier than it ever had been. She turned to Susanah who had tears in her own eyes and their arms went round each other in dumb comfort.

Emily Punchard let them hug each other for a minute, then pulled them apart by linking each by the arm. 'Now then, lasses, what say we have a cup of tea in the caff before we get our train back? The dear Lord helps those who help themselves, an' we need some help today, Lord knows.'

'So what was it like?' said Esther later, as Finn glumly gathered the remains of her supper on to a tray.

'What?'

'The p . . . place you went to today with Emily Punchard.'

'The prison? Much like you'd expect. It smelled like the Swamps. Bare walls. Clanging and echoing.'

Esther shuddered, pulling her bedjacket around her. 'You shouldn't be going there, Finnuola.'

'Then Michael'd have no one to visit him.'

'Your father and I knew he wasn't the right kind. Thought you might draw a line under it now.' Her voice dropped and her tone became very fierce. 'You can't be friends with a *criminal*.'

'He's my friend and he's not one of those *criminals*. Not a thief or a murderer.'

Esther pummelled the counterpane with her fist. 'But can't you see? He and that Farrell creature are worse. They are revolutionaries, just like those Bolsheviks who killed the Tsar – regicides – and he our own King's cousin. Threatening people in their own home like that . . .'

'He was just tired of sitting doing nothing. All this happening, unemployment, wretched lives. And they can do nothing about it.'

Esther threw up her hands. 'So they break into a man's house while he is having dinner and threatened him and his guests? What if he did it here?'

Finn looked round the sparse bedroom. 'There's nothing he would want here, Ma.'

Esther caught hold of her daughter's hand. 'Oh yes there is, Finn. There's you. Don't you see he's done the same here?'

Finn pulled her hand away. 'You'd not think that if you heard him talk to me today. You'd think I were a stranger,' she said bitterly. 'He seemed sorry I was there at all.'

Esther settled back against her pillow. 'Well, seems like there's some decency in him after all.'

She had secretly hoped that this disgraceful episode would indeed

157

draw a line under Finnuola's association with the Irishman. But now she was being made uncomfortable by her daughter's continued grief. Finnuola was going around in deepest gloom; she seemed to have lost pounds in weight and they'd had no smile from her in all these weeks. According to Patrick, the customers commented on it. The only time Finn's step lightened was when she went across to Plush Folly.

Esther wondered helplessly if the Loumis woman ever got a smile from her. All this worry about Finnuola was making her ill too. She was as weak as a kitten, despite the new tonic Patrick had got for her from a traveller.

Esther knew that Patrick too had hoped that Finn would forget the Irishman. They talked of it together at night in unusual harmony as they heard Finnuola striding backwards and forwards above them in her attic room.

Now, Finn turned down the centre light and lifted up the tray. 'Nothing else you want, Ma?'

Esther shook her head and snuggled down under the clothes with another of her novels of travel and romance. Some of these she had read five or six times over, until she almost knew them by heart. Sometimes they entered her dreams. Sometimes she had dreams which, written down, would be novels in themselves. She sighed as she pulled out her silk bookmark and settled down to read. What she would have liked for her daughter was a fine young man with money and a good job to come and take Finnuola off on romantic journeys. Then at least Esther would experience some reflected pleasure, some distant satisfaction. And at least Finn, unlike her mother, would not have to endure this cage of a life for the rest of her days.

But that did not look likely to happen. Not now. Not with this miner, this Michael O'Toole. Finn could end up no better than the other dreary downtrodden women round here. Not even as fortunate – ha! fortunate! What an ironic thought! Not even as *fortunate* as Esther herself.

Just over a week after her visit to Michael, among the bills and circulars coming into Montague's grocery, was a brown envelope scrawled in careful cramped writing with Finnuola's name. Inside was a sheet of thin off-white paper. The letter was topped with the prison address.

Dear Finn, I hope you don't mind me writing to you like this but things have been flying round my head. I have to endure this place for what I have done. It is very hard. I have seen Tom twice and he seems steady enough. Jonty's having a bad time as it

158

reminds him of a time he was in prison in the Great War. [There was something struck out next, probably by some official, with blocks of black ink. The letter continued.] It broke my heart to see you here in this place. It is not for you. So I have told them I don't want no visitors. None at all. Go on with your life. I dare not think of you. You want nothing with the likes of me.

Finnuola sat down hard on the chair by the counter and the letter fluttered to the ground. Patrick scooped it up and glanced at its contents. 'The lad has decency,' he said. 'He's right. That's no place for the likes of you.'

Finn took the letter from him and smoothed it out on the counter before she replaced it in the envelope. She looked dully at her father. 'I'll just go and get Ma's breakfast tray. Then there's the orders for my round to put up.'

'I'll do your round for you,' he said. 'You look worn out.'

'Suit yourself,' she said, and vanished into the back. He watched the curtain swing behind her and smote one hand against the other. Every night that week they had to endure Finn pacing up and down in her attic room above them; every morning after to be greeted by her strained face.

'She's in a terrible state over that boy,' said Esther.

'Do you think I don't know that?' said Patrick.

'She hasn't even been over to see her bosom friend Mrs Loumis for days.' Esther paused. 'That might bring her round a bit,' she said with great reluctance.

'I mentioned it to her,' he said, 'to go and see Mrs Loumis. But she keeps saying she's either too tired or too busy.'

'Can't you give her an errand across there? For the shop? Really, Patrick, you have no ingenuity!' she said sharply, turning over and pulling the eiderdown up to her ears.

The next morning, while Finn was seeing to her mother, Patrick made up a parcel of cotton reels and ribbon and labelled it in block capitals for Mrs Loumis at Plush Folly. In the afternoon, when the shop was quiet, he brought the package from under the counter with a casual air and pushed it across to Finn. 'Traveller left this for Mrs Loumis. Said would we give it to her when she called, but she's not been in. Could you take it across for her?'

Finn picked it up and looked at it. Her face was pinched and shadowed. 'I suppose so,' she said.

Toots came to the door of Plush Folly when Finn rang. Her face lit up when she saw who it was and she dragged Finn in.

'We're making gingerbread men,' she said. 'An' we went to Priorton on the train an' got some shopping an' came back in a taxi.'

In the kitchen Nancy was kneeling up on a chair, painting icing

159

eyes, noses and mouths on to the rows of gingerbread men. Jenefer was lifting a tray of teacakes out of the oven. There was a dusting of flour on her forehead where she had pushed back her heavy hair. The black and white cat watched the proceedings with absorbed interest from his perch on the high mantelshelf.

Jenefer smiled at Finn, veiling her shock at the sight of the girl's shadowed face, her fragile looks. 'Ah. The stranger. We were going to visit you this afternoon, weren't we, girls? Hasn't Hubert been nagging and nagging us?'

Toots had taken up her painting station beside Nancy. Two identical faces nodded.

'We've been very busy, Jenefer. I'm only here now because my dad sent me across with this parcel.'

Jenefer pushed the package with the back of her floury hand but made no attempt to open it. 'Very kind of him.' She peered at Finn. 'You look exhausted. Sit down and we'll—'

Finn turned away. 'I'm too busy.'

Jenefer caught her arm. 'Stay. I'm busy too, with these extra mouths to feed and bodies to keep in order. But stay. Just join us for tea,' she pleaded 'I am ready for it. And,' she eyed the giggling twins, 'ready for some adult female conversation.'

Reluctantly Finn nodded. 'Well, I mustn't stay long.' Even her voice was thinner, exhaled on reedy breath.

Jenefer nodded with satisfaction. 'Right. We'll have it in the sitting room. Toots, you go for the trolly. Nancy, you can put the cups on the trays. Finn, would you be terribly kind and go across to tell Hubert that tea's ready? Smiler's there doing his eternal whittling, so make sure he comes too.' She smiled the sweet smile which always emerged when she had got her own way.

Swept along even in her weariness by Jenefer's enthusiasm, Finn made her way across to the coach house. Smiler, sitting on the rickety chair whittling, grinned up at her. 'Miss Montague,' he said, 'here's Miss Montague.'

Hubert's welcoming smile was replaced by a frown as he saw the state Finn was in. 'Finnuola! Maid, are you all right? You look all in.'

She shook her head. 'No. No, Hubert. I am fine. Jenefer says you're to come for tea.'

'See Miss Montague,' said Smiler. 'Mr Loumis's been painting our Mick.'

Her glance strayed from Hubert to the wall behind him. The first thing she saw was a new image of herself, in her cardigan and her pleated skirt, with her tam-o'-shanter on her head. Inches away, large and strong-featured with his black shock of curly hair, was Michael. Their hands were reaching out to each other and trailing

160

from one of Michael's hands was a long chain.

Suddenly the dusty outhouse floor was coming towards her and all she knew was great silence and absolute blackness.

Hubert carried her slight body into the kitchen, followed by a bustling Smiler. 'Miss Montague came across to see us,' he announced, grave-faced. 'An' she fell dead on the floor.'

Toots screamed and Nancy, sitting beside her, had her mouth open wide as well, but no sound came forth.

PART TWO

16

Coming Round

The chain mesh underlay creaked as Finn turned over. She could hear echoes of voices from down a tunnel, rather than the voices themselves; the clash of tins and pans, the reverberation of hollow laughter. She tried to open her eyes but her lids refused to move. She could smell boiled cabbage and something sweeter, like the stuff they poured down the drains. Finally her eyes hauled open and she could see brown tiles, just like the ones in that place where Michael—

She sat up in bed. 'Michael! Michael!' She had been dreaming of him so much: the time in the apple loft was played out in her dreams over and over again like the chorus of a hymn. She put out a hand. The tiles were cold to the touch, solid enough. This wasn't a dream. She knew she'd had those. There was another dream with Michael. She was in that cold stinking place with him, reaching towards him, the iron links of his chain clanking as it reached the floor. No. No. That was the clash of tins and pans in this place. Where was it, where was she? 'Michael!'

The door clicked open and a large woman with beefy arms bustled in. Her broad beaming face was topped with a paradoxically frivolous butterfly cap, and her stout waist clenched itself around a substantial belt. 'There we are, pet. All awake. I told them it'd happen soon. You were on the cusp. I told them that, just . . .'

Finn's wrist was clasped firmly and fingers were lightly pressed on the inside of her wrist. The nurse lifted a neat watch on a chain on her belt. 'Hah!' she said, then tucked Finn's hand back under the coverlet and patted it. 'There, pet. That's more like it. I'll let them know, never you fear.'

'This is a hospital?' said Finn wonderingly.

The woman's laugh seemed to come from deep within her black laced shoes. 'It's not a railway station. Can't you remember anything of it, pet? You've been muttering and talking for days.'

Finn frowned and shook her head. 'I was in the coach house . . .'

'You were brought in here best part of a month ago, pet, with a lump on your head the size of a tennis ball. And you just didn't seem to want to wake up.'

'I can't remember . . . not since I was in the coach house . . .'

The nurse shrugged. 'Slept yourself better. It happens. Now I must go. I've got four ladies on this landing.'

'Who's paying for this?' asked Finn sharply.

The nurse laughed. 'Ah, we are feeling better, aren't we?' She shook her head. 'I don't know the answer to your question but somebody's paying. Now I must go.'

Finn slid down on her pillows and closed her eyes. Michael was there, in that long room with the tiles, the cruel wound still across his face. The smell. That smell was like the Swamps. Men crouched on their haunches on the corner, looking at you without interest as you passed. The barefoot children. It all made Michael so angry, so angry. He had done something about it, hadn't he? A pathetic gesture that was in itself a threat. Is that what the papers had said? The letter, there had been a letter hadn't there? He didn't want her, wanted nothing to do with her. The time in the apple loft counted for nothing. He had forgotten. More important things were afoot. 'No!' she shrieked, tears coming down her cheeks. 'No,' she said more quietly and she started to sob.

The nurse bustled back, carrying a tray with a cup of tea on it. 'Now, Finnuola, there are other ladies who . . .' Then she put an arm round Finn and held her weeping face to her well-upholstered shoulder. 'There now, pet, get it off your chest. You've been putting off crying for three weeks. There's a lot of tears inside there.'

When Finn had calmed down the nurse set the tea in her hand. 'Now, pet, you drink that. Nothing like a cup of tea to put things back in divine order.'

Finn waited for the door to click behind her, drank the tea almost in one gulp, then slid down in the bed, closing her eyes. Three weeks. She had been here three weeks? What was happening at home? How was her father managing with the shop?'

She swung her legs out of the bed and tried to stand up. Her head swam and her legs felt wobbly. She sat down. Then she stood up again and it was a bit better. Hanging on to the bed-rails she made her way across the room to the window and peered out. The landscape was familiar. Yes, this was Priorton Infirmary. She could see the road out to New Morven in one direction and the road to Durham in the other. At least it wasn't Sedgefield, where they took the mad people. At least they didn't think she was mad.

She went back to stand by the bed again and, holding the rail, started to move around the end of the bed in a systematic manner, gingerly lifting one foot after the other. She shook her head to get

166

rid of the fuzziness. She must get home. She must get home.

She sat down for five minutes, then set off again.

She was on her fifth circuit of the room when Jenefer, resplendent in feathered cap and cape, whirled in. 'Finn, what are you doing? You should be in bed.' She took her arm and tried to lead her back to the bed.

Finn resisted. 'What does it look like? I'm practising being human.'

'There was a message for your father and he caught me and asked me to come. He can't get away from the shop.'

'That's what I thought. How is he managing? I have to get back. How on earth can he manage without me?'

'Sit down, I tell you. You should be in bed.'

Finn wrenched her hand away. 'I've had enough bed. They say I've been in bed for three weeks. I want to go home.'

Jenefer looked around. 'You can't go home. You've no clothes here.'

'You can lend me your cloak. And they have blankets here. We can get a taxi. My dad'll pay. If you can bring your shopping back from Priorton in a taxi, you can bring me home in one.'

Jenefer shook her head. 'I'm on the motorbike.' She looked back at the bed. 'Look. Please, please at least sit on the bed. I'm terrified you'll fall again. I'll go and get the nurse and see what she says. If she says yes, we can go in a taxi and I'll come back for my motorbike.'

'Leave me your cloak,' commanded Finn, sitting down on the very edge of the bed.

Reluctantly Jenefer took it off and lay it beside Finn.

At Jenefer's request the nurse went off to find the doctor. He came, examined Finn and said that as far as he could see there was no reason why she shouldn't go home. 'Wrap her up well, Nurse, and see if an ambulance is available.'

'A taxi,' said Finn. 'I want a taxi. I won't go in an ambulance.'

It had been a long afternoon for Patrick. Sergeant Corcoran had brought a message from the hospital. Good news. There had been a change in his daughter's condition. Patrick's heart had soared. Finn's weeks in this deep sleep had defeated them all. In the first week Esther had visited the Infirmary several times. She had even hobbled down to the shop to mind it, while he dashed up to Priorton on the train to see their daughter. But this work in the shop had proved too tiring for her and she had vomited all through the night with exhaustion.

It had been Mrs Loumis who had gone into the hospital, most days, to see Finn, and to report back to him in her calm way that

167

there was no change, that his daughter was still lying there, being turned every hour.

He had even taken up Bella Smith's offer to mind the shop for him, only to return to find all her family, including Stacy, installed in the back room and his stocks of sweets, tobacco, liquorice and jam much depleted. He was making barely enough to cover his overheads anyway, and he would be in debt himself this week now because of the predatory Smiths.

He had lost business as well, when, on two days, he had to put the 'closed' sign on his door while he raced up the valley to do his deliveries.

Finn was a big miss.

As well as missing his daughter, Patrick had to deal with the plaintive voice of his wife, complaining of her discomfort and her need for perpetual cups of tea. His rest was also invaded by Esther's midnight speculations about Finnuola: where they had gone wrong? Why had all this happened? Would Finnuola die? She wouldn't die, would she, Patrick?

Oh yes, there was a lot of that. Just once the thought crossed his mind that Esther might be resentful of Finnuola stealing her thunder as the family invalid.

He'd had three travellers calling this afternoon, so he'd sent a boy to ask Mrs Loumis if she could spare him a minute. And when she came he had asked her humbly if she would go to the hospital for him. 'I've three travellers coming, Mrs Loumis, and I won't get away till much later. And I thought you . . . seeing as she knows you so well . . . And you've visited her anyway.' He paused. 'And you're paying for that room.'

She had smiled then, her funny secret smile that made him think of the cat that followed her round so much. He could never work out whether he liked her or not. Or for that matter whether she liked him. But it was as plain as a pikestaff that she, and that crazy husband of hers, liked Finn. They even liked that boy, the one in prison. Funny pair.

Now he heard the rumble of the taxi engine before he saw it. He peered out of the window, through the Cocoa sign, and watched with mounting excitement as it pulled up at the shop door. Then to his delight he saw Finnuola emerge, bundled up in blankets topped up with Mrs Loumis's cape.

He could hear Esther calling from upstairs. He opened the door wide. 'Finn,' he said. 'This is a surprise! Welcome home.' He pulled her to him and hugged her.

'Esther!' he called, 'it's Finn. Finnuola's home.' He drew Finn through to the back room where the fire, as usual, was burning bright.

168

Jenefer turned the shop notice from 'Open' to 'Closed' and followed them through. Esther had come down in her dressing gown and all three Montagues stood staring and smiling at each other.

Jenefer turned to go. Finn looked up. 'No, Jenefer. You need your cloak.' She struggled to get out of it. 'Thank you. Thank you.'

Esther took the cloak, folded it, and handed it over with cool politeness. 'We mustn't keep you, Mrs Loumis. We'll have to get Finnuola to bed.'

'Ma,' Finn smiled a watery smile, 'I've been in bed for three weeks.'

'Your mother's right,' said Jenefer. 'All this will be extra . . . Anyway, I need to go back to collect my motorbike. The taxi man's waiting.'

Esther turned on her. 'We don't need you, Mrs Loumis, to tell us what's right and wrong in our own home.'

Jenefer pulled her mouth back against her teeth and stroked her cape over her arm, then she nodded and swung on her heel. They heard the shop bell tinkle as she left.

Esther smiled at Finn. 'It's a great relief to have you home, dear. You've no idea how worried we've been.'

She looked from one to the other. 'You managed all right?'

'Your mother helped a bit in the shop,' said Patrick loyally. 'And the little O'Toole boy ran messages and swept up.'

'And your father got that Bella Smith in one day and you should have seen the havoc they caused,' said Esther grimly.

'Bella?' asked Finn smiling faintly.

'They were all in when I got back, the whole family. Children with their fingers in the sweetie jars, Stacy munching my ham, Bella with my Sunlight soap in her pocket. And then, when I started to remonstrate, Stacy became all offended and gave me a lecture on the state of the nation.'

'I can see you need me back,' said Finn.

He shook his head. 'Not till you're properly better. You look as though a breath of air would blow you away. An' I've an offer from Emily Punchard to help. That should be all right. At least she has a practical belief in the Ten Commandments.'

Esther put a hand on her shoulder. 'Now! Bed, lady, before you keel over.'

'Thrown out! Thrown out of that mean little shop by that shrew of a grocer's wife!'

Hubert looked up at Jenefer over his spectacles, a faint smile lighting up his craggy features. 'You? Thrown out?'

'And it was I who went and got her from the hospital.'

169

'The maid? She's awake?' Hubert sat up straight and leaned forward.

'What do you think? I took her home. She's chirpy, talking. Looks ghastly. But yes, she's awake. I brought her home, then had to trail back for my motorbike.'

He put away his book. 'I thought she might wait through the whole time, till young Michael came to wake her with a kiss,' he said, quite seriously.

Jenefer hooted. 'Oh Hubert, you think it's all fairy tales. Dragons and maidens, heroes and villains.'

He glared at her. 'There are dragons. I have told you. Sleeping now but I tell you there are dragons.'

She nodded slowly. 'For you there are.' She paused. 'Tell me, Hubert, do you ever think you are mad?'

He picked up his book again. 'Do you ever think you are?'

She looked round. 'Where are the children?'

'Aha! Quite the mama, aren't we? The twins are in the kitchen making bread. I showed them how. And young Smiler's in the coach house painting those things he whittles.'

She went across to Hubert and ruffled his hair. 'Quite the papa, aren't we? You're good at all this. Do you ever wish you'd had them . . . that we'd had them . . . children?'

He put his arms round her waist and pressed his head to her bosom. 'Not a bit of it. We are each other's children.' He pulled back. 'Do you ever think of the boy? Richard?'

'A man now. No boy. He crosses my mind. When we were in London I was looking for him. And I am thinking of him more now, with Smiler here, and the others.' She shook her head. 'He'll be a man now. He wouldn't even know me.'

'We should look for him,' he said in a firm voice. 'We will find him. It will be a good quest.'

She shook her head again. 'Pipe dreams, Hubert. Pipe dreams.'

Jenefer was just supervising the removal of two fine pound loaves from the fire oven when there was a thunderous knocking on the door. The sound was hard, as though delivered with a stick, and brought her heart briefly to her mouth.

She took the twins by the hand and shooed them out of the kitchen. 'Go across to the coach house and wait there till I call for you.'

She took off her apron and patted her wild hair. Then she answered the door to look into the top waistcoat button of the Reverend Hildebrand Marchant. Her eye moved upwards past the thin mouth to the sharp bright eyes.

He announced that he had come to see her on a matter of great importance.

She stood her ground, keeping the door only half open.

He looked up and down the street. 'It is not appropriate, madam, for us to have a conversation in this fashion.'

'Wait,' she said briefly.

Leaving the door as it was, she raced through the downstairs rooms looking for Hubert. He must have gone across to the coach house to supervise the painting of the carved animals.

She returned to open the door wide. 'Come in, Mr Marchant.'

She led him through to the sitting room. He refused to sit down and she stood behind a chair, her hands laid calmly on its back. 'So what can I do for you?'

He told her there were several things she could do for him. First she could go to church, as appropriate for a person of her station in the leading house in New Morven. That would set a much-needed example. New Morven people were getting lax in their attendance. Too much drinking and idling. Time on their hands. As well as that, of course, it would do her own immortal soul a deal of good.

She walked over and held open the door. 'Manners forbid my saying what is really in my mind at the moment, Mr Marchant. Suffice it to say I will not be preached at in my own house.'

He held up a hand. The next thing, he intoned, was that he had heard, from a very good source, that she was housing the family of a convicted felon. He thought that very ill advised, very inappropriate. Bad blood there. Her property would not be safe with such people under her roof. He was on the board of Carhoe Orphanage and could—

She started to protest and he raised his hand again. 'And thirdly, Mrs Loumis, I must beg, nay order, you to desist from the practices which are drawing people to you for ungodly purposes.'

Jenefer drew herself up to her full height. 'And what purposes might that be?'

'Ungodly, as I say.' He coughed his dry cough. 'Magic cures and spells. Primitive notions inappropriate in this modern age in a Christian society.'

She opened the door wide. 'Leave my house, Mr Marchant. And don't come back here with your gossipy opinions, your primitive, parochial busybodyings. I'll have under my roof those whom I choose. And I do not choose you. And if people come to me for the simplest old-fashioned advice because they have no one else to turn to, I'll not turn them away. Leave.'

'You will burn in hell for what you do, madam. Burn in hell, I promise you.'

She pushed past him and went to the hearth to pick up the biggest poker. She moved towards him. 'Leave!'

He backed off, clutching his umbrella to him. 'You will regret

171

this, madam. I came in good faith and see how you treat me. I tell you, you will regret it.'

She moved towards him and he turned and fled, clashing the front door behind him.

Hubert came in minutes later with a twin on each arm. He asked her what the clergyman feller had wanted. 'The twins said you gave him short shrift. They were behind the door.'

'He was making a collection for Carhoe Orphanage, but I told him I wasn't donating any orphans today.'

'That's what our Mick calls a close shave,' said Toots solemnly.

They roared with laughter at that and went through to the kitchen to try out the new bread.

The flare of energy which got Finn out of the hospital bed and back home was short-lived. She had to retire to her own bed and was asleep on and off there for three days. Her mother took quite good care of her; she actually started to get dressed during the day to do so.

She fended off all visitors, including Jenefer Loumis and Emily Punchard, although Emily stayed long enough to offer Patrick some help in the shop, should he ever need it. On the fourth day Esther was busy fending off another visitor. 'I'm sorry, Mrs Clelland, but Finnuola is not well enough to see anyone. She—'

Finn's voice called from upstairs. 'Mother, let Mrs Clelland up, will you? She's come all the way from Priorton.'

Finn was in the little upstairs sitting room, wrapped in a rug in a chair by the window.

'You shouldn't be out of bed,' scolded Esther.

'The roof was coming in on me up there,' said Finn. 'Can we get Susanah a cup of tea, Mother?'

'Well, I . . .' said Esther, rubbing her brow with genuine tiredness.

Susanah put a hand up. 'I want nothing, Mrs Montague.' She rooted in her bag. 'I brought this for Finnuola. Elderflower champagne, my mother-in-law's recipe.' She looked round. 'Is there a glass? It will do her good.'

There was a natural authority about her which ensured obedience. Esther scampered away to find glasses.

Susanah sat on the edge of the over-stuffed sofa. 'I won't ask how you are, as you look dreadful,' she said calmly. 'I was pleased to hear you were out of hospital, though. That was a shock. I have orders from Jonty to find out about you and write to him so he can tell that boy.'

Esther bustled in with her best glasses on a tray. Susanah opened the bottle with a slight pop and poured them all a glass. She wrapped Finn's hand round hers. 'Now drink it all up. You need building up, anyone can see that.'

Finn took a gulp, her nose wrinkling with the sweet hedgerow scent. 'It's nice,' she said.

Susanah sat back with satisfaction, then glanced up at Esther, who put her glass, undrunk, on the table. 'Well,' Esther said brightly, 'you two can entertain each other while I get about the business of running the shop.' The door clashed noisily behind her.

Finn looked at Susanah and shrugged. She lifted the glass. 'Makes me think of lanes and hedges,' she said.

Susanah was reaching back into her bag. She brought out a sheaf of paper. 'I thought you might like to read some of Tom Farrell's leaflets, seeing as they were the cause of the trouble. Those three didn't do it for nothing, Finn, though in itself it might seem foolhardy. They are men of principle, jewels in a dark age. Jonty's time is gone; he has fought his fight. But those two young ones will work on.'

'Has Jonty seen Michael? How is he?' said Finn urgently.

Susanah put the leaflets in order. 'He's surviving, as they all are, Finn. It's no picnic, Jonty's cough is back. To be honest, he says young Michael's a bit down. It's not the conditions: working in the pit is a good enough preparation for that. It's the confinement, I think. Jonty says there's gipsy blood in the lad; I wouldn't be surprised, with those looks of his. So it'll be even harder on him, poor lad.' She put the pile of papers on Finn's lap.

'I worry about him, Susanah,' said Finn, 'but at the same time he seems to be fading away from me in my head. We were just getting . . . close when he went in that place and now I worry about forgetting him too. I don't know what to do, Susanah.'

Susanah put a hand on hers. 'It'll come flooding back when you see him, Finn. Don't you worry. In the meanwhile remember, none of it's in vain. It's a necessary fight.'

Finnuola leafed through the pamphlets, nodding her head. 'I know it was not for nothing, Susanah. I do know that. Did you know Michael doesn't want me to go and see him in there?'

Susanah nodded. 'Look at it from his point of view, Finn. Like I said, it's hard in there as it is. And seeing you makes it harder.'

Finn nodded glumly. Susanah caught her hand. 'Your job is to get well, really well, so that when he gets out, you can be there at his shoulder, cheering him on all the way.'

Finn smiled then. 'Like you're at Jonty's shoulder?'

Susanah beamed. 'Always, There's no better place.'

Finn got better only slowly. Some days she was very low, bursting into tears at the slightest provocation, pushing away the admittedly sketchy meals concocted by her mother.

Desperately looking for something to cheer her daughter up, Esther finally and reluctantly let Jenefer in to see Finn. From then on Jenefer spent time every day with Finn, talking about Hubert and the twins, and Smiler's wooden animals, which he'd had up to Priorton and had sold door to door. He was very proud of the money he made with this, and with helping Patrick in the shop. He gave her every penny.

Jenefer brought old paintings of Hubert's to brighten the walls of the attic room, and photographs from the time she and Hubert were in France. She read to Finn from her own diaries at that time and Finn had a glimpse of the younger, more carefree Jenefer.

'You should go, Finn! It'd be the making of you. It would put the roses back in your cheeks.'

Finn laughed and told Jenefer money didn't grow on trees.

Finn gradually started responding to Jenefer's brightness, her goodwill. Now she wanted to go and feel the sun, see the bright skies. The flickering interest started to grow to a steady flame. But in her darkest hours, this prospect being so impossible made her feel even more wretched, her black moods even blacker.

One morning Jenefer stopped on her way through the shop and asked Patrick if she could take Finn across to Plush Folly for a few days. 'It's only a step away I know, Mr Montague. But there's the orchard and she can see down to the River Gaunt from there. I have this little wicker chair. The children are there, they can entertain her. And it'd give Mrs Montague a break. It's hard work caring for an invalid, I know.'

Patrick didn't want to let Finn go, but to his surprise Esther pushed for acceptance. She was finding it a bit heavy; she could do with a rest herself. 'And I can go across there, can't I? And check that she's all right?' She wasn't sorry to get the chance to see inside the old house, to glimpse the way these Bohemians lived. 'I can't understand what's so special about them, myself. Where's the fascination?'

'Well, Esther,' said Patrick, narrowing his eyes to make sure the sugar he was weighing showed precisely four ounces on the scales, 'now's your chance to find out.'

17

Coming Alive

It was strange to think that six hundred yards could make such a difference. Finn had spent a week cooped up in her attic room above the shop, where the only view from the narrow slit of the window was that of the slaughter yard of Joe Legge, the butcher next door. Then she moved six hundred yards to Plush Folly.

The bedroom which Jenefer put her in looked through high sashed windows back up the valley of the Gaunt, past pockets of woodland up to the Morven hills. The garden of Plush Folly was rampant with flowers and shrubs, once carefully planted, but now growing over, across, up and down each other in wild profusion. In front of the dining room Hubert, Smiler and the twins had hacked out a space and set up a wicker table, and chairs for Finn and Jenefer to sit in.

Beyond that, Hubert had erected a tent, part of his army kit, brought back with him from the Great War. He had set it about with climbing gear, camping stools and a petrol stove, so the children could play 'camps' under Finn's eye and amuse her.

Watching them from the window, absorbed in play in which they were soldiers on campaign in a foreign land, she thought again about how they and other children still played in the Swamps, living in a make-believe world of incident and fantastic event, almost despite the near starvation and dereliction around them. Here and now the twins were well fed and warmly clad but weeks ago they had been shoeless and ragged, as were the other children. But the miracle was that before, even in that grim place, they had played intently and with imagination, just as they did now. She tried to explain this to Jenefer who had laughed. 'Rich, old-fashioned souls, the pair of them. They would have thrived wherever they turned up on this earth.'

Hubert had been shocked when he first saw Finn in her pale fragile state. He urged Jenefer to get the doctor, but she waved his suggestions away. She gave Finn concoctions to drink which made her sleep deeply, and in the mornings Finn had to pretend to sleep – or at least lie on her bed pretending to sleep – till midday.

But in the afternoons, when it was fine, she sat out in the garden wrapped in rugs, watching the racing clouds in the changing sky, and the movement of light and shade on the far hills. The twins brewed up tea on their stove and offered her hard biscuits on a plate made from dock leaves. She needed her warm rugs to counter the snatches of mean cold that sometimes descended on the garden, transforming the season.

Jenefer insisted that she should rest so much during the daytime to facilitate the other part of her cure: Finn had to be fresh for the evenings which were always so special at Plush Folly.

Each evening was a kind of festival. Jenefer provided her wonderful herby stews and, with a little help, the twins now concocted puddings. Hubert mixed his cocktails in the sitting room, with special versions for the children. They ate in the dining room and Jenefer insisted they all dress for the occasion. She found ribbons and shawls for the twins to drape around themselves, and a red neckerchief for Smiler who looked every inch the traveller, sitting grinning alongside Hubert. Finn was allowed to stay in her dressing gown but she was obliged to put a ribbon round her fair hair, which was lank now, with night-time sweats and her mother's fear of washing hair when one was ill. Jenefer fixed the bow just above Finn's left eyebrow. 'You've been here two days to acclimatise so now we must do something about this dreadful hair. We'll get a roaring fire away in that bathroom and get you in the bath tomorrow. And we'll shampoo that lovely hair for you.'

The simple meal was eaten like a ritual feast and afterwards Smiler rolled up the sitting-room carpet and Hubert put his records on the gramophone. With Finn looking on, the others danced old round dances with Jenefer calling the steps. Smiler clumped round in his new boots, oblivious of the music, but Finn was intrigued as she watched the twins dance. They moved with the grace of birds in the air, dancing and responding to the rhythmical sounds with charm and a kind of integrated elegance where the movements of one complemented the movements of the other.

Finn clapped excitedly. Jenefer nodded at her. 'They're good, aren't they? Natural dancers. Something should be done about that.'

Finn glanced up at her friend. 'Aren't you . . . ?'

'Taking too much on myself?' She shrugged. 'Well, if they go back to Michael in that house across in the Swamps what kind of life will there be for them? There's room for them here, room for him too. If we scratch around we'll find some modest money to do what we want to do. It entertains Hubert.'

'They're not dolls, Jenefer.'

Jenefer laughed and curtsied deeply. 'I stand reproved, Your Majesty. But even at its worst, what is it? A chance of a bit of light and air, space to sleep for a few months. A few skills learned which might or might not be useful.'

Finn had to smile. 'I don't suppose I can criticise you for doing for them what you're doing for me.'

'I don't suppose you can.'

The days and evenings went quickly. Patrick slipped over for a few minutes every day to reassure himself Finn was making progress. Esther came once, but was so uncomfortable at the comparative grandness of the house and the easy superiority of Jenefer Loumis that she went home and, feeling faint, took to her bed herself so that Patrick had to call on the help of Emily Punchard.

Susanah Clelland came to deliver a short letter from Michael saying he was sorry to hear she'd been ill, but heard from Susanah via Jonty that she was improving and in the best of hands. She was to take care of herself and not overdo it. There was nothing in his letter about himself, or what he was doing, or anything about the way he felt about her.

Finn smoothed out the paper, trying to feel again the hand that had held the pencil to write the careful words. She put it to her cheek to try to sense him, his eyes, his own smooth brown cheek, finding savage relish in the thought that her need for him was growing rather than diminishing.

That afternoon Finn had better news from Emily Punchard, who told her, 'They're givin' them a bit of a hard time in there. But our Tom and Michael are reading lots and Tom's writing some new things, although they look at every blessed thing, dyin' to pounce on signs of treason. Treason! Our Tom! The Good Lord knows better. That lot should look to their own conscience, I can tell you.'

Emily also brought her the news that her mother was much better, benefiting from the rest. 'She's worked herself to a standstill, pour soul.' This was said in good Christian charity without a hint of irony.

Within a week, Finn was up in the morning, helping the twins to make their puddings and supervising some dancing sessions in the sitting room on wet afternoons. She felt fresher every day. After the first time, when Jenefer had to help her, she had washed her own hair. It was thinner, as some had dropped out, but Jenefer gave her another bitter drink and assured her that it would all grow back in, better and glossier than ever.

One fine afternoon she walked back across to the shop to visit her mother. The shop was crowded but her father gave her a delighted grin and Emily Punchard beamed at her.

Her mother was lying in bed reading. She looked up quizzically. 'Visiting, are we?'

'I thought I'd come to see how things are. I should come back to help. With Dad on his own and you out of sorts.'

Esther shook her head vigorously. 'We've had too much of a fright with you for that. Emily is a great help to your father,' she smoothed the immaculately made bed, adding complacently, 'and she's such a caring soul. I had not realised.'

Finn didn't know whether to shake her or hug her, but settled for half an hour's desultory conversation before setting off back to Plush Folly. She flopped, exhausted, into a chair when she got back.

Jenefer shooed her to bed. 'Sleep it off. You always feel stronger than you are. It's the one way to test your body. When he came back from the war Hubert was getting up and flopping down all the time.'

Finn lay under the top coverlet and dropped into an exhausted sleep. She dreamed that she was fighting with Michael to get out of this narrow tiled space and even as they fought the tiled roof was dropping lower and lower over their head.

She screamed and they all came running. Jenefer cleared the room of bodies and took Finn's trembling hand and listened to her stumbling account of the dream.

Jenefer shook her head. 'There is not enough light and heat here to heal you. I knew it from the first – that you would have to go where the sun is. Only that will lift you the last step to health. You must go.'

Finn shook her head. 'It's out of the question, Jenefer. My dad's on his uppers even now. Barely better off than Stacy Smith.'

'I'll find the money somehow.'

Finn shook her head vigorously. 'No. You know it's a struggle for you here even now. And you paid for the Infirmary. I would not allow it.'

Jenefer, looking at the firm line of her mouth, knew she meant it. 'But I'm sure you'll go. You have to go,' she said mournfully. 'There must be a way. I've seen you! It was there in my dream! Walking along the Promenade des Anglais in the sunshine. You're arm in arm with another young woman with red hair, flat on her head like ridges on a shell.'

Finn shook her head. 'Jenefer, you and your seeing! I'm not Bella or one of the others, you know. All it is, is wonderful wishful thinking.'

Jenefer stood up and away from her. 'Well, if that's what you think . . .' and stamped briskly out of the room.

Later that day Jenefer made her way down the street to the grocery shop. There were no customers and Patrick was leaning across the counter with the *Northern Echo* spread out before him.

Jenefer turned the sign round to 'Closed'.

'What . . .?' he said, folding up the paper.

'I'm sorry to be so . . . organising. But I want a few words undisturbed with you and Mrs Montague, and as your shop is open from dawn till midnight it seems to me that this is the only way to do it.'

He came from behind the counter. 'My wife's in bed, she's not so grand.'

'So Finn tells me. Perhaps she could lift her head for a few minutes. I would like to talk to her, and you, about the welfare of your daughter.'

Patrick rubbed his chin and nodded and silently led her up to the little front sitting room. 'I'll see if my wife . . .' he said.

'Bring her!' said Jenefer.

'Who is it?' whispered his wife, struggling up in the bed.

'Mrs Loumis,' he hissed. 'Something about Finnuola. Wants to talk to us.'

In a flash Esther was out of bed, digging into her clothes cupboard for her Sunday dress and her best corset. 'Go on! Go on! Talk to her! She'll be sitting there with her nose in the air, criticising my wallpaper.'

In fact, when Patrick went in Jenefer was standing at the window peering out. 'You have a very good view of the street from here.'

'I don't know about that. I'm never in here meself.' He stood by the empty fireplace. 'What is it about our Finnuola, Mrs Loumis?'

She looked at the door. 'Let's wait for Mrs Montague, shall we?'

They only had to wait three minutes for her. When she entered they all sat down.

Jenefer looked from one to the other. 'Your daughter's not picking up as she should. She needs to go away, to get some sun, some bright light to lift her out of these doldrums into which she has sunk. She's in a very nervous state.'

'She's always been strong as an ox. Can't think why she's like this now,' sniffed Esther. 'It's a hard fate for all of us.'

Jenefer looked at her coolly. 'Well, there was that dreadful experience with the Marchant boy, which is still giving her nightmares, and now this thing with Michael O'Toole who, whether you like it or not, is her very special friend. Finn's a sensitive soul, intelligent. This has all been too much for her.'

Esther put up her chin. 'Well, thank you very much for telling us about our own daughter, Mrs Loumis. I'm sure we're very grateful.'

'Esther!' warned Patrick.

Jenefer put up a hand, 'No, Mr Montague, your wife's right. I'm

179

an interfering stranger with no right to say all this. But Finn's my friend and I hold her in high regard. I know you both . . . well, have her welfare deeply at heart. But I think her mental health may be breaking down altogether and something should be done about it.'

'Very well,' said Esther sulkily, 'What would you do?'

'I'd get her to the sun. To the south of France. I know it very well. I'm certain it will do the trick.'

Patrick threw up his hands and laughed grimly. 'South of France? What about the South Seas? What about America? What about Timbuktu? Perhaps you don't realise it, Mrs Loumis, but we ourselves are living from hand to mouth here.'

'Patrick!' warned Esther. Her eyes narrowed and bored into Jenefer. 'Are you saying you would take her?' she said abruptly.

Jenefer shook her head. 'No I cannot. Could not. There's Hubert and I've taken responsibility for the O'Toole children.'

Esther had a flashing image of a figure leaning langorously over the rail of a large white ship, a shadowy figure at her side. 'But Finn couldn't go there on her own, could she?' For a second her tone softened, betraying her own longing to be that figure, sailing away into the sunset.

'Go?' Patrick exploded. 'On her own or with the Prince of Wales do you think? Have some sense!'

'She could do it,' said Jenefer stubbornly. 'I know she's young for her years. But she's a sturdy soul. And Thomas Cook's'd take care of her like a baby. They do that. I've seen it, with lone travellers.'

'I read that somewhere,' said Esther. In one of her novels the girl had travelled to Rome and fallen in love with a professor of antiquities who had turned out to be an Italian prince. 'They're there at every stage . . .'

Patrick interrupted her. 'Mrs Loumis, we can't afford it. That's the flat truth. We're barely better off than our neighbours, poor as they are. South of France? Ridiculous. Is that not so Esther?' He spoke with certainty of her agreement.

She scowled and shook her head. Her cheeks were pink with embarrassment at his parading their indigence before this woman. She looked at Jenefer. 'How much would this cost? To send her there for, perhaps two weeks?'

Jenefer shrugged. 'Thirty pounds. Perhaps fifty with everything taken into account. Perhaps less.'

'There!' said Patrick triumphantly. 'Impossible. I said so.'

Esther smoothed her skirt across her knee. 'She needs some sunshine. It would do her good. She could do it, Patrick. She has her head screwed on, our Finnuola. It's going to a decent school that does it. She should get a chance, even if other people never got theirs.' She looked up at Jenefer. 'Mrs Loumis, could you get the

180

tickets and help her to organise it? Make sure that Thomas Cook's watches out for her?'

'Yes. Yes.'

'Then she can go,' said Esther. 'I'll have the money for you by Friday. I need to get to Priorton. Fifty pounds.' She sailed out of the room without a backward glance at either of them.

Patrick pursued her to the bedroom. 'What are you playing at, you silly woman? You know we don't have that kind of money.'

'We don't, but Finnuola does.' She opened the drawer in her bedside table and brought out the money order. 'A gift anticipating her twenty-first birthday. From my dear brother.' She turned towards him then, and slapped his face hard. 'And if you plead poverty in front of anyone again, Patrick, I'll not guarantee the outcome. Especially in front of stuck-up ladies like that one in there.'

He backed out of the room and returned to the sitting room, his hand rubbing his hot cheek. 'Well, Mrs Loumis, it seems there will be money. As you say, anything for the good of our daughter. Perhaps you'd be so kind as to set the arrangements in motion? The sooner the better, I'd say.'

It only took two weeks for Plush Folly and Jenefer to work their modest magic and after that it seemed perverse in Finn not to go home.

In three weeks she was working behind the counter as hard as ever she had. Her early distress that Michael still refused to see her faded to a niggle; sometimes she was working so hard she even half-forgot his plight. There was a setback when Susanah came with the news that his and Tom Farrell's sentences had been further extended for causing some kind of affray inside prison. It would be nine months before they would see the light of day.

Now Finn was beset by her dreams again, of the cold tiles of the hospital, and the sense of being chained. For two days she could not rise from her little attic bed. Despite Finn's protests, Esther sat beside her throughout that time, reading to her from her latest novel: a touching account of a young girl who travels to Greece to be governess to the children of a rather severe widowed shipping magnate. In the end, to escape this suffocating attention, Finn dragged herself out of bed and got on with her work. She enveloped herself in a numb calm, the now dragging routines callousing over her sensitivity, so she could feel less of the pain.

In the event it took three months to set up Finn's trip. There was the passport to obtain, clothes to concoct from paper patterns out of fabric in the storeroom. By the time it was possible, there was truthfully no specific health reason now for Finn to go. The process of preparing had brought her back to life. Apart from the night-mares, she had entirely recovered from her bad attack of what she called 'the jitters'.

In the end it was her mother who pushed and pushed her to get her passport and use her uncle's money to pay the cost of this holiday in the South of France. Finn went along with it all, only half believing it would happen.

That resolve faltered once when, with the twins, she went across to collect the last of their things from the house in Primrose Court. Between them they had decided that there was no point in keeping the house on, paying the microscopic rent. They could pick up another house to rent when Michael finally did get home. There were lots of dark empty houses in the Swamps, vacated by luckier people who had got out of New Morven to places where jobs were more likely, even if they didn't exist in reality.

As she walked through the area, avoiding the gaze of the men squatting on corners, the women leaning on doorposts, she was overcome with guilt about the fifty pounds she was squandering on this trip. What good that could do here! How many empty bellies it could fill!

When she shared her worries with her mother, Esther shrugged. 'A jug of water into sand, Finnuola. You'd need to cut a river gully, sink a very deep well, to make a difference here. Anyway, the ticket's paid for at Thomas Cook's. Twenty-six pounds and ten shillings. And your dad has ordered your currency up in Priorton. The deed's done. And your uncle said it was for *you*, for your birthday, for something specific on my recommendation. And I recommend this.'

There the matter closed, despite Finn's continued unease.

One dark, wet Saturday afternoon she was taking an hour's break across at Plush Folly doing jigsaws with the twins while Jenefer sat mending holes in Smiler's socks. Going barefoot had made his feet hard and now he was wearing socks, his feet were hard on them.

Toots looked up from a muzzy piece of jigsaw which was part of the interior of a tree. 'What is there, at this journey you're doing, Finn?' Having been encouraged to call Jenefer and Hubert by their given names, the twins had begun quite naturally to extend this licence to Finn.

'There's the blue sea, Toots, and lots and lots of bright sunshine.'

'Can you send us a postcard of sunshine?' said Nancy.

'I can do that.'

'And one to our Mick at the jail,' said Toots. 'A lad at school said they have very little winders there.'

'An' bread an' water,' said Nancy. 'He said they only give them bread an' water.'

Finn's heart stilled and she looked up at Jenefer. 'I can't go,' she said.

'Oh yes you can,' she said grimly. 'You're going, if I have to drag you on to the train by your hair. You can send us all a card of sunshine and sea. And believe me, you'll bring a bit of it back in your case to light up this dark place. Oh yes, you're going.'

Finn made her way back home with her father's old umbrella up and her head down against the driving rain. She bumped into someone, pulled back, and found herself looking up into the face of Daniel Marchant.

He tipped his hat. 'Finnuola, I was coming to find you. I am just off the train. I want to say, sincerely—'

She pushed him hard in the chest and ran on up the street into the shop where her father was rearranging his scanty stock on the shelves.

'What is it, Finn?' He jumped off the steps. She was parchment-white and visibly trembling. 'What is it?'

She gulped for breath. 'I bumped into him. Daniel Marchant. He—'

The bell tinkled again, and Daniel Marchant was standing inside the door, rain dripping from his trilby on to his nose. 'Finnuola, I must speak to you. I want to apologise, make amends.' With his fine accent, his soft pleading voice, he was the personification of innocence.

Finn found her voice. 'There's no making up for that, ever.'

'I was carried away, Finn . . .'

Patrick went and stood in front of him, six inches too close for the comfort of either. 'You'll go now, Mr Marchant. You're not wanted here. If I'd my way you'd be in jail for what you did.'

Daniel clenched his fist and tapped Patrick very lightly, almost playfully, on his chest. 'I'd be very careful before you say anything about me, Mr Montague. There is a great deal I could say about you in this . . . er . . . fine village. He looked upstairs. In this . . . er . . . fine shop also. Remember I witnessed you on your – what do you call it? – round? Selling your goods to the personable Mrs Fenwick up at High Bank Farm.'

Patrick had landed a blow on Daniel's left cheek before he had thought about it. Daniel was caught off balance and twisted back against the counter. When he turned round, his eye was closed and his cheek bright red. There was saliva at the corner of his mouth.

From the inner doorway Finn laughed shrilly.

Daniel launched himself towards Patrick but the older man had picked up the long-handled shovel he kept behind the counter for problems which he occasionally had with late-night drunks off the Priorton train.

He held the metal blade of the shovel against Daniel's chest and pushed at him so he had to back towards the door. 'I know, Mr Marchant, you'll not criticise me for not fighting like a gentleman.' He pushed hard again with the spade. 'But you and I know you're not a gentleman. Not in one shaving of your fingernail are you a gentleman. So get out of my shop and stay out.'

Daniel felt for the latch behind him. 'But I only—'

'Out!'

Daniel backed out and Patrick, his shovel in his hand, moved across to close the door. Finn came to stand beside him and they watched Daniel walk up the street in the direction of the vicarage, holding on to his hat against the wind and the rain.

Finn was white and trembling. 'Bravo, Dad.' Her voice was very thin.

He touched her arm. 'Good thing you're going away, love. Very good thing, in my opinion. There'll be better things there.' He paused. 'Won't there?'

18

Woman of Business

The man watched, while the woman dressed very slowly. He was treated to three images, three angles of her in the long triple mirror by the window. He drank in the faint indentations of her spine on her long white back; the long full column of her neck; the cap of gleaming hair.

He leaned back on the bed. 'Exquisite body,' he drawled.

'I know.'

He watched the pull of her breasts as she dropped the fine silk petticoat over her head. She stood up and smoothed it down her plump thigh, then leaned across to lift the wool dress and shrug herself into it, attending to each button with great care, very aware that as each button slipped into place she was depriving him of his show.

He wriggled a little on the bed. 'Come here,' he said.

'No,' she said. 'There's no time.'

'You should do as you're told.'

'The arrangement was two hours.' She slipped into her soft suede shoes.

'You need taking in hand, my girl.' His tone was neutral; bereft of any humour.

She stood before the console mirror and twisted round to check the seams of her fine silk stockings. 'I've been told that before. But being taken in hand is not part of the bargain.'

He stood up and she recoiled slightly as he came just too close to her. She could see individual hairs of his dark moustache.

'How would you fancy,' he drawled, 'a trip to the old Côte d'Azure? I've some business down there that'll be bally boring. A little company could be some light relief from some awfully boring days.'

The woman was interested in spite of herself. 'You want to be careful. My father used to say only boring people were ever bored. Where on the Côte d'Azure?' She said it in the French fashion, and he felt a further ripple of deep interest in this strange woman.

'Nice,' he said. 'Do you know it?'

She nodded. 'There'll be a higher fee,' she said. 'It'll be a business arrangement.'

He kneeled up and caught her wrists in a painful grip and pulled her even closer to him. 'I'll pay your higher fee, madam. For absolutely exclusive rights, of course.' And he kissed her on the lips before she could stop him.

She was annoyed at that. She didn't allow kissing. Not ever.

What amazed Finn most were those towns where the buildings went on as far as the eye could see. From the window of the train all she could see was a great grey landscape of buildings: hills, valleys, rivers and trees, all engineered in stone and glass and metal: mountainous warehouses and factory chimneys, streets of houses curling like rivers, or long and straight, laid out like ploughed fields to the horizon: the meandering rivulets of streetlights and the watery glitter of tramlines retracing the streets in a more disciplined fashion.

And people. The streets near the railway stations were thronging with people, like great flocks of starlings at their autumn gathering; when the trains pulled out you could see them streaming away from or towards the station, like a many-legged insect with purpose in its step. She wondered where they were all going, who they were; how many they had in their families, where their homes were, where they worked . . .

They looked like people with jobs. They walked so fast, and to some purpose. It was a long while since Finn had seen workers in any numbers at all.

Just like the people in the carriage. She had never seen so many well-dressed people in one small space. Each face was different; hair was combed, hats were worn, faces were clean, except for the odd black smudge where soot had floated back from the chugging engine. She touched her own face, wondering if she too unknowingly had a black smudge.

She experienced a singular dart of knowledge, of all the millions of faces in the world. When you thought of it, they must all be different. No two alike, except for oddities like Toots and Nancy. How could that be? It made the brain tired to think of it.

On the long journey south she talked to no one, struck dumb by the sheer weight of the numbers of people and objects she had to take in; the newness of all the things she had to accomplish. The little train journey from New Morven to Priorton, which she was quite used to, did not prepare you for this: the masses of people; the swift forward movement of the great train; the infinitely rhythmic turn of the wheel; the shriek of the whistle as it went through the long tunnels; the huffing and puffing as the train slowed to a stop in the great stations of northern England.

The very newness of the experience had struck her dumb. One woman had asked her in a friendly enough fashion where she was travelling to as they drew out of Darlington. But Finn shook her head and the woman turned to another woman on the other side of her, who was much more responsive.

Perhaps the girl was deaf.

The two women talked, and Finn sat back listening to the details of their lives and their families' idiosyncrasies, all the way to Peterborough. Finn's mind wandered from the resonant clack of the women's voices back to Michael. She recognised now that he had stirred her from the first glimpse of his face, alight with righteous anger at her pursuit of Smiler. Then she had been pulled right into his world, getting to know him in his moods of prickly pride, his sudden gentleness, the dreamy forceful magic of the apple loft . . .

The train jolted and she was thrown against one of the women. 'I'm sorry,' she said.

The women exchanged glances. The girl certainly wasn't deaf. Perhaps she was just stand-offish. So young as well.

Jenefer had given her a list with detailed instructions of what to do and when. At King's Cross she nodded at a watching porter who took her bag. He plunged into the heaving crowd and she kept close behind, following him to the taxi-rank, the sixpenny tip clutched in her hand in preparation. 'Don't be embarrassed about tipping,' Jenefer had instructed. 'Just remember he probably has six children at home and the tip will buy the youngest her dinner.'

It took just minutes to get to The Coriander Hotel, a drab building facing on to a dusty green square which sported a tangle of trees and unkempt bushes at its centre. The hotel was only a single house wide and five storeys high. The bell on the desk was answered by a woman, tall, drab and narrow like the building itself.

The woman looked Finn up and down and requested her name. She checked the book and found, it seemed rather sorrowfully, that a booking had indeed been made for Miss Montague. 'You in business then? On business?' she said, most of her voice in her nose.

Finn shook her head. 'My father's a grocer. But I'm on holiday. I'm travelling to France tomorrow.'

'On your own?'

Finn coloured and nodded.

The woman sniffed and turned her head. 'Enterprising of you. Arthur! Room twelve.'

A man, smaller than Finn and wearing an improbable yellow knitted waistcoat, hobbled through a swinging curtain and, sighing, picked up Finn's two small cases. He led her up narrow flights of stairs to the third floor, let her into the room, took the threepence and left her to her own devices.

The room was tiny. Its only benefit was that it looked out on to the street and the square, rather than backed on to the blank wall of a garage. The smell of dust, damp cloth and old polish seeped into her.

Finn sat down hard on the worn plush chair. A wave of terror overwhelmed her. She must have been mad to do this. Mad. It was Jenefer's fault. She got carried away and carried everyone with her: even her own mother, Esther, who couldn't stand the sight of Jenefer, had got carried away with the enterprise of getting Finnuola to the South of France.

Finn put her toilet bag and her powder compact on the narrow shelf that did as a dressing table. This was the first time she had been so alone at night, with no one she knew within shouting distance. Within screaming distance. Folding her lips together hard, to stop the tears before they came, she took her new nightdress from her small case and laid it out on the bed. Then she went across and leaned up against the narrow window and looked down into the street and the square beyond.

The streetlights were modern and threw a sharp white electric light on the narrow pavement. Smart people in twos and threes were making their way along the street, in the bustling fashion of people who knew just where they were going. Workers. People with wages; money to spend. She put her finger on the pane and at this distance not one person was bigger than her finger.

Her face felt numb and lumpy from lack of use. She had neither laughed, spoken nor smiled to a soul all day, not since Jenefer and Hubert, the twins and Smiler had seen her off at New Morven Halt, on the very first stage of her journey. Her last memory of New Morven was of Jenefer astride her motorbike, waving her hat in the air as the train chugged out of the station.

The last two weeks had been a flurry of sewing and shopping as well as the shop work. This had left her no space to ponder on the stupendous fact that she was travelling halfway down Europe on her own. By herself.

The most enduring surprise of all this had been her mother's enthusiastic endorsement of the enterprise. One night Finn was just finishing putting her mother's hair into its nightly plait when Esther had clasped Finn's hand, held on to it, and started to tell her that she herself had always wanted to travel. 'It's educational, Finnuola. That's how you complete your education. I knew girls in Gateshead who went to *finishing school* in France. Girls I went to school with. My father had organised a trip for me as well. Then I met your father and my father wouldn't lift a finger for me after that. Not a finger.'

It took three hours on the train for it all to finally sink in. She was really travelling, by herself, all the way down England, all the way down France to fulfil not just her own desires, but Jenefer's nostalgic fancy, and her mother's unfulfilled dreams.

She started to shake. She had not felt able to speak to anyone on the train in England, and there everyone, porters and passengers alike, spoke her own language. So what would it be like in France? She had some bits of schoolgirl French absorbed willy-nilly from school, from Mademoiselle. *Je suis, tu es, il est . . .* But if she couldn't speak to strangers in her own language, how could she speak to French strangers?

She put her hot face against the cold glass and looked down into the square. A woman was walking alone along the pavement. She wore a small brilliant green hat with a curling feather, a fashionable swinging skirt and neat green court shoes. She looked like a *Vogue* fashion plate. As Finn watched, the woman approached several men. Some bustled past, others roughly threw off her engaging hand. Finally she got into conversation with a short, thickset man, who had been dawdling along, and slipped her arm through his. They walked towards the hotel and then they vanished.

It took Finn a second or two to realise they had vanished into The Coriander, her own hotel. In minutes she could hear them on the narrow stairs: the gurgling laugh of the woman and the puffing, grumbling chorus of the man. She heard the door above her slam and heard footsteps and chatter. Then silence, then a regular creaking sound.

Finn went bright red.

Then there was more silence. Then more footsteps overhead mixed with the grumble of the man's voice, then footsteps on the stairs.

She watched out of the window again and only the man came out, striding away with his hands in his pockets. Ten minutes later the woman came out, feathered hat in place, and recommenced her patrol around the square. This sight-and-sound pantomime repeated itself with four more men, and a stout woman in black. Finn was puzzled by this last visitor, but then decided that she must be a woman of the same kind, and they were comparing notes, or having a cup of tea or something. There was certainly no bouncing creaking sounds when the woman was in the room overhead. And she was up there for forty minutes, twice as long as the men.

Finn observed all this with a kind of fascinated embarrassment. She knew about such women. She had read of what were called 'disorderly houses' in the Sunday paper. And she had overheard Bella Smith tell of women like that, who frequented Priorton pubs: one of them even had her price chalked on the sole of her shoe, according to Bella, who was indignant that her Stacy might be 'ticed away' by such malignant creatures.

Finn started to smile, her depression forgotten in the fascination of watching this lady at work. Wait till she told Jenefer what kind of place she had somehow booked her into! Even she might raise an eyebrow at this.

Finn closed the curtain and got into her nightdress. But then Jenefer might just have booked her in here on purpose. She was a funny woman. She had told her gravely on the night before she travelled that this was an educational as well as a recuperative trip and she must, simply must, take advantage of every opportunity offered to her.

Finn opened the curtains a crack and watched the lady in the green hat trip up and down the street again. Now, just what did Jenefer mean by opportunity?

That night on the lumpy hotel bed she had the first dream that wasn't a nightmare since Michael had gone to prison: her dream was suffused with the smell of apples and the feeling on her fingertips of some man's hard shoulders and firm back, and the painful pleasure of him being part of her, her being part of him.

The next morning on her way to the bathroom she passed the woman from upstairs. Without her green hat she looked smaller and with her scrubbed face she looked younger. She had iron clips in her red hair and was wearing a black kimono with wide sleeves.

Finn smiled nervously in response to her, 'Mornin'!' and could feel the other woman's amusement like a sword in her back as she made her way downstairs.

Somehow her observation of the green-hatted woman at work made her braver the next day. Having watched and heard all that, she felt nothing could surprise her. At Victoria, as Jenefer had instructed her, she looked for the Thomas Cook man. Sure enough, there he was in his neat blue uniform, the paper in his hand fluttering in the wind.

He smiled at her, then looked down at his list. 'Miss Montague?'

She nodded.

'Hah!' he said, 'Never wrong, never known to be wrong. I'm Mr Jakes, your Thomas Cook courier. Very pleased to meet you. Right, Miss Montague, I've put you with Mrs MacMahon, another lady travelling on her own, I believe.'

Finn was first in the carriage and was well settled down in her seat when, through the window, she saw the courier in animated, even heated, conversation with a tall woman in a dove-grey coat with a fur collar, who was flanked by two porters carrying three suitcases and a hatbox.

Finn's heart sank as she watched them approach her carriage. It plummeted even further when the courier opened the door and jumped up to wedge the cases on to the rack. She kept her eyes to the floor as he jumped off and helped the lady on.

'Now,' said Mr Jakes, with practised jollity, 'Mrs MacMahon, this is your travelling companion, Miss Montague. Miss Montague, this is Mrs MacMahon who is also travelling to Nice.'

Reluctantly Finn raised her eyes to meet those of the woman and felt a shock go through her right to her toes. The face was familiar. Finely sculptured high cheekbones, wide hazel eyes, bobbed, permanently waved hair, now under a grey closefitting hat. Last night she had been wearing a green hat with a feather.

Her hand was being grasped firmly and a cool voice was saying, 'I was just saying to Mr Jakes that it's such a bore being twinned like creatures in the Ark simply because you're travelling alone, don't you think?'

The accent was a surprise. Finn had thought she would talk like Daniel or the vicar, in tones of the upper classes. But she had a Lancashire accent, somewhat refined at the edges, like the traveller from Blackburn who called once a quarter at Finn's father's shop selling overalls. Finn had always liked the way his voice lingered over the Ls.

Mr Jakes was scowling.

Finn nodded dumbly.

The woman went on: 'So I just wanted to say, dear, just ignore me. You needn't feel impelled to winkle out my lifestory. I'll certainly not winkle yours out of you.'

'Mrs MacMahon, if you wish for another seat I'm sure I can find . . .' Mr Jakes was offended.

She held up a gloved hand. 'Not now, Mr Jakes. It'll be the same wherever you place me . . . us. Isn't that so, Miss Montague? We're on our own and the world thinks it owns us, can pry into us.' She stopped and looked more closely at Finn and her eyes narrowed. 'No, this is perfectly in order Mr Jakes. Thank you.'

He stumped off, visibly miffed that his innocent plans of making all his customers happy were being perversely misconstrued.

Finn put her face down over her guidebook and kept it there while the carriage filled up, Mr Jakes doing his cheery duty several times before he was finished. There were couples and children, but no other person alone. At last the train was in motion and people sat back for the last phase of their journey in England.

The train had been travelling for half an hour when a quiet voice came from her right. 'They call it the Bay of Angels, you know.'

'What?' said Finn, forgetting her manners.

Mrs MacMahon put a gloved finger on Finn's guidebook. 'La Baie des Anges. That bit of the sea at Nice. On the coast of blue and gold. La Côte d'Azure.'

'You speak French?'

'No. Just what I've picked up.'

'Do you know it? Nice?'

'Well, yes. Been there a number of times. But know it?' She shook her head. 'Is this your first visit?'

'Are you trying to winkle my lifestory out of me?'

The woman laughed heartily at that. 'Touché. Sorry about all that, Miss Montague. But last time, Mr Jakes stuck me with this woman who was a religious fanatic and who tried to turn me into a nun all the way to Paris.' She reached over, shook Finn's hand heartily, saying. 'Hello, Miss Montague. I'm Kate MacMahon. You can call me Kate. I'm from Lancaster via London, am an entertainer by trade, but was previously a half-timer in a cotton mill from when I was twelve. Then put out of work. Then a clerk. Then an auditor by trade. Put out of work. Starved, then. Then in London where I do a bit of entertaining. Work as a mannequin sometimes. Surprising what you can turn your hand to. Me old dad used to say, "Needs must when the devil drives." And the devil's done some driving lately. There! No winkling required! Now you, what do you do when you're not staying at The Coriander Hotel?'

Finn's head came up, then. 'I'm Finnuola Montague. My father's a grocer so I suppose I am too, as I work in the shop. Not that we sell much. In the little village in County Durham where I come from the only people in work are the postman and the school caretaker. And the grocer.'

'Oh,' said Kate MacMahon. 'Well, young Finnuola, you're going to love Nice. A whole other world. The sunshine'll ripen you up nicely. Where're you staying?'

'A little *pension* called the Three Doves.'

'A *pension*?'

Finn glanced round the first-class carriage. 'I travelled first class because my friend Jenefer said that would be safest. But I can't afford a big hotel. I bet you'll be staying at a big hotel?'

Kate sat back comfortably. 'Hotel Négresco. The best. Work hard, play hard, that's what I say.'

Finn was glad of even the faintly mocking presence of Kate MacMahon on the long day and night which was her journey to Nice. Her pride stopped her from clinging to the woman, from looking for her at every turn. But at the docks, on the dipping and ducking steamship, on the unfamiliar territory of the French railway, Kate MacMahon would turn up at her elbow, making sensible suggestions in her faintly refined Lancashire drawl.

She even turned up with a large white handkerchief as Finn was leaning over the ship's rail delivering into the shimmering sea the last remains of her rather pleasant dinner. 'Rotten, isn't it? I remember my first time.' She rooted around in her neat grey handbag and handed Finn a small silver flagon. 'Here,' she said. 'Have a drink of this.'

Gratefully, Finn drank, welcoming the bitter cleansing taste of the liquid. 'What is it?' She smiled a watery smile at the other woman. 'I feel I should grow very small or very tall after drinking it, like Alice in Wonderland.'

Kate shrugged and returned the flask to her bag. 'Some mixture made up for me by this doctor I know in Chelsea. A client of mine. Perfect for settling a nauseous stomach. And no, you will get neither larger nor smaller and this is not a rabbit hole.' She put a cigarette into a short holder and lit it, then leaned on the rail alongside Finn. 'Talking of clients, there's something we should get out into the open.' She took a long draw on her cigarette and let the smoke trail from her mouth. 'I imagine you saw me plying my trade at The Coriander?'

Finn stayed silent a moment, her nausea forgotten. 'I wasn't sure whether . . . I was surprised that you . . . You didn't look the . . .'

'Type?' Kate laughed heartily. 'We come in all shapes and sizes, my dear girl.'

Finn dabbed her face with the handkerchief. 'Where I come from they wear bright red rouge and chalk the price on their shoe.'

Kate laughed at that. 'Aha. That's just the ones you know about. Some of us have our shoes handmade. As I say, we come in all shapes and sizes.'

Finn took a breath and looked out on the dark sea. She couldn't have asked this in the daylight, sitting face to face with this woman. 'What . . . why do you do it?'

Kate watched the end of the cigarette. 'In general, to live better than we did at home, with my father wounded from the war and my mother slaving over the boiler washing other people's clothes, and my two sisters who died of pneumonia and my brother who's coughing up blood in some sanatorium where they freeze them and feed them to find a cure for consumption.'

'There's lots of girls who've had a life like that in Priorton and New Morven where I come from, and they don't . . . do that.'

'More fool them, I would say. I must admit I wouldn't have started if . . . I was working for this man. Respectable family man, pillar of the community. He'd trained me as a book-keeper. I was always quick at figures. This feller was always flirting and trying his luck. My mother called all that kind of thing – sex, you know – "flies in the sugar". Funny, that. One night he had me stay back late to do extra work. And he attacked me . . .'

Finn cried out, chilled to the marrow with the memory of Daniel Marchant.

'Yes. It was pretty bad. He did just what he wanted, then he tied

193

me and left me.' She paused. 'Then the next morning he paid me very well, before he sacked me. Then said he would pay me a week's wages for one hour of my favours on a Wednesday night. Well, he'd trained me as a book-keeper and I could do those sums. Then other clients seemed to have found me by recommendation. I live very well. I've a bank account. Clothes, nice flat in Hampstead . . .'

'But The Coriander, there, you . . .'

'Were on the street like a common prostitute?' A gust of wind cut down the side of the ship and Kate stood silent a moment, pulling the fur collar closer to her neck. 'I sometimes do that as a kind of game to remind myself what I really am. The old bag at The Coriander pockets her share and pretends it's not happening. The night's work supplied me with my pocket money for the trip. More than that, it's a kind of vengeance.'

'Vengeance?'

'This jaunt to Nice's to do with a client, a new chap who's a bit carried away with himself. He's kind of bought me for the fortnight. He'll have tarts with titles falling into his bed at the villa where he's staying. But with me there's a risk, all kinds of risks. They like that, some of those bigwigs. Mind you, I come at a very high price.'

'What?' Another wave of nausea swept through Finn and she leaned over the side, retching.

'Yes, it does make you sick doesn't it?' said Kate calmly. 'That's why I did that thing last night, I think. To remind myself that I own my own body and no one has exclusive rights. It made me laugh. I went to sleep laughing last night, I can tell you. Now then, why not come down below and I'll get the steward to serve us some nice, American-style coffee? And you can forget everything I've told you.' She put her arm through Finn's and guided her towards the gangway. 'Do you know, it's the first time I've ever told anyone about all that? It must be the sea, and you offering your all to it. And the blackness of the night.' She laughed. 'And the sight of your face on the landing at The Coriander. You'd have thought I was a monster from the deep!'

Yes, thought Finn, as she crawled into her bunk one hour and three coffees later, Jenefer Loumis was right. This was going to be a very educational trip. Very educational indeed.

19

Light

By leaning out just a little and turning sideways, Finn could see
down the narrow street of the Three Doves, across the opalescent
white reflected light which dusted rue de France, to a jewel-bright
envelope of sea. Above it, the bright sky sat on the roofs of the high
buildings like an intense blue blanket.

She breathed in the perfumed evening air and thought of the dank
view from her attic room at home. Jenefer had been right about the
light. The very specks in the air were like gems; the glow was so
bright that the edges of the windows on the buildings were sharper,
the colours of the leaves more green.

And the heat. Like the oven when you open it to put in cakes.
She'd had to take off her cardigan in the taxi on the way from the
station, much to Kate MacMahon's amusement. 'Ha!' she said, 'it'll
be the liberty bodice next.'

'But I'm not wearing a lib—' Finn saw the look in the other
woman's eyes and laughed herself. 'I don't know that I've anything
in my case that would be right to wear here. My mother kept putting
in cardigans, and my friend, who lived down here at one time, kept
telling me to take them out.'

Kate MacMahon had the taxi-driver drop Finn off at the *pension*
of the Three Doves, in a narrow street not far from the Place
Massena. Kate shook her head at mention of payment. She grasped
Finn's hand. 'Perhaps we'll run into each other,' she said. 'If we
don't, I hope you'll ripen very well in the sun.' Then she tapped on
the glass and the taxi roared away.

In the little hallway of the Three Doves sat a small plump woman
of indeterminate age, in a black dress. She looked at Finn's booking
sheet, nodded her head vigorously and led the way to a little room
on the first floor. She waited for Finn to look around, then took her
arm and spoke to her, hands whirring around in an open palming
gesture. Finn worried whether she should tip now, and struggled to
get at her purse. The woman shook her head vigorously. '*Non, non,*

mademoiselle. The room, she is satisfactory?'

Finn looked around the tiny room with its shining bed, which looked more like a boat, and its low chair by the small window. 'And also . . .' The woman opened a second, longer curtain with a flourish. Here was a tall narrow window with a shallow sill. Outside was a pocket-handkerchief balcony adorned by a single pot of flowers.

'The English always like the balcony.' The woman almost pushed her out. 'Look, look! The sea.'

And there it was, like a bright jewel.

Finn turned to the woman. 'It's wonderful, madame.' She stumbled on. '*Belle. Belle.*'

The woman clapped her small hands with delight.

'*Et aussi . . .*' She took Finn's arm and pulled her back down the narrow stairs into a small dining room with just three small tables. 'The dinner and the breakfast,' she said.

Finn nodded. '*Belle,*' she said again. '*Merci beaucoup.*'

The little woman tinkled with laughter and Finn thought she was probably saying the wrong thing. But anyway the woman was smiling. Madame took her into the little front room where there was a yellowing country clock on the wall. She pointed to the number seven. 'Dinner, seven o'clock,' she said. '*Sept heures.*'

Back in her room, Finn unpacked her case, carefully laying her clothes on shelves in the long wooden cupboard, which was the only other piece of furniture in the room beside a table, the bed and chair. She let the satisfaction trickle into her, relief take over. She was here. Here and safe. She could communicate with her landlady, her room had a balcony and she could see the sea. Now she could look forward to the week. Now she could enjoy it.

Kate changed three times before she was satisfied. The note on the table, beside the orchid corsage, said, 'Dinner 8.30. A car will come. C.'

C.? She looked petulantly at her reflection in the grandiose mirror. She would hardly recognise him. She had this problem with all of her clients, even the very regular ones. And she'd only dealt with this one once. She could never picture their faces. Their necks, the breadth and strength of their arms; the bulging self-indulgent bellies; their more intimate endowments, (or lack of them) – all these she had efficiently catalogued in her head. But not the faces. And that was a blessing, in its way.

C.? Sir Denis Consadine was no exception to her rule. A firm man, narrowly made, with a taut body. He'd told her he hunted three times a week in the season, and he boxed. He had an interest in a boxing club in the East End. He seemed to think that the

196

solution to the problem of the poor was not to open factories or give them jobs. Just teach them to box, give them a sense of purpose and leadership, and all would be solved. She remembered from the one time they had met that Sir Denis had long hands. And very strong digging fingers. She remembered that. Smooth skin, very slightly olive. But what about the face? She could remember a dark moustache but nothing else.

There was a gentle knock on the door. 'Madame, your car has arrived.' A woman's voice came through the panel.

Kate shook her head to clear it of the inconvenient fug of thinking and picked up her small purse from the golden-legged console in the hallway. It was a short ride to a house in a quiet leafy boulevard. A dark man in some kind of livery came to hand her out of the car. 'This way, madame.'

The entrance hall had the impersonality of a hotel foyer, although there was no hotel sign outside. She was shown to what was obviously an apartment on the second floor. There were flowers everywhere, low tables and plump silk chairs to sit on. In the centre of one wall were tall double doors behind which she knew was a bedroom.

There was always a bedroom.

Beside the tall window was a table, set with crystal and lit by candles. The window had fine views of the twinkling lights of the bay and the Promenade des Anglais. Champagne was chilling in a great silver cooler and, without asking, the waiter poured some into a crystal glass and offered it to her on a small silver tray. 'I am Armand, madame, Sir Denis's servant. I am to take care of you.'

Kate took the champagne and sat down on one of the plump chairs, looking out of the window across the sea. Then she looked up at the servant, a tall sulky-looking boy of outstanding beauty, with an awkward cowlick of hair hanging down his face.

He bowed. 'Sir Denis says he will be a little delayed, madame. But I am to give you champagne, and per'aps hors d'oeuvres.'

She nodded and he brought a silver dish from the sideboard and served her a small selection on a plate and laid it beside her on a little table. Then he went and stood, not quite to attention, at the door.

Kate shook her head. 'You don't have to stay. I will just enjoy this, and the view.'

A shadow of annoyance marred the beautiful features. He shook his head doubtfully. 'Sir Denis employs me. I take care of the *lady*.' The dark liquid eyes had just the faintest shadow of contempt in them.

She sat up very straight. 'Well, if you've gotta wait round for Sir Denis, love, will you wait outside? I never could stand being watched while I eat me food.'

The servant darted her a sulky look, tossed his head and did as he was told.

Finn had dressed for dinner, following Jenefer's instructions, wearing a green silky dress with a sweetheart neckline, which they had cut down from one in Jenefer's travelling trunk.

The little dining room was empty except for Finn, whom Madame had placed at the little table by the open window, which looked out on the narrow street and the brief flourish of shops opposite. The tablecloth was white, with lace edges and the finest of mends here and there on its snowy surface. At the centre of the table was a narrow glass holding a single branch of mimosa.

Finn was served by a middle-aged man in mildewed black. He had been introduced to her as '*Paul, mon fils,*' but she had found it hard to think that this was the son of lively little Madame. They looked very much of an age.

She was served first with a dish of tomatoes which were sweet and fresh. Then Paul came with a short handwritten list. 'Wine, mademoiselle?'

She turned her hands out and shrugged. 'I don't know what kind of wine. I don't know anything about wine.'

Paul beamed. 'Mademoiselle will like sauternes. I have a good sauternes.'

Mademoiselle did like sauternes. She drank it with the delicious fish pastry with its salad accompaniments, and the small veal cutlets with the spicy rice which went with them, and the small round cheese which was runny at the centre, and the fruity compote which rounded the whole thing off. To Paul's evident delight she disposed of the whole bottle of sauternes before she got to coffee.

As she ate and drank she watched through the window as a steady stream of people made their way down towards the promenade. Paul whisked away her final dish and put a clean one before her. 'The food is satisfactory, mademoiselle?'

She was feeling flushed and very confident. 'Satisfactory? Paul, that food would have fed a whole family for a week where I come from. In one way it's just scandalous that I'm here eating this much food at a sitting.' She folded her snowy napkin and put it by her plate. 'But I've decided that, sitting here I'll enjoy it all, for them – for the twins, for Jenefer and Hubert, for my father, for my friend Michael, even for my mother. An' I'll tell them all about it, all about it . . .'

Paul held her green silk shawl for her, beaming, bemused by the swift, almost incoherent flush of words but generally satisfied that here was another delighted customer. 'And now, mademoiselle?'

She stood up and swayed very slightly. 'And now I will get my hat and I will walk along the promenade.'

Paul stood back and bowed. 'Mademoiselle will have a splendid time,' he said.

The promenade was thronging with people all bent on relishing the fine evening and the sophisticated setting. Men and women walked arm in arm, clusters of friends walked chirruping with excitement; more elderly couples made their stately progress. Other people, like Finn herself, sauntered along on their own; some more elderly women were accompanied by little dogs, either on leads or protectively in their arms.

Finn's eager eyes took in the smart cafés with elegant chairs and tables spilling on to the pavements and darkly bright mysterious interiors. She was glad that she had eaten at the Three Doves; she would have had no courage to enter those dark caverns.

She stood leaning on a rail looking out at the sea, a dark jewel in the dusk, moving and pulsing with deep power. Along to her left was the pier called La Jetée, its big casino like some Arabian Nights confection dolloped on to the end. It seemed to twinkle with a million lights and even from this distance Finn could hear the music and the laughter. As she watched, the final depressing assault of the wine hit her senses and her exhilaration left her. She wondered what on earth she was doing in this foreign place, among these strangers. Suddenly she wanted Jenefer beside her to talk of all these wonders, Michael's hand squeezing hers, sharing the magic. The tears started to fall.

The hours ticked by as Kate waited for Denis Consadine. She had refused further champagne offered by the supercilious servant. 'Lemonade, love. With ice,' she said. The words were friendly enough but the tone was sufficiently haughty for him to obey with instinctive alacrity.

When Sir Denis Consadine did come, he whirled into the room, bringing with him the fruity odours of port and very good tobacco.

He threw off his cloak and reached out for her. 'There, how splendid to finish the business of the day and get on with the business of the night. You're looking absolutely splendid tonight, splendid.'

He came towards her, his mouth open.

Kate evaded his grasp. 'I'm not your dinner. I've been here two and a half hours.'

'Aha! We are sulking, are we?' He laughed and lit a cigarette, looking narrowly at her through the smoke. 'I like a woman with spirit. Always have. Too awfully frightful of me being so late for our little assignation, I know, darling. But it is business; the fate of our nation. I could not leave the table of the highest in our land just to

199

come here to be with you, beautiful as you may be.' He moved towards her. 'But I'm here now.'

She moved behind a chair. 'I want to go out. The Casino,' she said.

He stared hard at her, then shrugged. 'I suppose you deserve a little entertainment.' He picked up her fur wrap and dropped it on her shoulders, stroking it down her arms. 'A very fine fur, darling. We have been a hard-working girl, haven't we? Working very hard at our loom?'

She met the impassive eye of the servant as they walked out of the room. He turned his gaze to Sir Denis. 'Fresh champagne for later, sir?'

Denis nodded. 'And make sure it's cold enough, Armand, or you'll get a whipping.' He turned to Kate. 'It's never cold enough. The boy never gets it cold enough.'

In the car Denis sat close to her. 'You're looking stunning tonight. Absolutely stunning.' He held her knee where the soft cross-cut fabric dipped towards her inner thigh. 'I've been looking forward to continuing and deepening,' he grasped her knee even tighter, 'to deepening our relationship.'

She looked at the hand, then peered out of the window. 'Stop the car!' she said.

'What is it?'

'Please, stop the car.'

He knocked on the partition with his cane.

She peered again. 'There's a friend of mine across there. I wish to have a word with her.'

She went to where Finn was standing by the rail. 'What are you doing here on your own, Finnuola Montague?'

Finn gave her a watery smile. 'I was watching the sea. I've never seen anything like it, Kate. It's as though a dark light is shining from under it, a dark light calling to this bright world.' Her voice was very slightly slurred.

'But you shouldn't be here on your own.'

Finn laughed. 'But I came on my own. I expected to be on my own.'

'How is your *pension*?'

'Wonderful. They're really kind.' She looked over to the car. 'Is that your . . .'

'My patron?' My paramour? My host? Absolutely. The rotter was two hours late and now as penance he has to take me to the Casino on the Jetée.' She suddenly clapped her hands. 'I know! You come with us.' She took Finn's elbow.

Finn twisted away. 'No. I want nothing in any casino. I'll go back now. You wouldn't believe how tired I am.'

200

'Oh. Well, I'll tell you what. Meet me here in the morning at ten and we'll go for a swim and then have *café et croissants* at one of the little cafés. And tomorrow night we'll keep his nibs waiting while we go dancing.'

Finn looked again at the car. 'He—'

'He's going to be late every night, I can tell. That's the game these fellows play. Keep you dangling. This way I'll tell him he *has* to be late. Puts me in the driving seat, see?'

When she got back to the car Denis was sitting back smoking a cigar. 'Is that your little friend?' he said lazily. 'You should have brought her along. Nice little thing. We could have had a jolly threesome.'

The chauffeur put the car into gear. Denis caught up Kate's hand, turned it over and kissed the palm, then very deliberately bit the fleshy part, called the Mount of Venus.

She yelped. 'Stop that. Stop it I tell you.'

Back at the *pension* of the Three Doves, Finn opened her bedroom window to let in the warm perfumed air.

All in all it was good. She was glad she had come.

Tomorrow would be fun, swimming with Kate in the morning and the chance of dancing at night. She took one more look in the twinkling street below, closed the curtains and went to bed. Lying there in the perfumed dark she was reminded of the scent of apples in the apple loft in the old cottage, and, curled up in a ball, she thought of Michael. Perhaps he would disapprove of all this extravagance and frolic. Certainly his friend Tom Farrell would see it as decadent. But not Michael: the lighthearted Michael who had come to her so joyously in the apple loft, he would approve. She was sure of it.

Kate and Sir Denis Consadine had a very late supper of peaches and champagne. 'Now,' he took her hand, 'my elusive bird, my factory starling, bed.'

She looked at the servant, lounging impassively by the door. 'Is that one staying all night?'

'Armand? Well, we may need something.'

She pulled her arm away from his. 'Well, Sir Denis, I'm not going through that door,' she nodded towards the double doors of the bedroom, 'till he's through the door behind him.'

'Armand?' said Sir Denis.

The boy smiled blandly and retreated.

'Now!' said Denis Consadine. He lifted her and carried her towards the door. She struggled slightly for effect. She'd played this scene many times with a whole variety of people. They liked you to struggle.

The bedroom was dominated by a great wooden bed with palest blue coverings. There was a huge mirrored dresser and, as Denis deposited her none too gently on the coverlet, Kate saw the mirror angled over the bed. She watched his reflection as he jumped on her, kissed her averted cheek and started to pull at her clothes.

She rolled out from under him. 'Wait. I'll take my own clothes off, thank you. They cost me good money and I don't want you spoiling them.'

She took them off carefully, one by one, laying them on the chaise which stood beside the dresser. She rolled down her stockings and finally unlaced the tiny, unnecessary basque which had supported them.

He lay back on the bed, watching with interest. 'Beautiful body, m'dear. Skin too. Such white skin.' He stood and came to stand beside her, running a hand down from her breast to her thigh. He had the hard palms of a horseman.

'Comes from being red-haired,' she said. 'You either have white skin or it's as red as a veiny orange.'

Then she put her hand on his cheek. He lifted her and lay her, more gently this time, on the bed. Then she turned on her side and watched him boldly as he undressed.

'You're not very hairy,' she said thoughtfully. 'I like that. Shows your muscles.' They all liked you to talk about their bodies. You could always concoct something to say even about the most revolting heap of flesh. It hadn't been necessary when she went with working men. But these bigwigs loved it. They looked to you for a mother's approval.

They especially liked you to talk about their endowment.

'Oh my goodness, what's this?'

He was already having an erection, and he stood as pleased as a child with a favourite toy, allowing her to admire him.

The climax, when it finally came, was all too swift, and had nothing to do with her pleasure. She waited for him to relax into sleep, so she could go off duty, but he didn't. After ten minutes his hands were over her and into her again, digging hard and kneading. She played up to him, only half her mind on the activity, the other looking thoughtfully into the mirror overhead, observing the pattern their bodies made against the blue sheets.

Then he was playing with the long cords which dressed the corners of the bed, teasing her and tickling her with the tassels. He tied one of the cords round her wrist and she sat up, pulling away from it. 'No tying. No tying. I told you I don't do that. I told you the first night.'

She loosened her wrist herself.

He lay back again. 'Well, my dear girl, there's always a first time. Now then, you are very, very naughty. You've roused me again. So just what are you going to do about it?'

Kate sighed and set about her work. Sometimes she thought it would be easier still to be working in the mill. But not so well-paid. Not half so well-paid. Then, as he turned her over, she glimpsed the mirror overhead and knew with certainty that the dark boy called Armand was there, seeing through it, watching them, enjoying the show.

20

Dancing on Glass

'What? You can't swim?' Kate's voice was disbelieving.

'Never had time to learn. They didn't bother about it in school at Gateshead. And we were too busy in the shop there, and then in the shop at New Morven. There's an open-air pool at Priorton, the town nearest us. The miners collected for it themselves. Dug the foundations during the '26 strike. People from Hew Morven use that for swimming. If they don't go down to that pool, they swim in the River Gaunt near us. I've watched them. Like fishes. Eels, even.'

'But not the shopkeeper's daughter?'

Finn shook her head. 'I used to envy the fact that they'd the time to do it.'

'No bathing suit?'

She nodded. 'I do have one of those. I thought it would be nice to sit on the beach.'

'Sit? You won't be sitting, girl! Go and put that bathing suit on.' Kate stood up, stretching her long legs. 'I'll teach you to swim.'

Finn smiled up at her, shading her eyes from the bright sun. 'You look like a film star.'

Kate patted her on the head. 'That's what I am. A film star in disguise.'

They were sitting on the verandah of the small hut Kate had hired. Inside, it smelled of the sea and very faintly rotting fish. Kate's elegant linen sundress hung neatly from its coathanger and there was a spare coathanger for Finn.

This peeling off your clothes all the time was so strange. At home, because of the perpetual chill, you hopped out of one set and into another double-quick; hardly ever saw your own body. Here, it was a relief to get things off, to cool down, to welcome the sun on to your skin.

Kate was already into the water when Finn came out of the hut. She reached out a hand to beckon Finn in. Finn kneeled, then sat in the water and felt the movement of the sea roll over her, the persistent flush and flow of salty spray over her body. She spluttered as the water hit her face and the rush and mutter of the waves invaded her ears. 'It's lovely,' she shouted to Kate.

'Right, now hold on.' Kate took her arm and started to strike out powerfully towards the bay.

'I can't swim,' shouted Finn, struggling and gulping a mouthful of water.

'Oh yes you can!' called Kate. 'A girl called Finn who can't swim! Of course you can. Now . . . relax, just kick your feet gently.'

Finn took a deep breath. And another. She moved her feet. Kate let go. 'There! it's holding you. The sea's holding you. Now just move your hands like this.'

The water was indeed holding her, floating her on the tops of its cradling waves, not pulling her down as she had thought it would. The slight kick of her feet and the flurry of her hands was keeping her afloat.

At the end of an hour Kate had her doing an embryonic breaststroke and they were both satisfied. 'Now I'll buy you the best *chocolat* in Europe,' said Kate. 'At Monsieur Fleury's.'

As they walked along the promenade, Kate put her arm through Finn's, a friendly gesture relished by Finn. They made their way through other smartly dressed visitors enjoying the promenade, the bright sunshine and the fresh breeze.

Finn remembered something that Jenefer Loumis had said, about seeing her walking along with a woman whose red hair curled round her head like ridges on a shell. Come to think of it, that was a very good description of Kate MacMahon and herself walking along this promenade at this very moment.

They arrived at the shaded café, Kate immaculately smart and Finn still slightly damp, her hair frizzing out in tendrils under the brim of her straw hat.

'The sea makes you much wetter than any bath,' she said seriously to Kate, who burst out laughing.

They had just had a glass of iced chocolate when a gaggle of men and women emerged from a large low-slung maroon car and spilled across the pavement into the café. At the centre of the crowd was a tall middle-aged man with a dark moustache, and a younger man with a high forehead and smooth hair. The rest were women, beautifully dressed in whites and creams. They wore their hair in the looser, slightly longer style which was fashionable now. They chattered in high voices: the most vocal was a girl with dark hair who lounged back into a chair beside the older man.

Finn watched Kate touch her own crisp permanent waves and was dismayed by the thought that Kate's splendid yellow sundress suddenly looked very bright.

Monsieur Fleury himself came out from the dark back caverns of the café to serve the group, with a graceful respect which was not servile.

Finn was aware that Kate was sitting stiffly beside her, staring hard at her tall glass of *chocolat*. 'Who's that? Who are those people?' she whispered.

'How would I know?' Kate whispered back fiercely, turning her chair slightly to get the noisy group out of her vision.

Finn watched as the man with the moustache leaned over to whisper into the ear of the dark lounging woman. The woman and the younger man turned towards their table, catching Finn's intense gaze. Finn blushed to the roots of her hair at being caught staring. 'Let's go,' said Finn. 'Do you know they're talking about us?'

'No.' Kate raised a hand. Monsieur Fleury scuttled across. 'Another *chocolat, s'il vous plaît, monsieur*.' She turned and put a hand on Finn's arm. 'Now what shall we do this afternoon, Finn?' she said brightly.

'There's a Cook's excursion setting out at half-past two. A tour of Nice. You go past that hill they call the Château, where you get the views of the mountains and the sea. Then up through Cimiez. Is that what it's called? Where all the posh villas are? And you see Hadrian's amphitheatre. We have Hadrian's Wall near where I live.'

'Do you, now?' Kate's tone was absent. Denis Consadine was staying at one of the grand villas in Cimiez. 'To be honest, Finn, I think I'll leave that to you. I've done it before. But on your way round, watch for my boulevard. Did you know they named a boulevard after me?' She laughed rather too shrilly. 'I tell you what! You and I will meet tonight. We'll go to the Blue Cat restaurant. Would you believe the floor's made of mirror? You'll like that.'

As they drank their second glass, the other party finished their drinks and rose to go, swinging past them in a capsule of laughter. The dark-haired girl smiled sweetly at Finn as they passed. 'Lovely hat, darling,' she said, and there was a gale of giggles from the others.

Red again, Finn pulled off the offending hat and her hair tumbled down about her face. The younger man, frowning furiously, stopped beside Finn, started to say something, then strode on after the dark girl, grabbing her elbow and talking angrily to her. The man with the moustache brought up the rear.

'Good morning, Denis,' drawled Kate.

He looked at her coldly, tipped his hat and followed his friends.

'You know him?' said Finn, smoothing her hair behind her ears.

'That, dear girl, is my patron, my sponsor, who thinks I'm good

207

enough to crawl into his bed, but not good enough to pass a civilised time of day with.'

Finn was pleased to part company with Kate as she left for the Three Doves, to change for her excursion. The older girl had become grumpy and incommunicative, a stranger again.

Finn joined two American ladies and a German couple on the Cook's car tour that afternoon. She avoided talking to them, wanting this first exploration of the city to be a solitary one. Now she could concentrate on the very strangeness of the place, with its wide boulevards and its narrow streets, its opera house and lawcourts. She spied the Boulevard MacMahon and wondered what a French city was doing with an English, well, an Irish name.

The car was travelling upwards now, near what the guide called the old castle; a great grassy mound scattered with rocks. The car stopped behind a little cluster of other vehicles, and the guide suggested they got out and took in the view. It seemed that the whole of Nice lay below them, skirted by the great bay, the Casino that childish confection on the Jetée; all contained by the great sweep of mountains like marbles in a cupped hand.

Finn had to widen her eyes to take it all in. The guide smiled at her enthusiasm. It was a change from the cool sophistication of other clients, some of whom had seen everything and done everything.

'Good morning.'

Finn looked blankly at the man who was tipping his hat at her. A young man with a high forehead and smooth flat hair.

'In the restaurant. We were at Monsieur Fleury's.'

She coloured, conscious that she was still wearing the little straw hat which had caused all the amusement.

'I just wanted to apologise for my . . . acquaintance's rudeness this morning. My name is Richard Evans . . .' He put out a hand.

Ignoring the hand, she took a deep breath and frowned. 'Monsieur Fleury's? I can't say I noticed you. Or any acquaintance.'

He nodded and stepped back. 'Just as well. Good morning.' As he got into his maroon car he looked back and smiled quite sweetly across at her. 'I'd watch that pretty hat up here if I were you. You get these gusts of wind. That's why they call it Rauba-Capeu. It blows people's hats off. Robs you of your cap. See? You mustn't lose your hat. It's quite charming.'

When Kate returned to the Négresco that afternoon she found Denis Consadine sitting in her little sitting room reading the paper. He stood up as she entered.

'Ah. A visitor! Did you come up the back stairs?' she said. She took off her hat and stood before the fine mirror, running her hands through her hair.

He moved across and locked the door, then closed the heavy curtains, cutting out the fine view of the bay. 'Discretion is everything. You were very improper in the dreadful Fleury's place this morning. Speaking to me. Against our agreement.'

She turned towards him. 'I can't say I think much of your friends. Vulgar, I call them. Come for our dues, have we?'

He looked around the rooms. 'You like the hotel? You said the best hotel . . .' He smiled smoothly. 'You're so aggressive, so direct, Kate. A sheer delight, my dear. Such a change from the simpering teasing madams with whom I am obliged to play games. I'd rather pay for it . . . for you . . . any day.' He walked through to the bedroom and across to the bathroom door. He wrinkled his nose. 'I thought you'd want a bath to get rid of the nasty salt water and that awful smell of Fleury's cold chocolate.' He looked at the bed. 'And a little rest before your evening activities.'

She went to the wardrobe for her silk wrap. 'I'm not waiting around for you in that . . . place tonight. I'm going dancing this evening,' she said, 'at the Blue Cat.'

'Ah. With your little friend? Not indulging in private enterprise, I hope? You know our little arrangement. An exclusive contract.'

As he watched she peeled off her clothes, then rubbed her fingers together and licked them, tasting the sea on her lips. She looked at him directly. 'There was nothing in our agreement that said I shouldn't enjoy my holiday.'

He shook his head. 'Quite right, my dear. As for tonight – that is convenient. There is a dinner at the villa this evening, guests from Italy and Germany, a deal of business to talk. Such an unnecessary flurry going on at the moment about Germany leaving the League. At least they don't shillyshally. I'll send a car for you at midnight. To take you to . . . that place. If you're not there,' he looked at his fingernails, 'you'll be in deep trouble. Now,' he took her hand, 'let us scrub the salt off that divine body.'

'You might not be able to swim, but you can certainly dance,' said Kate, as Finn was handed off the dance floor back to the table by an engineer from Coventry, friend to the one who had just danced with Kate. 'Where did you learn to dance like that? Are there lots of dance halls in that queer little place you come from?'

Finn shook her head. 'I have a friend. We dance to her gramophone, with her husband. It's much easier here, though, with that orchestra. There must be nine players there.' She laughed. 'And you don't have to wind them up all the time. And the floor! They won't believe me when I tell them about the floor.'

The dance floor was not large but it was made entirely of reflecting glass. Dancing on it was like gliding on ice. 'A bit . . . worrying, though.'

Kate put her mouth close to Finn's ear. 'Yes. You have to make sure you've got your best knickers on!'

'Kate! Can you see?'

'No, but people get a *frisson* from thinking you can.'

The band struck up a foxtrot. 'May I have this dance?' Finn looked up in surprise. It was the boy with the smooth hair, who had spoken to her on the Château. He had just pipped the Coventry engineer to the post.

Finn glanced at Kate, who nodded encouragingly. Over the shoulder of her own Coventry engineer, she was scanning the crowd for Denis Consadine. It seemed too much of a coincidence that the boy was here.

Finn and Richard Evans danced without speaking for a few minutes, fitting themselves to each other's bodies, and their movements to the marvellous music. She relaxed, just enjoying the dance.

He looked into her face as they turned. 'What luck to find you here.'

'Do you come here a lot?'

'No. Never been here before. Chap where I'm staying mentioned it. Said there's a good band. Right too.' He swept her round in a wide circle, tightening his grip as they dipped into the corner. 'I say, I don't know your name. As I said this morning I'm Richard, Richard Evans.'

'Finnuola Montague. They call me Finn.'

'Are you Irish? I thought that might be an Irish accent. Charming.'

'No. I'm from the North of England. Hardly an Irish accent.'

They talked on politely about her afternoon excursion, and where she planned to go tomorrow. The dance was over much too soon. He pulled her arm through his and walked her back to the table, where he hovered a little.

'Are you on your own?' said Kate.

'Afraid so. My party were indulging in a very grand, very formal dinner so I decided to play truant.'

'Well, we won't bite if you sit down here. You're staying up in Cimiez?' said Kate.

He cocked a speculative eye at her. 'That is so. And where are you staying?'

'The Négresco.'

'Mmm. Very swish.'

'Not me,' volunteered Finn. 'Where I'm staying is not swish at all. But it is really nice.'

210

The Coventry engineer came and asked Kate to dance again. Richard stood up and watched them dance away. 'Shall we?' he asked.

After that, they danced every dance together. Finn learned that he was here on holiday with friends of his father, that he had just finished a short commission in the army and was looking for something to do. It would probably be the City, though heaven knew that was not a lively place these days.

She told him about growing up in Gateshead, and the shop, and New Morven, where things were very hard now. Yes, he had heard that things were hard up North, but felt sure they would get better. They needed someone to take charge, to get the economy moving again. Just look what was happening in Germany. We could learn a lot from that.

She stopped dancing. 'They burn books there. That horrible man's out for war. It says so in the papers. My dad talks about it.'

He steered her back into the dance. 'We wouldn't do it their way. It'd be better, even more efficient. Bread on the tables. Jobs for the unemployed. Just get rid of the bureaucracies, the tangles of legislation, the exploiters . . . Anyway, we're here on holiday, to enjoy ourselves, not to worry about all that.'

When they got back to the table the Coventry engineer was standing there talking earnestly to Kate. She turned to Finn. 'George here wants to go to the little casino. Are you game?'

Finn shook her head. 'No. I think I'd better get back.'

Kate hesitated. 'I'll get you a taxi.'

'No need,' said Richard Evans. 'I've got my car. I'll run Finn back. Can I drop you at the casino?'

Kate shook her head. In reality, she and the young engineer were aiming for the Négresco. It would give her great pleasure to frolic with this young man for free, on the bed where just this afternoon Consadine had exacted his price. She picked up her wrap, then looked Richard Evans hard in the eye. 'You take care of her. And be the gentleman you obviously are.' She leaned down and kissed Finn on the cheek. 'Make him keep his distance, love,' she murmured.

They watched Kate and George go, and Richard sat down again. 'Did you say she was your friend?' he asked.

'Why do you ask?'

'You're,' he paused, 'very different from each other.'

Finn laughed. 'Well, my mother wouldn't approve of her. But I like her. I met her on the train. She's funny and very kind. And I like the way she talks. Reminds me of a traveller we had, in overalls. I mean, he brought overalls to the shop.'

Richard hid a smile. 'You came all the way here on your own?'

'Yes,' she said shortly. 'And please don't tell me its enterprising of me. The holiday is a gift from my uncle for my twenty-first birthday.'

'Twenty-one? I wouldn't have thought you more than seventeen.'

She started to protest just as the band struck up a waltz. He put up his hands. 'Shall we have one last dance before I deliver you safe and snug to your billet?'

That was just what he did, opening her car door and standing with her on the pavement. He did not touch her. 'There's something about you, Finnuola Montague, that I really like. I can't quite put my finger on why. Not just that you're so pretty. It's something else.' It was almost as if he were talking to himself.

'Don't go on,' she said, uncomfortable rather than complimented, suddenly nervous of where this was leading, the strands of panic going back to her experience with Daniel Marchant.

He took her hand and shook it heartily. 'Thank you for a lovely evening.' He held on to her hand. 'Would you say no if I asked to come to see Tourettes-Levens with you tomorrow? They say the views up there are simply stunning.'

She pulled her hand away. 'No. I mean yes, you can come.'

He touched his hat. 'Right. I'll be here two o'clock, outside Cook's.'

He got in his car and sat with his hand on the gear lever. 'And dancing tomorrow night?'

She smiled faintly. 'We'll see.'

She watched his car roar away in a swirl of dust. Madame was in her customary place in the little hall. She smiled benignly as she handed Finn her key.

'A pleasant evening, mademoiselle?'

'Oh yes, madame, a very pleasant evening.'

Kate flicked the pages of *Vogue* while she waited. She had just had another bath and was wearing a favourite low-cut green dress. She smiled down at the elegant images in the magazine. It had been a lovely evening: watching young Finn blossom and flower on the dance floor; then a very jolly rough and tumble with George the engineer on the wide bed next door. Good job he was off back to his beloved Armstrong-Siddeley engines tomorrow, or there'd be bother there.

A knock at the door. 'Your car, madame.'

This time, at the house, the smirking Armand guided her along a corridor to a long reception room where a heavy woman was playing jazz piano and twenty or thirty people were clustered in groups drinking champagne. The women were highly painted and mostly young. The men were mostly much older.

Denis came across to her, beaming, 'Kate, my dear. Come and meet everyone.' He pulled her into a small circle. 'Here is my old friend Sir Oliver Marchant. This gathering is to celebrate Sir Oliver's birthday. And here is his nephew, Daniel. And here is Sir Arthur Morgan Evans.' He looked round. 'Young Richard was to be here but he seems to have gone astray. Gentlemen, this is Kate!'

They smiled and lifted their glasses but did not offer to shake hands. Kate's eye lingered on Morgan Evans, who bore a remarkable resemblance to his son, Richard, and was, in his maturity, a much more handsome man. There were women in the group, but Denis did not offer to introduce them. They might have been wallpaper. They were smart, but too bright, too loud, too painted to be anything except hired women.

As she was.

The music changed. The chatter of the crowd stilled. The pianist was singing now, a low and throaty song about blues in the night. The air was suddenly zinging with sex.

Kate stared into her champagne glass, wondering, not for the first time, why she played these games. She looked up and found herself meeting the quizzical gaze of Sir Arthur Morgan Evans. She lifted her glass to him and he smiled very briefly.

When she and Sir Denis Consadine finally got up to their room at 2.30 in the morning, Armand was lounging by the door.

'Coffee, Armand, not champagne,' said Denis.

'It is ready, monsieur.'

'And you can come in and pour it.'

'*Oui, monsieur.*' He led the way in and poured coffee from a silver flask.

Kate sat down on one of the plump chairs and the boy handed her her coffee looking at her under his lashes.

Denis was standing by the ornate fireplace. He put his hand to his head, looking every year of his age. 'One moment, my dear. I'll just go and change,' he muttered.

From the bedroom he called for Armand, who threw a look at Kate and went in, shutting the door behind him. She picked up a magazine and began to turn the pages.

Five minutes later Denis bounced back through the door, his eyes gleaming and spots of bright colour on his cheeks. He caught her by the shoulders and lifted her to her feet. 'Now, beauty, it's time for our own little party.' He pulled the thin shoulder strap of her dress down and kissed her throat then took his lips down to her nipple. 'Now, lovely.' He led her into the bedroom, where Armand was calmly folding his clothes, pushed her on to the bed and started to kiss her again, his hand on her knee and travelling up towards her bare thigh, under her suspenders.

She sat up. 'Get him out,' she said, pulling up the top of her dress. Armand was now lounging on the chair beside the door. 'Get him out.'

Denis lay back on the bed. 'He's a very good boy, Armand,' he giggled. 'He has to have his sweets. That so, Armand?'

The boy inclined his head. 'Monsieur promised.'

'Well, madame says get out yer little twerp. I don't care if you do get him things . . . is it cocaine? You get out or I'll give you such a crack you'll need a party mask for a week to cover your bruises.'

He looked down at Denis, who shrugged. 'Very well, madame.' Then he flicked his eye upwards to the mirror, just to let her know that he would see it all anyway.

She locked the door behind him. 'Now, you!'

'Darling, you are such a peach when you're angry,' he said lazily. Then his voice changed, 'Now get your clothes off and come here.'

That stage was shorter than usual and as he lay back she felt certain there would be no repeat performance. She was very tired herself. She moved to her part of the bed. His voice came from behind her. 'Arthur Morgan Evans took a great fancy for you, dear girl.' He ran a finger down her arm. 'He's a good chap. I told him he could borrow you for a night. He's such an old stick, Arthur. He needs a good—'

She rolled over, brought herself upon her knees and slapped him hard across the face. 'How dare you, how dare you! You can't sublet me as though I were a villa or so much meat on the hoof. How dare you!'

He caught her wrist and leaped to his feet, dragging off her the bed. Still holding her in a painful grip, he shook her and thumped her in the stomach. Then he brought a hard hand across her cheek twice, dragged her across the bed and threw her down, tying her hand and foot with the cords before she got her wind back.

She saw to her horror that he had another erection. He got on to the bed. 'Being a common screaming tart might just have its attraction, my dear,' he said through gritted teeth, 'but one must draw a line somewhere.'

As he went about his painful business, she looked upwards at the smoky mirror and knew the dreadful Armand was there, savouring it all.

Finn was disappointed the next day that Kate wouldn't swim. 'Oh, Kate, I want another lesson. Please, please.'

Kate shook her head. 'No. Sorry. I'll sit here and admire your swimming style. You can have your practice on your own as long as you don't go out of your depth. Go on.' She sat back in her canvas chair. She was wearing a long-sleeved linen jacket and matching slacks and a silk scarf tied in a high fashion round her throat.

Finn came across and removed her sunglasses. Kate put her finger on the bruise high on her cheek.

'Kate! What happened? Who?'

Kate wrested the sunglasses from her and replaced them on her nose. 'That's nothing. You should see what's under the scarf. He wants his pound of flesh in more ways than one.'

Finn looked at her in consternation. 'Oh, Kate.'

'Let this be a lesson to you, young Finn. Never sell yourself, no matter how high the offering price. It's the selling that denies your status, your dignity, no matter what gold coins roll your way. It's my fault, my fault for getting in this deep.'

Finn sat down and picked up Kate's manicured hands. 'It's not your fault. Lots of people sell themselves, Kate. There's fellers with one leg in New Morven who've sold themselves to the army at one time, fellers who're choked half to death 'cos they've sold themselves to the pit owners. An' girls who go off into service, they sell themselves for five bob a week. Body and soul. An' they get injured and misused. Black eyes, slapped faces – worse if there's men in the house where they work. You see it all from my side of the counter.'

Kate put her hand back in her lap and gave her a watery smile. 'You'll have me crying yet. Now go and have that swim. Let me see the fruits of my labour.'

'You won't go back to him tonight?' said Finn anxiously.

Kate laughed. 'Of course I will. It's my job for the week and I don't get the second half of my money till Friday. Anyway, he'll be sorry when I've done with him. Squirming around in penitence. Now get in the water!'

But she watched Finn soberly as the girl splashed about. Usually she was confident of her business, very much in control. She had met some smart alecks and some 'wrong 'uns', but this was the first time she had been thoroughly frightened of a man. She knew that somewhere in his soul that man had a true black speck of evil. She would have to watch her step.

21

Confrontation

The following week went by very quickly for Finn: mornings with Kate, afternoons with Richard Evans, evenings with one or both of them. Richard drove her in his motor car up and down the coast to Monte Carlo and Grasse, into the mountains and villages. They bought food in the markets to make picnics, or ate in small restaurants, which could be found in the most surprising places.

Sometimes they would wander through the Old City, where the tall buildings must have been palaces at one time, but were now tenements. Some still retained the fragments of finely carved stone and faded exquisite decoration.

Battered sheets and bedding drooped from balconies like frayed white fruit in the sunshine; old women sat in doorways, children played. They entered a warren of streets where to Finn's eyes the sun and the light softened the poverty. Every so often New Morven did flash into her mind but the bare feet of the children in this place were dusty, not red and blue with the cold.

One day Richard took her into a building and up a staircase to see, among the detritus of crowded living, a beautiful wall painting depicting a god despoiling a maiden. She shivered at this and had to hurry out, refusing to respond to his concerned questions.

The two of them lingered in cafés and had desultory conversations of no particular substance. Richard was funny and attentive. He was interested in her stories, digging out the detail of her delivery trips up the Gaunt Valley and the idiosyncrasies of the customers. She told him about Michael and Tom Farrell, and old Jonty, who had been fighting for so long for what he believed in.

'And Michael's your . . . how would you say it, young man?'

'How would we say it? What do you mean? We're not a different species, you know.' Then she shrugged. 'He is my . . . well, my special friend, I miss him. But he doesn't want to see me while he's in prison. That makes it hard, really hard for me.'

'I can see why he doesn't want to see you. Don't you understand that? He won't want you in there, in that place. He wouldn't.'

'Would you go to prison for what you believe in?'

It was his turn to shrug. 'I was in the army for what I believed in, King and country. I'd have died for that. But Michael's not in prison for what he believes in, is it? He burgled a property.'

'He didn't. They walked in, to try to talk some sense into those numbskulls. And that was about what he believes in.'

'Same thing. Invasion of property.' He took her hand. 'Can't you see how dangerous it is? That's how all that Russia business started in '17. Those Bolsheviks. And see what a state they're in now.'

She drew away her hand. 'It's not so bad. They have bread. Jonty Clelland, who's a schoolteacher, says the Russians were slaves before. Serfs.'

'There are more civilised ways of putting bread in mouths, freeing people from penury. It can be done.'

She tossed her head. 'You're talking about Germany now. But how's that different? They kill their own people too. They burn books. And that man! Shouting away on the newsreels.'

'I admit he's a rum one. But this is only a stage while they get themselves sorted out. Believe me—'

'And you want England to be like that? Tom and Michael would say it's up to the people to sort it out, not some tinpot dictator.'

'But it takes training, intelligence, leadership,' he said eagerly.

She put a hand up. 'And how do you know that the people I'm talking about don't have these things? Because they're workers? Or, now workers without work? Adolf Hitler does have intelligence and leadership, does he? And anyway, what do you – and your friends – know about ordinary people, like them in New Morven where the children without shoes can't go to school? Where women lose their children through lack of sustenance? Where teachers read poetry to children who are still hungry.' She paused. 'And even me you look at like some specimen. The two of us lurk about in the hills, by rivers, in the streets, but I'm not up at the villa with you, playing tennis or whatever gets done there. Not that I'd want to,' she hurried on. 'I wouldn't go if you asked me.'

He coloured. 'Well, it's not quite . . . You're different, you . . . As for the country, we know what the country needs to—'

She stood up. 'Let's get on,' she said abruptly.

He watched her carefully as he handed her into his car. They were silent till they got to the waterfall and they set about their picnic. Then he started to talk about his father. 'Bit of an old stick, the old man. But he was a hero in the Great War.'

'What does he do now?'

Richard raised his eyebrows. 'Do? Oh, he lives in the country. Big place. Runs it like clockwork. Very military. His word is law there, I can tell you. He's a wonderful shot, Master of Foxhounds, and his farms are models. Showplaces. People come to see them.'

'Does your mother live in the country too?'

He shook his head. 'No. She's . . .'

She picked up his desolate tone. 'I'm sorry, She's dead? I—'

He interrupted her. 'No, she's not dead. Better if she were.'

'Oh, you can't say that, Richard.' She thought of her own mother, self-absorbed and sad. She could never, never wish her dead.

'I can say it. What she did to me.' He started to shred a hard bread roll till it had dropped like snow on the grass. 'I hate her. She left me and my father. In the war. Left him for one of his bally adjutants, don't you know?' He stood up. 'Anyway I don't want to talk about it. Shall we go?'

Then as they walked back down the hill to the car he pulled her to him and kissed her on the lips very briefly and let her go. It happened so quickly that it had barely time to register with her, and afterwards it was not mentioned.

That afternoon Denis Consadine called on Kate at the hotel. He made love to her in rather a hurried, distracted fashion, taking a mercifully short time, and afterwards they lay talking.

Denis mentioned to Kate that young Morgan Evans was never around these days. Kate yawned and stretched her arms. 'He's with young Finn. They go dancing and picnicking.' She bit her lip. The words were out before she had considered. She should not have told him.'

'Your little friend? Ah the young devil!'

Kate shook her head. 'No. It's not like that. Innocent as the day is long, she is. Him too.'

'He's a fool then. Needs to sow his wild oats.'

'Not with my "little friend" he doesn't.'

He raised himself on one elbow and looked down on her, running his finger down the bruise on her cheek, which was fading now. He'd been on his best behaviour since the day he'd beaten her. There had been no apology, but there had been a string of real pearls in a velvet case. 'You're very protective of that young woman,' he drawled. 'Almost sisterly. Perhaps I should tell young Morgan Evans that his little friend is best friends with a . . . woman who . . . Perhaps that will make him push his chances. After all, she's only some shopgirl. Her father's probably some little Jew. She's there for the taking.'

Kate sat up and pulled on her wrap. 'Oh, for goodness' sake, Denis. If you tell him anything about . . . this . . . I'll see you in hell.'

He lay back. 'Threatening, are we?'

219

'You heard. Now I need some rest. You can go back to your splendid villa and play tennis with your snooty guests.'

He put his hands behind his head. 'Well, you'll need your rest, darling. I want you there in the rue Colombier tonight, looking your exquisite best. We're having another little soirée with jazz.' He chuckled. 'I know! I was telling young Morgan Evans about it. The music, anyway. Said he should come. Perhaps he'll bring his little doxy along so that she can join in the fun with Auntie Kate.'

'I'm telling you, you do that and you can whistle for your nightly . . . pleasures.' She marched to the bathroom, then turned. 'And another thing: you can get rid of that little spying toad Armand. I've had enough of him. If he's there tonight I'll turn straight round and come back to the hotel. I'm telling you, money or no money, I'm sick of it.'

On their way out later that day, Kate put her arm through Finn's as they walked along the promenade. 'Do you really like young Richard, Finn?'

Finn nodded her head slowly. 'He has some funny ideas. But he's kind and clever. And there's a kind of . . .' She sought in her mind for what she really meant. 'There's a lot of difference between us but I kind of recognise something about him. I feel comfortable in his company even though we're so different. As though I'd met him before.'

'Has he . . .' Kate paused to find the right words, delicate but direct '. . . tried his luck with you?'

Finn shook her head. 'The perfect gentleman really.'

Kate and Finn were both subdued as they sat over their *chocolat* at Monsieur Fleury's. Kate was worried about any cynical revelations Denis Consadine might make to Richard about Kate herself, and by implication about Finn.

And Finn was thoughtful later, on her afternoon with Richard. She was suddenly full of thoughts of home, wondering how her father and mother were managing. And Jenefer and Hubert. And the twins and Smiler. She pushed her mind further. And Michael in his prison cell. Michael didn't even know she was here. She and he had not communicated in months. And she hadn't even sent the others the promised postcards.

'Penny for them,' said Kate.

'I was thinking that I should send some postcards. I've written them out. At this rate I'll be home before they will.'

Kate put out her hand. 'Give them to me. I'll put them in the post at the hotel.' She rifled through them, reading them unashamedly. 'At least you have someone to send them to. Not like me, the cat that walks by herself.' But she laughed as she tucked them in her

220

bag. 'Talking of cats, are you and that young Lothario of yours dancing at the Blue Cat tonight?'

Finn shook her head. 'No. He's taking me to the cinema. They're showing *Goodnight Vienna* – Anna Neagle's in it. Then a meal. And then he says he has a surprise. He says I'm to dress up.'

Kate pricked up her ears. 'What was that?'

'He wouldn't say. Well, he said even he didn't know properly.'

Kate stirred her spoon thoughtfully in her coffee. 'Don't you think you might be overdoing it, Finn? Perhaps you could do with an early night.'

Finn laughed at this. 'Can I be hearing right? That splendid night-hawk, Miss Kate MacMahon, recommending an early night? I can't believe it!'

Kate laughed and stood up. 'My great age catching up with me.' She touched Finn on the shoulder. 'Enjoy yourself tonight, love. We'll be on our way back the day after tomorrow.'

In the event Richard and Finn did not go to the pictures. As they walked down to the promenade, the day's heat buzzed back at them from the old buildings and the evening sky was dark sapphire-blue above the lapping waves. 'Let's walk,' said Richard suddenly. 'Jolly silly to sit in the cinema on a lovely night like this.'

They walked past the Rauba-Capeu where, on her first day Richard had told her to watch for her hat blowing off. Then they strolled on into the Old City. The narrow streets were darker here and he took her hand as they walked along.

They found a small café where they had a spicy dish, more African than French, and very rough red wine. She pulled her wrap around her; it was cooler in this interior dark space where the sun never penetrated.

He took her hand across the table. 'It's been such fun spending time with you here,' he said.

She smiled at him, not knowing what to say. 'Me too,' she replied lamely.

He gripped her hand. She thought absently how earnest and young he looked in evening dress, like a boy in a man's clothes. She frowned. There was something about him, some chord he struck in her.

'We have to go off tomorrow,' he said. 'My father and a few of them have some kind of conference in Germany. I'm to go with them.'

She withdrew her hand a little. 'Good,' she said brightly. 'That'll give me time to see the Fine Arts Museum. I promised my friend I would go. Her husband's a painter, you see . . .'

He gripped her hand harder to retain it. 'I don't want to go, Finn, but it's planned and—'

221

She smiled more freely now. 'Of course you've to go, idiot. But just don't take anything those Germans say as gospel. And keep your eyes properly open. Don't let them pull any wool over them.'

He shook his head. 'I'm not stupid. But I'm sorry to go, to bring this to an end.'

'That's what they say happens to all good things, isn't it?'

'I will write. I will come to see you.'

She shook her head. 'You can't do that. It's all different. There's no sun, no sea. You wouldn't like it. I'm different there. I'm the girl in the shop, not the girl at the Three Doves, or the girl drinking *chocolat* at Monsieur Fleury's.'

'You couldn't be just anything. You're always just yourself,' he said earnestly.

She laughed out loud at that, pulling her hand away altogether. 'Oh, Richard, you just sound like some old song. Now let's stop moaning on and enjoy ourselves. What's this surprise you're springing on me tonight?'

Taking her cue, he put up a hand to attract the attention of the waiter and reached for his wallet. 'I'm not sure. Some kind of reception before our party lights off. There's a new jazz ensemble from America – well, from Paris really, but they're Americans. And champagne. Should be pretty jolly. At a place on the rue Colombier.'

The house was elegant, with double doors, a cool tiled hall, and a sweeping staircase painted in white, picked out in gold. The tinkling sound of jazz piano drifted through a further set of double doors.

Finn shook her head when a black-clad maid offered to take her wrap. She clutched it round her, suddenly intimidated by her surroundings.

They went into the large room which was thronging with people, whose twittering, neighing and shrieking voices almost drowned out the music from the seven-piece ensemble on the rostrum.

Finn could smell rich tobacco and a sweeter, more fruity smell. The smoke hung in the air. A dapper waiter moved among the people with trays of champagne. He offered some to Richard. The contents of the glasses had long since stopped foaming. 'Come on, Finn.' Carrying the glasses Richard led the way to one of the small tables at the edge of the room and she sat down, grateful to reduce her visibility. He placed a glass in her hand and sat beside her.

As Finn steamed up the courage to scan the crowd more closely she realised that something was wrong. There were many more men than women. The men, mostly middle-aged, were smart, in evening dress. The women all young, were smart too. But when she looked more closely, she noted eyes painted like a ballet dancer's, dresses just too *décolletée*, voices just too loud, cigarette holders wildly

222

orchestrating too animated conversations, women winding themselves round, standing too close to the men. She looked closely at some heavily painted women who were giggling in the company of two portly men, waving large ringed hands in their faces. And she knew these were boys, not women.

She turned to Richard. 'What's this?' she said, standing up. 'Where have you brought me?'

'Ah, Richard! You brought your charming friend!'

They turned to face Sir Denis Consadine flanked by Daniel Marchant and his uncle, Sir Oliver Marchant. Finn clutched a chairback. Daniel came forward. 'Well, Dick, we may differ on many things but we do share one interest.' He took Finn's unresisting hand and kissed it. 'What an unexpected pleasure Finnuola.' He cast a glance round the room. 'Your true nature is emerging. I knew I was right.'

She wrenched her hand away. 'You!' she spluttered. Then to her horror she saw Kate appear at Denis Consadine's elbow.

'Denis, what's this? Richard, what have you done?' She put a hand on Finn's shoulder and turned to Denis. 'You viper, you destroyer!'

The music trailed to a halt. Now the whole room was hushed, eagerly witnessing the row. Rows were not unknown at these gatherings. Some considered them part of the cabaret.

'Now, now, Kate. All that's happened is that Richard's decided to join in the fun with his little . . . doxy.' His eye swept Finn up and down. 'So charmingly unaffected in her ragamuffin ensemble.'

Some women in the crowd laughed.

Kate brought up a fist and winged him with a blow which nearly threw him off balance. 'Viper. Evil man. Bloody fascist!' She spat the words out and landed a blow on the other side, which rocked him again. She turned on the crowd. 'Bloody fascists, the lot of you.'

Now there was open laughter in the crowd.

Then, Richard shouted, 'No!' as Denis brought back a fist and struck Kate, who fell, pole-axed to the floor. There was a chorus of protest from the other women but the men looked on with objective interest.

Daniel Marchant licked his lips.

Finn dropped on the floor beside her friend but she was firmly removed by the large hands of Denis Consadine. He pushed her violently towards Richard. 'You'd better get your little friend away, Richard. Miss MacMahon's fainted. I think we need to get her some help.' He signalled a dark boy, with a cowlick of black hair, who was standing by the door. The boy came across, lifted Kate as though she were an autumn leaf and bore her away.

223

Denis turned and signalled the band. The leader put his saxophone to his mouth and the music beamed forth again. The chatter restarted. The whole incident was like a stone which creates a ripple as it drops, but soon after leaves no sign at all.

Finn pulled herself from Richard's arms and started to run. She ran out through the wide doors, raced away from the echoing sound of the party. She heard his steps behind her, drew into the shadow of a sidestreet and watched Richard pass, then set off at a steady, more determined pace to the *pension* of the Three Doves.

Ten minutes after she had arrived Richard was on the doorstep. However Madame, flanked by her son, Paul, refused to let him in, saying Mademoiselle Montague had gone to bed and was not to be disturbed. He made the mistake of offering Paul money, and had the door shut in his face for his pains.

Watching him walk slowly back down the street from her window, Finn started to shake. She dropped on her bed and put her trembling hands to her face. What was happening? What was Kate up to? Was she dead now? As a true friend she should do something for her. But what could she do, a strange girl in a strange city?

Kate felt the water on her face and shook her head, waking up with a start. She struggled to move but the silk cords tying her to the bed prevented her. She tried to shout but only bit on the silk scarf tied round her mouth.

'Ah, Kate!' Denis's face loomed over her. 'Feeling better, are we, after our little bout of temper?' He handed the crystal jug back to Armand. 'I was just telling Armand here how you disliked being kissed on the mouth, so the silk scarf is a good thing, isn't it?'

Armand took the jug and placed it carefully on the console. He was naked to the waist and Kate could see a tiger tattooed on his left shoulder blade. She struggled against the bonds.

Denis sat down in the plump chair, took out a buffer and started to stroke it over his nails. 'Now I have a problem, dear Kate. Your cruel and unwarranted attack on my person this evening has made me a little dizzy. Thus I feel unable to fulfil my part in our . . . er . . . special activities. So Armand here, very kindly, has agreed to be my surrogate. It is a great concession, my dear, as he has informed me that he thinks you are somewhat ugly, and too thin, to boot.' He beamed at the boy who smirked down at Kate. 'I may get up the strength to join the pair of you later, who knows?' He lit a cigar and sat back in his chair smiling from one to the other.

Finn sat up in bed, shocked into life by the hammering on her door. '*Mademoiselle, mademoiselle, ici votr'amie!*' Madame's quavering voice was calling.

224

She opened the door and Kate fell into her arms. 'Finn, love, I'm such a fool, such a bloody fool,' she wailed. 'I can't go to the Négresco in this state.' Her face was bruised and there was blood coming from the corner of her mouth. Finn led her to the bed, lay her down, then turned to Madame, who was hovering at the door. 'Madame, is there some coffee? And a bowl of water, perhaps, with towels?'

Beneath her cloak Kate was wearing only her silk petticoat: there were more bruises on her shoulder and her upper arms; she had no shoes on her feet. Finn propped her on the snowy pillows, pulled over the sheet to cover her and sat holding her hand, waiting for the sobs to subside.

She thrust a handkerchief into Kate's hand so she could mop up the tears. 'It's that horrible man,' she said, 'isn't it, Kate?'

Kate snuffled into the hankie. 'I thought I could handle them, the bad buggers. But not this one.'

'He could have killed you.'

The tears had dried up now. 'He nearly did,' Kate sniffed, 'he and his catamite.'

'His what?'

'You don't want to know about it.'

When they had finished with her, Armand had hustled her down the back stairs. He had leaned her up against the wall, taken her wallet out of her bag and tucked the notes into the pocket of his short waistcoat. He pulled out a centime and thrust it into the wallet. Then he had put her out in the street.

Now as she lay in the small cottagey room, her hand in Finn's, her humiliation drained away, to be replaced by a familiar, much more bracing anger. She sat up straight and looked around. 'I thought I could get cleaned up and borrow something to wear so I can get back to the Négresco. All my things are there. I wouldn't put it past the bastard to clean me out. I need to get my things.' She looked round the room. 'I wonder if your little Madame has a vacancy.'

Finn shook her head slowly. 'How can you do all that, Kate? How can you do it? I hadn't quite realised . . .'

'Innocent.' Kate patted her hand and swung her legs out of the bed. 'It was always the devil driving. I see it as a kind of necessary thing. Do what they want and take the money. In one way I do to them what they do to me. I know their secrets. But after yesterday I am sick to the stomach of the whole thing. Maybe it's more necessary to stay alive.'

'Well, stop! Do something else before–'

'They do for me altogether? Mmm, you're right.' She stood up. 'Now we're not going to let the buggers win. Has your nice Madame got a bath in this place?' She started to strip off, causing Madame to gasp as she came in with her towels, amazed at the Englishwoman's rejuvenation in such a short time. She looked with clinical interest. The Englishwoman had a fine body, despite the bruises.

In the end Finn went to the Négresco with Kate. On the way she bought, on account, a new dress and an elegant veiled hat. Kate swept into the Négresco, with Finn in her wake, as though she owned the place, and though her absence had been noticed, it was not commented upon.

All her clothes and jewellery were intact and the two of them made short work of the packing. When they returned to the Three Doves two hours later there was a great bunch of flowers waiting for Finn, with a note from Richard.

Dear Finn,
I wanted to talk to you about last night's fiasco but you weren't here. I have to go now as we are all leaving on a very early train. I can't believe we won't meet again.
Richard Morgan Evans.

'They're gone.' Finn handed the note to Kate who read it and said. 'Good riddance to bad rubbish.'

Finn shook her head. 'Richard wasn't like them,' she said sadly, 'was he?'

'How do we know? How do we know anything about any of them? They live one life on the outside, one on the inside. Now then, did you say you wanted to go to the Fine Arts Museum? Might as well make the most of our last day.'

'You must have these.' Finn gave the flowers to Madame, who nodded graciously and passed them on to Paul.

Kate pointed at the cases, then put her arm through Finn's. 'Can Monsieur Paul take this to that little room you've sorted for me? Mademoiselle and I will be *touristes* today without the problematic incursion of *les hommes*. Shall we, Finn?'

After an exhausting day Finn and Kate were glad of an early night. Finn lay in a half-waking half-sleeping state, thinking about going home tomorrow, reviewing the last days and weeks. She thought about Kate squashed flat under the man's heel and even now bouncing back, her very resilience a vengeance on his cruelty. How much more quickly Kate had done it than Finn herself after that incident with Daniel Marchant. Now *he* was in the right company in that dreadful place. Showed him up, that did! Finn was pleased that suddenly she could think that without pain. Kate and this wonderful place, this bright dusty wonderful place, had taught her a lot.

And now tomorrow she would be going home to New Morven. It

seemed years since she had seen it. She wondered that she wasn't dreading returning home and the prospect of being enclosed by the routines again, the people. People. Suddenly names started to whirl through her head. Richard Morgan Evans. Michael O'Toole. Patrick Montague. Hubert Loumis, Jenefer Loumis. Jenefer Morgan Loumis. Richard Morgan Evans. Jenefer Morgan Loumis.' She sat up in bed, Richard's voice echoing in her ears. '*I hate her. She left me and my father. In the war. Left him for one of his bally adjutants . . .*'

The next morning in the dining room, Finn started her coffee alone, rehearsing, for Kate's delectation, just what she would say about Richard Evans's identity; how she was sure she knew . . .

But Kate preempted her, gliding into the dining room in an elegant pale green suit, subtle make-up concealing the worst of the marks on her face. She was smiling broadly. 'Finn! Guess what! I've decided to take your advice. I'm going to stop catering for those men with their foul and mincing appetites. And,' she nodded to Paul, who poured out her coffee, 'I'm going to come to that village of yours while I think what to do.'

'New Morven?' said Finn, dropping her knife.

'What better place? We're friends. I can entertain you. Nothing happens there. You said that.'

'But Kate, everyone *leaves* New Morven. Nobody *goes* there. It's dark, dingy. There's no bathrooms.' Finn's hair was standing on end at the thought.

'Well, I'm coming. You watch!' said Kate, laying very thick butter on to her croissant. 'You watch me, Finn. I'm coming.'

PART THREE

22

The Visitor

'This place has been far too quiet since the girl went away.'

Jenefer was watching Hubert paint. She was sitting in one of the wicker garden chairs in the coach house. She rubbed her hands together and put them towards the iron stove set up in there to ward off the October chill.

Hubert was working in the last corner of the smaller wall, painting the second of two identical whippets with jewelled collars, restrained by a double leash held by one of a pair of little girls, also absolutely alike.

'Mmm. Can't see how you can say that, with that young feller-me-lad clumping around and the two little birds twittering. See them here? Can you see them, Jenefer? Do you like their little dogs? They've given them names: Molly and Polly. I like that.' He smiled with some contentment.

'It's not the same,' she said. 'Finnuola, she's—'

'The maid. You're right.' He stood back, wiped his brush on the rag tucked into his Sam Browne belt, then came across to sit beside her. 'A comrade,' he said.

She poured tea from the teapot she had brought and the steam hung in the air. 'A little friend. What will she've made of it all there? Will she've swum in the sea? Will she've seen the waterfalls? Climbed the mountains?'

He smiled quietly. 'The joy of opening new worlds for the innocent. How careful we have to be that it is not Pandora's box. I've seen what emerges from that.'

She put a hand on his sleeve. 'Don't say that. You've been so well, Hubert. There in the sun you were boiling up in that strange fashion but here in this cold dingy place you seem so even, so steady.'

'It was the maid. I knew it was the right place when I saw the maid.' He turned to her. 'Do you really think I'm mad, Jenefer? Raving?' It was his old voice.

She stood up and ruffled his hair. 'Probably. But for the most part you exhibit a picturesque sanity which we'd all do well to emulate.'

He stood up and caught her in his arms and they kissed passionately, moving and nudging against each other for a long, long time.

'Ahem!'

They leaped apart guiltily and turned to see the Reverend Hildebrand Marchant in the wide doorway, holding a wriggling Smiler by the ear.

Jenefer went and removed the offending hand from the ear, and drew Smiler to her. 'What is it, Vicar?'

His eye gleamed. 'My housekeeper, Mrs Fosdick, caught this reprobate, and others, trying to light bonfires in the vicarage field.' He paused, his eye lifting to Hubert's great dragon, his bestiary of strange creatures and his scarifying images of battle. He continued, now in an absent tone. 'Fortunately, the kindling they were intending to ignite was . . . er . . . rhubarb leaves.'

Jenefer laughed.

'Aw, Jenefer, the bliddy priest . . . Ow!' Smiler recoiled into Jenefer as the vicar whammed him on the ear.

'No priest, you young Roman, you savage, but vicar of this parish!' Hildebrand gathered himself together and glared at Jenefer, then turned his gaze on Hubert, now standing stiff and wooden at her shoulder. 'Madam, it is evident to me that you are no fit woman to care for children. This is a place of lewd, lascivious activities; the child does not address people respectfully.' His thin finger pointed at the painted wall behind Hubert. 'And this . . . this is obviously some temple to the Antichrist.'

He reached to grab Smiler's shoulder and pull him away from Jenefer. 'Come. You will come with me to Carhoe. I am sure they will find a place . . .'

Smiler started to wail, 'Gerroff, mister, ah'm goin' to no workhouse.'

'It's a very respectable institution. I'm on the—'

Jenefer was tugging at the vicar's coat now, pummelling at his back. 'Let go. Let the child go.'

He was so surprised at the touch of a woman that he did so and Smiler catapulted away from him, falling on to the dusty floor.

'Get into the house, Smiler,' shouted Jenefer. 'And lock the door.'

He ran.

She wrenched the vicar round to face her. 'And you, you get away. Go! It's you who're lascivious, filthy-minded. It's you who're Antichrist. Anti everything that means life and love.' Jenefer was tugging at him, talking in a low determined voice.

Behind her Hubert covered his face with his hands.

232

'Madam!'

'I'll madam you. Go!' Now she was pushing at him and as he recoiled he had to stumble out of the door.

He backed away from her and she followed him. In his haste he stumbled over the black and white cat, which was lurking behind him, and fell headlong into the dust. He hauled himself to his feet, retreated to a safe distance, then stopped and said quietly, his voice a thin thread in the cold October air, 'This house is no fit place for Christians of whatever colour. It is no fit place for children. Any moral person would wonder what takes place here. You can be sure, madam, that the authorities will take these children. I would not be surprised if there were grounds for legal action.' He dusted his sleeves down as though her very touch polluted them. 'We will begin with charges of assault on my own person.' He marched off.

Jenefer turned and hurried back into the coach house. Hubert was crouched into a corner now, his hands still over his eyes. She pulled his hands away and led him to the centre of the floor. 'It's all right now, Hubert. He's gone.'

His face was utterly despairing as he looked down at her. 'He is such a bad man. I could not defend you, nor the child. I am nothing without my sword. You understand that? Nothing! That evil one can enter my realm, despoil my women and take my children and I am nothing.'

She pulled him down into one of the chairs and sat on his knee, bringing his face to her breast, stroking his hair. 'There, there, little one. It was only a silly old man, madder in truth than you could ever be. Don't disturb yourself, my darling, stay calm, stay calm.'

But this time even she could not stem the flow of tears.

In Montague's shop Bella was waiting impatiently for old Mr Hazelwood to scrape out the pennies to pay for the tobacco which Emily had just wrapped in a screw of paper. She shuffled her feet impatiently. 'Ah've pegged out, an' put the washer away. So can yer give us me money, Emily?'

Emily shook her head. 'That'll be up ter Mr Montague, Bella.'

Bella let out a snort. 'Ah need salt, Emily. Ah've got some stew on, me own washin' in the boiler an' fifty things to do.' It was unusual for Bella to be such a sourpuss. Emily dropped her eyes to the bulge beneath Bella's floursack apron and sighed. There was reason for it. 'Expectin' again, Bella?' she said gently.

'Aye, Em'ly, the bugger's got us up the stick again. Men – yer better off without one, Em'ly!'

Emily counted Mr Hazelwood's ha'pennies into the drawer and nodded at the old man, who picked up his screw of paper, thrust it into his pocket and shuffled to the door.

Emily looked up at Bella. 'Ah don't think so, Bella. Stanley didn't bother me like that, see. Once we'd had our three bairns, he didn't bother. But then he had his music, that blessed organ in the church, see? Eeh, Stanley he used to sing around the house like a bird, play with those music papers.' She brought up the corner of her pinny to wipe her eye, then sniffed. 'Ah know the Lord shows us we've got to forgive, but it's hard to forgive Mr Marchant for what he's done. Ah try, Bella, Ah do try.'

There had been a flurry of concern in New Morven about Stanley Punchard, after he'd hanged himself in the woods. But that soon died down. There were others to avail themselves of the generous well of scandalised local concern: the man who threw himself off Priorton Viaduct, another who had drowned himself in the Gaunt: both, like Stanley, overwhelmed by life without the meaning and sustenance of work. Then there was the woman who was carted away to Sedgefield, found raving in the street one washday because she had no soap to do her wash. The last straw.

Emily thought that, now, only she and the bairns ever thought of Stanley at all.

Bella's ears had pricked up, her mind on quite another tack. 'The vicar! Em'ly, does thoo knaa what May Lynn, her that scrubs for Mrs Fosdick, what she telt us the vicar said?'

Emily shook her head absently, her mind still on Stanley.

'He says to Mrs Fosdick that there were strange goin's-on at Plush Folly, bad things. An' that those bairns of the Irishman should be in the Home.'

Emily took down the salt from the shelf. 'Seems like a nice enough woman, that Mrs Loumis. Give me jam jars from the lofts, she did. Old Warburton was a hoarder, see? An' she give us boxes of apples from the trees for the soup kitchen.'

Bella nodded. 'Queer 'n, though.'

The bell rattled as Patrick Montague came through the door, his breath swirling on the cold air that belched in with him. He looked across at Emily. 'Are you still here? I thought you'd have been finished hours ago.'

Emily looked at the ceiling. 'Mrs Montague had one of her funny turns, so I said I'd stay on a bit.'

It was Patrick's turn to look at the ceiling. 'But what about your children, Emily? They'll be well back from school now.'

She shrugged. 'The bairns'll be all right. I left stuff out for them.'

'Anyway, get your coat on.' He opened the till. He paid her by the day, knowing the need for this money was that urgent. He thrust the coins into her hand.

She counted it. 'There's a shilling too much here, Mr Montague.' She held it out in the palm of her hand.

He shook his head, 'Extra time, Emily. That's for the extra time. You need it. For the children.'

She put it carefully in the back of her purse. 'It'll go to the Citadel,' she said.

Patrick shook his head and left it at that. Stanley Punchard's death still lingered in his mind. More than once he had wondered if, had he said more to Stanley that day he had picked him up in the street, if he had comforted or supported him in some way, that Stanley wouldn't have done that dreadful thing. Patrick pulled a little at his collar stud . . . that dreadful thing.

The bell tinkled as Emily bustled away to her children.

'Yes, Bella?' he said.

'Ah wus wantin' me pay for deein' the washin' an' ter pay for that salt that Em'ly Punchard put out,' she said. 'But neebody seems to listen round here.'

Later, when the shop finally cleared of customers, Patrick went upstairs to see Esther, who was sitting in the cold sitting room, looking out of the window.

'Emily said you'd had a bad turn,' he said.

She nodded and put the back of her hand against her brow. 'One of those dizzy spells, Patrick. Emily got me an Aspro and kindly said she would stay a little longer.'

'Yes,' he said, 'Emily's a good woman.'

She held up her hand with a card in it. 'There was a card from Finnuola. "Having a wonderful time in this wonderful place".' She put the card carefully on the shelf beside her. 'I'll keep it to show our Harold when he gets back from America. He'll be pleased his money's gone to such good use. Educational.'

Patrick started to say something about Emily, and about Stanley Punchard, then stopped. There was no point in saying anything to Esther. Her sympathies would not stretch that far. No point at all. He merely said, 'She's due back tomorrow, Finnuola, isn't she?'

'In England today, so home tomorrow, I should think.'

'It'll be good to see her.'

He had not realised just how much the child had done, just what kind of load she had taken on. He was worn out himself. The shop bell went. He returned downstairs, wrote a note for himself, to remember to bring the washing in, and propped it up beside the drawer that did service as a till.

As they sat in the taxi on their way for their overnight stay at The Coriander, Kate giggled a little at Finn's slightly harassed air.

'I know what you're thinking!' she said.

'What?'

'You're thinking what'll you do if I go flaunting myself round the square again.'

Finn coloured. 'No I wasn't!' She had been thinking just that, of course. 'And anyway, that would be your own business, wouldn't it?'

'You're right there, old girl. But I told you, I'm retired. Done with all that. Consadine gave me a sickener. Cheated me out of my pay, what's more, him and his catamite. My purse is just about empty. I'm coming North with you to see you safely home. I'll stay and have a bit of a think, then . . . I don't know what.' There was the faintest thread of uncertainty in her voice.

'I don't need no escort home. I came by myself, and I can go back by myself.'

'Are you telling me I can't come?'

'No. No,' said Finn hurriedly. Kate was right, of course, about the fact that she didn't want her to come. It was crazy to think someone like Kate could go back there to New Morven. Finn's heart was sinking at the thought of what might happen. How Kate would react when she saw the dark village and the black silent pitheads. It was all so different from France, and from London. She closed her eyes and tried to bring back the images of Nice: the bright blue sky, the gem-like sea, the promenade and the palm trees. She opened them again to see the rain coursing down the taxi window and the grey London world outside. Grey! And how black was New Morven beside that. 'You won't like it,' she said glumly, 'you'll think it's a horrible place.'

'I come from Lancashire, remember? You can't tell me nothing about dark satanic mills.'

'It's not terrible, you know, not altogether. And there's fields and rivers. It's quite green once you get away . . .' She broke off. 'I can't see why you want to come, Kate.'

'I think it was those cards you sent. I want to see who you sent them to.'

'And you won't be able to stay with us. The house is all shop. I'm stuffed up in an attic room as it is. There's hotels in Priorton, but you've no money. You said he didn't pay you.'

Kate squeezed her hand. 'I have a bank account. I told you. And I've those pearls that clot Consadine gave me. Are there any pawnshops in Priorton?'

'More than one of those! But they're more used to taking on some father's Sunday suit on a Monday to be redeemed on Saturday.'

Kate sat back. 'Well, that solves that problem. But I don't want to stay in Priorton. I want to stay in that place where you are. New Morven? Are there no hotels or boarding houses there?'

Finn laughed. 'There's pubs. No boarding houses. You could

maybe rent a house. Plenty of empty houses because of everyone going away. There's an empty house three doors down from the shop. It's dirty, though . . .'

Kate smoothed her immaculate hair and patted her tiny green velvet hat. 'That'll do fine. Us mill girls are used to a bit of hard graft. I'll have it clean as a pin in no time.'

Finn shook her head and sank back into her own thoughts about home. She was looking forward to seeing her father, even her mother. And Jenefer and Hubert. There would be so much to tell them. Should she tell Jenefer about Richard? It was a coincidence, that. She smiled at the thought of Richard. She would have had a different kind of holiday without him. He was a special person. She decided she would tell Jenefer, but not straight away.

And Michael. She would write a proper letter to him about where she had been and what it was like. And she would tell him how much she was looking forward to seeing him. It was clear to her now; she felt quite strong about it all. Her holiday, the rest, the sun, perhaps even Monsieur Fleury's *chocolat* had worked their magic. Just as Jenefer Loumis had said they would.

In the event Kate did stay in Priorton. She booked herself into the Gaunt Valley Hotel, and waved Finn off on the brief journey to New Morven Halt. Finn staggered with her cases the short distance from the station to the shop. Patrick was leaning with his elbows on the counter, as usual, reading the *Northern Echo*. His face brightened when he saw her and he came round the counter and took her case. 'You should have left it up at the Halt, Finn. I'd have got it.'

'Well, Dad, aren't you pleased to see me?' She stood helplessly in the middle of the floor glancing round at the dark, cluttered space.

He put her case on the dusty floor, touched her shoulder, and kissed her cheek. 'You don't know how much, love.'

He sounded so weary that Finn flung her arms round him and hugged him, and he hugged her briefly back, then disentangled himself. He cleared his throat. 'Now then,' he said heartily, 'you go upstairs and tell your mother you're here and I'll shut the shop for half an hour and make us all a nice cup of tea.'

In the back room she looked at the poster of Nice as he filled the kettle. 'It's much nicer than that, Dad. Much cleaner, brighter. You should see the sea . . .'

'Finnuola!'

'You'd better get up there. She'll have heard you.' He smiled faintly at her. Finn's heart sank. She had the idea that he didn't want to hear about how wonderful it all had been, that he was just pleased – very pleased – to see her back.

Esther, having enthused over her present of a bright silk scarf, was a much more satisfying audience, drinking in all the details about the promenade and the casino, the palm trees and the beaches, the cafés and the dance floor made of glass.

Finn waited till the next morning to go across to Plush Folly with her bag of presents. Patrick was put out at first, desperately wanting her straight back into the shop with him. 'But Emily Punchard's here, Dad. I'll just be an hour,' she heard herself pleading, and thought that the *pension* of the Three Doves was a world, not just a continent away.

At Plush Folly the twins flew at her, talking together about going to school and their new frocks which Jenefer had bought, new pinnies which kept the dresses clean, and how their teacher was so amazed that they could actually read . . . She looked over their head at Jenefer and Hubert, standing almost nervously in the doorway of the drawing room.

'Well?' said Jenefer.

Finn broke free of the twins and flew down the hall to them and the three of them hugged each other in mutual delight. Finally, 'Better!' Finn gasped. 'Even better than you said.' They led her into the room and she sat on the couch and looked up at them. 'That sea. And the sun. And those lovely old buildings. And the cafés . . .' She realised they were gazing at her with almost greedy delight. 'And I went to the Museum of Fine Arts and saw the paintings.' She paused. 'Yours're much better, Hubert.'

He roared with laughter at this. 'You know nothing, child. Nothing. But go on.'

'Did you get into the country?' said Jenefer.

'Yes,' she coloured. 'There was this person with a motor car.'

'A young man!' said Hubert with solemn delight.

'Well, no, he was young and he was a man, but . . . no. We didn't get into any countrywomen's kitchens, Jenefer, like you said I should. But we had wonderful picnics and nice meals in little cafés.'

The twins were sitting either side of her, pressing in towards her.

'Presents!' she said. She distributed them, simple mementos which were all she could afford, and they were taken with reverent awe, as though they were the finest jewels.

'And you feel well? You look well,' said Jenefer, sniffing her small package of two lace handkerchiefs.

Finn grinned at her. 'Never better. Better than ever.'

The door opened and Smiler clumped in, cleaner and tidier and plumper, but still with the sharp looks of the Primrose Court days. Finn's heart leapt as she suddenly noted his resemblance to Michael. She reached and pulled him to her. He wriggled out of her hug but stood grinning at her with pleasure. 'The vicar come ter tek us ter a Home, but Jenefer saw him off with a poker.' He announced. 'She's a bramah, is Jenefer.'

Finn smiled at Jenefer. 'So she is.'

'An' our Mick's comin' out of jail in two weeks. That Mrs Jonty wus here.'

Finn's buzz of pleasure faltered then blazed on. 'Right. Good. We'll have to get everything ready for him, won't we?' She wouldn't, couldn't write to him yet about all the amazing things she had seen. She could wait now and tell him to his face. To the face which was an older sharper version of that of the beaming Smiler, standing before her now. Her heart lurched, aching for yet fearing that moment now so near in the future.

When she got back to the shop her father was entertaining a visitor, a demure woman in a grey coat, grey lisle stockings and a neat grey wool beret. And red hair. 'Finn, here's your friend. Why didn't you tell me she was coming? Seems she's setting up as a book-keeper . . .' Patrick's face was alight with pleasure.

The demure woman turned round. 'Hello, Finn, dear. Your father and I are getting on famously,' said Kate. She came across and embraced Finn, whispering in her ear. 'You didn't tell me what a good-looking man your Pa was, did you?'

He heard this and pulled his shoulders back, standing even taller behind his counter. Shaking her head at Kate, Finn realised that it was all going to be even more difficult than she had anticipated.

23

Ménage à Trois

To the surprise of her husband and daughter, Esther Montague took a great shine to Kate MacMahon. Kate's demure, ladylike elegance appealed to her, as did her talk of London, Paris and Rome. Esther's puzzlement at why such a superior creature should end up in New Morven was resolved by Kate's shy allusion to a crossed love affair.

'So I did need to get away, Esther – I can call you Esther, is that all right? And then I met your Finnuola . . . what a nice girl! So well brought up, I could see it at first glance! So I thought, a quiet sojourn up in the North where nobody knows me, away from everything. I hoped I might get work as a book-keeper. That's my skill.'

Esther sniffed. 'Not many books to keep around here.'

'Well, we'll see. Mr Montague . . . Patrick . . . mentioned I may be able to help out here at the shop. He tells me you suffer from delicate health. I do have a small income. From . . . an uncle. If I live modestly I should be able to manage. I made enquiries about a little house along the street.'

Esther sat back with satisfaction. Here at least would be someone to talk to, whose mind rose above Sunlight soap and scrag-end joints.

On the third day back, Finn cornered Kate in front of the shop. 'What are you up to, Kate? Just what is it you're up to?'

Kate tucked her arm through Finn's. 'Now don't get agitated, love. I'm doing no wrong. I just wanted to try civilian life, you know? It's like coming out of the army. I need a place to start again and this is it.'

Finn looked around the street. 'I can think of better places.'

'No. This is fine.' She hugged Finn's arm to her. 'Now then, I'm just back from Priorton. The pawnshop was very busy. I got some money on the pearls and the promise of more. I bought a few maiden-aunt clothes and a few sticks of furniture for this house along here. And a tin bath, of course. They're bringing them on a cart this afternoon.'

Finn exploded with laughter. 'Kate, you won't survive here. A tin bath?' She thought of the Négresco, and its bathrooms with bright chrome taps and gushing hot water.

'So what kind of a soft life do you think I grew up to? There were tin baths in Lancashire, you know.'

'But do you want to go back to them?' asked Finn soberly.

Kate pulled her arm out of Finn's and she stood very still. 'I got a fright over there, Finn. That bastard Consadine gave me the fright of my life. I need some breathing space.'

Finn smiled at her, guilty at forgetting so quickly. 'Oh, Kate, you do what you fancy. Have a second holiday in New Morven if that's what it takes. Only don't play any parts, be yourself.'

Kate looked down at her neat coat and skirt, her sensible shoes. 'But which self, Finn? Looking like this, I'm just the same as I was before that first man turned me into a whore.'

Finn glanced hurried up and down the deserted street. 'As I said, Kate. You suit yourself.'

'I will, when I find a self to suit.' She smiled and turned into the shop. 'I've a book for your ma from the bookshop in Priorton, and your pa said he'd show me the ropes in the shop so I can do a stint here now and then.' She pushed the shop door and the bell rang. 'Bye, Finn.'

Through the doorway Finn saw her father's head come up and his shoulders go back. He beamed at Kate in welcome. It was a long time since Finn had seen her father so visibly happy. If ever.

Finn made her way to Kitchener Street, to the Salvation Army Citadel, where she found Emily Punchard alongside two other women, peeling vegetables for broth.

'I came to ask about Michael, Mrs Punchard. And Tom.'

Emily handed Finn a knife and she picked up a potato and started peeling.

'Due out a week on Friduh, pet. Tom says not to meet them. Thi'll make their own way.' She swilled her peeled carrot round in a dish of dirtying water and drew it into a large pan of water on the iron field cooker. 'It's not easy in there, where they are, pet. It's gettin' them down, the three of them. Hardly recognise our Tom. Don't expect Michael'll be any great shakes either.'

'I'll have to meet Michael. He needs to know to come to Plush Folly, where the children are. The house down Primrose Court is empty.' She was looking forward to seeing him free. She wanted to be there at the gates, whatever else happened.

'He knows about Plush Folly, hinney. Hasn't that Mrs Loumis got those kids to write a letter? Our Tom says the lad was in tears.'

242

But Finn was determined to go. She stayed with Emily until the vegetables were all done and the pots were bubbling. As she went through the hall the queue was beginning to form, clusters of rather silent women and yammering children filling the hut.

As she walked along to Plush Folly Finn tried to heave back to her mind the image of clusters of people strolling in the sunlight on the Promenade des Anglais. It was impossible. All the images were fading fast. She frowned and blinked hard, but it still didn't work.

Plush Folly appeared to be empty, so she made her way round the back and followed the sounds of laughter to Alan Newton's cottage, alongside the coach house. Inside, laughing and calling and chattering, Jenefer, the twins and Smiler were sweeping and clearing with gusto. The walls were white. Michael himself had painted them before he was arrested. There was some talk of Hubert doing more painting in here. Michael had mended the roof as well, up there in the apple loft. Finn thought of that and blushed, involuntary pleasure streaking through her.

'What's this?' said Finn, finally.

Toots, or Nancy, looked up at her. 'We're gunna live here with our Mick when he gets home from jail.'

'Well, our Mick and Smiler are. We're stayin' with Jenefer,' said the other twin.

Finn looked at Jenefer, who shrugged. 'Just a thought. Of course, Michael'll have to make up his own mind. They'll need somewhere. I can't see that young man wanting to live in the house after where he's been. He'll want freedom, independence. And I want this crew under my eye now I'm used to them.'

Finn looked round. 'Where's Hubert?'

'He's in the coach house mooning over his paintings. A bit melancholic now he thinks it's finished. He was going to do some more in here, but says there are no more images. Nothing in his head. That could be good or it could be bad. Do go in there and cheer him up.'

Duly dismissed, Finn made her way to the coach house. She smiled to herself. Her nose should be out of joint really. Jenefer was so preoccupied with the twins and Smiler that there was little room for the more grown-up Finn, who hardly needed her now. And Jenefer had been very guarded in her response to Kate MacMahon. Finn made the mistake of thinking they would get on like a house on fire, as they were in many ways alike, but, perhaps for that very reason, they didn't.

In another life, she thought, perhaps Jenefer would have been one of those women with hoards of children, all-in-all to them and they to her.

Finn's mind moved to Richard, her heart aching for the fact that

243

he had missed this wonderful intelligent mother-love and had to make do with the soldierly affection of his father and the whiskery doting of some crusty ancient nanny. She would have to tell Jenefer about meeting Richard. But now wasn't the time.

In the coach house Hubert was scraping away at a section of the wall with a sharp knife. She caught his arm. 'What are you doing, Hubert? You're spoiling it.'

He shrugged her arm away. 'The sword is not quite right, maid, the blade not sheer. It must be redone.'

Something dawned on her. 'Are you frightened to finish it, Hubert, frightened that it is all done?'

He turned his fine sparkling eyes towards her and nodded. 'When it is done, all is done,' he said.

In the next week there was quite a tussle between Patrick and Esther as to just who was Kate's friend. Patrick lingered in the shop when he should have been on his rounds, just to talk to the visitor. Some days Esther got dressed and actually came into the shop chatting gaily to Kate as she worked.

Kate's professional skills in reading people's needs and playing up to them were applied to some effect with Patrick's highly strung wife. Kate asked Esther's advice about curtains for the little house she was renting, number twelve Mainstreet. She asked Esther which novels she recommended and read them, so they could talk about the vagaries of the hero and heroine in Esther's highly developed private fantasy world. Then Kate would entrance Esther by weaving romanticised versions of her own adventures. Esther thrilled to the descriptions of Paris and Berlin, even Rio de Janeiro. 'You should write them down!' said Esther. 'That's as good as anything I've read.'

'I can't write them down,' said Kate. 'The only thing I can write down are sums. You're the one who knows all about books. I bet you could write them yourself.'

'I know I can write, I was the best at Composition in school. But I've never been anywhere further than Gateshead and this dratted little village!' wailed Esther. Never done anything.'

Kate leaned down from her ladder and tapped Esther lightly on the temple. 'What's a person's imagination for? It's all in there. That head is heaving with stories. Haven't I been listening to them for days? And there's travel manuals and encyclopaedias to check things up in.' She reached behind her to a high shelf and took down a dusty pack of six lined exercise books. 'You write them, Esther. It'll give you a change when you're resting, doing a bit of writing instead of all that reading.'

Esther brushed off the dust with her fingertips. 'Do you think so?' she said dubiously.

244

'Have a go, Esther. You've nothing to lose.' Kate beamed down at her protegée with an almost professional satisfaction. 'And I'll be your first reader.'

Finn had had to set out early on her delivery round to catch the daylight. On her return trip she found herself with an empty basket, at the top of the slope which led down to High Bank Farm. On impulse she freewheeled down the bank, parked her bike and knocked on the door.

Mary Fenwick opened the door, looked at her, smiled slightly and let her in. Roddy and Anthony whooped when they saw her and started talking at once about the farm and the fact that George the lamb had had to go to market and . . .

'Ye'll have a cup of tea, Finn?' said Mary, lifting the black kettle from the hob.

Finn nodded and eased herself into a chair. 'It's bitter out there.'

'Mrs Scargill down the dale said you'd been off away in France somewhere,' said Mary.

'Yes, in the south, near Monte Carlo.'

'The Prince of Wales goes there, did yer see 'im?'

Finn shook her head. 'Maybe caught sight of some of his cronies, though.'

'Fancy that.' Mary put a cup of tea in Finn's hand. 'Nice ter see yer here, love. Our Roddy's missed yer. Be sure ter come again. Ah'm needin' a new flue brush. Could yer put one on the bike next time yer come up here?'

Finn nodded. 'How's Tot, Mary?' she said carefully.

Mary shrugged. 'Usual. Though he was moanin' about how unreliable that Priorton grocer was, an' said he was sick of our Roddy asking after you.'

Finn nodded. 'Right, Mary.'

'I'm here to help you with the curtains. Esther said to come.' Patrick stood uneasily inside the door of number twelve Mainstreet, his toolbox in his hand.

Kate smiled broadly. He smelled her perfume as she leaned past him and closed the door. 'Isn't that kind? I've put up the nets, see? But the poles need some screws, perhaps I can show you . . .'

She climbed the stepladder and he was confronted by the slim curve of calf and ankle covered with fine silk. He swayed slightly, feeling drunk.

'Here, see? I think it needs two screws in here and two screws across there on the other side.' She raised her arm and her pretty blue pinafore pulled hard against her full breast.

Starting to sweat, Patrick took out his screwdriver and his screwbox.

He stood very clear of her as she came down the steps. Then he climbed up.

'I'll hold the ladders for you, Patrick. They're the slightest bit rickety. I got them from that second-hand shop in Priorton, you know.' She looked up at him as he fumbled with his screwdriver. 'You will be sure to screw it in tight, won't you? I can't have my curtains falling down on me. They're nice thick velvet, to keep out the cold.' She paused. 'And those prying eyes.'

Then she stood back and he did a very efficient job on each window, helping her to hang the curtains after he had secured the rails.

After the job was completed he lifted the stepladders into the back scullery. She was still close behind him. 'Thank you, Patrick,' she said. Then she took his hand. 'You know what's happened here, do you Patrick?'

With a great effort of will he let his hand lie there, not snatching it away, nor turning it and grabbing her till it hurt. He shook his head. 'We put up some curtains?'

She squeezed his hand. 'Not that. Of course you know.'

'Esther—'

'Will be quite happy. Have you seen her happier?'

He shook his head, his hand now clasping hers. He moved in towards her, she pushed him away and led through again to the front room. 'Will you go to The Eagle tonight?'

He nodded his head. 'A couple of hours, if our Finn can spell me. I didn't half miss it when she was away.'

She put his tool kit in his hands. 'Go there for an hour,' she touched his forearm. 'Then here for an hour. We could have some tea. I'll pull the scullery bolt.'

For the rest of the day he worked away in a dream. He gave the wrong change, he entered the wrong things into the tick book. He made Esther two cups of tea in succession. She looked up from her exercise book in some amusement. 'You brought me one ten minutes ago. Did you forget?' Then her head went down and she continued to scribble away.

Finn, preoccupied herself now with thoughts of seeing Michael at the end of the week, did not take this in at first. But when he started to weigh up twelve ounces of sugar into one pound bags she tackled him. 'What's up, Dad? You're like a man out to sea today.'

He shook his head. 'Don't know, Finn, maybe I'm out of sorts.'

It was Finn's turn to shake her head. 'You've never looked better, Dad.'

It was true. There was a spring in his step and often a smile on his face, even when you weren't looking at him. It was true of her mother too. Finn knew somehow it was all down to Kate. She called at Number twelve on her way out, and challenged her with it. 'It must be you. I've never seen them like it.'

Kate grinned at her. '*Ménage à Trois?* Are you saying it's a good thing, or a bad thing? Poor souls locked in there together twenty-four hours a day. Recipe for disaster, I'd say. No wonder your poor ma gets the vapours, and your pa trudges around like Atlas with the world on his shoulders.'

'No, I'm not saying it's a bad thing. Just a pity they can't . . . be like that . . . on their own.'

Kate hugged her. 'Such a puritan.' She turned her round to face the cosy room. 'Now then, what do you think of my little nest? My recovery room. My recuperation ward.'

Finn talked to Jenefer about meeting Michael. 'I want to meet him. He shouldn't come out to nothing, to nobody. None of them should.'

'What do Mrs Clelland and Emily Punchard think?'

'Emily'll do what their Tom says. But I don't know about Jonty's wife.'

'Write a note. Ask her.'

The answer came by first post the next day in a beautiful looping hand.

Dear Finnuola,
    Of course I'll be there for Jonty. I'm going for the first train from Priorton. I'm not sure what time they'll come out but I want to be there. Come with me if you will. No matter what they say, they will welcome our faces.
    Yours faithfully, Susanah Clelland.

Finn breathed out.

'And who's been writing to you?' Patrick looked up from the floor where he was noting the sizes of his remaining stock of boots.

'Susanah Clelland.'

'The schoolteacher's wife? They say in Priorton his school job's gone, of course, him being in prison.'

'They're coming out on Friday. I'm going to meet Michael with Mrs Clelland.'

He looked up at the ceiling. 'Your mother won't like that.'

'I'm sorry, but that doesn't matter.' She paused. 'She seems pretty content with herself these days.'

'Kate knows how to handle her. She's got her on writing these stories. Faraway places an' all that. Lot of nonsense, of course, scribbling away up there. But it seems to keep her mind off things.'

247

He smiled into the heel of a boot, then wrote down the size.

'Kate seems to cheer you up, too,' ventured Finn.

He beamed up at her. He was pretty content himself. 'She is a great help. I bless the day you brought her, Finn.'

Perhaps Kate MacMahon was handling *him*, but he didn't care. Two evenings now, he had slipped in through the scullery of Number twelve and shared tea and other greater delights with Kate MacMahon. He felt whole for the first time in years. He tried to think in his mind that it was wrong, but he couldn't. It felt so right.

'Anyway, can you spare me to go to Jenefer's? I want to tell her about Mrs Clelland's letter. Maybe the twins and Smiler would like to meet Michael.'

On her way along the street, she tried to picture Michael's face, but couldn't. Richard Morgan Evans' face rose before her. Then, suddenly, that of Daniel Marchant, in the flesh, just outside Plush Folly. 'Oh!'

He held her elbow to steady her. 'Ah, the lovely Finn Montague.'

She wrenched her arm away. 'Leave me alone.'

He chuckled. 'The innocent village girl now, are we? Not quite the sophistication of the demimonde in which we last met.'

She looked up and down the empty street. 'You want nothing here.'

'Oh yes I do. I've just delivered a letter from my London solicitor demanding apologies from that insane pair who live here, or I will bring a civil case of assault against them.'

'You'll gain nothing from that.'

Daniel was short of funds after his trip abroad, and was rather pleased with this wheeze, suggested by a recent escapade of a London acquaintance who had screwed a hundred pounds out of some old Jew who, on being told to clear off the pavement, had attacked him with his walking stick.

He laughed shortly. 'I'll make them squirm.'

'You'll never do that. Only worms squirm. You must have been squirming all your life.'

He took her arm then, and she brought back her other arm and delivered a great slap on his cheek. 'Get off me,' she snarled.

He dropped his hand to rub his cheek and she turned and walked through the half-open door of Plush Folly and slammed it behind her.

Jenefer was in the hall. 'Bravo! I was watching from the window, and would have come out with my poker, but thought you dealt with it perfectly well yourself. Best that way. Now wipe that little twerp out of your head.'

Which is exactly what Finn did. By the time she was in the kitchen telling Jenefer about Susanah Clelland's letter she had forgotten her encounter with Daniel Marchant, leaving space in her head for her to worry about Michael, and meeting him on Friday.

24

The Mob

In the end Finn left the twins and Smiler at Plush Folly, and went on her own with Susanah Clelland to meet Michael, Tom and Jonty Clelland out of prison.

She washed her hair the night before with some of Kate MacMahon's French shampoo. Then, as she set out, she filled her pockets with chocolates and sweets from the shop. On her way to the station she met Emily Punchard who handed her a parcel. 'It's a muffler for our Tom,' she said. 'An' one each for the other lads too. They'll be nithered, comin' out of that place on an October mornin'.'

Susanah Clelland, looking very striking with a deep red hat just perched on her upswept dark hair, was silent on the train. As they alighted from the train and set out in the heavy mist to walk down the hill, and on through the town to the prison, Finn ventured, 'I don't know about you, Mrs Clelland, but I'm dead scared of all this.'

Susanah kept up her pace. 'It'll be nothing to what they felt when they were coming down here first time. To go into that dark place.'

Finn, chastened, walked on in silence. Then Susanah put her arm through that of the younger woman. 'Don't mind me, pet. I was just thinking my Jonty's getting too old for this kind of thing. It's not the first time I've met him out of prison, but I hope it'll be the last.'

'He's been in prison before?'

Susanah nodded. 'In the Great War for being a pacifist. And in the General Strike for being in the way. The police called it obstruction.'

'Cares a lot about things, your husband. He does things, doesn't he? Marks himself out.'

'That's what those boys're doing too. Someone has to.' Susanah puffed a bit on the hill. 'Jonty's always done it. When we were very young I thought he was pompous. But I grew to respect him and love him for his ideals. A man of principle, Jonty.' She sighed. 'I

249

can't wait to see him. The house is so empty without him, even with our David in and out.'

Outside the prison, they waited for an hour sheltering in a doorway from the invasive drizzle of the October morning. Then the sun started to burn off the mist and shone out at last, providing a measured degree of warmth.

After another long thirty minutes the small door set in the great door opened, to disgorge a wretched-looking red-headed man and a smaller white-faced man, both hunched into inadequate coats, both clutching paper parcels.

The door clanged shut behind them.

Susanah stepped in front of the smaller man as he came towards them. 'Excuse me. Are there others coming out, mister? Do you know Jonty Clelland, Michael O'Toole?'

The man shook his head. 'There's other fellers in there, missis. Dinnet knaa whey they wor.' He pulled up his frayed collar and pushed his way past her.

Susanah stepped back into the doorway with Finn. 'They'll be in the next lot, maybe, pet.' She took Finn's hand and started to rub it. 'You're perished, girl. It's too cold out here for you to wait. Maybe we can find a café.' She looked around.

Finn shook her head. 'If it's not too cold for you, Mrs Clelland, it's not too cold for me.'

There was a grinding noise: the interior door opened again and three more shrunken figures stepped through. Susanah cried out and ran across the cobbles, to be swept into the arms of her husband who hugged her tightly. Jonty was more stooped than ever. His curly hair, under its battered black trilby, was now pure white.

Finn looked from one of the remaining figures to the other. Tom Farrell's head was bristly under his cap. Michael looked ten years older, his face deadly white, with deep lines scoring his cheeks. The men brought with them from inside the jail the rank smell of old sweat and urine. Finn wanted to rush into Michael's arms, as Susanah had run to Jonty, but Michael's arms were down at his sides and he looked anything but pleased to see her.

'There was no reason for you to come,' muttered Michael to Finn, making no move towards her.

She scrabbled away at the parcel in her arms. 'I had to come. Emily Punchard sent mufflers for all of you.' She lifted a long green scarf and held it towards him in a defensive gesture. He took it from her and wound it round his neck.

Tom Farrell took another scarf from her pile. At least he was smiling slightly. 'Canny woman, my Aunt Emily.' He held it up to the light. 'Drops a stitch here and there, but her heart's in the right place. Here, Jonty, this'll match your eyes.' He threw it at the older

250

man. There were weak smiles all round at this, and the atmosphere lightened. Susanah wound the scarf twice round Jonty's neck and tied it neatly at the front.

'Come on, lads and lasses,' said Tom grabbing the last scarf and throwing it around his own neck. 'We're out of that place now. Feller in there told us the best place for a good cup of tea around here is the café under the viaduct. A good cup of tea. That's what I need.'

'And a pie,' said Michael with feeling. 'I really fancy a pork pie.'

Finn found herself between Michael and Tom, walking along the pavement behind Jonty and Susanah, who were closely entwined.

It was Tom who first spoke to Finn. 'You're looking very well, Miss Montague.'

'My name's Finn, you know that. And thank you.'

'Seems you've been away on holiday, like.'

She felt uncomfortable. 'Yes. My uncle sent me some money. It had to go on a holiday. I know it seems—'

He shrugged. 'Choices. We all have choices. Once heard Leonora Scorton – Michael'd tell you about her, that MP woman – once heard her take on a heckler who told her her frocks were too posh. Betrayer of the working classes, he said. She said it's easy to be holier-than-thou about the trivial choices we make. It's the big choices where we may be judged. I'd think you'd stand up and be counted in the big choices, Miss . . . Finn.'

Praise indeed. Finn relaxed, glancing out of the corner of her eye at Michael, who suddenly spoke. 'A swim! Wouldn't I give me eyeteeth for a swim?'

Tom started to run towards the bridge, the first of two which spanned the looping river. 'No sooner said than done, old lad. There's the good old River Wear down there, just waiting to welcome us to her bosom.'

'You can't, Michael,' said Finn, 'You'll freeze. You've got no towel, no top coat . . .'

But Michael was away after his friend.

Finn and Susanah and Jonty stood on the bridge and watched as the two young men emerged from under the bridge with just their drawers on. They gasped with shock as they slipped into the blackish water and started swimming, turning somersaults in the water, racing each other from one bank to the other, laughing and shouting like children.

As the minutes went by the three on the bridge stamped to keep warm, shouting down to the boys to get out, get out. Finally the boys were persuaded to come back up the steps. Now their prison pallor was scrubbed off, their cheeks rosy with the cold, their hair wet and slicked back. The sodden scarfs, having done service as towels, were clutched in their hands, held away from their bodies.

'That's better,' said Michael, starting to shiver, his teeth chattering. 'The scum of that place swilled off. Now where can we get tea?'

'Here, have a toffee to be going on with.' Finn handed round the sweets from her pocket and they all set out for the café under the viaduct.

Daniel Marchant had obtained leave from college on the pretext that he had to return home on the anniversary of his mother's death. This permitted him his brief sojourn in the South of France to act as lieutenant for his uncle at the meeting of the international group. Then had come the irresistible opportunity for the short trip into Germany and the chance of meeting Herr Hitler. In the event, only his uncle and two others were chosen for that privilege. But he heard the tales on their return to the hotel so at least he could relish the flavour of the occasion.

On his return to the vicarage there had been letters waiting for him. One was from his tutor, the mentor of the group he played around with at Cambridge. Somehow, word of Daniel's true quest must have got back to them. The order in the fine cramped writing and the elegant syntax belied the violence of the content. The writer berated him as a traitor, a double-dealer, a spy, and told him to be very, very careful. The second letter in the same post was a rough brown envelope which contained a torn section of the deaths column from *The Times*. Superimposed on the black print in thick black crayon, was a skull and crossbones.

The third letter was an official missive from the university informing him of his rustication due to a combination of unpaid bills, the 'borrowing' of money without permission from another man on his staircase, undone work, and finally taking extended leave without proper notice to his college authorities. He sniffed. It was all trumped up, of course. If they applied those criteria across the board the place would be half empty.

On his first afternoon back he and his father made their silent annual journey to the hidden place where his mother's grave was marked simply by her name on a plain slab of stone. At dinner they drank wine sent across by his uncle, and Daniel reported back to his father about his recent trip, and the excitement of being on the edge of such a powerful circle.

His father smiled thinly, hiding the cataclysm of betrayal when it dawned on him what had happened. 'I feel I hear the sound of a changing tune here. The resounding chime of patriotism rather than the death knell of red flags flying?'

Daniel shrugged. 'True colours, father. I did all that, talked like that, because Uncle thought it useful for me to appear to be part of that mob. Good for intelligence. Never know when it might be useful.'

Hildebrand touched his dry lips with his napkin. 'Even here, at this table? Is this house such a nest of Bolsheviks?'

Daniel shrugged again. 'What they taught me was that I must be consistent. Must live it.'

'But now, the deception is over, even the deception of your father?'

Better not to tell the old boy about the rustication. 'They say I might be more useful in the mainstream. I'm to assist Sir Denis Consadine in his political campaigns, perhaps later be a candidate myself.' He speared a particularly large lump of beef on to his plate.

After dinner Hildebrand had Mrs Fosdick bring in the port 'in celebration of my son returning.' Whether it was to New Morven or to the ideological fold, was unclear.

Hildebrand sipped away at his glass, but Daniel filled his twice, talking excitedly about a new order of things. How in Germany they were at last putting into practice great plans to revitalise the nation, how they were clearing out the dullards and the troublemakers. There was so much energy there. Potency.

Hildebrand nodded, letting his sons words flow over him, quietly boiling up at the thought that his brother and his son had considered him too low, too unimportant to share their exciting secret.

Then they were both silent, staring at the flickering flames of the falling fire. Daniel stood up and poured himself another generous port. As he put back the stopper he looked across at his father.

'Why did she do it, Father?'

Hildebrand roused himself. 'Who?'

'She. Your wife. My mother. That stupid woman.'

Hildebrand nodded slowly. 'She was a very stupid woman. You're right. But I kept you from her, from the moment you were born, so you were safe. Do you see? They deceived me, you know, your mother and that mother of hers. Just as you have, in these months. I hate to be deceived. They did not inform me about it, your mother and that mother of hers. The doctor called it "stigmata of degeneration". It turned out that there was an aunt in an institution, and the grandmother, who was a Jewess, did the most savagely eccentric things. But I heard all this afterwards. People were kind enough to tell me, then.'

'What?' said Daniel.

'I wasn't told about all this until after your poor benighted mother died. The family doctor told me.'

'No . . . no, not that. Did you say her grandmother was a . . . Jewess?' Daniel's eyes were wide at the horror of it.

Hildebrand nodded, a slight glimmer of satisfaction in his eyes at

253

putting someone properly in his place. It was hard to stop the habit of a lifetime even if your victim happened to be your own son. He stood up. 'Now, Daniel, I have to work on Sunday's sermon. We're coming up to All-Hallow's Eve and I am doing a meditation on witches. Appropriate, in the context of our discussion, I think.'

Daniel got to his feet. His father's heavy skirts swished against him as he swept out.

Richard Morgan Evens peered out into the swiftly passing country-side, excited despite himself.

'It must be your first time north?' The woman opposite was looking up from her writing. She had been scribbling in a big foolscap ledger all the long weary way from London. The train was just drawing out of Doncaster Station and the two of them were finally alone in the carriage.

Richard coughed. 'I'm up here to look up . . . to find . . . a friend. I'm not quite sure where she lives. How did you know I'd never been up here?'

'I'm up and down this route all the time. You can tell the newcomers. Can't quite believe their eyes. They look at it like scientists in a rat laboratory.' Her voice, for such a small woman, was unusually deep and had a bell-like resonance. 'What do you see when you look out there?'

He looked again. 'I see hills. And houses. Churches in the distance. Factories. Warehouses. Roads. Collieries.'

'You see God's country. The engine at the very heart of the industrial revolution. The very crucible of the historic wealth and worldwide significance of Britain.'

He nodded, uncertain whether he could contribute to such rhetoric.

'You also see the shame of Britain. Neglect. Decay, Despair. Machines lying idle, shipyards still. Hungry children, starving women, men who've not worked for years . . .' She stopped, then smiled, the smile transforming her face from cross, tired anonymity into that of an attractive woman in young middle age. 'I'm preach-ing again. Habit of mine. But I hope you see more than the surface when you look out of that window. Look into the people's lives and consider how far you're responsible, and what you may do . . .'

Richard smote one hand against the other. 'Ha! I know who you are! Leonora Scorton, MP. You had your picture in last week's papers.'

She picked up her fountain pen again. 'You have the advantage over me, then.'

He put out his hand. 'Richard Morgan Evans.'

She shook his hand and then retrieved her pen. 'And what do you do in this world, Richard Morgan Evans?'

He coloured. 'Nothing at present. I'm just out of the army. But you're a pacifist, you won't like that.'

She frowned at him. 'No relative to that General Morgan Evans, I hope? They say he met Hitler last week. General Morgan Evans, the hero of all heroes mixed up with that pack of fascists.'

'He's my father, yes, but . . .'

She contemplated her hand. 'I'd not have shook your hand, had I known.'

Richard leaned forward. 'No, no. I've listened to them, I admit. I'm just back from a trip to Germany with them.' He looked her straight in the eye. 'I couldn't believe what I saw. I discover that I profoundly disagree with my father and his friends, but then I would probably disagree with you and your communist friends.'

She screwed on the top of her fountain pen and closed her foolscap book. 'So. Which part of Germany were you in? I was in Saarbrücken early this year . . .'

Michael would not come to Plush Folly with Finn, insisting that he would stay over at Emily Punchard's with Tom, to get his bearings. Leonora Scorton was in the area, talking to branches of the Unemployed Workers Union. Tom had promised Miss Scorton from prison that he would go to one of her meetings, and Michael thought he would tag along too.

Finn felt as though she were floundering up to her waist in muddy water. Not by word or touch had Michael O'Toole shown any recognition that she was there for him. She enjoyed more eye contact and more banter with Tom Farrell than with Michael.

'But the twins and Smiler, Michael. They'll be watching for you.'

'Send 'm across to Emily's. It's only a few streets away. I want nothing there at Plush Folly. No more do my sisters and brother, if truth be told.'

'Well,' she said frostily,' Jenefer Loumis's taken very good care of them. They're plump and bonny . . .'

'I'm sure they are. But they're not suckling pigs, you know. Human beings, that's what they are.' Now he did look at her, with the bland eyes of a stranger. 'I'm not saying they should stay at Emily's too, Finn. Just come across to say hello.'

She walked slowly on to Plush Folly, by herself. Once there, she sent the disappointed twins and Smiler off to Emily Punchard's and, refusing Jenefer's offer of tea, went straight back to the shop. There, a welcome scene of conviviality and laughter greeted her. Her mother, fully dressed, was behind the counter, handing up tins of peas to Kate MacMahon who was standing on the high stepladder. Patrick was lounging against the counter chatting to them both.

255

The laughter faded as they looked across at her. 'How was it, Finn?' said Kate.

'It must have been horrible,' said Esther.

'Are you all right, Finn?' asked Patrick.

'It was horrible, and I'm all right. The men looked pretty dreadful. Michael and Tom are across at Emily's. And we left Jonty Clelland with his wife in Priorton. He looked ill. On his last legs.'

'Well,' said Esther with unusual heartiness, 'we can cope here, if you want to go across there.'

Finn exchanged glances with Kate, amused in spite of herself. 'No. I think I'll go and get changed and give you a hand.' She glanced at Patrick. 'I thought you would be out on your rounds.'

'We keep telling him that, don't we, Kate?' said Esther.

Kate laughed. 'So we do. But we just can't get rid of him no matter how hard we try.'

Hildebrand's vengeful routing of his son had whetted his appetite and he was very pleased on the Sunday before Halloween at the turn-out in church. Through the years he had noted that in this benighted village there was a ridiculous amount of activity before Halloween and Guy Fawkes Night. In the middle of October the people, men as well as children started gathering kindling for two great bonfires at the north and the south ends of the village. There were masked callers at the vicarage, dancers with blackened faces, clothes backside first. People went by him without their customary doffing of caps or touching of forelocks.

Under normal circumstances anarchy was just a hairs-breadth below the surface in this village. But this was very efficiently kept in check by the sergeant and the faithful band of magistrates like his own brother. It had to be admitted that anarchy was also kept in check by the dulling effect of hunger and the laziness induced by years without work.

However, at this time of year, automatic respect of one's betters was thrown to the winds, and Hildebrand found the necessity to meet more than one insolent or critical gaze.

As if to make up for this, the church was always full on the Sunday before Halloween, and this year proved to be like the others. So it was with gusto that the vicar set about his sermon on innocents inadvertently harnessing the powers of darkness.

'Solutions to problems, pills and potions may be offered with soft words, kind glances. If they cure, then it is said they "must" be good. I say to you, no! In the hands of evil all is evil. Better to die than to live by an evil act. I say to you, beware witches, harry them, get them gone. Take the innocents out of their hands. And then they and we will be safe. And the balm of the virtuous way, the way

256

of Jesus Christ, may enter our lives, so that our pain is reflected and transformed by His on the cross.' He raised his voice so it echoed round the old church. '. . . Our hunger alleviated by His hunger for our sin . . . this to be suffered by Him so we may all enter the Kingdom of God.' His voice dropped now. 'I say harry the witches, eschew the demons on this devil's eve and enjoy the glory and forgiveness of the risen Christ.'

He stopped and saw with satisfaction the eyes turned towards him. He brought down his hand on the lectern. 'There are those here now in New Morven who think they're above our admonition, above God's law. So we are driven to act, to rout out those who use the powers of darkness against the innocents. We must act! I will take the first step myself, I know, with your support.'

Then he swept down the aisle and out of the church. The congregation surged around him, muttering with agreement, bubbling with excitement. A few of them wondered where they were going.

As the vicar, with patches of bright red on his pale cheeks, passed Stacy Smith, Stacy leaned and whispered into Bella's ear. 'Man's as mad as a hatter.' Then he and Bella, always game for a bit of entertainment, followed the crowd.

At Montague's shop, Bella peeled off to knock on the side door and tell Finn Montague that the vicar was on the warpath about her friend Mrs Loumis again and she'd better get down there double-quick.

Finn jumped up, followed by Kate, scenting a bit of excitement on a dull Sunday afternoon. Finn dispatched Kate to Plush Folly to hold the fort. At Emily Punchard's Michael answered the door and opened it wide for her to come in. He was looking better, much brighter than the last time she had seen him on the day he came out of prison.

He sat her by the fire. 'Here, get your breath back,' he said.

Tom looked up from the kitchen table where he was hand-printing posters advertising Leonora Scorton, MP, giving a talk on International Socialism in Bracks Hill Memorial Institute. The clash of crockery came from the scullery, where Emily was washing the pots.

'It's the twins, Michael, them and Smiler. According to Bella Smith the vicar's storming across to Plush Folly, preparing to wrest them from Jenefer's grasp, put them in a Home. He tried it before but she fended him off with a poker. Now he has a crowd with him. Sanctimonious lot. I'd have gone there to help, but thought even so the vicar might be able to take your family from Jenefer. But they couldn't take them from you, could they?'

Michael reached for his cap.

257

Tom stood up. 'I'll come with you.'

Michael shook his head. 'I'll do it on me own. Me and Finn here, anyway. You get on with your posters.' He leaned across, picked up a poster from the pile and gave it to Finn as she stood up. 'Mebbe you could put that up in your shop.'

'Yes, yes, of course I can,' she said hurriedly. 'Now come on, or you'll lose your family.'

'No fear of that,' he said quietly. 'I'm coming.'

They ran through the streets and took a short cut across a field to the back door of Plush Folly, where Kate was waiting. 'No one came this way,' said Kate, 'but there's a lot of shouting and calling out the front. The boy Smiler came, so I sent him into the cottage and told him to shut the door.'

'Go in there, hang on to him, Kate,' said Finn. 'Michael and me'll get the girls over here. They have to be a family, then they can't take them.'

Hildebrand had led the way to Plush Folly himself, his son Daniel at his shoulder. The crowd eddied and flowed around him like some stinking insalubrious river. Or like hunting dogs scenting a kill.

Inside, unaware of the approaching mob, Hubert and Jenefer were sitting on the sofa, heads back, half asleep, lulled by the chirruping of the twins as they played snakes and ladders on the floor. The gramophone was playing some piano jazz. It took some time for the shouting and noise outside to penetrate this cosy Sunday afternoon island. Then a great crash made them all jump and the twins were showered with glass as a pavement boulder landed neatly on their snakes and ladders board.

Jenefer leaped up, pulled the girls to the back of the room and stood with them by the door, out of range. Hubert let out a great bellow and leaped across to the shattered window. He pulled up the sash of the broken window and leaned out. 'Are you at it again, holy man?' he shouted. 'Harrying women and children?' "In peace there's nothing so becomes a man As modest stillness and humility." So where's your stillness, where's your humility, holy man?'

Hildebrand adjusted his sleeves and folded his arms across his chest. 'The casting of the stone is regrettable but the good people here in New Morven are angry. Angry that something evil, something despicable is going on here.'

There were jeers and cheers in the crowd around him.

'We come to tell you to give up the children. There are places for them at Carhoe Orphanage, a respectable institution.'

There were cries of 'Yes, Yes!'

'And we come to tell you that we have no space for you in this community. You are not welcome.'

258

Hubert started throwing things at the vicar then, heaving chairs and stools, books, boxes, even ornaments, out of the window. Jenefer clung on to the twins who were now crying. She started sobbing herself when Hubert picked up his beloved gramophone and this sailed out of the window, dropping with a clanking crunch at the feet of the vicar.

'Hubert stop!' Finn was there in the room with them, hanging on to his arm, hiding his hand, which was dripping with blood where he had ripped it on the window. She pulled him to the back of the room, then turned to Michael, who now had his arms round Jenefer and the twins. 'You take Toots and Nancy across to Alan Newton's cottage, Michael. Kate's got Smiler in there now. It's all set up for you. They can't take them from Jenefer if she hasn't got them.'

Michael nodded. 'Right. Come on, you two.'

As they turned and went, Hubert and Jenefer fell into each other's arms.

Finn turned back into the room. The shouting outside the window had reduced now to a rumble. She went across and leaned out of the window. 'What was it you wanted, Mr Marchant?' She avoided looking at Daniel who was standing beside his father, his eyes glittering.

'I intend to rescue the children from this house, miss,' he said grimly.

She looked behind her. 'Children? There are no children in here. Perhaps you mean the children of Michael O'Toole's family. Well, they are back with their brother now. So you have no need to worry.'

'We need to search the house,' said Daniel shrilly. He had been party to such an exercise on his German visit. It had its own satisfactions.

Finn shook her head. 'Mr and Mrs Loumis are too distressed by this attack to allow you or your father in their home.' She raised her eyes to the back of the crowd. 'But perhaps Mr and Mrs Stacy Smith may be your proxy?'

Hildebrand shrugged.

Stacy shouldered his way to the front of the crowd with Bella waddling in his wake. 'Look carefully,' growled Hildebrand.

'Right, Vicar,' said Stacy humbly. 'You can be sure I will.' This should be worth sixpence from the charity box, at least. Maybe even a shilling.

In five minutes they were back. 'Miss Montague took me right through, Vicar, and there were nee bairns. Not sight nor sound of them. Then out the back to old Alan Newton's cottage an' there they are, all three of them, set up nice an' snug with their big brother.'

259

There was a ripple of disappointment in the crowd. Hildebrand coughed. 'Well. So much less on the parish in that case.' He raised his eyes to Finn, who was still standing in the shattered window. 'In that case perhaps you will convey to Mrs Loumis the fact that there is nothing to keep her and her . . . husband in New Morven any longer. Nothing at all. We wish her to go.' He turned and stalked away.

With that the crowd dispersed, the younger ones to spend the rest of the daylight hours scavenging around in the fields and woods for wood for the two rival bonfires north and south of the village.

Michael, Toots and Nancy came back into the house, Kate in tow. Toots announced that Smiler had gone off to help with the north end bonfire. Kate said she would return to Patrick and Esther, to fill them in about what had happened. The strain was showing on Kate's face. 'It's a terrible thing to happen in a little place like this. Frightening people half to death. I've seen nothing like it. And respectable people doing it, not a mob. Respectable people in their Sunday clothes.' She turned and went, closing the door quietly behind her.

Nancy and Toots raced across to Jenefer and Hubert, touching them on their arms and shoulders, and asking if they were all right. Hubert stood still as a stone, but Jenefer hugged them and said of course they were all right and they were not to worry.

Michael came up behind Finn, who was still at the window watching the stragglers leave the road outside. 'Bravo,' he said. He put a hand on her arm and the scald of it heated her whole body. 'Sure, you're a quick-thinkin' girl. Good of you to rake me out, me being such a sourpuss. The prison does things to you, Finn. Hard things.'

She turned towards him. 'You'll stay with them now, in Alan Newton's cottage?'

He nodded. 'To be honest it was a bit crowded down at Emily's. An' I got the slightest bit bored by the litany of virtues of the musical Stanley. God rest his soul, though.' His hand moved over her arm. 'No, I should be here with those three. It's a nice wee place. Isn't that the place where the sleepin' loft smells of apples?' She blushed a fiery red. He pulled her round to look her in the eye, adding under his breath. 'I don't forget, you know. It's all there for us. In time.' He turned to the girls. 'Come on away now, girls, and leave poor Mrs Loumis in peace. You can help me get me things from Emily's, an' show me where I can sleep.'

He walked across and, rather awkwardly, shook both Jenefer and Hubert by the hand. 'Words can't thank you enough. I can't repay but I'll never forget. You can be sure of that.'

The three of them left, the twins clinging to his arms. He popped his head back round the door. 'You couldn't get to that Leonora Scorton meeting on Wednesday, could you, Finn?'

Finn nodded slightly and he vanished. She turned her attention to Hubert and Jenefer, who were now collapsed on the sofa. Hubert was staring unseeing in front of him and Jenefer was sobbing her heart out. Finn went and sat down beside her and clasped her hand tightly. She knew that it had not all ended yet. Not at all.

25

The Meeting

Daniel refused the offer of his uncle's driver to return him to the
vicarage, and set out to walk. The sky was bright and the yellow
leaves, which still clung to the black branches, fluttered and rustled
in the fresh wind. Even so, hunting had been no more than a good
hard ride this morning. The foxes, inconveniently, seemed to have
gone to ground.

This had put Daniel's Uncle Oliver in a savage ill humour, leading
him to threaten to sack his groom, his gamekeepers – the whole of
his outdoor staff – on the spot. And he'd had the gall to criticise
Daniel for being gloomy. A rare criticism from his doting uncle.
'Don't say you're takin' after that joyless brother of mine, Daniel. I
have to tell you, the old boy's as much company as a half-dead
cockroach.'

'I say, Uncle . . .'

His uncle had held up a hand. 'I don't say your father don't have
virtues, Daniel. He's an upright feller but he's not the most cheering
of fellows on any day.'

This cast Daniel into even deeper melancholy, leading him to
refuse his uncle's offer of lunch, so as to spare Sir Oliver the
boredom of eating with a cockroach. This comment restored Sir
Oliver's good humour, bringing forth a shout of laughter. Then the
hearty alacrity with which his uncle accepted his refusal simply
added to Daniel's gloom.

Walking south into the village, he came upon a group of lads with
blackened faces hauling long boards in the direction of the north
end bonfire. He caught the last one by the scruff of his neck. 'What
thieving is this?' he said. 'Where did you get these boards?' The lad
looked up at him, wide-eyed and scared. His face was dirty and,
over the lower part, smeared with slaver.

'What, mister?'

Daniel clouted the boy across the head. The boy squealed, then
started to cry. The other lads dropped their boards, then the

smallest one, better dressed than the rest, approached Daniel face on. Like the others his face had been blackened with coal dust or cork. 'Sure there's no need to clout the feller, mister,' he said, grinning widely. He glanced back at the others who came up to join him. They stood in a circle round Daniel, just out of reach. 'The feller's done no harm. Us've done none either. Aren't the boards just ones from the old ironworks, an' hasn't that been empty twenty year?'

'You keep a civil tongue in your head, or I'll have the constable after you. Property is property.' They were staring at him now and very slowly started to circle round him, just out of arms' reach. He cracked his boot with his riding crop.

'Feller's done no harm, mister. Let him go. Let him go,' said the smiling one.

The others took up the chant. Whites of eyes were staring at him out of blackened faces. 'Let-him-go-let-him-go-let-him-go-let-him-go . . .'

'Stop!' He thrust the snivelling one out, away from him, to break the circle, flung him to the ground and started to run.

Smiler hauled the sniveller to his feet. 'You all right, charver?' he said.

Daniel stumbled on, slashing away at undergrowth with his crop. Through his tears he glanced around him. He was at the edge of the woodland. Even after the leaf-fall the sticks and branches made dense cover. He realised he was not ten steps from where his mother lay under her plain slab, on her unconsecrated plot.

Disturbing more undergrowth, he nearly fell over a small wooden cross nailed to a board. He leaned down and peered at the poker-burned lettering: 'Stanley Punchard you will delight in the music of the spheres.' Now that name seemed familiar but he couldn't quite remember why.

Slashing on, he found his way again to the little place with its iron rail. He looked at the name carefully carved in Gothic lettering. 'Harriet Marchant.' Not *beloved wife of* . . . *much loved mother of* . . . no *music of the spheres* for her.

Not even a proper graveyard, for his mother. Oh no! She put herself away from him in death, just as she did in life. He was the naughty boy because she'd not see him. Didn't she realise that? But he wasn't. Nothing wrong with him. They said he was very promising, but they didn't know, did they? About the mother who'd been mad and the great-grandmother who, unbelievably, had been one of the Chosen Race. And a father who was first cousin to a cockroach. Degenerate stock, they'd called it, when Daniel was in Germany. They had ways of dealing with it, and there'd been applause in the room. Daniel himself had applauded, but he wasn't safe, was he? The cockroach would use what he knew when it suited him. To get the upper hand. Cockroaches did. That was happening in Germany too. Disclosure. To cleanse the race. Didn't his mother see? Necessary for progress, so they said. It made sense to him.

Daniel climbed over the low rail, got down on his knees on the hard slab and lay down on it full length, his lips close to the crisp Gothic lettering. 'I'm tired, Mummy, really tired.'

Finn had to do battle with her mother to put the notice for Leonora Scorton's meeting in the shop window. 'We can't have that, Finnuola. I've read about her in the papers. They say she's red. A communist, like those monsters that killed the King's cousin, the Tsar Regicides.'

Finn shook her head. 'She's a socialist, mother. That's what she is.'

Tom Farrell had left some newspaper articles about Leonora Scorton in the shop, in case anyone was curious.

Kate was at the counter reading them. 'Sounds all right. She's for fair shares for all, says here. Work for all. The government making sure that happens.'

'Not just that!' said Esther triumphantly. 'Direct action. It says there one thing she talked about in that speech in Derby was "direct action"! Isn't that how that Michael O'Toole got himself thrown into prison?'

'They do it for what they believe in,' said Finn lamely.

'They'll plunge the country into chaos,' said Esther. She'd read that in the newspaper too.

'You put up notices about meetings at the Institute in our window,' said Finn stubbornly. 'And about the unemployed work-shops. This . . .'

'Oh, please yourself,' said Esther. 'I'm going upstairs. I'm not feeling so well.' She glanced at Kate, who, deep in the article, ignored her, then flounced out and clattered up the stairs.

Kate finished the article and looked up. 'Are you going to this meeting?'

Finn shrugged. 'Michael asked me to.'

'This woman looks interesting. Talks about fighting fascism, not treating it like a sickness that'll go away of its own accord. You know what fascism is, Finn?'

'Well, I . . .'

'It's bastards – pardon my French – it's bastards like Sir Denis Consadine and that gaggle of twerps he was fawning over in France.' She grinned. 'Well, are we going to this meeting or not, young Finn?'

★ ★ ★

265

Michael, having no money, walked along the river to the meeting at Bracks Hill. Tom had already gone first thing that morning to call on Jonty Clelland in Priorton, who was too ill to attend. Tom said he would try to persuade Susanah to come. He was relishing the thought of the meeting. At Jonty's urging, he'd a short correspondence with Miss Scorton from prison, to comment on one of her articles. Tom was dying to meet this woman. 'Carrying a torch for her already,' as Jonty told Susanah, with some satisfaction.

Michael himself was not quite so keen. Scorching his fingers on the raid on Banville House and ending up in prison had shaken him. But it was a fact that this woman had very sound ideas. And it was a fact that she was a Member of Parliament. She was nearer some kind of explanation about the state of things than most people, and nearer to those whose fault it was, and conversely those who had some idea of what the resolution might be.

In the meanwhile he could enjoy the walk by the black water on this crisp November morning. He could listen to the dense rustle and twitter of tree and bird, see the wide blue sweep of sky. An eddying breeze was throwing up leaves and, as he watched, seemed to be shooting handfuls of gathering birds into the sky. They rose into the blue like a shower of black flakes before settling again on their roosting tree.

Michael had been terrified by his experience in prison. The confinement, the dull hopelessness, the lack of real light and air had squashed the life out of him. Tom had used all of this to fuel his political anger and set light to his enthusiasm. Jonty had endured it with the gentle valour of a true pacifist. Michael had been full of fear, had felt reduced, diminished. He was only now getting back again to being human. It would be a long time before he would risk prison again. Even in this just cause.

On the river bank he passed the vicar's son, looking uncharacteristically dishevelled.

'Afternoon,' said Michael, without tipping his cap.

Daniel glared at him and ambled on, muttering away to himself about cockroaches and insolent thieves.

Michael arrived at Bracks Hill Memorial Institute an hour early. Even so, the hall was already half full. He found a seat halfway down and put his cap and a paper on the two seats close by. One was for Tom, and the other, he hoped, was for Finnuola Montague. The hall filled up and though he had to endure one or two black looks from people, he hung on to the seats he had saved.

By ten minutes to three the hall was jammed and a murmur rippled through the people as the platform began to fill with well-known people from the miners' and ironworkers' unions. One

266

or two of them wore three-piece suits, which belied the weather-beaten faces and broad capable hands of men who had once made their living from manual work.

Michael was just feeling guilty about the empty seats beside him when Tom came in. Beside him was a finely made woman with bobbed black shiny hair. Unlike all the other women in the hall she wore no hat. She was wearing a brown tweed jacket which had seen better days, and had a sheaf of papers under her arm. From her other side a tall young man with a high forehead, in well-cut clothes, surveyed the proceedings with interest.

Tom stopped beside Michael and the woman did too. Michael stood up. 'This is me marrah, Miss Scorton, Michael O'Toole. Michael, this is Miss Leonora Scorton, MP. I found her at Jonty's. Seems they're old marrahs themselves.'

Michael caught sight of Susanah Clelland standing placidly behind the group, waiting for them to walk on.

Leonora Scorton beamed at him, shaking his hand vigorously. 'Wonderful. Another one who bearded the old fascist lions in their dens. You'll be getting yourself elected to the Priorton Soviet before you've finished!' She patted the hand in hers. 'Don't look so startled, Michael O'Toole. Just my little joke.'

She insisted that Tom came to the platform with her, elaborating on some point about the old guard and the new guard sitting together. 'We need a young face up there.'

Michael sat down and gazed after them as they swept up the aisle and watched as Miss Scorton rearranged the whole platform so that she could sit with the tall young man and Susanah on one side of her and Tom on the other.

Michael grinned to himself. That Miss Scorton was a cunning one. She had a slave for life now. Perhaps not just one.

'Excuse me.' He looked up, a smile already on his face, and moved up to let Finn in. She had Kate MacMahon with her, that Lancashire woman who was so pally with her parents now.

Finn settled down to the speeches, happy to be there beside Michael, shoulder to shoulder, thigh to thigh. She strained to listen to the introductions in the packed hall. But when Miss Scorton stood up to speak there was no problem in hearing her bell-like, ringing tones as she talked about her recent visit to Germany, how the socialists there, despite being imprisoned and proscribed, were a force to be reckoned with. Now they were girding their loins for a last battle with the fascists, and she had confidence, yes, confidence, that with their brothers and sisters in the wider socialist movement they would win the day, that same movement which would defeat unemployment, assert the immorality of the gap between rich and sated, poor and starving, yes . . .

267

Kate nudged Finn. 'Look who's sitting with her. Just beside the dark older lady.'

Finn moved her head to get a better view, squeezed her eyes, and found herself gazing at the elegant figure of Richard Morgan Evans, head on one side, listening intently to Leonora Scorton. 'Richard!'

'What?' whispered Michael.

'Nothing, nothing.'

After that, the fine rhetoric went out over Finn's head, which was swimming now with thoughts of France, the bright sea and sky, of dancing on a floor of mirror glass. And a single kiss. Now, she was even more aware of Michael beside her.

Then her thoughts went to Jenefer Loumis. If he had come this far Jenefer must meet him. At least just once.

There was great applause. Leonora Scorton was cheered to the echo. In the true spirit of County Durham hospitality, there were cups of tea afterwards. Some of the women went streaming back to their own houses to bring extra cups for the unexpected numbers.

Miss Scorton made her way through the crowd, shaking hands with an old comrade here, making a new conquest there. She was flushed, charged up, by the time she got to where they were. 'You see, Michael O'Toole? Your friend Tom Farrell has whipped me a fine crowd up here.'

'Finnuola!' Richard was reaching past Miss Scorton to get to Finn. 'You here? What a surprise!' He shook her hand warmly. 'Finnuola. And Kate, too!' He shook her hand too, unfazed by the dramatic modification in her appearance since he last saw her.

Kate grinned. 'Hello, Richard. Now will you introduce me to Miss Scorton? I've never heard such sense talked in years, wonderful stuff.' She rung the politician's hand warmly. 'What you said about the fascists fits every one of them I've ever met.'

'You've come across them, then?' asked Leonora Scorton. 'Here in . . . er . . . Bracks Hill?'

Kate laughed her hearty laugh. 'Not here. Lancashire. London. Paris. Rome . . .' They were walking down the aisle, heads together, as though they'd known each other for years. The crowd moved along behind them.

In their wake there was an awkward silence for a second.

'Oh,' said Finn, 'I should . . . Richard. This is Michael O'Toole.'

Richard nodded. 'The man of principle. I heard all about you.'

'Did you now?' Michael's tone was even.

'And this is Richard Evans, Michael. I met him in France. We . . . it was a very jolly time.' She turned to Richard. 'What are you doing here of all places?'

'Well,' he rubbed his chin, 'I came to look someone up.' He glanced at Michael. 'You, actually, Finn. We seemed to part in such a hurry and then I went to Germany. Can't tell you how awful that was. Then I was coming up here to scout you out and met Miss Scorton on the train.'

The crowd around them was thinning now. Michael coughed. 'I'll just get after Tom Farrell. He said sommat about a smaller meeting of the union blokes with Miss Scorton. Sommat about a government deputation . . .' He drifted away, avoiding Finn's gaze.

Richard looked at her. 'Have I stepped into something?'

Finn shook her head. 'All that'll wait. Now! What are you doing?'

'Well, I said to Miss Scorton . . . but no, she'll never miss me. What is it you want to do?'

'I want to take you to meet someone.'

He frowned at her. 'Who?'

'It's a secret. But it's someone you should meet, even if it's only once.'

He threw up his hands. 'Well, I'm all yours. Lead on!'

Since the Halloween attack on Plush Folly things had been very quiet in that house. Toots, Nancy and Smiler lingered with Michael in Alan Newton's cottage, although they slept at Plush Folly. Jenefer sent the twins with notes to do her shopping as, since the attack, she had not felt safe leaving the house. She called to the cat from the door, not going into the road to coax him in, as was her wont. Hubert could not paint, as his hand was heavily bandaged from the broken-glass injury. In any case, he said, it was finished. The sword had been repainted, and there was an end to it. He sat most of the day in the shell chair in the sitting room, sometimes with his eyes closed, sometimes staring into space and occasionally clearing his throat.

One day when Jenefer came into the room he was humming a tune under his breath. She stopped in her tracks. 'Oh, the music is such a big miss, Hughie. And the gramophone in smithereens still on the lawn.' She kneeled beside him and took his hand. 'I tell you what, dear boy, when Finn comes I'll ask her to order a new gramophone from one of those catalogues Mr Montague has. And then at least we'll have our music.'

He looked at her, his eyes blank, and took away his hand.

There was a great knock on the door and she opened it to find Finn herself there, with a young man at her elbow. She smiled with relief. 'Finn, dear, we were just speaking of you. Come in, come in!'

In the hallway she looked from Finn to her companion. 'Now, who may this be?'

'This is Richard, Jenefer. I met him on holiday. I told you. Richard, this is Jenefer, who set the seed that made me come to

269

France in the first place. Jenefer's a change-maker, a woman of magic.'

He bowed over Jenefer's hand. 'For that we all thank you . . . er . . . Jenefer.'

'So you came all the way up here to seek out our Finn, Mr . . . Richard?'

He liked the direct look, the broad, upright, elegant figure. He smiled ruefully. 'It seems so, Mrs . . . Jenefer, it seems so.'

Jenefer stared very hard at him. 'Come in, come in, both of you. Say hello to dear Hughie. It'll give him a lift. He's so far down it's all I can do to keep him afloat.'

When Hubert saw their visitor he stood up from the chair, glared at them and walked to the window, put his face close to it and stared out.

Jenefer laughed uneasily. 'Well, perhaps you two could come into the kitchen and tell me where you went in Nice, what you did.' her voice was uncharacteristically shrill.

She made them sit at the table while she laid it with a colourful cloth and sharp-yellow earthenware cups and saucers. Then she sat down to pour the tea from the yellow teapot. She looked up to smile brightly at Finn. 'Now, my dearest Finn, you're about to tell me you have brought to me my dear son, long lost to me.' She turned to Richard, her bright voice belied by the slightest of tremors. 'It can only be Richard Morgan Evans. I met your father when he was just your age. You are your father's very image and your voice chimes with his in my memory.'

Richard stared at her with disbelief, then turned an agonised and angry look at Finn. 'How could you?' he said.

She stood up hastily. 'I – I'll just go to see Hubert,' she said. Then she fled.

The kitchen clock ticked into the silence as Richard Morgan Evans and his mother sat like statues on either side of the table.

Then they both spoke together. 'I knew nothing of this,' said Jenefer.

'I didn't know. How could Finnuola . . .?'

'She would mean the best,' said Jenefer. 'She knew how much I have longed, longed for—'

He stood up, his chair scraping back, 'Longed! What a joke that is. You are a great blank in my life. Not a word from you. I've wished you dead, the picture would be clearer.'

'But the letters all the years. Those letters into a blank space! I thought . . . knew . . . they must have taken them.'

'Letters? I've had no letters—'

He was interrupted by Finn slamming back into the room. 'Jenefer, it's Hubert. I can't find him. He's nowhere in the house and every single blessed window is open.'

270

★ ★ ★

The cloud were building themselves up in menacing piles, like castles of the bad king. The houses leaned in on him and he whacked the walls with his sword to keep them off. He made his way out of the city into the open countryside, regretting the fact that his horse had been shot under him. Dead now, a faithful servant.

He strode down towards the river, slashing away at the thinning winter bushes as he went. His spirit calmed a little as he walked beside the whispering brook, but even the water seemed to murmur to him to take care, take care. Beware demons.

The river path was narrow, encroached on by dead black sticks of old hedgerow and overhanging tree. Ahead, the torrent narrowed as it coursed under a hump-backed bridge. Across the bridge swirled a dense black figure, attended by fluttering demons with hooded heads hanging in the air like great moths.

Hubert lifted his sword high and paused, hardly daring to breathe. Then his heart sank to his boots as he saw the black figure swirl down the steps, alight on the path and walk along towards him. His hand tightened on his sword and bravely, he stepped forward. The dark thing shouted words and spells he could not understand and the smaller demons started to flutter towards him. He raised his sword to defend himself. The dark figure drew his own sword and advanced, the stream of words and spells from the mouth rising to a scream of invective. They engaged, the dark figure all the time having the advantage, thrashing Hubert about the head with a black weapon. Hubert pulled back to get his breath. The small demons flapped and fluttered and got right in his face. He brushed them away just in time to see the dark figure launching itself at him. Instinct overcoming reason, he took a slight side-step and turn, a ploy learned a world ago at Sandhurst, and the figure whirled past him into the water. As the figure sank, some of the smaller demons sank with it, leaving behind only the slight sickly smell of sulphur. Other small demons rose in the air again and settled in the trees, to await the next victim.

Hubert sheathed his sword and walked on, whistling, ignoring the single shout of rage gurgling up at him from the water.

Richard Morgan Evans felt lost in the flurry of panic which surrounded the disappearance of Hubert Loumis. He had been shocked at the way Loumis looked: a great ruin of a man, who though many years younger, looked older than his own father. And here was Jenefer, who in his mind had become a kind of demon queen: a comfortable, colourful, enigmatic character with not a whisper of Mata Hari about her. It was all so confusing.

Jenefer and Finn came into the house from yet another foray,

271

followed by the black and white cat. Richard stood up.

'I think I should go. I'm no help . . .' He looked at Jenefer, who took his hand. He left it there but did not grasp her back.

She looked deep into his eyes, right back to the stalwart lonely child at the core. 'Come back, Richard. I know you will come back to give me a chance . . .'

He pulled his hand away. 'I really can't say.' He turned to Finn and said coolly, 'I don't know if I can thank you for this . . . surprise. But I can see one would have to try it. I'll come to find you tomorrow.'

Finn and Jenefer stood staring at each other. Jenefer kissed Finn on the cheek. 'Thank you for having the courage to do that. If you'd told either of us we'd have prevaricated. It's hard, but . . .'

Richard pulled on his gloves and put on his cap. They followed him to the hall and he lifted his cap to both of them, then they all turned as the front door clicked again and Hubert breezed in. He smiled broadly from one to the other, removed his stick from where it was tucked into his Sam Browne belt, and placed it carefully in the hall stand.

He beamed and came to shake Richard heartily by the hand. 'It must be Richard Morgan Evans. I must tell you, my boy, you are the image of your father. And your father was a fine soldier. A fine soldier.'

Michael trudged back along the river track to New Morven. He had enjoyed the energy and optimism which Leonora Scorton had infused into the union meeting. He could see what Tom was on about. She made things seem possible. She made you sense that you owned your own fate. And if you joined your fate with that of other 'common men' then you would gain the power to do what seemed impossible. Quite the revolutionary. No wonder Tom Farrell was carrying a torch. Not that Miss Scorton would see him, or most men, in that certain way. What fired her up, made her so vibrant, so attractive despite being nearly the age of Emily Punchard, was that inner life that lit her up like a blazing beacon.

The last time Michael had seen that was when he was working in Scotland and, wandering around one Sunday to kill time, he had come upon an open air mission outside a Presbyterian church. There, a man had been preaching about the glory of God and the transcendent goodness of Jesus Christ. His face had shone with conviction and simple delight. Michael had had to suppress the desire to go up and kiss him to share in that delight. He smiled at the thought. If he had given in to that impulse they would have known him for the papist he was, probably called him drunk, and thrown him into the sea.

But not for Leonora Scorton or for any priest, any rabble-rouser, would he risk again that death-in-life of prison. He had lost so much in there.

He stopped on the bridge and leaned to look down over the night-black waters of the River Gaunt. From the preacher and prison his mind leaped to Finn. Finnuola Montague. He stroked his hand along the smooth damp stone and thought of Finnuola as he had lifted her to him in the dusty light of the apple loft.

Suddenly he was distracted by the strangled scream of a calling fox. He waited for the response, which didn't come. Then his eye was caught by something lifting and falling in the water as the river swished round the foot of the bridge. He pulled himself onto the parapet to get a better view and focused on a flash of silver in the moonlight. 'Jesus Mary and Joseph,' he said.

The dark figure of a man was down there, face down. His white hair was floating like thistledown on the black ripples. Michael scrambled to the bank and heaved the body out, his own boots sinking into the soft clay. The body felt enormously heavy as he turned it over. At first, because of trailing river weed, the mud and bruises and the livid shine, he didn't recognise it. Then the moonlight caught the sharp nose and he recognised the Reverend Hildebrand Marchant. He dropped the body and had to grab it again as it started to slide. 'Jesus Mary and Joseph,' he repeated. 'So are the mighty fallen.'

26

The Fight

Jenefer was rushing round the kitchen at Plush Folly with her hair even more awry than usual, odd shoes on her feet. She made tea without the tea in it and left the innards in the chicken when she cooked it.

Toots and Nancy, across from the cottage 'helping', were delighted by her gaffes. 'Fancy that, Jenefer! No tea in the tea!' said Toots.

Jenefer drained off the water, dried the pot thoroughly, then heaped tea leaves into it.

Nancy was sitting at the table. 'Our Michael would say you're like a "man off", today.'

Jenefer smiled faintly. She was trying to bring properly to mind the baby Richard, skinny and solemn, with delicate fingers and a long face below a large smooth forehead. He would be presented to her after tea by Nanny, with the admonition to mind Mama's skirt. Once, Jenefer had held her arms out for him and he had hung back. Nanny had grabbed him then, slapped his legs and plonked him on Jenefer's knee. 'He can be very stubborn, madam. You need to be firm.'

Strangely the child had not cried, only set his bottom lip very hard. Then the door closed behind Nanny, and Jenefer turned Richard to face her. He looked at her with wise eyes, put down his head and butted her twice in the face, causing tears of pain to rise in her eyes. 'Go 'way', he had said. 'Go 'way. Bad lady.' Then he wriggled off her knee and raced out of the room after Nanny.

'Jenefer,' said Toots now, 'there's no need to cry. The kettle's nearly boiling and we can make a new cup of tea.'

Jenefer blew her nose. 'Where's Hubert?'

'He's in his chair,' said Nancy. 'He's either asleep . . .'

'. . . or gone deaf,' said Toots. 'We shook him and shook him.'

Quietly Jenefer made her way to the sitting room. He was slumped in the chair. 'Hubert,' she said quietly. He stirred, but his

275

eyes stayed closed. She noticed bruising down one side of his face and wondered where he had got that. She backed out of the room and returned noisily to the kitchen. Since he had greeted Richard so cordially Hubert had said nothing to her at all. He had prowled round the house, doing several circuits, taking in the back yard, across to the coach house then back to his shell chair in the sitting room.

'I'm afraid he's gone back into his shell properly,' she announced in the kitchen, pouring the bubbling water on to the tea leaves.

The twins frowned at her in puzzlement, then swung round as Smiler burst through the kitchen door. 'Our Mick's back an' he's wet through, an' he found the vicar drowneded in the river. That vicar feller's dead-serve-him-right,' he said breathlessly.

The girls jumped down from the table and ran towards the door, followed by Jenefer.

In Alan Newton's cottage, Michael was crouching before the fire removing his boots and his sodden socks.

'What is it, Michael, what's happened?'

He shook his head. 'I was comin' back from that meeting in Bracks Hill an' I found him, the vicar feller, pushin' up against the footin' of the Roman bridge. Dead as nails. Wet an' cold.' He shuddered.

Jenefer stood very still. 'How did it happen? Was he drowned?'

'There's no telling, Mrs Loumis. He was face down in the water. His face was marked, from the stones, I think.' He shook his head. 'One minute I was coming from that woman's meetin', thinkin' the world's out there for the takin', the next I find that man, that terrible man, slimy with death. An' the rest doesn't matter a jot. He thought he could tell us all what to do, an' now what?' He had a world of weariness in his voice.

'Yes, it puts—' Jenefer stood stock-still and closed her eyes. She could see the swirl of black and hear the thud of stick on bone. She swayed. Michael stood up and grabbed her elbow. 'Are you all right, Mrs Loumis?' he said.

She stood up straight again. 'I'm fine, Michael, fine. Don't worry about me. Why don't you send Smiler across to get Finn? She'll want to know what's happened to you.'

Smiling slightly, Michael nodded at Smiler, who streaked away.

'An' we can sleep back in our old beds in Plush Folly?' said Nancy. 'It's crowded up there in that old apple loft. An' if Mr Marchant's not . . .'

Glancing at Michael, Jenefer nodded. 'The beds are turned down, ready,' she said simply.

It was easy for Finn to get away from the shop. Kate, Esther and

276

Patrick were in the little back room. Esther was reading out her story from her little notebook and the others were listening. She broke off when Finn put her nose through the curtain. 'Young Smiler says Michael found the vicar drowned by the bridge.'

Esther let out a strangled cry. 'Dear me.'

'I'm going across there,' said Finn, 'to see they are all right.'

Kate stood up. 'We'll do the shop, won't we, Esther?' She turned to Patrick. 'Why don't you go down to The Eagle, Pat? There'll be some news there, of the old duffer.'

Patrick was already reaching for his hat.

Quietly Finn let herself into the cottage. Michael hadn't heard her come in. He was sitting on a small stool beside the blazing fire. His head was in his hands. She went and touched him on the shoulder. He jumped up and turned towards her, and she put her arms around him.

He talked into her hair. 'I've never seen it, Finn, a man dead like that. Injured from the pit, yes. Beaten in the strike, in prison as well. Yes. But not that, like so much matter, the life out of it. No life in it at all. Dead fish. Ugh.'

She rubbed her face against his and hugged him to her.

He muttered. 'I want you, Finn, I want you with me always. Always. I want a ring on your finger and the words said over us.'

'Yes,' she said, 'I know.' Turning her face towards his, she brushed his lips with hers. 'I know where there's life, Michael.' She drew a hand down the side of his face. 'Do you know Smiler went across to Plush Folly. Michael? He said the girls were there.' Then she whispered, very close to his ear. 'What I want most in the world, Michael O'Toole, is for us to go up into the apple loft and make a life.'

He pulled himself away from her and groaned. 'Aw, Finn, haven't I still got the stink of the river on me, and that man's . . . that man's . . .'

She looked around. 'Where's the bath?'

'On a hook in the back yard. Why?'

'Go and get it.' She lifted the lid of the boiler in the black iron range and stood back from the steam. 'This is full and the water's scalding. We'll give you a bath.'

They laughed as they filled the bath with a long-handled pan and the ladling can. 'There's some Sunlight soap in the scullery, go and get that,' he ordered.

By the time she came back with the soap and an old iron cheesegrater, he was in the steaming water. He looked at the cheesegrater with alarm. 'What in heaven will you do with that?' he said.

She laughed. 'My father used to do it for me when I was little. I loved it.' She grated the hard soap into flakes and it settled all over him, into his black curly hair, on to his muscular shoulders and arms, into the steaming water. She stood back. 'My dad used to call it a snow storm.'

He laughed and started to rub himself, creating soapy tides and circles on his arms and shoulders.

'I'll help,' she said, 'but first . . .' She pulled her jumper over her shoulders, then her thick skirt and petticoat.

He was delighted. 'Finn, you hussy.'

She held up a hand, 'I only do this because I've no wish to get my good clothes wet. Now, where's that brush?'

He lifted himself up on one knee. 'Come here! Come here! I want you here.'

She laughed. 'No. Here is for cleaning. The apple loft is for wanting.'

It was eleven o'clock by the time she let herself back into the side door of the shop. The shop was closed but Kate was still in the back room.

Kate put a finger to her lips and glanced at the ceiling. 'Ssh, Finn. Your ma's just gone to sleep. I told her I'd wait for you. Have you walked back at this time on your own?'

'Michael walked me.' He had clung on to her hand, not wanted to let her go. Up in the apple loft they had made love, at first violently, then in a softer, more exploratory fashion, and then they had lain and snuggled and talked. Michael talked of the optimism he'd felt when listening to Leonora Scorton, how if they worked and fought for it, the future was theirs. He'd talked of the ring he would buy her. He'd pawn his life to get her one, she could be sure of that. Nothing now would keep him away from her. Nothing.

She told him how blue was the Mediterranean, how bright the sky, how perfumed the air. How she had danced on glass.

He had turned on his elbow then, and looked down at her, pushing her muzzy hair away from her brow. 'An' how could you face to come back to this place?' he asked. 'How could you face this after that?'

She touched his strongly marked cheekbones. 'That was a fine bright dream. I loved it while it lasted. It put the sun inside me for ever. But how could I stay away?' she asked. 'My people, all the people I care for, are here.'

He had kissed her then; her lips were almost bruised with his kisses. 'An' what about the feller Richard Evans?' he said against her mouth.

She sat up. 'He was part of it. Blue skies. And he turned out to be part of what's here, an' that makes it more interesting. But I like him like I like Hubert, or Jenefer. Probably always will.' Then she kissed him for the last time, that night.

'Hey! Hey!' Kate was saying now in the shop. 'Come out of that dream. Now what have you been up to, little minx?'

'What do you think?'

And Esther upstairs stirred as she heard their joined laughter down below.

Kate put on her coat. 'Lock the shop door properly after me,' she said. Outside, she turned up the fur collar to walk the few yards down the road to the little house where she knew that Patrick Montague would be waiting, with well-concealed impatience, for her own particular ministrations.

'Of course,' said Emily, 'they're sayin' it's suicide, but Ah know better than that.' She was leaning on the counter talking confidentially to Kate MacMahon, who was sorting out the pennies for the jam jars.

Kate made a tube of her fingers to stack the pennies neatly and pushed them across the counter. 'Why's that, Emily?'

'The vicar's not the kind of man. No conscience. No sense of right an' wrong.'

'So what are they saying?'

Emily put the pennies into the back of her battered purse. 'Did he fall or was he pushed? That's what they're sayin'.' She glanced at Finn who was serving old Hazelwood with an ounce of tea. 'They're sayin' that Michael O'Toole had sommat to do with it.'

'Michael just found the body,' said Finn. 'Went and told Sergeant Corcoran.'

Emily shook her head. 'Ah'm not sayin' anything about Michael, pet. Nice lad. True friend to our Tom. Treasure the ones who are true. Priced above rubies. No. Ah'm just tellin' yer what they're saying. Me. Ah've been doin' battle with meself, on me knees in the Citadel askin' forgiveness.' She adjusted the scarf under her chin. 'When Ah heard, me first thought was serves him right, sour old man. But it doesn't. Serve him right, Ah mean. Miserable cringin' sort of feller he was, but Ah doubt if he'd had a day's real content in his life. My Stanley, he got more joy in the music for one Sunday service than the vicar had in all his time in that church. My Stanley died unhappy, but, by and large, he lived happy. Not many of us can say that.'

Daniel Marchant nodded with approval as he looked at himself in the mirror. 'Smart turnout, old boy. Uncle will approve,' he muttered, touching each item in turn: the black suit, the high stiff collar, the black tie, black overcoat, soft grey gloves and the black Homburg in his hand. He thought about his father's body, at his and

279

Uncle Oliver's insistence, lying on its own bed here at the Vicarage, guarded over by the hysterically tearful Mrs Fosdick. 'Stupid woman's going berserk, secret lusting after the old boy, shouldn't wonder. Lusting after a cockroach. Quite enough to make one vomit.' He giggled to himself. 'It'll be a pleasure to send her packing. I'll do it directly after the funeral. Always a bit above herself, old Fosdick. That'll show her.'

Sergeant Corcoran had talked of his father's body going to the mortuary at the Infirmary, but Daniel and Sir Oliver would have none of it. The doctor, then some other official, had been to view the body but no certificate had been sighed. There was some talk from them too, of insisting on the removal to the hospital.

Sir Oliver had soon shown them off. There should be no breath of scandal. Not this time.

Daniel went into the bedroom and looked at the elongated contours of his father under the draped sheet. He would no more have lifted the sheet than tweaked the devil's tail. He went to the mirror and looked at the body in reflection.

You've done it too, father, he thought. Gone. There could have been no better timing. Now there'll be no treacherous talk about tainted grandmothers and madness. At least now I am safe. And have no fear, dear father, dear cockroach, I will do right by you. You'll get justice. I've an errand to see to that, then I'm to lunch with Uncle. Go to Banville House for good now, shouldn't wonder. Son of the house. The Bishop'll be wanting this dreary place back; put some worthy in here.

Daniel tweaked the edge of the sheet and addressed the body.

'The Bishop'll put some proper Christian in here, shouldn't wonder. Not some charlatan like you. A nice man who likes people, loves his sons and believes in God.'

Later that morning he stood in the police station with lowered head, while Sergeant Corcoran extolled his father's virtues and voiced his regret at the good vicar's demise. 'He'll be missed in this village, Mr Marchant, I can tell you that.'

Daniel took out a snowy handkerchief and blew his nose. 'Very kind of you, Sergeant. Most kind. But I must tell you I'm here for two reasons. The undertaker has been calling every hour on the hour, asking to set about his business . . .'

Corcoran shook his head. 'The doctor and the coroner's feller is still ditherin' on. They still want yer pa up at the Infirmary, sir. They're talkin' about . . . beggin' yer pardon . . . signs of a struggle, that yer father mayn't have slipped. Talkin' about gettin' an order to get him there to the Infirmary whether or no Sir Oliver wishes it.'

'A struggle?' Daniel stroked his chin with a grey gloved hand. 'It is odd that you should say that, Sergeant. But this is the second reason for my errand. I was considering this thing. Do you know I was there, on the river bank? In the afternoon, just before this thing happened, I imagine. For a walk. I didn't see my father. But do you know whom I passed, skulking down there? Michael O'Toole. The man who, I believe, is said to have found him. Am I correct?'

The sergeant nodded.

'Well, Sergeant, I have to tell you that that fellow was very rude to me on that occasion and has a great grudge against my father – my family, in fact. He was in prison for burgling my uncle's house. And my father, quite rightly, made great moves to get his sisters and brother into the protection of Carhoe Orphanage. Which O'Toole manifestly loathed. And took steps against it. Although,' Daniel sneered, 'he did hide behind a woman's skirts.'

'I am aware of all this, Mr Marchant. It is under consideration.'

'Good, good. My uncle will be pleased. I'm off to Banville House now, to lunch. I will mention it to Sir Oliver – your co-operative attitude.'

Daniel walked down the road with a light step, relishing the glances of curiosity, and the shallow expressions of sympathy cast in his direction. He called into the village shop and was surprised to see a stranger behind the counter, a rather plain woman with a very good figure, crimped red hair and calm wide eyes. He asked for cigarettes. 'Is Finnuola around?'

She shook her head.

'Will you give her a message?'

'Certainly,' she said.

'Tell her that Irish roughhouse she's attached to'll end up back in jail or at the end of a rope for what he's done to my father. I have seen the sergeant. I am Daniel Marchant.'

Kate smiled, her smile turning a plain face into one of beauty. 'Oh. I know who you are,' she said.

'You!' he said. 'Here, in—'

'The door's behind you,' she said. 'Be careful to close it after you. There's a foul-smelling wind blowing through there.'

He was grinning a wolfish grin. 'Now here's a bit of colour for this godforsaken village. Wait till I tell Denis Consadine.'

Kate came round the counter then, took him by the arm and thrust him roughly through the door. 'Get out of here, you little twerp. And don't you bother Finn. She has enough on her plate.'

Outside he pulled at his sleeve to straighten it and glanced round, to see if anyone had witnessed his humiliation. The street was deserted. He breathed a sigh of relief.

His steps lengthened as he made his way out of the village. He was proud of the way he ignored the sneers and catcalls of the group

281

of lads who were putting final touches to the north end bonfire. He was pleased that he could dismiss the memory of the contempt in that whore's voice as she threw him out of that scruffy shop. You had to rise above these things. They would get their just deserts, those insects.

He hesitated on the edge of the wood near his mother's grave. No, she would know about all these things already, wouldn't she? And her poor old heart, in heaven or wherever she was, would be sinking at this very minute at the thought of the imminent arrival of his father. He laughed out loud at the thought and started to hum 'Land of Hope and Glory' under his breath at first, then very, very loudly at the top of his voice as he strode along.

27

Suspicion

'Go and talk to Hubert,' said Jenefer to Finn. 'I can't get a word out of him. Not a word.'

'He's in his shell,' said Nancy.

'. . . gone back into his shell,' echoed Toots.

Hubert was in the sitting room, in the chair, his long fingers stroking the black and white cat on his knee. Finn went to kneel by him and looked up into his face. His eyes were as clear as the Mediterranean. 'How are you, Hubert?' she said, touching his worn cuff. 'Are you well?'

'I'm very well, little maid. Never better than this for many years. I am trying to absorb that fact. Test it to see if it squeaks.' He stood up and the cat leaped from his lap. He took Finn's hand. 'Come. I wish to show you something.'

He led her through the house, through the front door and round to the back, avoiding the kitchen. They went to the coach house. The afternoon was dark and the room was in shadow. He went round and lit his lamps, one by one. 'Look. What do you see?'

The images were still there: intricate and skilfully painted.

'Your pictures of the dragon, and images of battle. Scenes from your life. People you know.'

'Look closer.'

She worked her way across the wall. Something was happening. On the body of the dragon and other parts of the wall the paint had flaked off altogether so that the dragon looked moth-eaten, and the detail on the rest was muzzy: faces blanked out, limbs lost. In addition, the whole range of colour had dropped in tone. She frowned. That first layer of paint which had covered the old walls: the paint that Hubert and Michael had slapped on all those months ago, was very old stock from the shop. Her father had been glad to get rid of it. That was the cause.

The effect of all this degeneration of the basic paint was to remove the passion and the pain from the whole execution; the message of terror had faded. The soldiers were toys, the weapons sticks and stones. Her glance dropped to the corner, to the sensual image of herself which had so upset her. Even that was fading, neutralising. It could be any girl, anywhere. In the later image of herself and Michael, the chain dangling from his hand had vanished. They might be any boy and girl.

'The dragon has fled. The demons are gone,' Hubert said simply.

'But, Hubert . . .' She should explain about the paint. The cat was winding itself softly round her legs. Finn touched Hubert's hand. 'Oh, that's wonderful. That is so wonderful.'

He went and peered out at the dark day through the uncurtained window. 'Yes. I think so.'

'But why? Jenefer is so . . .'

'There was a price, I think. I believe I may have killed that Marchant feller. That holy man. Can't remember, of course. Raging at the time. Against the demons. And they're gone. Jenefer knows. I see it in her eyes. So I try not to look at them.'

She took his hand. 'At least come and talk to her. She's desperate that you don't speak to her. Unhappy.'

They went directly to the kitchen this time. Toots looked up at them from the table where she was sitting cutting carrots. 'Our Smiler's gone out raidin' the south end bonfire. And Jenefer's got a visitor in the sitting room,' she announced. 'That posh lad. The one you know, Finn.'

Jenefer was shaking. 'Can I get you something, Richard? A glass of Madeira?'

He shook his head.

'It's wonderful to see you, Richard, wonderful . . .'

He sat down and took off his gloves. 'I've had very hard thoughts about you all these years, Mrs . . . see I don't even know what to call you.'

'My name is Jenefer. You call me that. My young friends here do.'

'You just went. Nothing after that. Left us. Left with your . . . Hubert Loumis.'

'But I wrote – cards, letters, presents. Every week for five or six years.'

'I know nothing of that.'

'I thought that you mustn't have received them at all, in the end. Of course, they would keep them from you.'

He stood up and started to prowl the room. 'How could they? How could they? I asked them about you, you know. Got quite obstreperous about it sometimes.'

'What did they say?'

284

He laughed shortly. 'Father would glare and go out of the room. Nanny would say that Mummy had been rather a naughty girl and had run away.'

'She would mean it for the best, you know, Richard.'

He shook his head. 'I needed you. And could have had at least that part of you, the letters. And they kept them from me.'

'For five years, Richard, I used to come at the beginning and end of term, when they left you at school, or collected you. Just to get a sight of you, see you fit and well and laughing with your friends. Then it all got too painful and I had to stop. Except for once. I did see you on graduation day at Oxford too.'

He shook his head. 'Waste. Waste. I'll go and see Nanny, get those letters.'

Jenefer laughed. 'That would waste your time. She'll have burned them. Very tidy mind.'

He shook his head again. 'But you knew her. Think how rigid the old girl was about the law. It's illegal to steal His Majesty's Mail. But to destroy it! A hanging offence.' Now he had a faint smile on his face, his belligerence all gone. 'She'll have them, unopened, shouldn't wonder. She had . . . has some integrity.'

'And she was all the mother you've had in these years. Don't undervalue what she's been to you.'

He shook his head. 'I couldn't do that.'

She looked up at him. 'I hope you find them. And read them. Then you'll know how much I was thinking about you. And continued to think, even after I gave up hope and stopped writing.' She was turning a handkerchief round and round in her fingers.

He nodded. 'Jenefer, I—'

There was a knock on the door and Finn came in with a tray. 'I thought you two might want some tea. This talking is a thirsty business.' They watched her gratefully as she busied herself pouring tea and handing it to them.

She looked from one to another. 'I'm really sorry if this is a disaster. Maybe I shouldn't have . . . It seemed so meant . . .'

Richard coughed. 'No. We should be grateful. Unfinished business. We can't rewrite the past.'

Jenefer, who had been holding her breath, nodded eagerly. 'That's true. But we don't have to go on living it.'

Finn gave them an approving motherly smile. Then she turned to Jenefer. 'I talked with Hubert,' she said. 'He seems fine, well in himself. He says the demons have gone, the dragon has fled. We looked at the paintings. It seems they have.' She paused. 'But he says he thinks he may have killed Mr Marchant.'

'I knew it.' Jenefer turned to Richard. 'I saw it. Dark figures. I heard it. Wood on bone. But Hubert has bruises. I thought it might be his bone.'

'Jenefer sees things,' explained Finn. 'In her mind, her imagination.'

'It's especially so here in New Morven. I don't know why. I knew I had to come. Hubert, my h— husband's been ill from recurring shell shock since the war. It's recently been very bad, which is why we came to New Morven. To give him some breathing space,' she laughed, 'and to conserve our resources, of course . . .'

Richard leaned towards her. 'That's one reason why I had to come and see you, now I knew you were here, Jenefer. There're some papers that've been swilling around in our London house for years now. I asked my father about them a year or so back. Two old cousins of your father died. There was a house, some shares. Well, a lot really. Father's executor, but he couldn't find you. Said you lived abroad and his searches were fruitless.'

Jenefer smiled thinly. 'The General was too good at intelligence for that to be true. Perhaps I'll have to—'

Finn glanced out of the window and saw Sergeant Corcoran making his ponderous way along the front path and down the side towards the cottage. 'There's the sergeant. He's going to see Michael. I must go.' She flew out of the door banging it behind her.

Richard turned to Jenefer. 'I think a great deal of Finn, you know?' There was a question in his voice.

Jenefer smiled and shook her head. 'There are things I've always been certain of about young Finn. That she would make a difference to me and Hubert. And she has. That she should go to France and it would make her blossom. And she did. But I didn't know, not in a thousand years, that she would bring you back. It seems to me now that I sent for you. Perhaps the unexpected event will prove to be the most intended of all.'

He smiled and sat back more comfortably in his mother's chair.

Michael was opening the door to Corcoran when Finn got there. She followed them into the small space. The sergeant turned to face Michael.

'The situation's this, O'Toole,' he said. 'The vicar's now been taken to the Infirmary an' they think that mebbe it wasn't a simple slip on the bank. There's two marks on his face that's mebbe been cracks, like. Like somebody's walloped him. Vicar's brother, Sir Oliver, an' the son, Daniel Marchant, reckons murder could be the order of the day. An' wants justice. These fellers have some pull when they want sommat. I've felt that iron hand before. Meks me hot under the collar.'

Michael shrugged. 'All I did was find him.'

Finn moved to put her arm through his.

'I have it on good authority that you were on the river path earlier in the day, O'Toole.'

'So were half a dozen more. I passed them.'

Corcoran took out his notebook and licked his pencil. 'If you could just give me names.'

'Daniel Marchant was one of them. Can't say about the others. Familiar faces, but no names. I'd think it's Marchant said he saw me?'

'Well, yes.'

'And I saw him, so where does that leave us?'

'Ha!' Corcoran tucked away the notebook. 'It leaves us with the fact that you and yer family,' he paused to glance at Finn, 'and yer friends, have more 'n one reason to have it in for Mr Marchant an' his family. To be honest, in relation to Miss Montague here, I can see some—'

'But Michael couldn't do a thing like that. Wouldn't do that,' said Finn.

'I hope yer right, Miss Montague, but there's a canny ferment goin' on about it now. High-ups involved. Makes no difference if he didn't do it o' course. Nothing to worry about. I'm not after a scapegoat even if others may be in that game.' Corcoran fastened up his cloak and put on his helmet. 'As you say, in that case it's make no difference. But the feller who did it's lookin' at jail. Or even the rope, if it were done with malicious intent.'

Finn went to close the door after him. She turned to Michael, who was standing before the fire, a grim look on his face. 'Prison. I couldn't take it, Finn. Just couldn't. I'd die.'

'You won't have to. You didn't do it.' She squeezed his arm. 'We both know that and they'll find that out. But it's nearly as bad. Michael, I think Hubert did it. In the middle of one of his turns.'

'Think?'

'He can't remember. But Jenefer's seen it.'

'Seen it? In one of her visions? Ha! I don't think she's half the witch that either of you make out.'

'She saw Kate with me, before I ever met her, Michael. She can do it. I'm certain.'

He threw himself on to a hard chair. 'So there we are. It's either me in prison or Hubert Loumis. It'd kill either of us.'

She sat on the chair opposite. 'Something'll turn up. It could still have been an accident,' she said, without any conviction at all.

They sat there quietly for ten minutes watching the fire go down. Then Michael stood up and pulled her to her feet. 'I have to stir meself,' said Michael. 'There's a Leonora Scorton meetin' up at Darlington tonight. Tom asked could I be there. He has news of some big lads who'll be paid money to break it up.'

'I'll come,' said Finn.

'Can you?'

'No reason why not. Kate's across at the shop. She might want to come, of course. She's fallen a bit under Miss Scorton's spell herself.'

He frowned down at her. 'Well then, I'll see you at Darlington Station at half past five. I've to go to Tom's to help him carry his blessed leaflets, then on to old Jonty's to see if he can make it. Tom says he's on the mend. Susanah thought she would lose him this time.'

Finn grinned at him. 'Well then, that's one good thing. You can wipe that scowl off your face. Can't let you get back into those bad habits.'

He smiled reluctantly. 'Wouldn't you scowl, if you were lookin' in the face of ten years in jail? Or worse? Wouldn't you?'

Daniel had been doing his uncle's bidding all day. Collected Uncle Oliver's repaired gun from the gunsmith. He had read sections from *The Times* to his uncle while he was attending to his morning toilet. Uncle Oliver was interested in the State and its machinations but was no great reader. Had been thrown out of school because of his difficulty with reading.

Then Daniel had checked the quality of a repair on a distant fence on the estate, kicked it down and told the workman to go back and do it properly. He'd had to sort money from his uncle's cash-box into small packages. These were payments of a particular kind to be made, to be delivered and distributed by him at a meeting later in the day. And he had strict orders not to pay until he had seen them do their job. Sir Oliver might not be able to read, but he knew about men.

That would all be a fag.

Daniel had suggested that they go hunting, but Uncle Oliver thought that might be indelicate in the circumstances. He himself would be buried in much-needed discussions with one of his farm managers. Then there were papers from Germany and France to deal with – perhaps Daniel would be on hand to help him read these? And a letter reporting one of Sir Oswald's London meetings to reread.

Daniel felt at a loose end at Banville House. There were no guests and he was forced to participate in sporadic hypocritical talk with his uncle, regarding the virtues of his father and the need to bring his killer or killers to justice. All the time he was hugging himself with the sheer delight of it all. That at last he was free.

Free of the cockroach. Free to do just as he wished.

288

He laughed suddenly, and scrabbled in his wardrobe for the suitcase, still not unpacked, from his sojourn in France. He dug underneath the shirts, so beautifully laundered by one of Denis Consadine's French skivvies.

'Hah!' He grinned to himself and pulled out a small sack in royal-blue silk. He opened it and set about the newly learned and not unpleasant ritual of attending to its contents.

Esther was beside herself with pleasure at the sight of Richard Morgan Evans in her shop. Now here was a catch. More intelligent than wonderful-looking, it was true, but by the very gloss and polish of his person, the cadences of his speech, this was a young man of quality. Of affluence. It made her so glad she had been fussy about Finnuola's speech: the extra elocution lessons at school; those ha'penny fines for leaving the Gs off the end of her words. Finnuola would need her nice voice in the world into which this young man would take her.

Kate had, to Esther's annoyance, taken herself off to Darlington to have a permanent wave put in her hair before going on to the MP woman's meeting that night. When Richard Morgan Evans came through the door, Finn had refused to let her mother take over the serving for her to go up to the sitting room to attend properly to her caller.

So Esther had sat on her stool, which was her regular perch now since Kate had come to help. Lounging around on the bed had become so boring nowadays. As Patrick said to Finn, her mother did more perching than working in the shop, but she did lend a hand when there was a rush on. And she was so much perkier these days.

Now she perched, grilling Richard with questions about the army, and his life in London. It was twenty minutes before Finnuola finished with the last of the customers and turned the dangling notice round to 'Closed'.

'There,' she said. 'We'll have an early tea.' She looked closely at her mother. 'It's nearly ready, Ma. I'll put the potatoes in. Maybe you could go up and pour us some of that sherry the traveller left for Christmas.'

Esther looked from one to the other of them and unhooked her bottom from the stool. 'A lovely idea. I'll leave you two here to . . . er . . . sort things. I'll call down when it's poured.' She went off humming under her breath.

'Phew!' said Richard.

Finn laughed. 'She's all right when you get to know her.' She paused. 'Well, she isn't really, but we're used to her. She's a lot better than she was. Kate's bringing her out of her shell.' She

289

thought of Hubert 'going into his shell'. 'Did you talk at all to Hubert across there?'

He shook his head. 'I'm a bit – no, *very* – cautious about Hubert Loumis. Don't forget that mad, poor and broken as he is now, he has been the black angel in my dreams since I was a boy. All this takes some getting used to.'

'I wish he could remember what really happened on the river bank. But even if he did that awful thing, nobody could say he's properly responsible.'

'It wouldn't be the rope, or even prison. An asylum, perhaps.'

'That would be worse. He would get madder. He'd die without Jenefer. But then if they don't get him, they'll get Michael, won't they? It has to be either him or Michael.'

Richard took her hand from the polished counter and she let it lie in his. 'I didn't come to talk about any of them. Well, not directly. I came to ask you a specific question, Finn. I'd have done this whatever happened here, I promise you. All this about Jenefer and so on. I want to ask this question before things move on, but I don't want you to answer it now. I know you have other . . . options.' He took a breath. 'What you said in Nice, Finn, about all that shameful lurking around, that's haunted me. In doing all that I was being true to the way that people like me see, or saw, the world. Unthinking. Taking a certain way of seeing things for granted. D'you see what I mean?'

'Richard, what . . .?'

'I want you to marry me. I want to take you into my life, into my world, and flaunt you, not lurk around—'

'Richard . . .'

'No, I don't want you to answer now. I want you to leave it. Are you going to Leonora's meeting tonight?'

She nodded numbly, her brain whirling.

'Well, why don't I take you? I'm borrowing Jenefer's motorbike. It'd be a good wheeze to turn up on that, don't you think?'

28

The Bonfire

Michael was waiting at the big iron gates of the railway station when Finn rode up with a flourish, perched behind Richard on Jenefer's motorbike. Finn's face was stiff with cold and her lips were chattering. Michael put an arm round her till she stopped shuddering.

'I got a lift here,' she stuttered.

'Sure, I can see that,' he said, eyeing Richard, whose glittering goggles reflected the streetlights, denying his face any expression.

Richard made a half-salute, turned the bike downwards towards the town centre, and roared off. Michael's arm came down, away from Finn. 'You should have gone straight to the hall with him,' he said flat. 'Just your sort of feller, that, sittin' there like Baron von Richthofen.'

She put her arm through his. 'Didn't want to,' she said.

'We're to meet Tom an' the others at The Commercial Hotel. Leonora's staying there.'

'Leonora? That sounds very friendly.'

'It's easy. She's that kind of person.'

The lounge bar of the hotel was crowded with Leonora's supporters. Finn looked around her with some curiosity. She had never been in the bar of a public house in England. Not even The Eagle, where her father spent so much time and not a little of their money. This didn't look too much like a den of iniquity, more like somebody's overfull and rather greasy sitting room.

A vision in a holly-green velvet suit, a little hat with a feather on its head, came towards her. 'Dearest Finn!' she said, kissing her on both cheeks.

'Bloo—' Michael swallowed the swearwards.

Finn laughed. 'Another transformation, Kate?'

'No, love, a reversal. I decided to come as myself. Leonora Scorton invited me to tea and I decided to grace The Commercial Hotel with the real me. Gave her a bit of a jolt I can tell you,' she said with satisfaction.

'You do like the drama, Kate MacMahon. This means you're going, doesn't it?' said Finn.

'Nail on the head, Finn. Ghosts vanquished, recuperation over, rejuvenation complete. Ready again to take on the world. You and your ma and pa, and New Morven have done your magic. And, dear girl, now I'm in receipt of an offer I can't refuse.'

'What . . .?' said Finn.

But the crowd, with Leonora at its centre, was moving off. As at Bracks Hill, the MP had Tom Farrell on her right and Richard Evans on her left. Finn, Kate and Michael joined in at the back of the crowd beside Susanah and a sparky-looking Jonty Clelland. Those two were holding hands.

'You're lookin' on form,' Jonty,' said Michael.

'You look really well,' chimed Finn. She smiled across at Susanah.

Jonty adjusted his tie in a gesture which was almost too flamboyant for him. 'Can't keep a good man down,' he said. 'Wouldn't have missed all this for the world, my boy.'

'Good thing, sir,' said Michael earnestly.

For a second they were schoolmaster and pupil again.

There was quite a crowd outside the hall, which Finn thought must be a good thing. But as they got nearer it was obvious from the jeers that this crowd was here to threaten, not to praise. The men shouldered their way forward and confronted Leonora. One man stepped up very close to her. 'Traitor!' he said. 'Know her name, lads? Lenin Scorton. The woman's a bliddy communist traitor.'

Tom moved in front of Leonora, and Michael pushed forward to stand by his side. Others moved with them. But Leonora hauled the screen of bodies to one side. 'No violence, boys,' she muttered. 'No violence or they win.' She moved in so close to the man he had to take half a step back. She looked him in the eye. 'Why?' she said. 'Why do you think I'm a traitor? Where's your evidence?'

He took a whole step back and looked back towards his mates. 'On the side of them Russians, this bitch. Regicide!'

They started to mutter and mumble and swell towards her again.

'Regicide,' Michael butted in, elbowing his way again in front of Leonora. Tom and Richard stood beside him. 'That's a big word for a workin' man.'

The man scowled at him and threw words back over his shoulder. 'Yer know what they say, marrahs? That we should not fire on our enemies, be they Huns or Russkis. An' we fought in the war, didn't we? Our mates dyin'. Brothers. Sons as well. Didn't they? Traitors, that's the top an' bottom of it.' He pushed at Michael.

'What we say,' said Leonora from behind Michael's elbow, 'is that

292

other working men are not your enemy. They're your class. They could be your brothers.'

'What'd you know anyway?' He expelled a gob of spit in her direction. 'A bliddy jumped-up woman.'

Finn ducked under Michael's elbow and faced the man herself. 'We know as well as you, as well as anybody. It's up to us no less than it's up to you. It's our vote as well that puts in them that makes this mess of things. It's our vote that can put in people to mend it.'

'Bravo!' said Leonora and Kate in unison. Behind them Susanah clapped her hands.

Richard's clear, aristocratic voice cut into the air. 'You say you fought in the war, man. Which regiment?'

'The DLI, sir.' The *sir* was out before he could stop it.

'Then you should be ashamed of yourself, abusing ladies like this, and other people going about their legitimate business.'

Whether it was the determination of all the people they were facing, or the authority implicit in Richard's cut-glass, professional soldier tones, the aggression seemed to leak away from the mob then. The muttering continued, but the crowd parted and let Leonora's supporters through, grunting and swearing at them as they passed.

'I'll stay here,' said Michael. 'See they keep their distance.'

But once the door was shut the interest of the crowd faded altogether. The leader made his way across the square to the corner of an alley and the rest followed. Michael strolled across after them and recognised the man they were clustering round as Daniel Marchant.

'You didn't do it,' Daniel's petulant voice pierced the threatening rumble. 'You didn't do it. You were supposed to break heads. Frighten them properly. I've orders not to pay unless the job's—'

'Why, look at that, lads,' called Michael from across the square. 'These fascist bosses don't pay up either. What you need is a bloody good strike. Or a bit of direct action. I say take what's yours.'

The men were starting to push Daniel about, to try to do just that. He pulled himself out of one burly grasp and started to run. The last Michael saw was Daniel fleeing up the back alleys of Darlington pursued by a hired mob.

Grinning, he turned, went inside the crowded hall and closed the double doors behind him. Then he took his place beside Finn and settled down to listen to Leonora.

'He asked you to marry him? Richard Morgan Evans? Phew! I'd take his hand off,' said Kate.

'Would you?' They were walking back from New Morven Halt, still flushed with the excitement of the success of the meeting.

Michael had gone home with Tom Farrell.

'Richard's a nice feller, Finn. Right sentiments. Open mind. And all that money. Phew! I'd be the last to doubt your fascination, Finn, but are you sure he meant *marriage*? He *mentioned* that word?'

'I'm sure.'

'Then I'd take his hand off,' she repeated.

'What about Michael, what do you think of him?'

'Well . . . he's the best-looking feller I've seen in years, if ever. Not just in his face, but his body. Those shoulders. That loose-limbed body. And in his . . . kind of seriousness. Courage. And he thinks the sun shines from your fingernails.'

'So?'

'No contest, love. Go for the money and the class. Think of the life you'll be able to lead. It'll stand you in good stead on those rainy days.'

'Talking of rainy days . . .' said Finn. They were standing outside the shop. The row that was brewing inside penetrated the plate glass. As they opened the door and the shop bell tinkled, Esther and Patrick looked round like two children caught stealing.

Esther turned to her daughter. 'Finn, I was telling your father once and for all that all this credit has to come to an end. From now on we deal in cash and nothing else. They'll not starve—'

'But they will!' yelled Patrick. 'That is the point, you stupid woman. They will!'

Then they both looked even more startled as, behind Finn, they saw Kate MacMahon in all her elegant finery.

'Well, I never!' said Patrick. 'Kate, you look—'

'Wonderful,' said Esther. 'Where did you get that suit?'

The next day at eleven o'clock Finn made her way across to Plush Folly. Behind her she left Kate, demure again, helping her father in the shop; and her mother, still in bed, calling down for Kate, dear, to bring her some tea.

Smiler, who had been sweeping and piling and counting for Patrick since the dark dawn, walked back across with her. In the garden she met Michael and Hubert who, with glowing faces, were tackling a massive withered hornbeam with a two-handled saw. They grinned like panting children at her, then turned back to their task. Smiler went to stand behind Michael like a small sentinel.

Over his shoulder Hubert gasped. 'Go and see Jenefer, Finnuola. She's really down. Needs some company.'

Finn was just entering the house when she realised that for the first time Hubert had called her by her name. He did not need to see her any more as "the maid". Jenefer and the twins were in the kitchen, as was usual now. Their eyes were streaming. Before them they had twin mountains of cut onions and apples.

'We're making chutney,' said Toots.

'I i'nt never had chutney,' said Nancy. 'What's it taste like?'

'Like people,' said Finn. 'Sweet and sour at the same time.' She sat down, took up an onion and started to peel it. 'How're you, Jenefer?'

'Fine!' said Jenefer brightly. 'Worried about Hubert, of course. Sergeant Corcoran's been to talk to Michael again today. I'm sure Hubert's on the cusp of going to the sergeant and confessing, even though he doesn't remember a thing.' Her face brightened. 'Richard's coming later today.'

'He's asked me to marry him.'

Jenefer wiped her eyes with a clean tea towel and threw it over the heap of onions. 'Toots, Nancy, why don't you get your recipe books and copy down the recipe for this chutney? Best writing, mind you!'

'I've got eleven recipes in my book,' said Toots.

'Eleven in mine too,' said Nancy. 'An' one drawing of Plush Folly.'

'I drew Jenefer,' said Toots. 'With odd shoes on.'

Jenefer pulled up a chair by the fire and sat on it. She looked at Finn. 'Will you do it? Marry him? What did you say?'

'I said nothing. He said not to say anything just yet. That Leonora Scorton's taken quite a fancy for him. Talking about a job, work anyway, for him down in Westminster.' She giggled. 'That's a turn-up for the books. Or, as my ma would say, a volte-face. Him working for Labour after the company he was keeping in France.'

'The General among them, I suppose?'

'Looked like that.'

'Richard was saying there's money of mine, some inheritance, lying idle in London.' Jenefer snorted. 'Arthur failed to track me down, apparently.'

Finn hesitated. 'Is the money important?'

Jenefer shrugged. 'Means we're no longer poor as church mice.' She coloured slightly. 'Although here in New Morven that is very relative. To talk about being down to your last thousand is a bit insensitive.'

'What will you do about it?'

'Well, with this hanging over us, nothing. In an ideal world it would free us to travel again. London. Back to France. Even America. As it is, it may have to come in handy for clinics and hospitals, if they say Hubert did kill that old duffer and is really as mad as a hatter.'

'Jenefer, I've never seen him saner.'

'That's the trouble. Neither have I. If *that's* the case it wouldn't be hospital. Could be prison. Or worse.'

The twins had stopped writing and were staring at them with wide knowing eyes. Toots' lip trembled and a tear reformed in Nancy's eye. In the silence that ensued Finn struggled to find something helpful, something constructive to say. Then she had her brainwave. 'Jenefer, once you told me you could transfer your dreams to Hubert, to calm him down, to cheer him up?'

'Yes. Yes. It was very hard work, very tiring.'

'Couldn't you somehow transfer his dream to you, so that you can remember it? So you both know what really happened? Then at least you'll be able to do something based on what you know rather than whistling in the dark.'

'That's not so easy. How? How would I do that?'

'Same as before,' said Nancy.

'. . . ame as before.' Toots was on beat behind.

'Like we said, he's never seemed better,' said Finn.

Hubert, when they proposed the scheme, was all for it. He put on his cloak and his hat, and, when Finn gave him his stick, he thrust it in his Sam Browne belt, crosswise, like a sword. Then, in a little troop, the black and white cat bringing up the rear, they followed Hubert's route down towards the river. Jenefer was by his side, and the others a step or two behind.

Before they got to the river Hubert took out his stick and started slashing the undergrowth.

'Now what are you doing?' asked Jenefer softly.

'I am walking along, There are demons either side of me and I am keeping them off. They are fluttering and swooping just above the branches. Screaming at me. The road is narrow. The river is calling. The water is so black.' He stopped.

'What is it, Hubert?' She pressed his arm.

'He's there on the bridge. That dragon. The black one. He's coming. Coming. But I'll take him on. I go forward. Now is the time.' Hubert flailed around, then cringed almost to the floor as an invisible blow winded him. He hauled himself to his feet, dodged an invisible blow, flailed around a bit more, then stood very tall and turned sideways.

Then he was peering in the water.

'What did you do then, Hubert?'

'He was coming at me, the black one, his sword high, coming down on me. So I side-stepped. And he catapulted past me into the water.'

'You didn't throw him in? You didn't kill him?'

Hubert sighed very deeply, then took Jenefer's hand. 'No, my darling, I didn't. I'm both very glad and sorry to say I didn't. The real dragon was dying on the walls of the coach house. I know that. I put him there and he died.'

'Hooray!' The twins, picking up the delight and satisfaction in the atmosphere, were clapping their hands. Jenefer was hugging Hubert and the twins were hugging her. Michael put an arm round Finn.

Then Smiler set up a great bellow. 'Bliddy hell! Look at that! The buggers've fired our bonfire.'

Over to the right, just beyond the belt of woodland, the flames were leaping into the sky. Smiler started to run and the others followed. There were more boys at the bonfire when they arrived, looking on in dismay as the work of weeks was destroyed. Smiler picked up a big stone and heaved it into the heart of the fire in frustration.

'You buggers! You bastards!' he shouted. The others followed suit. A hail of stones crashed uselessly into the crackling wood.

Toots tugged at Smiler's sleeve. 'There's a trail,' she said, pointing.

'Yeah,' he said. 'Look at this.' A trickle of matches, scattered singly on the grass, lead out of the clearing and through the bushes into the woodland. Smiler set off and all of them followed him.

They had only been walking a few minutes when the bushes opened out again and they were near the edge of the wood, where it butted on to the ancient stone wall which was a boundary for New Morven Cemetery.

'Bliddy hell.'

'Smiler! Enough of that language,' said Michael before he saw what Smiler saw. Then: 'Jesus, Mary and Joseph.' He clutched Finn's hand. Behind them the bonfire boys came into the clearing and made a circle around what could only be a gravestone.

There, lying within the low iron railings surrounding his mother's grave, was Daniel Marchant. His clothes were in a neat pile beside him, as was an empty matchbox and a blue silk sack with pills and powder spilling out of it. Beside it, small brown paper packets were laid neatly in a row. Red ribbons, tied round his wrists, lifted slightly in the November breeze.

Daniel was stark naked and he looked, to all intents and purposes, as dead as a doornail.

'He hasn't got much of a willie, has he?' said Smiler thoughtfully.

'I thought you looked really nice yesterday,' said Patrick. 'Really nice. You should wear that suit more often. Yes. Green really suits you.'

Kate dimpled and dipped a slight curtsy. 'Thank you, kind sir.'

There had been a continuous trickle of customers and this was the first time they'd had time to talk.

Patrick stared hard at her. 'Are you in disguise, Kate? What are you doing here? What are you?'

'Patrick, I have to tell you something. I'm going away.'

'Going away? You've just arrived.'

She put a hand on his where it lay on the counter. 'I came for a quiet time, Pat. Something awful happened and your little Finn was such a brick I wanted to come back with her. To get myself, well, better, see.' She laughed. 'Now, what with you and Esther and Finn, I am better. Raring to go!' She paused. 'To go.'

'Oh Kate!'

She squeezed his hand. 'No glum faces, Pat. You're a lovely man. The nicest I've ever been with. There's some bastards out there, excuse my French. But you're good and kind. A softie but none the worse for that. Too many hard'ns around. But things move on. I move on.'

'What'll you do?' His voice trembled with the effort to make it seem disinterested.

'Well, seeing as you ask, Leonora Scorton's asked me to go down and help her down there, in London. Secretarying, book-keeping and all that. Looks like she's on a recruitment drive. She's lassoed young Richard Morgan Evans and she has her eye on Tom Farrell. People like me and Tom are her credentials, see? We can talk about what it's really like, out there.'

'She's using you, you mean?'

Kate shrugged. 'Looks like that. But it's for the greater good.' She took her hand from his. 'Anyway, people always use each other. What about you and me?' Then she grinned. 'But wasn't it nice? Hey, what's that? Big car at your door. Now here's a man who could buy up your shop.'

Sir Oliver Marchant swept into the shop like a ship of war, Mrs Fosdick in his wake.

'Can I help you, Sir Oliver?'

Sir Oliver raised an eyebrow around the crowded scruffy shop. 'Hardly in the provisioning line, I think. But Mrs Fosdick here says that you may be able to assist with some information.'

'Anything, Sir Oliver.'

'My nephew, Daniel Marchant, is staying with me after the recent tragedy regarding his father. He did not return to Banville Hall last night. I came here to enquire of Mrs Fosdick and it seems he was not at the vicarage. But she says the boy was carrying a torch for . . .' he cast an eye round the shop, and it came to rest on Kate, standing foursquare now beside Patrick '. . . the daughter of the shopkeeper.'

Patrick took a step forward. 'It was no torch, sir. He—'

Sir Oliver slapped his smooth leather gloves into his palm. 'Is he here, man? Is my nephew here?'

298

'No, we have not seen him. And I'll tell you he's not welcome—'

But Sir Oliver was already turning away. 'Then I'll bid you good day.'

'Don't you . . .' Patrick darted towards him but his own door was shut in his face. When he turned back towards Kate there were tears in his eyes. 'You see, Kate? I can't even protect my daughter against them, against any of them.'

She put her arms around him, her face against his. 'Don't think about it, Pat. You're a good man, a kind man. Men like him aren't worth the dirt on your shoe. Your daughter's lucky to have you.'

There was a noise in the back room and they pulled apart, turning away from each other.

'That was Sir Oliver Marchant, wasn't it?' Esther was standing in the middle doorway in her best dress. Her hair was pinned up quite neatly. She came across and perched on her usual stool. 'What did he want?' Her face was quite smooth. There was no telling whether or not she had witnessed the touching scene between her husband and the woman who had recently become her friend. 'It was something about Finnuola wasn't it?'

29

Deliverance

Michael carried Daniel Marchant back to Banville Hall wrapped in Hubert Loumis's capacious cloak. They debated as to where to take him but they decided Banville Hall was marginally nearer to the grave outside the cemetery wall and the bonfire, than the vicarage.

Smiler and the north end bonfire gang remained behind to mourn over their lost fire. The others accompanied Michael on his journey, short enough under normal circumstances, but quite a trek weighed down by an unconscious man. Hubert carried the packets of money which Daniel had not paid to the bullyboys. Jenefer carried Daniel's clothes. Finn carried the blue silk sack, its neck tightly tied. The twins walked one either side of Michael, occasionally glancing at the shrouded shape of Daniel Marchant with clinical interest.

Sir Oliver's sleek motor-car was on the drive of Banville Hall, and the door half open when they arrived. Michael shouldered the door fully open and walked into the house, followed by the others.

Sir Oliver himself was in the hall, handing his coat to an elderly maid. 'What's this?' he blustered. His eye fixed on Michael. 'I know you. You're one of those criminals . . .' He ventured forward and looked at the vacantly sleeping face of Daniel. 'What have you done to my nephew?'

Michael walked past him, on through an open door into the drawing room where he lay Daniel on a sofa. He rolled him to one side, heaved Hubert's cloak from under him and handed it back to its owner.

Oliver stared at Daniel's naked body, his eyes bulging. Then he grabbed his own coat from the maid and covered him. The rest of them were crowded into the room; the maidservant had hustled in after them, not quite sure what to do.

'Yes we have met, mister,' said Michael. 'Last time, with me mates, wasn't I trying to teach you something about the world you live in? This time it's another bit of the world you live in. I've done nothing to your nephew except come on in him in the woods, dead

301

to the world in his birthday suit. So I brought him here.'

'He's fired our Smiler's bonfire,' said Toots, who had been following all this very closely. 'He didn't like that, our Smiler.'

'. . . bonfire,' said Nancy.

On the sofa, Daniel started to mutter, threshing around as he rose to a lighter level of sleep.

'He was at the edge of the wood, lying on what must be, I imagine, his mother's grave,' said Jenefer, her voice involuntarily sympathetic. 'If it was a try at suicide, thank goodness it failed.'

Very carefully Finn placed the blue silk sack on a low table beside the couch. 'This had pills and powder inside. He must have taken them.' She picked up a strand of the red ribbon where it fell away from his wrists. 'I don't know what this is about.'

There was a small shriek from the maid in the doorway. 'Blood. His mother. She cut her wrists.'

'Drugs? Are you're suggesting my nephew indulged in—'

'Those people he was running with in Nice, they did.'

'How would you know, you . . .'

'Shopgirl? I know 'cos I was there, Sir Oliver. I know for a fact that Denis Consadine—'

Suddenly the old man was roaring at her, 'Sir Denis Consadine? *Sir* Denis Consadine? How dare you! how dare you! Insolent girl. I'll have you . . .'

There was a groan from the couch as Daniel turned slightly to one side, and spewed a fountain of vomit half on to his uncle's coat and half on to the carpet. Then his eyes opened slightly and he started to mutter. 'Mummy, Mummy, is he there yet? The old cockroach is coming to get you. You thought you'd got away, didn't you? He's coming. I was coming myself to save you . . .' He started to laugh, then the laughter turned to wild sobs.

Michael looked at Sir Oliver Marchant. 'I wouldn't say his word'd get very far in a court of law, would you?'

The other man drew himself to his full height. 'I think you should go, all of you. My nephew needs a doctor.'

Quietly they filed out. Finn was last. She turned. 'You'll excuse me for saying this, Sir Oliver . . .'

He glared at her.

'But common good manners say you should thank us for bringing him here. He really could have died there in that state.' She closed the door firmly behind her.

At first there was an air of quiet satisfaction in the group as they trudged their way back into New Morven. Jenefer and Hubert set off arm in arm, with a twin hanging on to either side. Jenefer started to say that now they knew the truth, that the old duffer had died by accident, they could get on properly with things. She felt sure in her heart that Hubert would be safe now. 'There's some money, Hubert. Richard was telling me. Lain there for some time. Means we can go . . . anywhere. London. Back to the South of France. America.'

Hubert laughed. 'Wait, wait, O impetuous queen! Give me time to savour the return to a life without dragons and demons.'

'Wouldn't you like to go somewhere?'

'Of course I would, but where or why is unclear as yet. Give me time.'

'Where are those two?' said Jenefer, looking round. The twins had loosened their grip, and were now behind Finn and Michael, their small dark heads close together.

Finn and Michael were walking along without touching. Finn was acutely aware of him. She hadn't been able to work him out in the last few days. This man who had cried with joy as they came together, who had told her that she was a 'true beauty, a true delight', was treating her politely, with respect which itself created a great chasm between them. She might have been a distant cousin. And her body longed for him. She was afraid to touch him even casually in case she exploded with feeling and disgraced herself. And now she had Richard to think about. His offer had its charms. If she had never met Michael, perhaps . . .

Michael cleared his throat. 'That was a good show you made back there, Finn.'

'Pleased you think so.'

'Did I say it before? You've got spunk.' He paused. 'Did you really see people with drugs when you were in France?'

She shook her head. 'No. I just spent time with people who drank coffee and chocolate. But Kate, she did. Had a bad turn with one of them, a horrible man who took cocaine, I think. That Sir Denis Consadine.'

'Hard to read, that Kate.'

'Yes,' she said. They were on Mainstreet now. 'Seems she's going off to London with that Leonora Scorton. To help her.'

'Her too? She's 'ticin' Tom down there, an' all. Writin' stuff, an' witnessing what goes on here at the hard end, to make them comfortable bourgeois audiences uncomfortable.' He paused. 'The union want me to do some of the things he does up here. Not the writin', like. But helpin' Jonty an' them to organise an' all that. Money in it. Not a real wage, but . . .'

She squeezed his arm then. 'That's perfect, Michael. Worthwhile.' Her hand dropped to her side.

He turned to her. 'Finn, is there something wrong? I—'

Toots' cross voice came at them from behind. 'Mick, will you get on? That's the second time we've bumped.'

He was silent then, and only gave Finn a vague smile as she left them to turn towards the shop door.

In the shop she found only her mother, perched on her stool. Esther told Finn that her father was off on his rounds and Kate was packing. 'She's going to London with that politician. Did she tell you?'

'I knew something was up. She said she'd had an offer she couldn't refuse.' She looked at her mother's strained face. 'She was only ever going to be here a short time, Ma. She's not the type to—'

'Do you think I don't know that? This filthy village, this dark county. She's a person of refinement. Sophisticated. Did you see that green suit? She's moved in society . . .'

Finn bit her lips on a revelation of the true nature of Kate's professional relationship with that society.

'. . . Kate's travelled, Finnuola. Of course she couldn't stay here. Nothing to keep her here. Not me, not even your father. Not even you.'

In desperation, to escape her mother's misery, Finn blurted out what was on her mind at that moment. 'Ma, Richard asked me to marry him . . .'

Immediately Esther brightened. 'Finnuola, how wonderful! Wonderful. Now then, when will you want the wedding? Now don't you worry, money may be stretched but your Uncle Harold wouldn't have his niece shamed . . .'

'Woa, Ma, hold your horses. I haven't said yes.'

'You refused him? Finnuola, you—'

'I didn't do that either.'

'Finnuola!' wailed Esther. 'What am I to do with you?'

In number twelve Patrick was sitting in Kate's easy chair, twirling his trilby between his knees. He smiled faintly. 'I should have known it was too good to last, Katie. And I knew you weren't what you cracked up to be. More to you than that.'

She nodded. 'We've had some nice times, Pat, you and me. And I've had some nice times with Esther. I like her. She's a funny stick and there's a lot swirling round in that head of hers. And she hasn't much of a life.'

He put his head down.

'No. It's not your fault, Pat. It's the times, these wicked times. And from what I hear, it seems you two got off on the wrong foot anyway.' She put a hand towards him. 'Be good to her, Pat. At least you've got each other. Me, I've a feeling I'll be on my own for ever. No, don't shout me down. I feel it's true.'

He clasped her hand as though her grip would stop him from drowning.

She touched his shoulder with the other hand. 'If we'd met when I was twenty, before you met Esther, who knows? Maybe we'd have a string of children and a string of shops between us? But like I said, you're the nicest man I've been with. That I've made love with. And I don't know whether you realise this, but I've been with quite a few.'

'Oh, Kate!'

She stood up, pulled him to his feet and kissed his cheek. 'Don't "Oh, Kate" me, Pat, with that face like a mile of bad road. Now come on. You get along to the shop and cheer Esther up. You're to tell her her hair's very nice like that, and she suits that dress she's wearing. Do you hear me? I've an errand of my own to do, then I'll come and join you.'

They stopped outside the shop and she looked up at him. 'I want you to do something for me, Pat.'

He put his hands in his pockets to prevent himself touching her. 'Anything, Kate. Anything.'

'Give young Finn a wage. Then she'll be free of you and Esther and the shop, even when she's with you. And she won't end up like Esther, curled in over herself for want of space.'

He nodded his agreement, even though he didn't understand what she said.

She left him at the shop and made her way down the street and up the little pathway beside Plush Folly. She knocked on the door of Alan Newton's cottage and a surprised Michael let her in, asking her to sit in the one comfortable chair.

He looked at her enquiringly. 'You're very welcome, Kate, but I'm sure you're here to some purpose.'

'You know how fond I am of young Finn, Michael. She's come to be like a little sister to me in these weeks.'

He nodded.

'Accepted me for what I was. No questions. Well, almost. And she stuck by me. Seems like the first person I've met in years who wanted nothing from me. Who gave without calculating the getting.'

He smiled. 'Sure, don't I like her more than a bit meself, Kate?'

'Well, I wanted to give you this.' She handed him a white envelope. 'In it is a legal paper to say that number twelve belongs to you. Not rented, or borrowed like this one, but owned. And there's twenty pounds in there for . . . expenses . . . if you do what I think you should.'

Michael was peering into the envelope frowning slightly.

'And here.' She gave him a small box. He opened it and a broad gold band winked back at him in the firelight.

She stared at it. 'It was my mother's. She pawned it when we were on extremely, the worst of, hard times. I redeemed it, but I couldn't

305

let her know, as the pawning was her dark secret. They were happy, Michael, my mum and dad. Even through the hardest times they loved each other. I thought you might find a use for it.'

He looked at her, understanding dawning in his eyes. Then he shook his head. 'I could be in prison this time next week, Kate.'

She shrugged and stood up. 'I'll have to be off now. By the by, you do know, Michael, that if I found anyone – anyone – doing the dirty on that girl I'd screw them into the ground till they squeaked?' She swept out, then popped her head round the door again.' Oh, I forgot to mention it. Did I tell you Richard Morgan Evans has asked Finn to marry him? I'd 'a thought that'd please both Jenefer and Esther down to the ground, wouldn't you?'

Hurriedly Sergeant Corcoran buttoned up his jacket and put his hand over his sparse short hair.

'Come on! Come on!' said his wife from the door.

He went through the door and across the hallway to the little office. His hand went up in a salute which was half military, half touching of forelock. He cleared his throat. 'Afternoon, Sir Oliver.'

To the sergeant's surprise, Sir Oliver Marchant tucked his polished stick under his arm and shook his hand heartily. 'Ah, Sergeant. Good of you to make the time.'

Corcoran's glance narrowed slightly. The last time he had met this man was to endure a bullying insistence that the death of the Reverend Hildebrand Marchant, Sir Oliver's brother, was obviously foul play and if the sergeant was too laggardly to pursue it as such, then he knew higher powers who would be mightily annoyed.

'What can I do for you, Sir Oliver?' said Corcoran evenly enough.

'Well, I have been giving some thought regarding the tragic demise of my poor brother. And have been speaking to two coroners of my acquaintance.' He touched his moustache. 'This is just between you and me, you understand, Sergeant. Anyway, to be perfectly honest, I have come to the conclusion that, my brother's death being so clearly an accident, to pursue any other possibility would be inappropriate, distressing even, for his family. My dear brother must be put to his rest with Christian solemnity, with due dignity as he would have wished. This is all going on far too long. It is undignified.'

Corcoran relaxed a little. 'I don't know about that, Sir Oliver. I've been pursuing my enquiries and it seems that Irishman had grounds for a grudge against your brother. And with Mr Daniel Marchant's testimony– – '

'There is no question of my nephew giving evidence, Sergeant. He has been through such a great deal lately and is now quite ill with . . . quinsies. So he will not be able to say anything.'

'But he could when he's better, Sir Oliver,' said Corcoran, enjoying himself now.

The stick came down and struck the floor, hard. 'No! No. I cannot have it. My nephew suffers from a fragile constitution which is to some degree inherited. And the drama of recent weeks has lead him to be . . . overwrought. You have been in this village long enough, Sergeant, to know that his mother also had a fragile constitution.'

'Ah,' said Corcoran thoughtfully, 'you're sayin' that Mr Daniel Marchant would be an unreliable witness?'

Oliver Marchant was now very red indeed. 'I am saying nothing of the sort. I am saying that he is—'

Corcoran let him off the hook. 'Well, Sir Oliver, if that's yer view, I must take it into consideration. To be quite frank I thought it a shaky proposition in the first place.'

'Hmmph. Well. You are very wise. In that case, I will proceed with the arrangements for my brother's funeral.'

'Yes, Sir Oliver, I think that'll be in order,' said Corcoran, giving permission which was not really sought.

He escorted Sir Oliver to the door and watched him as he got into his sleek motor-car, tapped his driver on the shoulder and sat back in the deep cushions. Then Corcoran walked back through to his kitchen, loosening his jacket again and undoing his collar stud. 'Horrible feller, that, Bridget, never liked him. Thinks he's God Almighty. I've more time for Stacy Smith, an' that's sayin' sommat. Now, pour us some tea, will yer?'

'Was he talkin' about that nephew of his?'

'You know he was. You were listenin' at the door.'

'Well, I an't surprised he can't let that lad speak out. Bella Smith's middle lad was there when they found him. Hadn't he fired their bonfire an' gone off to his mother's grave to do himself in? They found him stark naked, good as dead, with red ribbons tied all over him. Can yer imagine?' She filled his mug to the top. 'I saw poor Mrs Fosdick in Priorton Co-op. An' she says the lad's ravin'. Callin' her unmentionable things. Insultin' his father. Now you know Mrs Fosdick wouldn't like that. Thought the world of Mr Marchant, did Mrs Fosdick. I sometimes think . . .'

'Is there any of yer fairy cakes left, Bridget? I could just fancy one of those.' Corcoran lounged back in his chair, profoundly happy with his lot. 'Then I'll make my way across to that O'Toole feller an' give him a last fright before I let him off the hook.'

She dumped the plate, graced by its fragile cake, in front of him. 'You have it in for the Irish, all of them.'

He bit into the cake, a look of bliss lighting up his square face. 'Not for the ones that can cook, Bridget. Not those.'

★ ★ ★

Michael closed the door behind the sergeant and leaned against it. Then he went across to the table, took the house deeds and the money from the envelope, and placed the gold ring on top of them. 'Now!' he said.

He looked across at Smiler, who was sitting by the fire whittling. 'Will you go across to the shop an' ask Finn if she has a minute, Smiler? Well, ten minutes.' He raked around in his pocket and handed a threepenny bit to his brother. 'An' maybe you could get some sweets for you an' the girls. Take them across to Plush Folly for them? An' tell Finn it's urgent. Tell her it's a matter of life or death.'

30

Departures

'Can Ah have thet in the book, Mrs Montague?' Bella fixed Esther with her most appealing gaze.

Finn was perched up a ladder cleaning the inside of the plate glass window. She watched with interest as her mother surveyed the collection of small packages and parcels in front of her, then opened the greasy book with the very tips of her fingers. 'You already owe two pounds fourteen and elevenpence ha'penny, Mrs Smith. How can I let you have more?'

'If yer dinnet lerrus have it on tick wuh'll go without wuh teas, Mrs Montague. There's not a scrap in the pantry save three taties our Ernest picked up off the back of a potato wagon. An' wi' this new bairn on the way Ah canna stand washin' for folks, an' Stacy can pick up nee work since he was let in with the authorities. An' ah've pawned everything except what we stand up in, an' . . .'

Esther pushed the packets towards her. 'Just take them, Mrs Smith, take them! I'll put them in the book, but you'll have to find some way to pay some of this debt off. This can't go on for ever.'

'Ah know that full well, Mrs Montague. Neebody better.' Bella pushed the packages into the floursack she was carrying. 'Good of yer, Mrs Montague. There could be sommat at the end of the week. Our Stacy's diggin' the hole for the vicar, an'll help to carry him at the funeral, shouldn't wonder. Our Stacy says he's a heavy man, Mr Marchant, for all he was so thin and spiky. Pity Stanley Punchard's not there to play him out with one of his big anthems. Emily'd a' liked that.' She glanced at Finn. 'Time they buried him, like. It's a disgrace to keep a dead man above ground so long. An Ah tell yer what, old Alan Newton – ye knaa he works at Banville Hall? – well, he telt us he'd seen them take off Mr *Daniel* Marchant, bundled in a blanket. Can yer believe it? The cook telt Alan the lad was for Sedgefield. A strait-jacket for him, shouldn't wonder. A private room, though, the cook said that.'

'Too good for him,' said Esther with sudden violence.

'Mother!' warned Finn.

'Thank you, Mrs Smith. I've got them all down in the book.' Esther watched as Bella gathered her bag to her chest and waddled out.

Finn came across, wiping her hands with a towel. 'There, Ma, not so easy to refuse credit even when you want to, is it? Not with the person there in front of you.'

'They're so improvident, so careless, these people, even with what little they have,' sniffed Esther. 'I've seen Stacy Smith coming out of the Puddler's Arms more than once. Staggering.'

'They're not all like that. Some are too ground down even to play the odds like Stacy Smith does. And even that, it's not Bella's fault, is it? Bella's a trier, don't you see that? The children have to have something. We can't let the children starve, can we? And they do pay off a bit when any money comes in, all of them.'

The bell trembled again and Kate MacMahon walked in, glowing in her green suit and feathered hat. Esther came from behind the counter.

'You're off, Kate,' she said, folding her lips tight to stop them trembling.

Kate nodded. 'Yes, Esther. Clarry Tazewell's out there with my luggage, waiting for me. Seems he's set up a bit of a taxi-service with the vicar's car until things get sorted out. A nice bit of enterprise, don't you think?'

Tentatively, Esther held out her hand. 'All the very best, Kate. It was good to have you here. I'll . . .' she took a deep breath, '. . . miss you.'

Kate ignored the hand and hugged her, enveloping her with soft fabric and scent. 'Thank you for making me so much at home, Esther.' She put a slip of paper into Esther's apron pocket. 'There's my address in London, love. You finish your story and send it to me, and I'll type it on Miss Leonora Scorton's typewriter and see if I can flog it to someone down there. It's as good as any of those you've been burying your nose in for twenty years, I can tell you. And I'll be up here, again, never fear. Leonora Scorton's up here at the hard end, all the time. And now I'm like Ruth, me. Whither she goeth I goeth . . . goeth, is that right?' She turned to Finn and winked. 'Well, Miss Changemaker, I'm off now. Not to the life of a Professional Lady, but to the life of a professional lady. Get my drift?'

Finn laughed and kissed her cheek. 'You behave yourself, mind, Kate. And come and see us. Do you want me to do something about Number twelve?'

'Don't you worry about that. The house is in safe hands. By the way, did you decide what to do about Richard Morgan Evans?'

310

Finn glanced at her mother. 'Still thinking,' she said.

Esther had her mind on other things. 'Patrick's at the whole-saler's, Kate. He'll be so sorry he missed you going. He's appreciated what you've done here.' Both Kate and Finn looked at Esther, wondering whether somewhere under fifteen layers of innocence, she really knew what had been going on. Esther's face simply reflected genuine concern.

Kate plonked a kiss on her cheek. 'Just give him that from me, Esther, and tell him he has to take care of you.'

As she went out of the door she bumped into young Smiler O'Toole. In the road, Clarry Tazewell, who had been lounging against the bonnet of the car, stood up straight. Then he bent to fit his starting handle into its hole and grunted as he turned it. From inside the shop Kate could see Smiler staring at her and her grand car, through an O in the word COCOA, which was painted on the glass door.

Settling into the back of the car, Kate dwelled with some anticipation on thoughts of a tender little farewell assignation with Patrick in the Gaunt Valley Hotel before she got her train in Priorton. The car engine started to chug and Clarry was just releasing the handbrake when Finn emerged from the shop and raced across the road. Kate smiled and waved vigorously at Esther, who was now standing in the shop doorway like a lost soul.

Finn raced on, past Jenefer and Hubert, who were swirling away on the motorbike as she arrived at Plush Folly. She looked at them twice, noting that it was Hubert who was in the driving seat. He must be feeling better.

Alan Newton's cottage was deserted when Finn arrived. The fire was burning brightly in the grate and steam was floating gently from the forked spout of the black kettle. The ladder was up against the loft. She climbed up and put her head through the hole. Michael was sitting at the far end of the loft, leaning against the wall beside the shamrock window.

'What is it, Michael? What did you want?'

'I watched you come, Finnuola. All the way down the street and round by Plush Folly. You got bigger and bigger. Prettier and prettier.' His face was in the shadow of the eaves.

She hauled herself into the loft. 'Smiler said it was a matter of life or death.' She crawled towards him until she could see his eyes. 'What is it, Michael, this life or death?'

'My life. My death. To live with you will be a life. To live without you will be a death.' His voice was flat, emotionless. 'Do I hear that the soldier feller's asked you to marry him?'

'That's true.'

'An' what will you be doin' about that?'

311

She pulled herself along so that she was sitting beside him. 'Well, Michael, considering the way you've been retreating from me in these weeks I have to admit I gave it some thought.'

'An' what did you think?'

She leaned her shoulder hard against his. 'Well, I thought he was a very nice man. You have to agree with that, Michael. He's jolly, good fun to be with. Prepared to listen and learn. He was polite to my mother and respectful to my father.' She put her arm round his shoulders and turned him towards her in the dim loft light. 'He's the son of my best friend, so I knew that at least part of his heritage was right.' She wriggled her knees so she was kneeling up in front of him. 'He's very rich, so I knew that I and mine would never know the desolation of want that I've seen here in New Morven.' She smoothed the dark curly hair away from his brow. 'I knew he and I'd always be friends, even after we'd been lovers.' She placed his arms around her waist. 'But the thought of him didn't light me up the way . . .' she had to pull away from his tightening grip now, '. . . that thoughts of you do.' She escaped his mouth. 'He doesn't turn my knees to jelly and my inside to molten lava. And I find that I'd rather scrub shirts like Bella Smith, or sell jam jars like Emily Punchard, and be with you. And with Smiler and the twins . . . Michael, wait, let me say this. All of it. Stop it! And all this year, throughout our trials and tribulations, I've watched Jonty and Susanah Clelland. Their love shines out like the brightest beacon. That is, it says it in the Bible, to be prized above rubies. And it's there for us, just us two, to take, to relish.'

'I have something. Kate gave it to me.' He dipped in his pocket and brought out a handkerchief which was threaded through a ring and tied in a knot around it. With clumsy fingers he untied the knot. 'She's a good woman is Kate. And her ma and pa had a good marriage, so this is a good ring.'

She nodded. 'We'll make it a good ring, Michael. Good for us, I'm sure of it, whatever the times to come.'

He lifted her hand and placed the ring on her finger. She turned her hand and held his hand tight, then brought it to her lips and kissed first his knuckles then his palm.

He was kissing her then, and there were no words. There was touching and the tender brush of lips and tongue. There was stroking and the tease of fingertips. There was the raising of head, the arching of back, the involuntary closing of eye to aid the inner focus, the distillation of self and other that makes for love.

A world in time later they heard sounds down below. Michael pulled on his clothes in seconds and made his way down the ladder. It took a little longer for Finn to dress and when she made her slower progress down she was faced with Smiler, who had the black and white cat draped round his neck like a scarf; and Nancy and Toots, who had parcels and packages at their feet, clothes over their shoulders.

'What's this?' said Finn.

'Toots says they've gone, Jenefer and Hubert,' announced Smiler. 'Gone away.'

Finn frowned. 'Gone?'

'They've gone to the South of France,' said Nancy sadly. 'They've got some money now, and can go away.'

'Go away,' said Toots, her usually bright face white and strained.

'So they left you there? At Plush Folly?' said Michael, frowning. 'Alone?'

'That can't be true. Toots! What did they say?' said Finn.

'They didn't say nothing. Just went off on their motorbike.'

Finn was shaking her head. 'No, no. That can't be right.'

Nancy looked more closely at her. 'Finn, do you know you've got your jumper inside out?'

'And your hair's really messy,' said Toots, fondling her own neatly braided hair with pride, her recent distress momentarily forgotten.

Finn went beetroot red and Michael took her hand. 'There's something you need to—'

He was interrupted by the roar of a motorbike outside. Toots shrieked and Nancy shrieked: a tenth of a second later they piled outside and viewed the vision before them.

'Jesus, Mary an' Joseph,' said Smiler.

It was Jenefer. And Hubert. And their motorbike. And to one side of them stood a contraption balancing on one wheel.

'Our sidecar,' said Hubert, beaming. He leaped off the pillion.

'We'd ordered it. They were holding it at Priorton Central Garage for us.' Jenefer pulled the bike back on its stand and alighted. In a second the twins were inside the sidecar, and Smiler was on the pillion.

'The twins thought you'd gone off from here, to London or somewhere,' said Finn.

'Without telling them?' Jenefer shook her head. 'Never.' She hesitated. 'That's why we bought this . . . thing. We have to go to London. They must have heard that. There's some legal business to sort out, about some money.'

'Jenefer wouldn't go without them,' said Hubert, still muffled by his scarf.

'So I thought,' Jenefer turned to Michael, 'with your permission, we'd take them with us. Smiler too, if he has a fancy. Could be a bit of a squash, but . . .'

Smiler was shaking his head. 'Ah stay with our Mick. And Finn.'

313

'How long . . .?' Michael and Finn spoke in unison.

Jenefer shrugged. 'As long as necessary. A week, a month? Let them see a bit of the wicked world like you did, Finn.'

Finn laughed. 'Very educational, as my mother would say.'

Jenefer continued. 'And if the money's what Richard says it is, Hubert has this wonderful idea.'

They all looked expectantly at Hubert, who was unhooking his goggles and taking off his scarf. 'Buttons!' he said jubilantly. 'What do people inevitably need, rich or poor, at peace or at war? In depression and in plenty? Buttons. When I was a poor student just before the war I worked in a button workshop just outside Paris. Wonderful lovely things, buttons.'

'Buttons . . .' said Finn uncertainly.

'What we think we'll do, if the money is right, is build a button workshop here, in the garden of Plush Folly. Work for ten, fifteen, maybe twenty people. Make buttons for the nation.'

'Pitmen won't work in a button factory,' said Michael bitterly.

Jenefer nodded sympathetically. 'No. I know that. But perhaps the wives and mothers will. Think about it. Finn here could be forewoman . . .' Her eyes dropped to Finn's hand. 'What's this? Have you two got married while our backs are turned for five minutes?'

'He gave it to me. Just . . . earlier.'

Finn held up her left hand and the twins peered at the ring. She shook her head. 'But we're not married just yet. But very soon.' She glanced at Michael. 'I tell you what, Jenefer. You go to London and sort your business out. Take the twins and show them the wider world. Even the brilliant blue of the Mediterranean. And then you come back here to New Morven and build your button workshop. On the day it opens we'll get married. Isn't that right, Michael?'

He picked the hand up and kissed it. 'Do you know, Finnuola, me darlin', for a minute there I could have sworn you were Irish?'